FATHERS
and
CHILDREN

Judah Stampfer

FATHERS
and
CHILDREN

SCHOCKEN BOOKS · NEW YORK

First published by Schocken Books 1983
10 9 8 7 6 5 4 3 2 1   83 84 85 86
Copyright ©1983 by Judah Stampfer

Library of Congress Cataloging in Publication Data
Stampfer, Judah, 1923–
  Fathers and children.
  I. Title.
PS3537.T1754F3   1983   813'.54   83–42707

Designed by Nancy Dale Muldoon
Manufactured in the United States of America
ISBN 0–8052–3835–2

I would like to thank
      BARBARA MERSON and MANY FRIENDS
for their help in my work

PART ONE

Chapter One

IN THE MIDDLE of the last century, at a crossroads junction called Radich, east of Melon Village and sixty kilometers south of Warsaw, flourished an inn called the Flying Goose, with a gabled roof, shuttered windows, and a yard walled in against thieves. A pond in back, frozen over in winter, had a shaded hut alongside it, half underground, built of layers of heavy timber, where ice was stored for the entire year. Fine trees enclosed the entire grounds, sheltering a secluded lawn where, at the dawn of history, early tribes enacted the rites of spring.

Radich was at a crossroads overlooking a spread of gentle hills. It was fox-hunting country, filled with manorial estates, where winds blew from all over Eastern Europe. Nuthatches nested in the linden groves, flying out to Crimea and the Black Forest. There was a constant movement of horses: village mares pulled wooden huts on wheels, moving ice to Warsaw, bandits rode with secrecy and dispatch, Russian cavalry galloped up the road on maneuvers, Polish nobility jumped walls and streams, chasing their prey and planning the next rebellion.

A regular stop of the Bucharest coach, the Flying Goose was built when a romantic spirit breathed across Europe, when Imperial Poland was still a frontier of the west. In the great room, two rows of oak tables offered schnapps, a hot sausage, schav with cabbage leaves, and a deep vat of beer. Seated over dinner, visitors gave reports of seeing Byron in Switzerland. A secluded room in back serviced a clandestine Warsaw romance, a private entertainment with music and dancing, or just a traveler sleeping over so as to reach the city the next morning at a proper hour. A special suite with a heavy door sheltered now an old man and a little girl, again a wealthy Warsaw lady and her music teacher, or two cavalrymen riding each other in their sleep.

3

The inn flew the Polish colors; but Poland was in a decline, occupied and under foreign rule. Napoleon had come and gone, leaving behind a deadly romance and bunches of graves in the historic cemeteries. Under a hostile Church, the Catholic nobility, stuffy and defensive, concealed their mortgages, hoarded their jewels, and hosted entertainments where they circulated, dressed in frock coats; pawnbrokers mixed with card readers, and houseguests played the piano. The ancient nobility had died off, leaving their stiff, proud children graves to decorate and a choke of national fury. Meanwhile, the old Russian governor never forgot a slight. He gave amnesties neither for Christmas nor Easter. Whoever entered his jail died there.

When a canal was proposed for the Melon district to create cheap, reliable commerce and a reserve of water in case of drought, the nobility blocked the proposal, bickering over the exact route and water rights. Then a local nobleman diverted the Bucharest coach to pass his manor for the convenience of his occasional guests. Travel to the Flying Goose became more spotty; private drivers followed the route of the coach. Dancing was now at the dacha.

With the area in a steady decline, a Warsaw developer converted the inn to a boarding school for girls. He hedged the road with thick bushes, raised a school banner and in the woods hung swings trailing flowered vines. As enrollment swelled, musicians were hired and the stable got a shiny wooden floor. Select sons of nobility came to dance with the bourgeois maidens of Warsaw. The school's list of applicants lengthened.

Then a local nobleman gave a student a ride on his horse, holding her steady with a rough skinny hand. She sat, frightened, flattered, intrigued and returned the next morning, hysterical, barefoot, full of deranged accusations, and was sent home, gagging. The nobleman glowered at all his questioners.

The episode made the school somehow available. A week later, a highwayman waylaid a coach carrying some girls and took their clothes as spoils. The school soon emptied out; the girls were moved to safer, more drab surroundings.

The closing of the school left the Flying Goose deserted for more than a year. The shutters worked loose; dust blew through the loose windows. Then a Bucharest tanner raised the red flag of a tannery on the flagpole. He spread sawdust for the blood, hung iron hooks, and installed a vat of curing liquid, and from Bucharest brought his sister Anna, a kitchen slut, to keep house for him. But because he was a foreigner, the local slaughterers con-

4

signed their hides to the Warsaw tanners. The tanner thought himself cursed. Superstitious and a drunk, he finally died in the icehouse, drinking, singing, pissing, his behind blue with cold, calling himself a devil. His sister and a priest managed his burial.

Trapped in a ghost house and lonely for her brother, the sister kept the stable as a tanning room, with its hooks still hanging over the bloody sawdust. When she caught the attention of local noblemen, she used the red flag as a sign for another trade; but the halls became shabby, foreign, and unreliable. Jews were infiltrating the area, opening small shops. They spoke darkly of the Pharaoh, blood on the Nile, and the exodus from Egypt. Approaching a church, they spat, and crossed the street to pass.

A drought killed the local corn that summer, and one night Jewish thieves broke into the Flying Goose. Hearing their Yiddish curses in the rooms below her bed, Anna began packing to return to Bucharest.

That evening, Anna stepped along an alleyway in Melon, asking if a Jew wanted to buy the Flying Goose. The shopkeepers were suspicious; but finally somebody sent her to a chicken farmer newly arrived from Galicia—a country Jew, riding north with his family in a wagon loaded with clothing, bedding, and pieces of furniture.

Anna strode back toward Radich. Wrapped in her shawl, she turned onto an abandoned field. A fine dust rose under her feet. As she approached a campfire, a burly Jew rose in her face, wearing a rough field jacket and a knitted cap over a bushy, uncombed red beard.

Unlike the Melon Jews, Nehemia smiled cheerfully as he heard her out. To Anna, he didn't seem to care overmuch, but the inn intrigued him. He sweated a lot and only with difficulty controlled his feelings. He cautioned his wife Geula about the children and promised to return in a few hours. Geula watched him going off with Anna. Satisfied that there would be no incident, she returned to her daughters.

A gentile woman out at night with a Jew, Anna kept her shawl carefully around her shoulders as they took back roads to the inn. Nehemia asked if the stable was on the ground or on blocks—if it were on the ground, rats would always burrow in. She told him it was on blocks. In the stable, the horse trough was good for perches and as a dropping board; there was a spot near the floor for a pophole to the yard. Nehemia got on his knees and examined the floor under a lamp. It was fresh wood and dated from when the Flying Goose was a school. The tannery blood was a blemish—old wood carries diseases—but the tannery was hardly in operation. And how much could they use it, the little dancing ladies?

Nehemia stood up. "Enough. The asking price, building and grounds?"

Anna hesitated, feeling off-balance and insecure. "Eight hundred rubles?" she asked, and put up a bottle of schnapps and two glasses.

Nehemia smiled. "And perhaps two hundred?"

Anna gasped. "Two is plain thievery!"

Nehemia poured two glasses of schnapps. "And eight is right?"

She chewed her nail, and then snickered. "No, it isn't."

Nehemia lifted his glass; she lifted hers. They gulped their schnapps. He pulled her outside. "I'll give you three. Come, it's not an insult. I'm a farmer, not a banker; we all do what we can do. We'll draw up a contract; I'll put the money in your hand."

Nehemia found a Polish notary back of the Jewish alleyway in Melon, and woke him up, as Anna hung back in the shadows. Nehemia closely watched as the crabbed functionary copied out their contract with a quill, working by candlelight. He seemed indifferent to a Jew acquiring Radich land. Nehemia took it as a good sign.

At their campsite, Nehemia crawled under the wagon and unstrapped the money from between the planks. Sensing Geula watching his every move, Anna snatched her pay and darted off, giggling at her oafish customers.

Nehemia smiled helplessly at Geula. She nodded with a patient smile. Irritated, he doused the fire and loaded the wagon.

Nehemia drove his family to their new home with a peasant's smile. He nudged his five-year-old son, Shaya, sitting with him on the driver's seat. "The house had bad luck, but we'll nail a *mezuzah* by the door. Use a broom and the dust flies out the window." Shaya nodded gravely.

Geula glanced at the two, nodding and talking. Her husband was strong, honest, and direct. He was her choice; she would share him with no one.

Chapter Two

NEHEMIA'S EARLIEST MEMORIES were of Bessarabia, a forest area northeast of Bucharest that opened into White Russia and the

Ukraine. The Turkish Empire was drifting toward collapse. Borders were desultory, the police collected taxes and their crack troops, the Janissaries, were a Turkish foreign legion, child converts, and captives, every one a fanatic. In these occupied Balkans, the traveler paid his way into a hotel and out of jail.

Sephardic merchants handled the Bessarabian timber. Mediterranean Jews from Italy and Greece, used to jewelry and spices, had in their leisure movements a Latin softness. They knew no Yiddish; Ladino was their patois, the Zohar their book. In their mystical traditions, they floated into illumination, balancing systems of numbers in their heads. They passed medical skills from father to son, and they memorialized Maimonides, the great medieval legalist and philosopher, physician to Saladin. Nehemia was, with northern European Jews, descended from slaves shipped west after the Roman legions sacked Jerusalem. Their children, the legalists of Paris and the German ghettos, spread east into Poland and Lithuania. Sensing the Sephardic prejudice against his kind of Jew—in their eyes he was a barbarian, Ashkenazic Jew—Nehemia clung to his Yiddish, rejecting their Latin ways with a proud isolation.

Bessarabia was a verdant province, with stretches of rock fault and timber platforms on high wooden stilts. It stood on a Balkan shelf where locusts winged up from the south, and the weather carried in a sweep of atmosphere from the Urals. An only child, raised by an older couple, Nehemia wandered in the woods, drinking in the air of the wilderness. Restless and lonely, he felt God in the flow of sunlight splayed across the Russian pines, love in the liquid cool of a mountain stream.

Once Nehemia felt an earth tremor. He ran home and demanded of their Ukrainian housekeeper what had happened. She said the world began as a rooster; but it crowed while God was sleeping, so he changed it to earth. The tremor was a last twitch of the rooster's body that ever refused to die.

Once, moving through the woods, Nehemia spotted a flock of blackbirds. He killed one with a slingshot. The flock whirred off in a rush of wings. He felt sorry and wondered why he had done it. The flock settled down again. He killed another. This time the flock didn't come back.

A religious civil war ravaged the Balkan Jewish community. Shabbetai Zevi, the false Messiah who wrote poetry and sang with a lyric tenor voice, was imprisoned by the Sultan and converted to Mohammedanism rather than suffer martyrdom. Imitating him, his followers abandoned Jewish law. They sought God's body in the act of sin, eating swine flesh, violating the Sabbath, performing incest and adultery. The rabbis fought them with bitter determination; whole communities numbering in the hundreds of thousands swung back to Orthodoxy without a trace of their apostasy; but the heresy hung on. Entire Bessarabian towns lived a double life, pretending a strict observance and remaining Shabbatean cells. In a nearby village, every Jew lit a candle in synagogue after the Sabbath service, and uttered a prayer to God in sin.

Nehemia thought them all maniacs, twisted and demonic, with their Messianic dreamworld; and yet he felt a kinship. Their free search for God echoed his barbaric independence and mistrust for society. He would find God for himself, in his own life, his ability to work.

When Nehemia was a boy, Nazirites visited Bessarabia from as far off as Vilna and Danzig. They were hermits with a Jewish restlessness to fulfill the commandment: "Fill the earth and subdue it." In the forest behind his house, Nehemia spotted a skinny one sitting cross-legged in torn pants, his hair cut short and ragged. His eyes laughed without a stop. Nehemia sat down opposite him, feeling a compulsion to join him, but the Nazirite recited the same mystic book at high speed over and over, his whole body shaking rhythmically like a woodpecker against a tree.

The Nazirite looked hungry. Nehemia went home and piled together a sack of food, but when he got back the Nazirite had disappeared. For days Nehemia wandered the forest looking for him. Nehemia was closer to God than he was to any human being. Lonely, Nehemia longed for mystic experiences; but God was never that intimate with him.

Then, on his thirteenth birthday, the Bessarabian couple who raised him told Nehemia that he was a foundling; they weren't his real parents. He asked if he came with a name. They showed him the name Kramer on an attached piece of paper. When he asked why they had raised a strange child, they answered that to care for a foundling was their religious duty. Nehemia felt a fury of rejection inside him: this couple was just doing a job.

The next day, Nehemia climbed on a wagon of garlic headed for Vilna. On the way, something got scorched inside him—a softness, an ability to connect. Feeling bleak hollows inside him, he insisted on his sanity; work would be his penance.

After two days, tired of the garlic wagon, Nehemia got off in a wild stretch of the Galician Ukraine, where the thin settlement and open, innocent fields might give him a new life; and yet he felt a morbid quiver. He knew from the Shabbateans that innocence and malevolence were shadows to one another, that the hurricane is mothered in a center of lyric calm. These innocent fields veiled horror, but the Eternal should protect him from all harm.

Were he inducted into mysticism, Nehemia might have become another Nazirite, but that called for books and a teacher. Nehemia plunged into work with a harsh laugh. He belonged in Galicia, a barbaric spread virtually without people. He was the ultimate Shabbatean, turning everything on its head—but he would keep his own head straight. Work, that would be his way.

Chapter Three

FOR THE NEXT FOUR YEARS, Nehemia shifted about in the Galician Ukraine. An abandoned child, he did his own abandoning, avoiding human company, but he couldn't escape the miscarriage of his life. It was all a violation. The space in his mind had a wounded, frightening emptiness. He could get near to no one. He blinked at strangers with wild, helpless eyes. Whatever he had made him a thief. The blank air became a sheet of guilt on which atonement should be written. After a stay in a town or on a farm, he again wandered, fleeing something unclean.

The Nazirite haunted him. Like him, Nehemia was another penniless wanderer, with God all around him. The sky had a strange music that never stopped playing. The universe was a great vessel that was the body of God, but the Shabbateans had ripped the body of God apart to worship the pieces. Tramping about, Nehemia felt God's presence thrashing about in the sky, out of his reach. Stranded, he wanted to contact the earth, but he felt blocked off everywhere.

Nehemia was big for his age and matured young. As he traveled, bosses had him dragging stones, or pulling a plow like a horse. Nehemia did it, but he could be pushed only so far. He had a patient sanity, but sometimes he ran away from a job in the dead of night, afraid of his own loneliness and violence. His pride lay in never being dependent on anybody.

THE day Nehemia crossed into the eastern Ukraine, a compassion for his unknown mother burst loose inside him. However it was done to her, she was a wanderer as he was. Whoever forced such desperation on her, that she had had to leave him, even if it was his own father, he performed an act of ugliness. He would have his own family to heal her pain. Nehemia swore it; and mysteriously, his mother's spirit flowed down from the sky and filled the space around him. He was lonely as before, but he was no longer the thief of God. He was surrounded by a silent healing. Over and over, walking away from a settlement without any road, Nehemia felt a catch of fear, relief, and a vast communion. Sometimes he climbed a slope for an hour and reached the rim of a crater a kilometer across. Its round edge was too perfect to be natural. God must have taken out a scoop of the earth here, and brought it to Himself.

Nehemia picked up melodies in his wanderings—he didn't know from where. Once he started awake in back of an abandoned stable to the smell of smoked meat crackling on the fire. He glanced up, terrified; four Cossacks, three of them half-naked with shaven heads, the fourth with a sheepskin on his back and a scalp lock, squatted singing and drinking. Keeping absolutely still, Nehemia shaped their melody to the words of "*Lekhah Dodi,*" the song opening the Friday evening service. It was crazy—the Cossacks singing in a drunken gibberish while he arranged "*Lekhah Dodi*" in his head—but to tear the song out of their throats had a Shabbatean rightness. He could hardly keep from bursting out in laughter.

People trusted Nehemia on sight. He looked like a healthy mule or a trained watchdog. Since the climate was warm, he would give away the clothes from his back; it was not his time to own things. His hair grew wild. Women liked him; he never knew why. He could crack a whip like a Cossack; he couldn't remember who taught him how.

Once Nehemia stood inside a chicken barn, its four walls of cages full of hens clucking and brooding, all with frizzle feathers. Then a hen kicked a pellet of shit into his hand. Startled, he gripped it, then threw it away in annoyance. He remembered how as a child his housecleaner had told him the world began as a chicken. Wiping his hand clean, he decided to become a chicken farmer, and stayed long enough to learn the trade.

After he had moved on to Crimea, where the waterways joined and divided and the trees trailed their leaves to the ground, a barge captain's wife adopted Nehemia. For two days he worked, wondering when the captain was coming home. When Nehemia kept to himself, the wife asked how old he was.

10

He said, fifteen. Surprised at his youth, she told him to leave his door open that night. As the full moon played over the surrounding waterways, she slipped into his room and taught him the secrets of intimate pleasure.

For a month they slept with one another. She brought him meals like a servant girl and patched together clothes for him. Then she told him she was having his baby. Nehemia thought, I have one God; I have one life. He would share it with a partner made out of his rib, not a stranger's wife. Half an hour later, he disappeared up the road.

Treading over the steppes, Nehemia brooded over his baby that he abandoned. Did she really have a barge captain for a husband? Would his child be abandoned as he was? He remembered the two blackbirds he killed. Wandering, he felt in himself a waste and void. God's breath stirred over the abyss. The wind rippled over the spring mud; he was rubbish from the first creation, a botched attempt before God finally made Adam.

In an empty settlement, Nehemia found a black shofar, turreted like a medieval castle, with Hebrew inscriptions on it. Practicing as he walked, he became an expert blower. When he blew, he felt his mother's spirit around him, once again healing him, and God's spirit flowed around him; they were one. He walked in a wash of God's presence. He knew himself to be a holy man.

A peasant came by in a wagon. Nehemia climbed on and lay back, rocking in the rhythm of the wagon. He wanted to die, to kindle and dissolve into smoke for God to breathe. He was sixteen and his name was Kramer; but if he was Jewish, he was a child of sin and family weakness. Nehemia decided to marry young and be a father.

Getting off the wagon, Nehemia met Geula, carrying a pitcher of water. He remembered the Bible. She looked so like Rachel at the well that he couldn't stop smiling.

Chapter Four

AN ONLY GIRL after five boys, Geula Horowitz was fifteen when she met Nehemia. Her mother Yael was tiny and bald, always with a kerchief, and scurried around like a tree animal. Yael never washed; she put on a sweet perfume and always dressed in silks. She was jealous and spiteful after Geula's birth, but Geula was very sure of herself and adjusted her attitude to

11

make each situation work. She sized up the men in the family as Yael never dared. At five, she cut her mother out of her life to go her own way.

The Horowitz family were Ashkenazic traders who constantly moved south over the Turkish border. The Sephardic Jews they came in contact with fascinated them. Geula's father, Gershuni, was forever on the road, fulfilling commandments and relating to the world. Even his name Gershuni was after a Sephardic *chacham,* or wise man, of whom his father was enamored. A Chasid and follower of the Gerer Rebbe, he had a sense of elevation and Mediterranean beauty in his life, but his constant absence from home tore something loose in Yael.

Gershuni's snobbery overflowed into Geula. She knew what her life needed and was impatient with her sluggish home. She studied Hebrew like a boy and read the Bible on her own. She did what she wanted in her mother's kitchen; it was her kitchen too. She was smarter than her brothers, but to her that was no great compliment. Much as she loved her father Gershuni, he irritated her. She could tell that he wanted to cuddle and be close to her. It gave her enormous pleasure to keep him at arm's length, but he never dared try anything. Yael intimidated him with her craziness. The whole situation made Geula restless.

Spoiled as she was, Geula had a spunky honesty. She was lazy, yet she stirred with an impatience for something better in her life. Ignoring Yael, she turned pages in the Bible, fascinated by its self-reliant women. Deborah inspired her, but she had no real husband. Ruth was more of a model for her, picking herself up and moving with Naomi to Beersheba, not clinging to family, yet finding herself a man—and what a man!—Boaz, rich, loyal, a man who treated her with respect. But where was there a Boaz in Galicia?

Geula's stubborn streak turned to impatience at the softness of Sephardic men. They never gave her a flat answer to anything. She knew how to work in a way that Yael would never work. If she wanted, as a girl she could keep her own house.

Geula would have gone her own way, but the Horowitz family was too intensely clannish. At home, they were Gerer Chasidim to a man. In their trading expeditions, south into Turkey where the money was, they used flattery, small favors, and unexpected gifts, always shifting in manner with the people they met. At home, when not gathering at the rebbe's table, they visited each other for weeks on end, bringing wagons of food, wine, and gifts. The men then gambled compulsively, returning their winnings and starting all over, drinking vodka and fruit juice as their wives sampled each other's gefilte fish for the lightest and most fluffy. Gershuni brought home a nargileh that the men took turns smoking. On Friday night, they sang the same table hymns week after week, dissolving with pleasure at each other's voices. They married young and stayed in the clan. Children who held back were politely shoved at each other to pair off or simply pushed into bed and called man and wife.

When the Gerer Rebbe gave audience, hundreds of followers came in pilgrimage, *shtreimels* on their heads, white stockings to their knicker bottoms. A Gerer Chasid set a tune to the psalm about approaching the Jerusalem Temple: "Open up, ye gates of righteousness." The Chasidim sang it at the Rebbe's door, dancing and flinging their hands in the air.

The Horowitzes usually joined the Rebbe's table at Purim, to receive wine from his holy hand. A seat of honor was given to Gershuni, with his auburn hair, bushy white temples, and jowls that quivered with sensitivity when the Rebbe spoke. He murmured proverbs like, "What the wind writes, who can read?" "Pleasure is such a simple thing," or "Man was created by God, but he is not divine." The Rebbe called the Horowitzes "*Maineh sheineh Yuden,*" leaving them all smiles. That's what the Horowitzes were, his beautiful Jews.

Nehemia arrived and got a bed, a blanket, and basic books. A wild boy off the steppes who spoke a flat, hard Yiddish, he did his *mitsves* with little concern for cultural nuances. When Gershuni was away in Bucharest, Nehemia found some chickens, tiny bantams with black plumage. He fenced off a section of the yard, and built boxes in the corner for them to brood in. Gershuni called Nehemia his *Tohu Vavohu,* the Biblical "waste and void." Yael called him simply "that creature."

Nehemia was the first man Geula met who completely ignored her. She sensed his contempt for her family's Sephardic ways, a contempt that echoed her own insecurity. With a quiet shudder of surrender, she opened up to him inside herself in an act that was treachery to her father and all he stood for; and yet the treachery felt deliciously right. Nehemia's abrupt, violent mannerisms left her relieved and strangely happy after Gershuni's endless flattery and posturing. She caught in Nehemia a hunger for love, a sense of music, and a compulsion to run away. He was such a strange man—proud, Jewish, primitive, a worker with his hands, so innocent that his entire life seemed in her hands.

Geula was a little annoyed that her father did not notice her heart straying elsewhere. Didn't he care about his little girl? But he was so distant and inert, all wrapped up in his vanities and his humility, his gifts for the Rebbe, and his snorts on the nargileh, that he could never see anything. His innocence was totally different from Nehemia's. Gershuni's Garden of Eden in the Balkans was a bore. Geula could manage a house better than Yael; and with Nehemia so undemanding, she could manage him with a minimum of headaches.

But it irritated Geula that Nehemia was so self-sufficient. While he was on one of his compulsive hikes, rats worked under the fence and killed his chickens. When he got back, Nehemia dug the fence deeper and put in a fresh flock. He worked with a single mind, the way he prayed; he didn't need a woman for anything. Being ignored annoyed Geula. Did he judge her second-rate? She could manage a house as he kept a chicken coop. She had nothing to apologize for. They were a match.

Nehemia bothered Geula more and more with his passivity. In her heart, she knew he adored her; but he made himself passive so as never to do anything wrong. She would punish him for his weakness. And yet Nehemia intrigued her more and more with his indifference and passive strength. She kept going out and bumping into him in the yard. Once she asked why he marched off the way he did. He looked at her with such fear that she quickly changed the subject.

Geula spent hours in her room staring out the window and brooding. Catching sight of Nehemia, she jumped into bed, afraid he would notice her watching. Yet Geula had her reservations. Nehemia was a troubled wanderer, primitive and solitary. He was avoiding her in the way Jacob stood in line for fourteen years waiting for his Rachel. But she was no Rachel; she was more like Ruth. And Nehemia was no Boaz.

Then one day, standing in the kitchen, Geula saw Nehemia running through the yard and out the back door. She was frightened that he might be running away. The Bible was the Bible, but life was life. And in life, a Ruth could settle with a Jacob. In fact, if Jacob had met Ruth instead of Rachel, things would have gone a lot more easily. When Nehemia came back, Geula began following him around all the time.

14

Chapter Five

GEULA ACCEPTED NEHEMIA in her head but she was in no hurry to consummate a marriage. She knew that to love him lowered her, and yet it bothered her each time he took off. His body intrigued her—the way he could just suddenly go. She was homebound; women had no freedom. A boy that loose, all his life a wanderer—sooner or later he would be back on the road. Then where would she be? She would feel like a fool.

One afternoon, frustrated and jealous of his freedom, Geula played the dutiful, obedient woman and began following Nehemia at a distance, in the way of a Gypsy wife. His not looking back made it all her doing. But she was unable to match his pace. He kept getting farther in front until he disappeared from sight.

Geula refused to turn back. The road was clear enough; she would catch up when he stopped for a minute. But as she began passing fields heavy with white alfalfa, she became uncertain what was the road and what a field divider. She followed a wheel track for half a mile. When that disappeared, she climbed a long hill to get perspective, but thorn bushes and slippery rocks covered the crest. She descended a dry stream bed and looked around. Lost, she stopped on a patch of clover.

These were the wilds, but Nehemia was a wild man. If he found her, fine; if not, she would die and make no trouble for anybody. Unsure what to do, she lay down and fell asleep.

Geula woke up after a long sleep and saw Nehemia standing over her, big as a bear and grinning mischievously.

"What are you doing here?" Nehemiah finally asked.

"I was looking for you."

"Let's go back."

Geula got up and took his hand. She didn't have to, but he didn't seem to mind. Headed back, she looked up and told him to marry her. He smiled in silence. The air had a mustard freshness. Laughing with pleasure she ran her hand down his chest, and then stopped, unsure. An impatient anger gathered in her throat.

Nehemia embraced her and kissed her suspiciously.

Geula was charmed at how vulnerable she was, how she was open the way boys are open and yet perfectly safe. The air around her had its own protective magic. She kissed him back. He kissed her again. She kissed him more warmly, brushing against his body, feeling already like his wife. She could feel his arousal.

Having no reason to wait, they lay down, opened their clothes, and began to make love. But lying alongside him, her clothing undone as if she were in her room at home, Geula saw a swimming look come into Nehemia's eyes, a sudden twitch of fear, a sense of entrapment and bleak isolation.

Geula broke into a fishing giggle. "Nehemia?"

His eyes opened from another world."Yoh?"

Geula kissed him, almost singing it. "I'm your loving wife."

Nehemia closed his eyes, his isolation torn open. He crushed her against him with a powerful embrace. The passion exploded inside him, big, primitive, and very distant. Geula sensed something inside him in hiding that refused to come out, but this plowman's love was fine with her. His babies would soon begin doing the same, hiding in her body until ready to come out.

They finished; Geula washed her blood away in a stream, watching, distracted, as it thinned and ran off over the pebbles. Her crotch hurt a little; it felt right somehow.

"I'll wear a kerchief after the chuppah but I won't cut my hair. Yael hasn't any hair, and doesn't Gershuni know it. She'll try to cut my hair. Can I fight her?"

Nehemia smiled in bewilderment. "Do whatever pleases you."

Geula swung up and kissed him. "You're so good. Wouldn't it be funny if she's actually bald and pretends to cut her hair to cover it? It would be just like her."

Walking back, Geula kept shifting from side to side to touch him in some new way, unable to let him go. Something inside her jumped in the air and kicked its heels. She despised her family, their pretentiousness, their snobbery. If Gershuni rejected the match, she would have Nehemia's baby and force his hand. Besides, she knew her father: a trader, indirect, full of nuances, he could not stand up to a determined woman.

Geula guessed it right. At home, she marched in and said in plain language that she and Nehemia were being married. Gershuni coughed, smiled in scorn, and said nothing. With his silence, the marriage was on.

The Horowitz family organized itself for the family ritual. A tent was raised behind Gershuni's house. All the clan gathered. Then when Geula sat in her dressing room, surrounded by blue silk drapes for the wedding, wearing the family wedding gown, she heard Yael sneak in behind her and start to cut her hair.

Geula sprang around and pushed her back. "No!"

Yael came at her, her lips opening and closing, working the scissors like a hungry fish; but Geula threw her off. "You're selfish! You want me to lose Nehemia like you lost Gershuni! But I'm keeping my husband!"

Yael squealed. "You'll disgrace us all! You have no shame!"

Yael came at her again with the scissors, her blue gown shimmering to her ankles. Geula wrestled with her, tearing her mother's dress and twisting her scissors away. "Nehemia told me to do as I pleased."

Yael shrank back with a scream. "Your life is a disgrace!"

Geula tore off Yael's wig and threw it in the dust. She headed out of the tent in stubborn determination. Yael pinned her dress together, knocked her wig clean, and put it back on, and followed her.

The entire Horowitz clan had come for the chuppah, in wagons from all over the area—even the cousin Yael had picked for Geula. The family enveloped Nehemia like the sea. Four brothers held the chuppah poles; the fifth read the marriage contract in Aramaic. A group of cousins sang a hymn sung at Safed weddings about union with the celestial spirit. An elegant cousin with flowing locks recited the *Shma* from beginning to end with exact intent on every word, guaranteeing immortality to Nehemia and Geula. Geula kept looking at her chosen cousin during the chuppah, delirious with relief that she had escaped such a fool. But then all her relatives were fools.

Nehemia brought Geula down several pegs, but he touched to life a barbaric free woman trapped inside her. Her dream was to be trapped and enjoyed, then escape to a new life. Who was enjoying her? God, Nehemia? Her life was a bottle of wine to be drunk or spilled out, never to go dry. She spent her wedding night deliriously in love, addressing herself entirely to Nehemia's appetites, her children already rising to life inside her.

Chapter Six

NEHEMIA GOT A COTTAGE by Gershuni's home and became his handyman, building up his grounds. The slope was warm, the area safe and open. Gershuni gave him a *chalif,* or ritual slaughtering knife, and a stone to sharpen it with. He had him trained in ritual slaughter at a nearby farm so as to supply chickens for the Horowitz table. Within three years, Nehemia had

17

three daughters, Gita, Feigeleh, and Esther. After a few years Geula became pregnant once more and had a son, Shaya.

Living adjacent to her father, Geula comfortably passed back and forth between the two homes wearing a kerchief. She bared her head only for Nehemia and Gershuni and cooked for Gershuni when Yael was indisposed. Gershuni visited her Sabbath table once he finished with his own. Then Nehemia sat him behind him at the head of the table. Sometimes Yael was indisposed as Geula was about to feed her baby. She then wrapped Shaya in swaddling clothes, walked over, and nursed her baby as she gave food to her father. Father and daughter repressed the same smile. He enjoyed being babied; there was no harm in that.

Gershuni made a point of bringing something back for Geula from each of his business trips—the Mediterranean fabric was so much finer than the local weave, a shawl from Genoa, a robe from the Aegean Islands. Geula's sense before her wedding of having to choose between the two men now seemed childish and extreme. She even made her peace with the Horowitz family. If their stupid rounds of visits kept them distracted, who was she to complain? The family was comfortably together and she a fulfilled woman. And yet, lying in bed with Nehemia, she felt in his body his old compulsion to wander; his was the embrace of a vagabond, making everything feel makeshift in her life, and giving her a permanent cast of foreboding that she ignored as best she could.

Nehemia allowed Gershuni's gifts even if such goods were beyond his wherewithal. Living on Gershuni's grounds and tending his estate, he choked with anger that his own father had given him neither money nor self-respect. The Horowitzes were blind sentimentalists, with their wagonloads of family gifts, the hours they shared at table, slurping hot soup and cracking chicken bones with their teeth, their slow, heavy hymns dissolving over each other's voices. At their feasts, he controlled a hysterical laugh. He had no training, but he knew what music was. The family had almost the same body—a herd of overweight gazelles with *shtreimels*. Not respecting them, but constantly surrounded by them, Nehemia kept to himself. He kept remembering the baby he abandoned in the cottage of the ship captain's wife; accepting his bitterness as a form of penance made it a shade less bitter.

At a religious holiday, one of the Horowitzes always served as the family scout to collect the necessary paraphernalia for every-

18

body—a citron and palm branch, horseradish for Passover, honey for the New Year, noisemakers for Purim, a sukkah—even if visitors had to enter the hut in shifts. So they traveled, dabbled, and collected, carrying odd furniture pieces on their wagons, scrolls, preserves, Hebrew books, and children's clothing, *bakvem*. They were thoroughly comfortable with one another. Even wearing silk, in the winter Yael backed against the fire and lifted her skirts in back to warm her legs. When a Horowitz spotted a strange object, he saw it as a present. The family system stayed afloat in exile. Distant visitors stayed for days, bringing Gershuni news of an available forest, a shipment of spices, when the next war was due between Russia nd Turkey.

The great family commodity was *koved,* a blend of honor, pride, and simple vanity. They made treks in the summer heat, chafing in holiday clothes, swarms of flies surrounding their wagons. Then at the feast, in their slant wood halls of rough timber, all sang with a single voice, fifty strong: "*Lo mir aleh in einem, in einem, Tante Rochel mekabel ponim sein, und trinken a glegeleh vein.*" "Let us all honor Aunt Rochel and drink wine together." Aunt Rochel would burst into a surprised giggle of pleasure at the *koved.* For an hour, they circled the room with elaborate protocol, honoring each person there with the same song. Each person honored responded with the same surprised giggle.

Nehemia was a marginal son-in-law. Marriage with an outsider ensured a business connection, access to another city, a family they felt comfortable with. Nehemia was not only an outsider but a barbarian with no connections, but the family harbored no grudges. He sang well and worked like a horse. Their shofar blower had just passed away, and for a successor to show up like this was a wink from heaven to allow the match.

As the years went by, Nehemia became increasingly impatient with the way the Horowitz family herded together for business, repeated the Rebbe's words, and passed around his amulets. Feeling corraled and hemmed in, he grumbled endlessly, brooding over his lost child—it was a son, he was sure of it. It made him treasure Shaya all the more. He swore in his soul that he would give his life for this one.

Never having attended school or grown up with his own family, Nehemia felt awkward as his daughters grew up. Since he hardly read beyond the prayer book, he left their education to Geula. He had their complete trust and yet felt in some way

19

he failed them and was not giving them genuine fatherly guidance. As for Shaya, Nehemia sensed in him a depth of soul that held him in awe. Whatever the cost, he would allow nothing to harm his son. In the evening he walked outdoors with Shaya perched on his shoulders to drink in the night air. Afterward, Nehemia brought his son inside and put him to sleep.

A Warsaw lumber merchant, Zfania Binstock, visiting Gershuni, twisted around at table on hearing Nehemia's name. "Kramer? Kramer?" he muttered to his host. "The Kramers are Warsaw Belzer."

"He's married to my daughter," Gershuni hastily murmured.

"You have family in Warsaw," Binstock said with decision, and turned away.

Nehemia fell quiet. The Belzer were another Chasidic dynasty, like the Gerer. He knew about them secondhand but he felt a family bond. Geula saw his reaction and felt a twinge of helpless panic: Nehemia never really joined her family and was now slipping out.

After the merchant's visit, the sky turned raw and chill, exposing the blue bowels of the firmament; Nehemia took compulsive hikes. Galicia was hardly settled; torrential rain already washed away the soil. Vagrants occupied the abandoned farms, burned the furniture there for firewood, and then vanished.

Nehemia sometimes disappeared for an entire day; then at night, he hid inside Geula's body, afraid for his own existence. Geula patiently received him. By now her dreams of magic protection had dissolved into a quiet fatalism. She knew how fragile her securities were. Anything could destroy the things her life clung to; sooner or later, something would.

"When will it be?" Nehemia whispered in bed, blindly hugging her.

"Whatever will come, will come," Geula murmured, loyally caressing his head, but afraid even to think of what was frightening her.

Chapter Seven

WHEN NEHEMIA'S OLDEST DAUGHTER turned twelve, in the same month that she had her first period, a Shabbatean cell two villages away from Gershuni's holdings succumbed to the Frankist insanity. The once revolutionary Shabbateans had stabilized themselves and gone into hiding. They were a safe heresy, a part of the establishment; whatever they did occurred in private. Touched off by the partitions of Poland, the Frankists were a crazy offshoot of the Shabbateans. An apocalyptic movement tuned in to the spirit of abandonment spreading through Poland, they cast away all caution, aggressively sought converts, had communal sexual orgies, and converted wholesale to the Catholic Church to practice mock adoration of the Pope.

Such a village was dangerous. If the Russians got wind of it, they might rid the entire province of Jews. A strong Kahal government would have fought them relentlessly, but the area was disorganized and no one seemed to care. The heretic Frankist villagers even remained Gerer Chasidim with an elaborate rationale of hidden and revealed truths—lies that are seeds of higher truths—sending missionaries to spread the word, zealots armed with a system of double answers to every question. They used the homes of several of Geula's relatives as stopover stations.

The sudden activity in Galicia set Nehemia's mind in motion. His daughters were twelve, eleven, and ten, and his little boy had eyes like saucers. Shaya was vulnerable to every passing wind. A province as primitive and scattered as Galicia needed strong Kahal government. The Horowitzes weren't to be trusted; they were all idiots with a borrowed Sephardic softness. They had no deep family honesty. The ground felt unsafe as he walked. Nehemia was a Belzer; he belonged with the Belzer community in Warsaw.

The first news about his father that he had received from the Warsaw merchant filled in a cloud empty of memory. If his father was a Warsaw Kramer, and Nehemia himself had been abandoned in Bessarabia, then his father would be a traveler, perhaps a businessman like Gershuni, or a consultant engineer. Out in the provinces on a job, he had an affair with a local girl and then returned to Warsaw. If she became pregnant and didn't get in touch, then he was probably married. She chose to shame herself rather than shame her love. Again Nehemia felt a burst of loyalty. She attached the Kramer name, to the foundling, not her own, out of loyalty to the man she protected. God should shelter his mother in His arms. Nehemia swore in his soul to protect his own family if it cost his life. Nehemia told Geula it was time to leave and move to Warsaw. In the back of her head, she had a faint seed of guilt about her own divided loyalty, and made no demurral.

In a community as small as theirs, every departure is a defection. As soon as Nehemia made the announcement, the Horowitz clan began conferring with one another and passing out pronouncements. Geula was told to demand a divorce. She refused to consider it. She was asked to leave her children with family to make the trip easier. She insisted that question was for her husband to decide. Nehemia had had twinges of insecurity about Geula's loyalty; seeing how closely she followed his lead, he felt vindicated in his marriage as he never felt before.

Disturbed at Geula's stubborn resistance, Gershuni hurried off to the Gerer Rebbe for support and returned with five delegates from the nearby Galician congregation to pay Nehemia a formal visit. Nehemia made them a community of eleven male adults. With his departure, they were scratching a bare *minyan* of ten. One plague, a war, another defection, and God forbid, the community would fall apart. They might have to sell their land after all their years of labor, and settle elsewhere. Without a *minyan*, there was no communal life.

Nehemia poured each a glass of wine. They each took a ritual sip and started in again. Had they offended Nehemia in any way? Nehemia shook his head; no, they hadn't. Could they make him change his mind? Was he avoiding saying something? He should be open with them; they would do whatever they could. Nehemia shook his head. They were fine men. He had nothing against them; he just wanted to move to Warsaw. They left depressed; he couldn't help that.

While Gershuni conferred with the Rebbe, the Horowitz clan brought a scribe on a covered wagon. They all pushed into Nehemia's home together, practically splitting open the walls. With the entire Horowitz family behind him, the scribe showed the passage in the Bible where Jeremiah told the Jews in Babylon to settle there and raise their children. In other words, once in exile, stay where you are; do not go to Egypt, or Greece, or back to Jerusalem. And if followed logically, stay away from Warsaw.

The entire Horowitz phalanx bristled and pushed forward, waiting for Nehemia's reply. He glared back at them. If Jeremiah's exiles had settled in Galicia instead of Babylon, the prophet would have told him to pack up and get out fast. There were too many maniacs around, bullies and moral idiots. Even his chickens were dying of the heat. Galicia was clearly headed for punishment. Nehemia wanted sanity for his children; well, to get sanity, you have to get out of Galicia.

As he finished, Gershuni burst into the house, waving the Rebbe's writ, black on white, that announced Nehemia should stay. Nehemia, the Belzer, defied them secretly, but the Rebbe's writ intimidated him.

Seeing her husband at bay, Geula stepped alongside him, coming out of the shadows at last. A true Biblical scholar, she said in a strong voice, "My husband gave you his verse: 'Get thee forth.' And my verse to him is: 'Whither thou goest, I will go; and where thou lodgest, I will lodge. Thy people shall be my people, and thy God my God. The Lord do unto me and more if aught but death part thee and me.' "

"Idiot!" Yael shrieked.

The scribe was outraged. "Those two verses are unrelated!"

But the Horowitzes understood. A Horowitz had turned her back on the clan. Outraged, rejected, depressed, they fell over each other pushing out the door, and climbed back on the wagon.

Gershuni stepped directly in front of Geula and refused to move. She hesitated. He blinked at her, like a child being abandoned, saying nothing, his face a sheet of pain and bewilderment.

"Wherever we settle, come and visit," Geula finally murmured.

He nodded in silence and stepped outside.

Squirming like a cat, Yael confronted Gita, Geula's oldest girl. She stepped half around her, caressed her cheek, tapped her lips, and then snatched up her hand, the perfume oozing from her body with the body odors:

"You're leaving us? No, you can't leave us. Your groom is Yitzik, your dear cousin Yitzik. You'll come back to Yitzik. We love you and you love us. You'll write to your *bubbe.* But keep it a secret from Mummy; I have to run." And Yael ran out laughing and climbed on the moving wagon.

As the wagon rolled away, Nehemia began to make his plans. Gita and Feigeleh were healthy, quiet, likable girls. With luck, they could manage in Galicia. But Esther was his wild one, the family misfit, perhaps even smarter than his son Shaya, with more dreams in her head than any human being could handle. She always trailed after her father; nothing escaped her. If he stayed in Galicia, she would end up a witch like his mother-in-law. For her, he needed a city where she could grow and come to herself. Shaya also needed larger surroundings; at twelve, eleven, and ten, his three daughters could still be moved securely—they would ignore the road and the road would ignore them—and at five years old, Shaya had been weaned for two years now and could travel.

Geula's loyalty to him in the confrontation with her family made him jubilant. And she was right: "Get thee forth" was his verse. He was Abraham to this family. Abraham got out of Mesopotamia and started on his way to Canaan. Nehemia would get out of Galicia and head for Warsaw. Maybe he would meet his family there and melt into them as the Horowitzes melted into one another. And if that did not happen, humiliation was not his way of life. Exile was a condition one grappled with.

What did the Talmudist say when earth and sky, the sun, moon, and stars, and all the signs of the zodiac refused to help him in his hour of deepest need? He sighed out of the depth of his soul, "In that case, it depends on me alone."

Before dawn the next day, Nehemia's family was packing and getting ready for the road.

Chapter Eight

TO THE BACK OF HIS WAGON Nehemia attached a second section with its own rear wheels, nailed it tight, and put fencing around the front of the wagon, for security and a little privacy. He collected straps and coverings. All day, he smoked sides of beef and lamb. As Geula separated clothing and luggage, packing for the trip, Nehemia got out his own pieces of furniture, tools, supplies, and sets of dishes, and tied them all down in front of the wagon. Geula made sure she packed her new clothes iron, with the hollow inside to hold hot coals.

The next morning before dawn the family prepared to leave. Nobody came to see them off. The Horowitzes didn't fight over every tool and piece of furniture. They weren't malicious—they just cut the Kramers out of their family.

Nehemia didn't care. He hid his money in a pouch strapped under the wagon between the planks and tied a mule to follow in back carrying fodder. He spread a tough canvas quilt on the wagon floor in an open space in back for some privacy, so his ladies could lie down while the wagon moved along the road. The shoals of stars were still swimming free in the pitch-black heavens as Geula and the three girls curled up on the quilt and went to sleep. Nehemia cracked his whip and got the wagon on the road.

An hour later, as flecks of red light quivered up from the east and the sky came alive with shivers of silver spreading over Galicia, Nehemia stopped the wagon, put on his prayer straps and tefillin on his left arm and the crown of his head, wrapped himself in his full-length tallis, and said his morning prayers, rising on his feet on the unsteady wagon to chant the *Shma* as the sun rose over the horizon.

They rode all day at a leisurely pace, not even stopping under the heat of noon to rest in the shade, so as to make a distance between them and the Horowitz area. The women stayed in back but Nehemia kept Shaya in front with him on the driver's bench. Having traveled so often on his own, he felt a starvation for Shaya's company.

It was late summer. After a month of rain, the air sparkled; the ponds were at the full. The wagon splashed through more than one puddle, bouncing over rocks hidden in the water as the family shrieked and groaned. When the wagon got stuck in the mud, everybody climbed out. Esther, the lightest one in the family, held the reins; the mule carrying fodder was tied on in front for his added pull. The family all pushed together and got the wagon rolling again. Esther was delighted momentarily to be the family driver. It felt right since she saw herself as their guardian spirit. They all then stopped at the next pond to wash, keeping on their cotton underwear with its sleeves and leggings.

Climbing out, wet and half-dressed from one such washing, they spied a wagon at the top of the next hill, smaller and sturdier than theirs, with a simpler, more durable cover, rolling toward them at a brisk pace, driven by a solitary peddler. As the women shrieked and ran to dress in hiding, Nehemia strode in front of the wagon in his wet *gatkes* and waited. He shook his head in amazement at its load of old books, pamphlets, and broadsides. But the driver was a Litvak, a husky young Jew from Lithuania, lean and leathery, in clothes black as an undertaker, a stripling Yeshiva boy, frowning aggressively under an old fedora.

"*Sholem aleichem,*" Nehemia muttered guardedly.

"You want a book?" the stranger said by way of reply.

His garlicky breath annoyed Nehemia. "First I need some pants."

The stranger roared with laughter.

"There, I carry only my own."

Nehemia shrugged. "We don't meet on business."

"The name is Mendeleh; I sell books."

"My name is Nehemia, if I can trust a piece of paper."

"Trust it; a paper with a name is not a joke."

"Not a joke? I think it's one of the plagues of Egypt."

"All Poland is a plague of Egypt. We suffer it because we deserve it, being pigheaded idiots. Where are you going?"

"To Warsaw."

"You should go to Odessa; it's warmer."

"I'm a Belzer. The Belzer have a school in Warsaw. You should sell oranges and lemons."

"If I grew oranges and lemons, I would sell oranges and lemons. Since I write books, I sell books. Have luck in Warsaw."

"And you in Odessa, growing oranges and lemons."

"If I sell no books, I may starve on the road."

"Who asked you to write books to begin with?"

The men saluted, parting with grudging smiles of respect.

Although Nehemia had food in the wagon, he had grown up a scavenger and knew how to live off the land. Nehemia gazed about him as he moved through the hazy warmth, squinting over the fields. Sometimes as he rode, he spotted edible leaves, wild radishes, a growth of mushrooms, or even a straw-yellow hillside covered with blueberries. Then the entire family climbed out and started collecting. Once, in a field choked with asparagus, they had an orgy collecting the giant heads.

An expert with a hand net, Nehemia kept one tied beside the wagon. Whenever they passed a pond, he locked the reins, stripped to his *gatkes,* and waded in, jumping, twisting, fumbling for footing, scooping the net in the water. Having nothing to do, his children watched from the side, commenting on his style and admiring his hairy legs. He always caught something; always the children applauded.

Geula sat on the wagon and watched with a patient, skeptical smile. It was all very innocent and romantic to wed such a primitive show-off, and she thoroughly enjoyed her marriage; yet she heartily congratulated herself for having the generosity that this match called for.

The weather was sultry, with only a wet haze to filter out the sun. Ribbons of rainbow wobbled over the weeds. Nehemia advanced slowly, trying not to weary the horses. He had spare wheels tied to the side of the wagon in case one broke, and yet he knew that if Geula weren't there, he would take off like a vagabond and disappear over the horizon, leaving the wagon and everything in it, Shaya riding on his shoulders and his three daughters trailing behind him, the daughters of a Jewish Gypsy.

The New Year was a month away; they could take their time. When the sun was at its fiercest, they stripped as much as they dared and lifted parasols against the sun. Even Shaya had his little blue-and-white umbrella. Nehemia trusted only his thick knitted cap to protect him from sunstroke, and kept his two hands for driving.

Every once in a while, remembering the coming New Year, Nehemia took out his black shofar with the inscription and the turrets at the end, and blew a practice blast: *Tekiah Shevarim, Teruah*. As if in response a miasma of dust would lift from a stretch of burned-out fields.

Chapter Nine

NEHEMIA KEPT SHAYA BY HIS SIDE on the driver's bench. His feelings were complicated and strange. Grumbling and complaining as the wagon rocked slowly forward across the changing landscape, Nehemia saw Shaya as the ghost of the son he abandoned in the Crimea, as well as the family baby, his heir, father of the next generation of Kramers, Isaac to his Abraham, a man whose life would be full of laughter:

"God made Adam last of all. For six days, He made the whole universe, the sun, the moon, and all the earth; and then he made Adam, the crown of creation. After the six days, when creation was finished, and Adam was in the garden, and the animals all got names, He made Eve. So by the time He got to Eve, He should have known what He was doing. And yet they're funny, women. You take a chicken. How does a chicken spend her life? Producing eggs. The rooster is beside the point. If there's a rooster, then the egg is fertile; if not, it stays just an egg. But a chicken doesn't chase after roosters; it just produces eggs. A chicken is a lot saner than a woman, where if there's no rooster, there's no egg. On a good chicken farm . . ."

Shaya gestured for Nehemia to wait; he suddenly missed his mother. He crawled to the back of the wagon, making his way over boxes and pieces of furniture tied together under the stiff, rocking canvas. Seeing him coming, Geula shushed the girls. As Nehemia waited patiently, Geula took Shaya on her lap. She held him close, rocking him in her arms and giving him an occasional kiss. When he had enough, he crawled back up front over the canvas; and Nehemia continued as before:

"The life of a chicken is a lot saner than a woman's life. A woman is always wasting her time making connections, having babies, hanging on to family . . ."

Shaya leaned against him and began gently snoring. Nehemia

carefully laid him down on the bench, took off his coat, and spread it over his son, making sure he would not fall off the wagon.

A tool keg worked free of its rope. Nehemia stopped the wagon, worked the canvas free, and tied the keg down afresh with double the number of ropes. He had brought extra, as he had brought extra wheels. He thanked God it was only a keg; had a wheel broken, he would have had to strip their possessions off the wagon to replace the wheel. He would have lost a day.

To ward off insects Geula had several bottles of a smelly family liquid. Once they saw what resembled a low cloud of moths spreading over the road in front. Moments later, a haze swarmed all around them—not moths, but insects. An hour later, a swarm of locusts kicked over one another, fighting to land on their bodies. The family slapped more liquid on one another and rode on, making faces. No insect would touch them, nor any human being.

Shaya glinted up slyly. "Are locusts kosher?"

Nehemia frowned. "I'll have to ask a rov."

Shaya grabbed one on the fly, shoved it in his mouth, and chewed it down with a crunch. "Yeah, do that," he giggled.

As the locusts thinned out and disappeared behind them, Nehemia heard Esther's voice, from the back of the wagon, singing Gershuni's Belzer hymns, imitating his rocking lilt; Geula and her sisters finally slapped her quiet for mocking her grandfather.

In the early afternoon when the sun began to scorch the earth, the family pulled off the road, slept for a few hours, and then continued. They kept wine for a Sabbath kiddush, but otherwise Geula frowned on drinking on the road. Isolated in front and smelly with insect juice, Nehemia drank from a jug of raisin wine under the driver's seat.

That night, Nehemia stopped the wagon to camp by some body of water. There he watched his four darlings strip and bathe, splashing and washing each other clean. His eyes widened to take in this patriarchal feast of family. He couldn't tear himself away to unpack for the night. A barbaric appetite took hold of him and swept him into a froth of lust. He giggled without thinking. He wanted to take a bite out of Geula's body, and the girls too, he loved them so.

Feeling out of control as his family came out of the water, Nehemia strode forward, swinging his arms. Shrieking, they told him to stay away, as he pinched their cheeks, smacked their rumps, bussed their foreheads, and told them to behave themselves. Esther shrieked for him to be a good daddy. Finally, she pressed in front of the others, jumped into his arms, embraced him, and scolded him for the way he behaved.

Nehemia smiled in pretended bewilderment. "Why are you so smart, Esther?"

She giggled happily. "I don't know."

Nehemia then set up camp; Geula looked after Shaya.

His three daughters adored Nehemia, even if he remained something of a stranger. Having their own family, they broke loose from the larger family of Horowitzes; it was so romantic, to be a family on the road. Only Gita remained loyal to her *bubbe*. Nehemia was their barbarian father, comic, skeptical, dangerous, but absolutely trustworthy and self-reliant. Geula didn't mind his raunchy appetites, as long as those appetites stayed at home. They might be a harem, but finally only she possessed him.

After the women bathed, and Nehemia unpacked for the night, he sat down to supper, a little sheepish. In his own way, he was making up to his daughters in love what he lacked in learning or social status, but he knew how vulnerable they were and how little protection he gave them. He had peasant ways, working, for him, was the equivalent of the hunting and riding the Polish nobility enjoyed. He did what he could for his family; that was why there were three patriarchs, Abraham, Isaac, and Jacob—because one man can do only so much. So Shaya would take over from him. Already he felt his life passing over to Shaya.

Looking at his daughters, but lacking a language in common with them, Nehemia wondered how, with all his ignorance and guilt, his family could approach a wild man like him. If he could, he would give them his life as an act of repentance. Whatever they did, however they abandoned him, his home would always be theirs.

But a leisurely supper restored his spirits. As they relaxed, he leaned over Shaya by the fire. "Your grandfather is like an angel, isn't he? He moves, he talks, he overflows. But nobody ever mistakes your father for an angel, that you can be sure of."

Shaya blinked up in silence; Nehemia broke into a grin. "Moses went up Mount Sinai, and nobody mistook him for an angel either. Too big a temper. And you know what the angels did while he was climbing? They threw balls of fire at him, he should turn around and go back."

"They were jealous," Shaya lisped.

"It didn't stop Moses. Dealing with God, he didn't have to worry about all the little angels."

"They were like the Horowitzes," Shaya lisped with satisfaction, curled up with a huge grin, and went to sleep.

Nehemia blinked at him. Shaya adapted beautifully to the road, keeping to himself and never jarring Nehemia or the others. And yet it was a rugged trip; Nehemia worried about his stamina.

At night, when they were sleeping, Esther sometimes crawled under Nehemia's blanket and clung close. She breathed so hard that Nehemia wondered if she was having a bad dream. A fever played under her skin. She lived in too many worlds. She was fragile; as always, she knew more than anybody could handle. The trip was too much for her. He sighed and let his daughter quiet herself against him.

Chapter Ten

JEWISH COLONIES WERE SCATTERED across the Galician plain. The Warsaw road sometimes skirted one; others a traveler stumbled on only by accident. They were too ephemeral to be shtetlach; they were just floating social islands that changed shape and format according to their needs, on the southern frontier of the Pale, that vast eastern spread of Czarist Russia where Jews were allowed to live.

Settlement was always provisional in these colonies. Sometimes a stranger appeared, able to teach Hebrew; then a neighboring colony might move alongside it to make a school. Several miles away, another colony could split up, its members tired of each other. Then the settlers meandered over the horizon in every direction, each group of them searching for a watering place. Sometimes an area became too desirable and the Cossacks moved in; the Jews left fast for another try at a home.

The colonies kept themselves scattered in order to avoid detection. Having virtually no rights, they seemed safer in those places where they could disappear fast. Charity collectors, political agitators, and false Messiahs circulated about on the Galician plain, scarcely knowing in what direction to turn; there were official and unofficial maps, all with the sketchiest of directions. They lost track of who was the Czar; Napoleon and Genghis Khan blended with one another. One settlement became confused what year it was on the calendar and lost count of the leap year. In another, two leaders argued which day was Saturday; in twenty-four hours, the colony split up.

Each had its own peculiar version of historic memory, its skills, its dead to be remembered, its craziness and ways of survival. Their pooled stories made a homemade history that their badchanim rehearsed to sing at the holiday table. Their stories needed no devils for color; the Cossacks were enough. The Ashkenazic Jews remembered the Crusaders, Ivan the Terrible, and the Teutonic Knights; the Sephardic Jews recalled the ships fleeing Spain where sailors ripped open women's bellies seeking jewels swallowed for safekeeping, and sold the survivors as slaves. Both remembered the Cossack butcher, Chmielnicki, who carved a path of fire and sword as he marched north toward Warsaw, leaving no one alive behind him.

In rural Galicia, politics broke down to folklore. Yellowed Yiddish newspapers were passed around, smudged to illegibility. The inhabitants hung tatters of news on old folktales. They were living the forty years in the desert: Elijah the prophet was seen wandering in Minsk; the Golden Calf was rising bigger than ever in Warsaw; another *oisvulf* of a Czar had taken the throne of the Pharaohs. If God didn't answer their prayers soon, everything would fall apart so even He couldn't fix it.

Driving the wagon, Nehemia explained the various types of Jews to Shaya, sitting on the bench next to him.

"Shaya, you know what a Galitzianer Jew is?"

Shaya nodded. "He's a Jew from Galicia."

"And do you know what a Litvak is?"

"A Litvak is a Jew from Lithuania."

"And we're Belzer Jews from Warsaw, and never forget it."

"I won't."

"The trouble is that the Pale consists of German Jews who were knocked out getting here. When pogroms sent the German Jews flying east, the heaviest brains landed first, in Lithuania. The winged creatures flew to Russia. But the empty heads flew and flew until they reached Galicia."

Shaya nodded with a weak smile. "Yeah."

"That's why Galicia has the worst false Messiahs, because its Jews are such desperate idiots. The Messiah is their last hope of ever escaping Galicia. Could they make a wagon like we did and get out? No, because they're Galitzianer Jews, lazy and weak-minded, and so far out that only a Messiah can bring them back."

Shaya nodded with an eager smile. They got more and more excited as they talked by the hour.

At each colony where he stopped, Nehemia got a grilling:

"You read a scroll?"

"No."

"You carry amulets?"

"No."

"You slaughter kosher?"

"Only chickens."

"You got a line on Rothschild money?"

"No, nothing."

"Then what are you good for?"

"I can blow a shofar."

"The colony waits for five years, and all we get is a shofar blower who can slaughter chickens?!"

"We live in exile."

Once, leaving a colony, Nehemia nudged Shaya, hunched next to him on the seat. "If all of Galicia were for sale, how much would I have to pay for it?"

Shaya blinked at him and waited.

"I'd get it for nothing. I'd go up to the Czar and promise to get rid of all his Galitzianer Jews in exchange for Galicia. He'd grab at it. Then I'd go back to Galicia and announce that the Messiah in Jerusalem called for all Jews to come and join Him, and especially the Jews from Galicia. In five minutes they'd take off for the Turkish territories in the tens of thousands, no questions asked. They'd disappear forever. And for that favor, I'd get Galicia as my reward."

Shaya smiled weakly and said nothing.

Passing through a strange colony, Nehemia listened like an animal to the rapacity of the colonists, and what they would permit themselves. Too many colonies had designs on him. Nehemia always camped out on the field, ready to take off at a breath of danger.

In one colony, the locals milled around him. Their first settlers were four couples who produced five sons and seven daughters, now old enough to pair off and have families. But this gave only nine males. Eventually one couple would add a tenth male and make a *minyan;* but by then the first settlers might begin to pass on. And what if they all had girls? You never know what a pregnant woman will deliver. Even if it's a boy, after being without for fifteen years, they would wait for another fifteen years—unless of course a stranger would join them and make a tenth.

32

They looked not only at Nehemia as a possible recruit, but at each other in suspicious resentment. They congregated around Shaya's wagon with sour resentment. God had given them twelve children, intending six boys and six girls. But five boys and seven girls, that was perverse; that was cheating. Somebody produced a girl that God had intended as a boy. They could almost figure whom; one of those girls should have been a boy, but she wasn't; and two girls were now at loose ends, unless somebody took two wives. Still it was awkward; it was simply— well, awkward. But if Nehemia were willing to stay, they would give him the two surplus daughters as second wives. Didn't Jacob marry Rachel and Leah? He could even pick what pair he wanted. It would be worth it, to complete their minyan. They would be good girls. With him there, the colony would feel somehow complete.

Nehemia shook his head at the *meshuggener,* if they were this crazy they could do anything. He made camp, piling thick logs on the fire to burn all night, so they should think he was still there. At dusk, he loaded his family on the wagon and started at a fast pace rolling toward Warsaw.

Shaya yawned under a shimmering sweep of starlight.

"We'll sleep?"

"When it's safe."

Shaya curled on the bench against him. Nehemia spread his greatcoat over him, but the slippery, jarring pebbles under the wheels jarred the boy. Shaya crawled back over the rocking canvas and fell asleep in Geula's arms. Nehemia put his coat back on and rode in silence.

The next settlement was larger and considerably older, with sun-dried walls and thatch roofs. The settlers had lived years in this location with nothing to do but be fruitful and multiply. Children popped out of every window. By now they had six *minyanim,* and another six on the way. Nehemia still touched off a stir that gathered in to a charge of excitement as he approached a group of colonists. They kept so busy with each other they had no time to talk to him.

"He's here."

"He's finally come."

"He had white horses."

"My father died, waiting his entire life for this."

"Last night, I saw blood on the moon."

"He had to come today."

"Look—white horses!"

A farmer rolled a wagon out of his barn and began hitching his horses. Another screamed to his wife to pack faster. A teacher called for class and sent the children jumping out the window to race home screaming. A man in *gatkes* jumped out of a second-story window and ran for his horses. Three old ladies stood side by side, giggling hysterically at Nehemia. Across the way, children's voices began singing in chorus, "When Israel Went out of Egypt," amid cries of rejoicing.

Nehemia gagged. His hair stood on end. It was a Messianic cult. If he didn't get out fast, he would have forty crowded wagons following him to Warsaw to build the new Jerusalem. He leaned back and cracked his whip over his horses. They leaned into their harness and started the wagon rolling. He cracked it again. they heaved forward, speeding up.

As the settlement Jews screamed to him to wait, Nehemia yelled back to Geula to watch the girls. The wagon now moved faster, with the mule running behind, trying to stay on its feet. A moment later, Shaya crawled back between the bouncing boxes and took his place beside him.

Nehemia slowed down after the third crossroads, letting the horses take wind, trusting anybody following to take a wrong turn.

Shaya looked up. "What happened?"

"They thought I was the Messiah."

"What are they, crazy?"

"What can you do. Galitzianer Jews."

Chapter Eleven

As NEHEMIA CROSSED INTO POLAND, a visionary blue haze hung in front of him so powerful that he could feel it with his fingers. Inside the light, a huge wagon rolled toward him, drawn by a single horse. The driver was a gaunt Talmudist, impoverished, with empty eye sockets, in a worn black suit and black felt with a worn brim. The horse was lean and black as the rabbi, its belly hanging like the rabbi's clothes. Both had the same face.

The wagon dragged alongside, the rabbi whipping the horse as if he knew where he was going, yelling in a hoarse Yiddish, his voice a dry wheeze: "Go, stupidity! Go, meat and bone! Horse, do your job!" Then the rabbi pointed his whip at Nehemia and gestured for him to stand alongside the horse and help pull the wagon.

Nehemia gasped and flinched back. At Shaya's hand on his elbow and his quiet "What?" the blue light dissolved. Nehemia rode on in a troubled silence.

In Poland, solid farms were carved out of the stretches of waste country—fields with drainage, enclosed pastures, and walled meadows. Each valley had its cluster of stone cottages with thatched roofs, wells with long pump handles angled into the air, and women with wooden shoes carrying a pair of baskets at either end of a pole across their shoulders. Everywhere priests led groups of children.

Soon Nehemia's wagon bounced over the stone streets of a medieval town. Its dwellers flicked glances of appraisal toward Nehemia, but refused to engage in conversation with a Jew. The city wall had been blasted out during some ancient war. Hardy children climbed it to walk along the top. Bats hid there, and owls perched on the broken pediment at night. A dark velvet moss clung to the breaks in the stone.

Past the town, Nehemia encountered some Jewish farms and Polish shetetlach that were sturdier than the Galician colonies. News moved more easily. They were less isolated and possessed by rumors, less inclined to pick up and move.

Polish roads were busier. Nehemia regularly passed vagabonds, bandits, political dissidents, or just beggars. They sometimes called up to him but Nehemia never slowed down. They let him pass.

At one campsite, a bare-chested man, with a Cossack mustache, his head shaven, ran alongside the wagon, jumped on, and sat down next to Shaya on the driver's seat.

Nehemia looked ahead, driving in silence. When the stranger said nothing, Nehemia asked in Polish, "You have a name?"

The stranger smiled. "Why not tell me your name, Jew?"

Controlling himself, Nehemia tapped Shaya, who crawled in to the back, frightened. Nehemia then said evenly, "Stranger, this wagon carries my wife and my four children. They are my family. Go in peace."

The man refused to move.

Nehemia cracked the whip far out, just touching first one horse's nose, then the other. He cracked the whip on the road, lifting a pebble. He rose on his feet and stepped away, the whip angled back, the handle in his right hand, the whiplash in his left, and waited, his powerful body crouched, ready for a jump.

The stranger gave him a long look and slipped off the wagon with a lazy smile. Nehemia put the whip back in the holder.

Shaya crawled back up front and rejoined him on the driver's bench.

Driving, Nehemia shook with indignation. Such a fight always brought a Jew reprisals. And what if the man carried a gun? He felt the tears running down his cheeks. Let him arrive already. The trip was taking too long; hidden dangers were strung along the road. But there was no reason to despair. The Warsaw Belzer had Kahal government, a school for his children, husbands for his daughters, a minyan in walking distance, and sanity.

That night, he again saw God's wagon rolling along the road toward him, more huge than before in its visionary blue, against continuous black smoke. Now, however, the horse drove; the gaunt rabbi was in harness. But the horse was blind too, whipping the rabbi to pull faster and whinnying incomprehensible orders in the hoarse voice of the rabbi, as the rabbi moved like a corpse pushing to its own grave.

The horse gestured with its hoof for Nehemia to help pull the wagon. Nehemia woke with a choked scream. What was waiting in Poland? But it was too late to turn around, and he had nowhere else to go. Besides, he had family in Warsaw. He was a Belzer. He gave Shaya a quiet hug.

In the next walled town, Nehemia stopped before a fortress synagogue with a peaked lead roof, round windows blackened with soot, and scorch marks on the wall. Two rows of letters arched over the recessed door: HOUSE OF ISRAEL, I PLACE GOD EVER BEFORE ME. No Jew was visible anywhere; it was still a Kahal building.

Nehemia gestured to Geula to keep the children close, and stepped around to the attached cemetery. Slate tombstones leaned in every direction; two winged angels, thin as scratches, blew trumpets of resurrection over the inscription. But every stone had the same date of death, a hundred years before. Some stones bore no names. Those lying in this cemetery had all been massacred.

Nehemia approached a white bearded Jew in a white *kitel* who was sweeping the walk. "Peace be unto you."

"Unto all who come in peace."

"One can live in Warsaw?"

"You have a trade?"

"I raise chickens."

"A few shtetl before Warsaw are opening up."

"For a laboring man?"

"A laborer is not a thief. Ask before Warsaw; the Jews there will help you." And he resumed his sweeping.

Nehemia left the town behind. The fields became rocky and soon disappeared into open country. The road swerved behind a spur of mountains. Very quickly, he was in the wilds again. Then, after an hour's riding, three Russian army scouts galloped past. One trotted around the wagon, eyeing it, and then galloped off to join the others.

Nehemia immediately turned off the road before the advancing army. He put on additional canvas covers, and strapped everything down firmly. He put Geula on the quilt, angled out of sight behind boxes, with two daughters on one side and one on the other; he cautioned them not to move.

Nehemia got back on the road with Shaya, cracked the whip, and got the wagon rolling, singing under his breath: "Though I walk through the valley of the shadow of death, I fear no evil; for Thou art with me. Thy rod and Thy staff, they comfort me."

Nehemia fell silent as a contingent of several hundred Russian foot soldiers approached, then another, and then another, marching in step. It was an army corps, redeployed from St. Petersburg behind the Turkish border. Occasionally a column broke into a Russian folk song that spread from column to column until the earth itself was marching.

With two wheels of his wagon off the road, Nehemia drove at a slow, steady pace, and left the road altogether when a row of caissons approached. Whenever anyone glanced up, Nehemia raised his hand in solemn salute, staring dead ahead. The army was in battle formation, marching toward a strange war. Nehemia and his family could have been on another planet.

After the bulk of the foot soldiers passed, a platoon of Cossacks appeared, riding bareback, with tufted boots, shaggy coats, and drooping mustaches. Nehemia pulled off the road against a hugh bush, and waited, singing the *Oleinu* and preparing to die, as the Cossacks galloped up.

One Cossack yanked his horse to a pitched stop directly in front of the wagon. He lifted a hugh pistol in Nehemia's face and cocked the trigger. Nehemia shrugged and pointed to the mule in back. Laughing, the Cossack shot the mule dead. As it collapsed, its blood running in the sand, the Cossack galloped off in high spirits.

Nehemia stepped around the blood and retrieved the last fodder, chanting a *Shehecheyanu* of thanksgiving that his family was unharmed. It was his good fortune that the Russians marched

37

south, disciplined and in full armor. Were they running the other way, leaving half their number crippled and dead on the battlefield, they would have gone over his wagon like ravens, kites, and vultures.

Nehemia now met more Polish Jews. They had a God different from the God of the Galician Jews. God in Galicia was looser, more enigmatic, a creature of wayward contradictions, at home on a weedy plain and in the heresies and giddy dreams of His believers. God in Poland was institutionalized and morally relentless, at home in a law court and in the ark of a fortress synagogue. These Polish Jews intimidated Nehemia. They had holdings greater than those of any Galician colony, but they always looked dissatisfied. They were better craftsmen, slower and more deliberate; their tailors knew how to make a coat. Stubborn in their caftans, they talked a legal jargon, reinforcing each other like a hutch of noisy chickens: "What do you raise? Chickens? I never heard of such a thing, a chicken farmer from Galicia? Keep moving; we have enough of our own Jews on charity."

Hearing the Polish Jews talk to one another, Nehemia caught news from the West, countries whose names he scarcely knew. Confused he was, and afraid to ask for explanations. But if Rothschild was one man, why was he in so many places? Another name, Herzl, spread more furtively; here the name of a new Messiah, there a piece of abomination.

Nehemia passed another scorched medieval synagogue, but also newer synagogues, symmetrical wooden structures that angled out log on log, with spacious porches. Polish Jewry was on the ascendant. His move north was happening at a good hour.

Hard-bitten Warshavers cracked open a peasant like Nehemia like a ripe walnut, to get at the soft meat inside, but Nehemia had too tough a crust, a stubborn common sense, and a way of landing on his feet. He took care of himself and his dependents, never asking anybody for anything. He was evasive, slippery, mistrustful.

His fodder almost gone, his children travel-sick, Nehemia remembered the cemetery beadle. He stopped asking questions and spread the word everywhere that he was a chicken farmer, looking for a place to settle. He camped, waiting for an answer, confident that God would not forget him.

When the tanner's sister approached his campfire, Nehemia took one look at her face knew she had a home to offer him. He would take that home and raise his family there. Any stranger would get only so close to him.

Chapter Twelve

A WANDERER ALL HIS YOUTH, Nehemia strode restlessly from room to room in his own house, one he would never leave until he was carried to his grave. Here, he replaced broken handles; there, he scraped away wood rot. Everywhere he made doors open and windows close. He permanently closed the doors to more exotic rooms without bothering his head with their use, working all day with a patient exasperation. He had made his great decision to move north. Now a part of him wanted the women to run the house, just let him enjoy his family and raise chickens. He was like Noah after the flood, who got drunk, enjoyed the earth, and took pleasure in his daughters.

In the kitchen, Nehemia koshered all the iron pots, pans, prongs, and skillets. He checked signs for rats. He burned the wooden dishes that could not be koshered and buried the earthenware in the ground. In a hundred years, his grandchildren would uncover them, vessels once again kosher. He unpacked two sets of dishes and another two for Passover, mumbling under his breath about the mountains of cutlery.

The stable had a hard wooden floor from the days when the building was a school, the stable used for school dances. Nehemia spread a load of sawdust, built layers of shelves and cages, a watering trough and perches. He installed a kerosene stove and plenty of water. From another chicken farmer he bought a rooster and six healthy pullets, carefully probing each bird under the wing and across the chest to make sure it had straight bones.

The children wasted no time taking over the house. On arrival the three girls marched from floor to floor, opening doors. Frightened of being alone, Gita and Feigeleh took over the largest guest room, insisting on rooming together. Gita called them visiting royalty. It didn't matter which was king and which was queen; it was enough that they were a royal couple.

Ignoring her sisters, Esther took a corner room halfway up the stairs to the third floor. Smaller than the guest room, it overlooked the road and had a yard window, a balcony with a view in back, and a rail over which she could eavesdrop all over the house—Esther, the family spider.

Esther had furniture, but no linen. She marched in on her two sisters and dragged out all their bedclothes, screaming that they were hers. The two jumped her on the stairs and dragged them back indignantly; but Esther attacked them once again with screams, so Geula hurried up the stairs and ordered them quiet.

Esther then demanded that her mother decide; anything she said was fine with her. Geula heard them out. As the three sisters stood, trembling with tension, Geula decided they should pool their bedclothes and divide everything three ways. Gita and Feigeleh agreed morosely, having no choice. As for Esther, she had planned exactly this from the beginning. She put a straight face on her satisfaction and carried her booty to her room.

Nehemia and Geula gave Shaya a bedroom adjacent to their own. Their son and heir had been a fantasy for so long that Shaya was now accompanied by an atmosphere of achievement; he was the family treasure. Every Friday night after kiddush, Nehemia put his hands over the heads of his three daughters together, blessed them in the spirit of the matriarchs, and kissed them. Shaya then got his blessing by himself—in the spirit of Abraham, Isaac, and Jacob.

To quiet the local nobility's suspicions about a Jewish landowner, Nehemia removed the flagpole, painted the house a dull gray black, locked the gate permanently, and arranged a side entrance for wagons into the yard, nailing a sign, CHICKENS, over the kitchen door. A Galitzianer barbarian, he gave no credit; he took money or local produce in barter. The Jews accepted him into their community; the Poles grudgingly respected their *zhid*.

The Radich area was more settled than Galicia. The Jews managed their own affairs with little contact with the authorities. The Belzer sent a specialist who built a mikvah in the yard back of the kitchen, with a sunken tile booth, tile steps, and a source for special running water. Geula descended into it once a month to cleanse herself a week after her period, accompanied by Feigeleh, her middle daughter.

Once Nehemia was loading the wagon for a trip to the Warsaw market, with Shaya helping hand up boxes of eggs, when a local Polish nobleman galloped up the road, his riding jacket buttoned up to the neck, his skinny hand chafing the head of his riding crop, fishing for offense.

"Do you know me, Jew?"

Nehemia bowed slightly and looked away. "I have the honor to speak to Prince Jan Potofsky, lord of all our villages."

The prince nodded curtly. "So the Galician stranger is changing the Flying Goose into a Jewish chicken farm."

Nehemia nodded patiently. "I respect its noble history. I bought the building from a Bucharest woman who lived here alone. I have people in Bucharest. If the prince is curious, I can inquire from them about her."

The prince snorted, cracking his whip. "Never mix in my affairs."

Nehemia bowed carefully—then Anna was the prince's mistress. "I am always at the prince's service."

He took a huge breath of relief as Prince Jan galloped off. The prince was occupied with other things; he had not struck fire.

Geula was always taken aback at how hard Nehemia worked. She felt alienated by it, as if he didn't altogether trust her and couldn't allow himself to relax. A religious peasant worked that way. Gershuni never exerted himself that much. But she worked in her own fashion, ignoring his compulsions.

After all his years around Shabbateans and mystics, Nehemia had a touch of the demonic in him. Sometimes a downpour of rain was a stream of invisible angels, dissolving all idolatry in a rain of heavenly fire. He liked the massive furnishings of the Flying Goose, with oak knobs, chests of drawers with partitioned sections, heavy brocades, and the samovar that he could sit next to for hours, his children asleep over his head, sipping tea from a saucer. This was burgher solidity. Raising his family in the house of the red flag touched awake the Shabbatean secrets of his boyhood.

He built a sturdy platform in the chicken house, put a mattress on it, and lay there by the hour, restlessly watching his flock. When he found broken, empty shells, he hovered on the watch, caught the cannibal chicken breaking an egg, and slaughtered it for the table. If a brooding hen seemed restless, he put its egg beneath a quieter hen. He could have sat by the samovar with his daughters, sipping tea and enjoying being a father; but women were quality. He didn't really belong.

Sometimes, lying in the chicken house, Nehemia got horny. Unsure of himself, he clambered off the platform, pushed blindly outside, shambled back to the house, and climbed the steps. Whichever daughter was with Geula took one look at him coming in and got out fast, as Geula prepared herself. It wasn't even that Nehemia wanted particularly; he wanted a raft on which to ride out the random tumble of a strange country. Yet he wanted sex, clinging to Geula's body in the stupid heavy push of cattle and fish.

In the winter, Nehemia cut ice in the back pond, bringing out the children so bundled up they could scarcely move. They all pitched in with measuring lines, ice picks, hatchets, hammers and levers, hooks and ropes, sliding slabs of ice over one another into the icehouse, using straw to separate them so the slabs wouldn't stick together.

As the children moved the slabs, screaming at each other not to slip, to keep their mittens on and their feet to themselves, Nehemia felt a pressure mount inside him. He began singing, "When Israel Went out of Egypt." For an hour, they sang and worked together, until they began to tire. Shaya wailed that his fingers were frozen; a block of ice slipped on Esther's toe.

Then Gita slid into the water. Nehemia snatched her up. As he carried her back into the house, shivering with cold, he wondered why he avoided the Kramers in Warsaw. They were his family; he came north to be near them. But what did a close, dignified family need with an ignorant Galician farmer? There was time to meet them when he got established.

Nehemia carried Gita inside. As Geula put her to bed, she murmured, "Why don't you get a helper? Afraid I'll spoil you if you have time on your hands?"

"Try me and see for yourself."

They broke into slow grins, full of secrets that made them happy.

Chapter Thirteen

ONCE A MONTH in balmy weather, Feigeleh and Gita put on walking shoes and Sabbath clothes, and accompanied Nehemia to the Melon synagogue. Vain and self-conscious, the two sisters huddled together, peeping through the curtain as Nehemia sang the service, checking off shtetl Jews and finding them all pathetic. The Polish Jews looked down on them, and Nehemia's daughters withdrew with a touch of defiance. They found their Jewish neighbors petty, ingrown, full of bad manners, and lacking in soul. The service over, they accompanied Nehemia back home, relieved, having kept their self-respect and advertised their female wares. Now they need not leave their homes again for a month.

Gita secretly longed for Galicia. She couldn't bear their isolation. In the winters it was a battle to step into the yard, no wagon ever pulled in with visiting family, and meals were just a Kramer affair. Nobody arranged a marriage for her. In Galicia, her family were quality people, Mediterranean travelers who dressed in silk. Her father made her ashamed.

As for Feigeleh, the most restless and forthright of the three, she sensed even more than Gita how stranded they were. She kept talking about other towns, Warsaw, and the west, and felt she couldn't hide in a basket. She was too restless to know the world, to strike out, and establish that she was there.

Her sisters practiced being ladies, but to Esther, it was all a bore and a waste of time. The smartest and most wayward of the three, she sensed that her parents were not that close, and dreamed of growing up and marrying Nehemia herself. If Geula sighed, Esther smiled with satisfaction; if she coughed, Esther scrutinized her for signs of tuberculosis. It was all very sinful, of course; but she knew Nehemia's secret. Underneath all his patriarchal dignity, he was a scamp, just like her.

Seeing Esther, his pet, forever near him, Nehemia nudged her and pointed to a bluebird. "That bird comes from Jerusalem."

Esther glanced at the bird and smiled happily, refusing to answer. Nehemia had made it all up, but his talking like that made her very happy.

Esther was watching when Nehemia found an abandoned harpsichord behind some boxes in a closet. She instantly pounced on it and insisted that Nehemia have it tuned for playing. With knowing fingers and Nehemia's feel for music, she practiced until she played as well as her sisters plucked chickens. Evening after evening, she got Gita and Feigeleh to sing with her as Nehemia rolled his eyes, wondering when work would be done. He felt Esther's pressure on him and finally fled the room; but she was in seventh heaven, banging louder and raising her voice so it filled the house. He would never escape her.

As for Shaya, arriving at Radich with only dream memories of Galicia, he swam and ran outdoors like an animal; yet something in him was always adult. He was a shade more religious than his sisters, more civilized and careful in his blessings. He was patient, guarded, self-assured, with a deep generosity and a quiet sense of what parts of himself he would never let be violated. He worshiped his mother, yet their relationship was very formal. He and Nehemia spoke little but they thoroughly trusted each other. Shaya understood his place in the family. Coming north out of Galicia, Nehemia got them into motion; he was the next step forward. Twice, working in the garden, his father had kicked him for being a fool. No third kick was necessary; Shaya was never a fool again.

Shaya liked wandering their grounds alone. To Nehemia, God filled the vast waste of the steppes; to Shaya, God was the dew in the air, the green shoots along the river in March—a hope, a birth, a constant beginning.

On a frozen night, under heavy, shifting clouds, Shaya crossed the yard in his greatcoat, to get a fresh egg for his mother in the morning, swinging a lamp for security in the pitch-darkness. When he slipped his hand under the hen's sleeping body and took the warm, fresh-laid egg without waking the mother, he was the thief of heaven, putting it on Geula's plate.

The village of Melon was several miles away. Having some of his father's waywardness, Shaya made his mother his teacher for Hebrew and Bible. He didn't want the village Jews and their Hebrew classes. A creature of intuition, he absorbed music like a blotter, Shaya sensed early his father's ongoing solitude. It made him a meditative. With all Shaya's overflowing happiness, he kept alone, riding inarticulate hungers and talents he would never explore. A blind need to trust gripped him with a starvation.

Feigeleh already knew Hebrew. Now that Shaya had begun Esther decided to study too, and soon outstripped them all. Esther sensed Gita's excuse for not studying, that she was just a woman. But she was so vain about her humility—she clearly thought herself a superior person, being so humble; Esther couldn't stop laughing at such idiocy.

Aside from his father, Shaya felt close only to Esther. She sensed his closeness; his aloof withdrawal so like his father's awkward distance with women, drew her irresistibly to him. After an hour plucking chickens with her sisters, Esther would chase off and start plucking the family darling. He promptly started screaming, but Esther persisted until Geula waded in and extricated him, screaming and half-dressed from her hands. Geula insisted that Esther respect her brother. Esther made herself contrite. An hour later, Shaya popped up at her side, ready for another plucking.

Once Esther hid behind a door and fell on him like a hungry cat, dragging him to the floor. "Lokshen-face, answer a riddle before I eat you up: will you marry your choice, or Poppa Momma's?"

"Poppa Momma's," he answered instantly.

She ground her fist in his nose. "That's the wrong answer, lokshen-face. Before Poppa Momma, you marry who I choose for you."

"Why can't I marry who I want to marry?"

"You have to want who I want, lokshen-face."

"But I want what Poppa Momma want," he wailed.

"You're a fool, lokshen-face, a fool, a fool, a fool."

Another time, she grabbed Shaya and started to spank him. "What did I do? What did I do?" he wailed.

"I'm spanking you for being lazy. You should have been born first. Then I could have met all your friends and picked the one I wanted. But you were lazy, so you're completely useless to me."

"I couldn't help it! Hit Momma! Hit Poppa! They did it, not me!"

"No, you're to blame! You're to blame!"

Esther found an abandoned sign behind the woodpile, a great wooden shield with a flying goose painted on, faded and weather-beaten, but still heavily flapping its wings. Awed, Esther leaned it back and flapped her elbows as in the sign of the inn. She ran inside and asked Nehemia why the flying goose was their emblem.

Nehemia picked her up and swung her back and forth in the air. "Because the goose is an edible bird, and I'm raising three more edible birds of my own that will grow and fly away."

Esther kissed him and gave a huge sigh of impatient satisfaction. She went out and lugged the shield to the sliver of lawn in the woods, shimmied up a tree with a rope, and pulled up the shield to dangle from a branch. She then lugged out a wooden tub.

With her usual relentless insistence, she coaxed her two sisters out. In the summer heat, they stripped and bathed in the woods, then danced around the tub, self-conscious about their bodies. They clambered on the swings and pushed each other, pitching up naked, kicking their heels and laughing. They felt wicked for such scandalous behavior, virtuous for knowing how wicked they were, and fascinated at being so complicated and having so many feelings.

Suspicious of the way Esther disappeared with her sisters, leaving the house empty, Shaya snooped around until he found their lair, now complete with stones from an ancient herb garden, swings, the flying goose, and the tub. He climbed a tree and waited. They skipped out, stripped and started to bathe. He watched, fascinated as they jumped in the tub, soaped each other, and danced.

Carried away, he let out a tiny burp. Esther squinted around, then shinnied up the tree, pulled him down, stripped and soaped him mercilessly, taunting him to watch Geula in her mikvah. He had no mother to protect him now; he was completely in her power.

Gita and Feigeleh quickly dressed and left, but Esther couldn't stop herself. Shaya was too delicious, just a sliver of God's body. When she finished washing him, she lifted him out and kicked him in the rump; he dressed as fast as he could. He returned to the inn, screaming and delighted; she scampered after.

Nehemia shook his head that night in bed. "Esther is becoming impossible."

Geula grinned slowly. "It happens to many girls. When I was Esther's age, I was always walking in six directions at once. Pay attention and you'll only make problems. It'll pass; she'll pull together."

Nehemia sighed. "I hope so."

Strangers who brushed against Nehemia's daughters found them engaging, ardent, uninhibited, full of life, with an innocent winning generosity. But they lacked an animal toughness that comes from sinking one's roots in the locale. They needed protection. Three impulsive girls, they needed more luck than one has a right to expect in this world.

Chapter Fourteen

WINTER PASSED, then summer; it was another fall. More and more, as they settled permanently on the chicken farm, Gita saw the move north as a disaster. She stayed docile and well-behaved; but her grandmother's words stayed hooked in her mind. She missed the Horowitz clan. Remembering the tension between Yael and her mother, she aligned herself with her grandmother. Her mother was smarter and more effective, but she had them stranded among a bunch of peddlers and village farmers. The Radich area was just too cold, too isolated. There was no common ground. In Galicia, she always had things to join in, family to visit. She kept getting distracted, frustrated, with nobody to talk to. Often she bit the side of her mouth as she chewed. Spoken to, she didn't always hear. Sometimes she washed her face a second time, not remembering what she had just done.

Gita was secretly ashamed of Nehemia. He was just too arrogant. Her zayde was such a refined man. He set her father up in life but Nehemia showed no gratitude at all. And the way Nehemia showed feeling, suddenly giving gifts without an occasion so you didn't know how to react. It was embarrassing, like the way he suddenly stopped and stared at her with that huge grin. He did it when she was in her wrapper; but even when she was clothed, it didn't feel right. He was a man; and men are, well, difficult. He was a peasant, he was primitive. But being his daughter, she couldn't spell out her worry. She sulked, had obscure longings, and refused to talk.

Feigeleh also had misgivings about Nehemia. The part of her already woman felt at once approached too much and altogether rejected, with no sure footing to make her able to love. But this only made her turn more emphatically to Geula, a full woman, with only her sane, practical mind, who liked having her with her in the kitchen and let her accompany her to the mikvah. Nehemia was generous to the family and completely devoted, and she adored him, but Feigeleh wasn't sure Nehemia thought about her at all. And he had that sardonic smile, that dreamy look in his eyes when he sang, a violence in him that was not altogether under control. Geula thought herself generous in marrying Nehemia, and Feigeleh completely agreed. Geula was generous because women know how to be generous, and Feigeleh would be too.

Feigeleh studied Hebrew with her mother and became a Bible reader. She felt especially for Shulamite in the Song of Songs—a farming girl whom everybody ignored, and yet she spurned King Solomon for her village sweetheart. She read over and over: "I am black but comely, O ye daughters of Jerusalem, as the tents of Kedar, the curtains of Solomon. I am black because the sun looked upon me. My mother's children were angry with me. They made me the keeper of the vineyard, but my own vineyard I have not kept." When she read that passage Feigeleh burst into tears.

Her father was a compulsive worker and so was she. She was his daughter, even if he ignored her completely. Pushing out on her own, she became a fine housekeeper and tended her own garden; growing vegetables for the family table felt like a constant healing. Nehemia loved the whole family. She did too, and spelled out her love in food she set on the table for everybody to eat. At the Passover seder, she relished her satisfaction. The bitter herbs her father ate were fruit of her garden.

Only Esther stayed completely loyal to Nehemia. His strange smile and dreamy roving eyes only made her love him the more.

And if his movements were unpredictable, she always managed to track him down. She would have him in her web yet.

Nehemia's children shrank from the nearby shtetl as provincial, but Nehemia found much in its way of life congenial. The Melon Jews were stubbornly content and enormously secure in their holdings. They combined a grass-roots determination to survive with a mistrust of any change, sharing local events and reports from Warsaw at synagogue. The town elders made realistic decisions for the shtetl with a constant sense of how exposed they were. A gang of Jewish thieves occupied a stable five kilometers away; if the Poles didn't object, the Jews left them alone. They didn't want turmoil.

The Melon Jews cautiously sniffed out passing travelers, many of them Yeshiva boys, dazed and bewildered after too many years of Talmud. In despair of ever graduating to become rabbis and unready for trade, they read Yiddish translations of Goethe and Schiller in secret until something inside them cried, enough! It's up to here! They took off to smell the fields, meet human beings, and start making a living.

Each visitor got a bed, a seat at prayers, and a kosher meal. If he seemed a professional beggar, a permanent vagabond, or just crazy, he was moved on swiftly. A more agreeable wanderer got a job, as a clerk, a teacher. A shiddach was arranged; he was absorbed into the shtetl.

The Melon Jews were particularly on their guard with transients before Passover. At that time any stranger with a suitcase might be accused of carrying gentile blood to make matzoh, and so would cast a pall on the entire shtetl. Provocateurs might come, converted Jews out to trap them. Passover was the time of the great migration, a restlessness stirred from house to house. Sniffing the Angel of Death, Nehemia sat at his seder table, his greatcoat on, staff in hand, ready at a word to begin his wandering again.

In a distant way, the Melon Jews knew of something called modern life in the West. The Rothschilds pushed for a Suez Canal. France had a revolution. The railroads were beginning to expand across Poland. Over the Atlantic, a strange nation was growing. They sniffed at it, yet something had gone limp in their characters. Once an inspiration, the Messiah was now a poltergeist who smothered every question and every impulse to change. He would bring redemption, if they could just hang on long enough.

Nehemia fitted in slowly and carefully. On a free afternoon, he loaded ice onto his wagon layered in straw with a thick rug on top, and rode it to Melon to sell. He had his own sardonic sense of patient humor and with a peasant's indifference shrugged off those of his customers who found his accent jarring. With his natural tenor voice and abundance of melody, he always served as cantor.

Nehemia always liked to size up those he did business with. A workman once stepped into the yard, asking for a job. Nehemia smelled him out as a thief; he welcomed him on the farm, gave him a pick, and started him digging a trench, following him with a shovel. After an hour, the man asked how far the trench went. Nehemia told him to keep digging. The man was strong, but after another hour Nehemia was shoveling him out with the dirt. The man disappeared up the road, cursing under his breath.

Nehemia noticed his fenced-in chicken yard was getting holes in the ground. His flock was growing and was too big for so small a yard. All were digging in the same spot. He needed a helper to carry the work. He would build an adjacent pen, and shift the chickens back and forth.

Seeing Esther eyeing him, Nehemia gave her a huge grin. "Go tell your sisters that if they'll pluck it, I'll slaughter a good chicken for tonight." Esther darted off, pleased to do her father's bidding.

One Saturday morning, Nehemia spotted a vagabond in the Melon synagogue —gaunt, with a long, wispy beard, a driver's hat, and a tallis over a heavy workman's coat.

Nehemia strode over. *"Gut shabbes."*

The man blinked without answering. He didn't seem altogether sane, but his bearing had enormous dignity.

Nehemia smiled. "You're a traveler?"

The man joined his hands. "My name is Shimon Cohen. When I was ten my father sold me into the Cossack army to release another man's son. Twenty of us went to the Urals for training. Nineteen died of colds; only I survived that first winter. A question kept me alive. I was a cannoneer against the Turks. We subdued the Mongols. I was released five years ago; but I lost the name of my town, so I became a wanderer. If you know of a Cohen taken into the army forty years ago, my search will be over."

Nehemia smiled gently. "What question kept you alive?"

"Moses sent twelve spies to scout out the land in a time of war. I want to know, did they give him an honest answer when they returned?"

Nehemia shook his head. "Caleb and Joshua did; the others had no courage. They said giants lived there, too strong to be conquered."

Shimon slammed his fists together. "They said that about the Turks, but we crushed the Turks. Nobody could stop our army! Who told the truth? Caleb and Joshua? We could have used them in Mongolia."

Nehemia frowned. "What powder protects chickens against nits?"

"You mix lye with a pot of powdered chalk."

"Can you use a hammer?"

"I built a tent with my bare hands in a hurricane."

"Come home with me after services. You can sleep in the chicken house. Work for me and you'll never go hungry."

Shimon lifted Nehemia's hand and kissed it. Nehemia began services breathing a sigh of relief. He had an assistant he trusted.

With Shimon's arrival, Gita and Feigeleh, and their scamp sister Esther, invaded the chicken house to harass him, but he charged about, cheerfully ignoring them. He was unable to sit idle; old army ideas were always possessing him. Thrashing about, lonely, he gave his chickens orders; his hens were a work detail whose job it was to produce eggs. If they faltered at the job, he'd report them to headquarters.

But after a period of excitement, the idea of army went dead in his head. The chicken house became a military prison. Shimon was once locked in a Turkish jail for a month, with caged cells one row over another, just like these chicken coops. He barely got out alive. When this occurred to him Shimon sat down under the weight of the memory, wailing and dabbing his cheeks. Then, after a period of weeping, the hen house became a barracks again, the chickens a work detail following his orders.

Geula stopped Nehemia. "Find Shimon a wife in Warsaw. Gita spends too much time in the chicken house. He's not all there in the head. It's your own fault, insisting on somebody you can totally trust. You should have been satisfied with an ordinary farmer. Shimon isn't a farmer at all. He's a retired soldier. What does he do in there, guard duty?"

"Enough. I'll see what I can find."

Chapter Fifteen

ONCE A WEEK, Shimon and Nehemia loaded the wagon before dawn with eggs and cages of live chickens, tying down the cages so they wouldn't jostle apart on the road. Nehemia gave the family his last instructions for the day and took off for Warsaw. From her lookout window, Esther always watched Nehemia start off and then went back to sleep.

Nehemia rode in pitch-darkness to Melon, and from there to the next shtetl, Kabol. Twelve kilometers above Kabol, he joined the road of the Bucharest coach. By now the sun was rising. It was too early for travelers but on the road were other chicken farmers, vegetable farmers, a rolling hut of an icehouse, and one-horse runners carrying containers of milk. Boys with long switches kept herds of cattle on the road. An Orthodox farmer gave his son the reins, put on tallis and tefillin, and prayed standing on the wagon. When he finished he took the reins again and his son began to pray.

Soon the sun stood high in the heavens. Passenger coaches began to pass, with curtained windows. Nehemia's path broadened and grew more congested as they joined the main road to Bucharest. One wagon edged aside to avoid a fight, urgently anxious, another watched for friends. A dust began hanging in the air, not the raw dust of Galicia, but human grime, filled with smoke from a thousand chimney pots.

After a substantial trip, the travelers passed through the crowded courtyards of Warsaw. Finally, in the high morning, Nehemia rolled in a congestion of coaches and wagons onto a market by the Belzer synagogue and other institutional buildings, harnessed his horses, and put them by a water trough, and prepared for a day's selling.

A month after Nehemia began visiting the Belzer market, a war broke out between groups of ritual slaughterers. The Belzer didn't trust the Gerer, or the Gerer, the Belzer; the Litvaks trusted no one. Wild rumors flew about, of sanctions and retaliation, secret atheists contaminating their kitchens with horsemeat, scandals about to burst, bribes that passed behind closed doors. Jews bought only from butchers they knew personally; the more timid went altogether vegetarian. The whole meat business was shrinking.

That morning, a delegation of butchers in slaughtering aprons, their beards bristling with outrage, each with a black yarmulke, marched down the street, carrying their axes, and invaded Kahal Council, demanding respectable work conditions, and an end to this bickering. Kahal Council heard them out. After three hours behind closed doors they sent a delegation to the rabbis, demanding, on penalty of fines for their schools, an acceptance of Kahal authority over ritual slaughter. Fearful of controversy, a crowd rushed to the market to buy live chickens to slaughter at home with the ritual knife. The demand for beef declined; the demand for chickens soared. That visit to the market, Nehemia was sold out in half an hour.

On the next wagon, a Jew sold eyeglasses, with a choice of twenty lenses all with steel frames to last a lifetime. He fitted the glasses on his customers, one after the other, demanding that they make a choice. Twenty glasses! Not another wagon in the market had so many to choose from. As Nehemia harnessed his horses and cleared his wagon for the trip home, the eyeglass salesman fought off a customer who complained of headaches. A choice of twenty lenses should be enough to find a pair he could use, so what was he coming to him with headaches?

As Nehemia left the market, making his way out of the city, Jewish craftsmen circulated on the street —a carpenter with a saw, hammer, and nails; a sweep with long-handled brooms; a scissors sharpener, carrying a stone; a used-clothes buyer carrying a big sack. A row of porters carried huge boxes on their backs, held by a strap over their chins. In every courtyard, craftsmen cried their wares.

The next week, the fight was still on. Nehemia brought three times as many chickens in rickety cages that they had spent an hour tying down. They sold at double the usual price. Having money in his pocket, Nehemia circulated about the market, buying salt, tar, nails, and yards of fabric. But he refused to buy a bracelet he liked. To take it home would mean he was competing with Gershuni, and in such a competition he would finally lose.

Late that night, Nehemia drove a laden wagon back to the Flying Goose. He glanced into the chicken house. One careful look around, and he knew Shimon had followed the schedule he gave him before leaving.

When Nehemia entered the house everyone was asleep. Only Esther sped from her window to the rail over the stairs. She had spied Nehemia coming in. Now she leaned over the rail, straining for his conversation with Geula.

"You didn't stay up for me?" Nehemia asked, crawling into bed.

Geula made room. "It was so late, I thought you'd sleep over. It's not good to travel after dark. Shimon can manage. The night roads aren't safe for a Jew."

Geula's mistrust of the night road made Nehemia uneasy, but he didn't change his routine. Then, one night, he saw a burned wagon by the road. Its sides still smoldered. Nehemia continued riding, afraid to stop and look for the driver. Had this wagon not preceded his, his wagon would have been plundered. Next time he resolved to sleep over in Warsaw after all.

On his next visit to Warsaw, Nehemia wrestled with his guilt at sleeping away from family. It was necessary, but at least he shouldn't enjoy it. A hotel felt immoral. For three kopeks, he arranged to sleep on a tailor's bench when the tailor stopped work, but the tailor worked sixteen hours a day.

Waiting for the tailor to go home, Nehemia stepped into the Belzer synagogue for the evening prayer. There, three hundred Chasidim stood facing the ark and bimah, or central table, while the Rebbe had his own private chapel; smaller, more informal, minyanim kept forming against the side walls, and dissolving.

After service, the wizened beadle pushed through the throng, with an orange yarmulke and owl eyes.

"You want a turn at the Torah on Saturday morning, Kramer?"

Nehemia shook his head. "You don't know me."

The old man smiled. "Aren't you Kramer?"

"This is my first synagogue visit. I was all my life in Galicia. You have no Galitzianer accent. How do you know me?"

The beadle smiled dryly. "After nine years in Hebrew school with your father, I shouldn't know Aharon Dovid's voice in his son?"

Nehemia bent over, closing his eyes. "Aharon Dovid?"

"He spent a year over *Baba Metzia,* exploring land law under a foreign government, and if it lasts into the Messianic days."

Nehemia bit his lip. "And is my father still alive?"

The beadle tugged Nehemia to the side. "Speak softly; there are listeners everywhere. You lost all touch with family?"

"Lost touch? I never had any. I was left a foundling with the name Nehemia Kramer on a piece of paper."

"We live in exile."

Nehemia shuddered in indignation. "We live in exile? In a world of accidents, we do what we can do! Does my father still live?"

"He lives in the world of truth."

53

"And my mother?"

"Your father's wife here in Warsaw was without children. Family pressed him to divorce her, remarry, and have a family; but she was a sickly, gentle woman. He was an engineer who sometimes traveled. You're your father's son. Your uncle in Vienna has a garment store. Our Belzer representative visits Vienna. He'll make a stop and tell your uncle that you were found. His answer will come in a week, God willing."

"This brother was all his family?"

"A third brother became a maskil, everything for Hebrew. Shall I find him for you?"

"Everything in God's own season."

"Aharon Dovid was a fine cantor. He often took the table. Would you, next week, when you come again to market?"

"If I sleep over, I would be honored; but I go back to Radich."

The tailor had finally left his bench. Nehemia lay down and pulled his coat over him, but the bench was narrow and hard. He fell off twice. He felt guilty, not being on duty at the farm. A soldier can go on furlough, but farming is relentless. After one day without care, and half his flock could die. He didn't trust Shimon and should check for himself.

Lying unable to sleep, Nehemia remembered that the barge captain's wife knew him as a Kramer. Did she abandon Nehemia's son as a foundling with the name of Kramer attached? The stain would never disappear.

On his next Warsaw visit, the slaughterers' war was still on. Nehemia sold out quickly and returned home, but the ebb and flow of city life absorbed him more and more. On the road, Nehemia asked himself why he didn't ask the beadle to find the maskil for him; but some sense of family was burned out of him. He wanted family nearby, but only so close.

By the following week the slaughterers' war was settled. The public returned to meat with a vengeance. Nehemia sold his last chicken very late. The tailor's entrance was closed for the night, so he headed back to Radich under a full moon, barely brushing the trees overhead—and passed a campfire where three vagabonds huddled over the coals. He continued, not looking left or right, steadily cracking his whip over his horses.

Back home, Nehemia was too choked with the violence of the night to go indoors. Helpless, but refusing to be frightened, he stepped into the chicken house, sharpened his knife on the stone, grabbed and held a chicken between his legs, and slaughtered it. He then threw the body in the basket to be plucked.

When he came inside, Geula sat wrapped in a shawl in her chair, waiting. She insisted with real concern that he not come home late at night. If he couldn't sleep over, then he should stop going to Warsaw. They would manage somehow and Nehemia made his peace with sleeping over.

Chapter Sixteen

LATE ON A SEPTEMBER EVENING, beginning their third year in Melon, as the family relaxed, a large black carriage with two horses pulled into the yard. Esther first heard it and flew to the window to peer out. Moments later, as Nehemia approached the door, Gershuni stepped down from the carriage in a long black leather cloak and a field hat over a dignified sweep of hair and white temples.

Nehemia was taken aback, but he welcomed him courteously, helped him settle his horses, and brought him in to the family table, all the time working to control his own emotions at this ghost from his past. With disarming simplicity, Gershuni explained he was picking up a business connection with Zfania Binstock, the lumber merchant who first told Nehemia of his Warsaw family. If Nehemia had a spare bed, he would sleep over and go on in the morning. Nehemia had the bed.

While the men settled things outside, Geula spread a meal for her father. He gave Geula regards and bits of news about each of her relatives. He wanted to make peace with Nehemia, and stay in touch with his children and grandchildren; he should have been more generous when Nehemia left. Nehemia had good instincts in coming north. He regretted the position he took.

As Gershuni ate, and the conversation unfolded, the darker aspects of his recent life appeared. His best Bucharest contact lost a ship full of merchandise returning from India, and retired to Padua. Another was arrested by the Sultan for no reason, and all his wealth was confiscated. The Horowitz family business was in a decline. To recoup, Gershuni had to cultivate contacts in Warsaw, where things were on the upswing, and where middlemen who intimately knew the southern provinces were badly needed.

Nehemia listened uneasily. If Gershuni was shifting his line of travel to Warsaw, then he would make regular visits. Nehemia didn't like it, but it couldn't be helped. He had to give him hospitality.

"You wanted to keep my children when I left, didn't you?" Nehemia suddenly muttered, with a bitter smile.

Gershuni lifted a patient, elegant hand. "You might have wanted to get settled and bring the children later on."

Nehemia choked. "Don't take a man's children from him."

Gershuni hastily began to admire the Flying Goose. He marveled at how solidly Nehemia had established himself. He had underestimated his son-in-law. Nehemia sat without moving. Gershuni looked up at Geula. She patted his hand in appreciation of his compliment.

Gershuni had a heavy fruitcake for their table. One by one, he brought out gifts for all the children, beginning with a silk fabric for Geula. Esther stayed at table to watch, but saying nothing and sitting far away from Gershuni. She let nobody grab her by surprise.

Feigeleh sweetly kissed Gershuni, accepted her gift, but slipped out of his reach and went immediately to her room. His bringing all those gifts in that carriage was like King Solomon in the Song of Songs—when Esther wanted a sweetheart her own age, and a worker.

Shaya mistrusted Gershuni even more than Esther, but he wasn't so alert. Teasingly curious, he shuffled up to the table. There Gershuni swept him in the air and began feeling his face, exclaiming what a personality Shaya had, the presence of a born diplomat. Oh, he would negotiate like a prince! Shaya blinked at him in absolute silence. Behind his silence, impenetrable to the world, lay a total loyalty to his father.

Only Gita held back; finally Gershuni chased her around the table, snatched her up, and held her close, exclaiming in her ear, "Oh, what a lady you are! You are a real lady!"

That night in bed, Geula asked Nehemia, "You don't mind him too much, do you? If you say it, he'll never come here again."

Nehemia stiffened. "Do whatever you feel is right."

Geula kissed him in loving thanks.

At dawn Gershuni left for Warsaw. Gita stayed the whole day in the chicken house. She couldn't bear her father in the house, and Shimon was so dignified and respectful, sleeping on that platform. He never complained, even though he was cut off from family. Gita lay down on Shimon's platform. Her *bubbe* wanted her back, to marry her cousin Yitzik. Her *bubbe* seemed a figure out of the Bible, just like the four matriarchs, Sarah, Rebekah, Rachel, and Leah. Gita already had a relationship with Yitzik. Of course it had come to nothing so far, but Bubbe would keep it going.

Suddenly Gita started up. Shimon crouched at the edge of the platform, hanging on by a rope, staring at her so intensely he looked cross-eyed. God help her, was he possessed? Gita whispered her *bubbe*'s charm as a protection. Feeling secure, she got up and luxuriously stretched herself. She then daintily climbed down and went out with a charge of excitement.

Gershuni returned in midafternoon, his trip a success. Why had he moved south all these years? Warsaw was the place to do business. He brought Geula a shawl just arrived from Paris and chocolates for the children. He accepted a packet of food and continued south, to travel as far as he could before dark.

The next day, Shaya noticed Geula had dressed in the morning, the way city ladies did, instead of going half a day in a robe and then dressing for her husband when he came in from work. Was she expecting another visit from Gershuni? He was frightened, bewildered, insecure, but too guarded to complain.

Gerhsuni's visits oppressed Esther. Loyal to her father, she played the most infectious melodies on the harpsichord until the family gathered around her. Then she had Gita and Feigeleh dance a *shereleh* as she swung one hand, conducting and keeping Nehemia's family together.

Ever inventive, diffident, sly, she devised her own song, *"Du Bist Mein Ketzeleh"*—"You Are My Pussycat"—that she repeated over and over, giving each member of the family a round, and the last to Nehemia, when she reversed it and sang, *"Ich Bin Dein Ketzeleh,"*—"I Am Your Pussycat." She then burst into a giggle.

Nehemia lifted one eyebrow to Geula. She smiled helplessly. "Ignore it; it will pass. It takes time."

Nehemia nodded and continued reading.

During Gershuni's next visit to Warsaw, a quarrel erupted between the wine suppliers. A Gerer saw a gentile handle an open wine bottle in a Belzer store, giving it the taint of idolatry. The storekeeper insisted before Kahal Council that he boiled the wine and then cooled it, eliminating any risk of accidental handling by a gentile, since boiled wine is allowed. The Gerer refused to believe it and stopped buying Belzer wine. The Belzer retaliated by refusing any Gerer wine. The Litvaks rejected both their wines. To avoid confusion Kahal Council then passed a decree forbidding the boiling of wine before sale in a Jewish store. It made no difference to the Litvaks; when it came to wine, a Litvak trusted no one.

Nehemia came back that night. In the yard, he spotted Gershuni's black carriage. Gershuni was now sleeping over in a guest room, before continuing to Warsaw, but he picked the day Nehemia was in the Warsaw market. Gershuni said he wanted to make peace; but he avoided Nehemia, who ended up feeling used. Why give a free bed to a relative who avoided him?

Gershuni now came up sporadically about once a month and spent long hours with Geula. Far from Galicia, he permitted himself to talk about Yael, things he kept buried inside himself all through their marriage, as though, in the slack of distance, he could safely let his marriage fall apart. Geula knew it all already; she was still appalled to hear from her father how Yael never washed, but used perfume to cover the smells of her body. She wore silks but served food on unwashed dishes; more and more, she read books of superstition, spin-offs from the Shabbatean visionaries, one more idiotic than the next. Gershuni doubted if she was altogether sane.

Gershuni reached out hesitantly. Geula held back, and then she patted his hand. He gave her a grateful smile, somehow able to return to Galicia once more.

Once Nehemia returned at night when Gershuni was there. He sensed that Geula was awake. He turned toward her. "Why does Gershuni come only when I'm not home?"

"It's nothing; he comes when he can come. But I don't want you on the road so late at night. You have to sleep over."

Nehemia nodded and fell asleep. Then in the middle of the night he started awake, insecure in Geula's wanting him to sleep over. She had her children, Shimon to manage, and her urbane father ready to move in. Memories stirred in him of being a castaway, penniless and wandering from settlement to settlement. In a choke of excitement, he made love to Geula. Geula sighed patiently in his arms, as if bearing some burden. He fell asleep with his face to the wall, tears in his eyes.

Gershuni began bringing up a *shiddach* between Gita and her cousin, Yitzik Horowitz that always ended in a bitter argument with Nehemia. Gershuni insisted that Gita and Yitzik were bound in soul; the betrothed were not to be severed from one another. Nehemia told him only the father of the bride made a betrothal; Gershuni insisted a *shiddach* was a family decision, not for one man alone. It was the decision of two families. Nehemia countered that the Kramers had a voice, and he was the Kramer family. Gershuni smiled and muttered that one man doesn't make a family.

Nehemia sprang to his feet. "You'll die with a father's curse on your head, stealing his children." He stumbled out in the yard in fury, as Gershuni smiled at Geula, shaking his head in urbane helplessness.

Chapter Seventeen

VISITING WARSAW week after week gave Nehemia a strange sense of being on a ship afloat without a rudder in the dark waters of history. His scorched solitude remained, but his sense of abandonment was gone. A Jew, he had slipped back into the perils of history. He had a father, Aharon Dovid, a son Shaya, who were links in a chain of generations. He would pass his life on to his son.

Word passed in the market that a strange Pole had spat in a Jew's face. The area was in a turmoil. Without insult or provocation he spat in the face of a Jew?! The details were repeated, checked. What was his name? Was the argument over money? How was the Jew dressed? Did this happen before? The excitement soared, and then passed away; the Pole was dismissed as a maniac. One cannot generalize from a single example.

Nehemia began sleeping in a small hotel adjacent to the market. For four kopeks, he got one of three beds in a basement room. Since he got up early, he always took the bed nearest the door.

One evening, his last chicken sold, Nehemia entered the Belzer synagogue. Over the ark, the smoke rose from the oil-fed eternal light into a circle of blackened soot in the ceiling. Smaller groups were already forming minyanim in the side halls. By now, he knew Reb Reuven Dressler, the beadle, and several of the elders. Reb Reuven saw him enter, but stayed away; that meant there was no letter from Vienna. His uncle had become a Yekke, a German Jew, and would take his time formulating a letter.

Reb Reuven gestured to Nehemia to conduct services. Nehemia took the bimah and smacked into the evening service, his Galician accent flailing out with a lilt and a quaver. A barbaric freshness caught at the listeners' ears; Nehemia read the words as if for the first time.

Many prayed standing up, a pattern of grays and blacks like scroll lettering, swaying at their lecterns, intense at prayer, in a constant motion. At one point, Nehemia fitted in the Cossack melody he used for "Lekhah Dodi." Heads stiffened at a new melody. Half the congregation accepted it, humming and tapping their lecterns in accompaniment.

The word was already passing about: a son of Aharon Dovid Kramer had appeared out of nowhere. Strangers tugged at Nehemia's sleeve, peering in his face for a resemblance. There was here a smile, there a smack of the lips, a rolling eye, a hint of scandal, a quiver of upturned fingers. The implications dangled teasingly in the air. But Nehemia was too loose-ended. Where did he live? What were his connections? Their curiosity was piqued and demanded more.

Moments later, another item spread. This was the chicken farmer who sold at the back of the market. *Rachmono Litzlan!* Aharon Dovid had a son a chicken farmer! Men fished for connections; Nehemia's outline became distinct—his chicken farm at Radich, his purchase of the Flying Goose. But did the Polish nobility allow the inn to go into Jewish hands? What money did he bring from Galicia? Whom did he pay off? How powerful was he?

On Nehemia's next visit his place was kept free in the market. The shadchonim all knew of his three unmarried daughters and a son, and all had a shrewd sense of how marketable they were. People made a point of buying at Nehemia's wagon. His chickens had a reputation of being healthy, and were more likely to be kosher since he came from such a fine family. As customers milled about, bits of family history came out. His father was a tempestuous figure; his uncle in Vienna was the mathematical brain of the family. The maskil was so retiring that some people wondered if he was normal. A building engineer, Aharon Dovid did jobs outside Warsaw. He was a patron of the old-age home behind the synagogue.

Nehemia's elegant melodies gave his singing a distinct flavor. He was asked regularly to conduct services. Then, after several weeks, Reb Reuven slipped a letter in his hand and stepped away. Nehemia opened and read the following in a flowery Hebrew script:

"To my beloved nephew, my brother's son, Nehemia ben Aharon Dovid, God give him long life, Torah, and good deeds. We have a path, we take it, we arrive at our destination; we wander and our wandering has no end. A light has

60

risen in the east, and in this light lies the truth. We know it, and we have peace. My dear brother, Aharon Dovid, who now awaits me with joy in the world of truth, has implanted God's image that his name not be blotted out. The Ruler of the Universe kept the truth hidden until Rivka passed away, she should feel no pain. The family is to be denied no more. My arms long to embrace you, but I cannot come to Warsaw; my heart longs to know you, I can only kiss you from afar. Let us stay in touch through messengers, share our families and our feelings. If the werewolf lunges in Vienna, I will seek your help in Warsaw; if God forbid in Warsaw, my Vienna roof will be your home. You are family; take my life if your own needs it. Jacob met Esau after twenty-one years; Joseph embraced his father after wasting his life in a foreign country. Family cannot be kept apart. In expectation of the imminent arrival of the Messiah, I am, Tevya Kramer."

Who had time for letters with such style? The man must have spent weeks composing it. Depressed, Nehemia placed the letter in his pocket and put aside all thought about his other uncle's family.

Nehemia slept in a hotel, but sullenly. He begrudged the price of a better hotel and disliked the accommodations in a cheap one. Lying in bed, it bothered him not to be at home. In spite of all his family, he was finally a wanderer. Geula was too good for him; she would finally leave him he was sure of it. Thinking this way made his mood savage.

On his next trip, the chickens moved briskly. Nehemia was down to three unsold chickens. He was looking around to sell them at half-price and return to Radich that night, when the market nudnik started his way, swinging the panels of his caftan, his side curls jiggling, as he rehearsed bits of scandal in his head. A man with a heavy limp, he was called a *hinkedink*.

There was no time for a cut-rate sale. Nehemia decided to donate the remaining chickens to the old-age home his father once helped. Nehemia climbed off the back of the wagon with the last chicken cage as the *hinkedink* swung up, frantically waving. Nehemia stepped through the milling throng, and knocked at the service door to the old-age home.

A tall, blind woman opened, about thirty, with almost an albino skin, half-dressed, wearing several petticoats but no skirt, in a heavy lace blouse that opened over her bosom. Her long head had pinched, fixed eyes, a slack mouth, and a wen on her chin; her hair was piled loosely on her head.

61

"I thought I'd give my last three chickens to feed some old people and then start for home."

Startled, she shifted, releasing a musky smell. She angled her head, shifting: "You're Kramer, the chicken man in the market. Very nice, very nice. I'm Shaineh Nissel; I keep the kitchen, and also the rest of the house when I bother. You wonder how? There's nothing to wonder. God put eyes in my hands. They talk well of you in the market. Your father was always bringing my aunt Hinda things. Aunt Hinda showed her appreciation, but who talks of such things? You're new at Melon. How do I know? Everything about you is chewed over and over."

"I think everybody in Warsaw is chewed over and over."

She reached out sure fingers, like a cave animal, and took his hand. Her nails were flat with sharp corners, shortened with a single scissors' cut:

"You'll sleep over; the roads are bad after dark. We have an extra room. You give me three chickens? You'll get a bed for the night. It'll be a pleasure to serve you, and you'll go back in the morning."

"God willing, I'll have a bite out and not impose myself."

Shaineh pulled him inside. "It's no imposition; it's a pleasure to serve you. These old people talk and talk, but they don't chew what's on their plate. Complaints? But here I go, a *drai-kopf* with all the Warsaw *yentas,* all day chewing the cud with gossip. Your father was good to Aunt Hinda. She handled the kitchen here. Oh, she knew quality in a man."

A cry came from the stairwell. "Shaineh, *gevald!* They're biting me!"

"Just make yourself comfortable!" she cried back upstairs.

Nehemia sat down in her kitchen, with a huge stone and cupboards everywhere, everything arranged in an exact spot so she could reach it without hesitation.

"I have a piece of flanken and some tsimmes. Your father had such a name, and he had a son? Who would believe such a thing? But here I go again. You must think me terrible, with such an appetite for gossip. Come, sit down. Shall I say how Aunt Hinda talked about your father? Sometimes she said God kissed his eyes, and sometimes she said God kissed his hands. With so much kissing, I think maybe sometimes she forgot about God."

"Shaineh, I'm dying," came a cry from the stairwell.

"It happens!" she cried back.

"How long have you been here?" Nehemia asked with a patient smile.

"Why do you ask? You got a proposition?"

"My assistant, Shimon Cohen, is honest, hardworking, a hero, one of the forced children in the Russian army. If it's a *shiddach,* you can come home with me in the morning."

"Shaineh, there's fire!" came a scream from the stairwell.

"Spit on it!" she screamed back.

"I'm waiting for your answer."

Shaineh swayed in her chair. "He's an *alter kocher,* isn't he?"

"Better one *alter kocher* than the six rooms of *kochers* you got here!"

"Shaineh, I'm choking on something!" came a scream.

"The doctor will look in the morning!" she cried back.

Shaineh rested her hand on his. "You're so intelligent. Share my room tonight, if you like. It's just to save linen."

"I'll pay for the extra linen."

Shaineh turned her hand over his on the table, then back again. He waited patiently.

"You're a workingman?"

"I have my own chicken farm."

"I'll come in the morning."

In the morning, driving the wagon back to Melon with Shaineh Nissel at his side, Nehemia suddenly looked up. "I have a son in Galicia; he's a foundling."

"Any son of yours would be a prince."

Shaineh pointed her blind head this way and that, drinking in the smells, the bumps, the shape of the wind, creating a landscape in her head. Rolling with the wagon, she reached back to steady the cage with the last three chickens.

Chapter Eighteen

WHEN HE LEFT WARSAW, Nehemia picked up a *ksuvah,* a wedding contract, and put it in his money box. After several hours, he rolled the wagon into the yard at Radich. Esther first spotted them and ran out smiling, clasping her hands over the addition to the household.

Nehemia gestured to Esther as he climbed off the wagon. "Go get Shimon from the chicken house. I have his wife for him."

Geula came out and gave Shaineh a long look, examining her

attire, and the way she looked blindly about. She helped her off the wagon. Shaineh was much too young for Shimon; and besides she was blind; there was work she could never do. A shadchan would have found a better match, but Nehemia was the manager.

Shimon marched out of the chicken house. He looked at his bride with distaste as her patient, vibrant fingers stirred in his direction. Nehemia and Geula were already arranging a *chuppah,* with some wine and food afterward. Nehemia drove his carriage two kilometers down the road and asked the nearest Jewish farmer to serve as second witness. The farmer followed in his carriage, planning to return to his farm immediately. Shaya and the three girls held up the four poles, using a tablecloth for a top. Nehemia sang the service and read the *ksuvah* with speed and fervor.

When Shimon had to take the oath, Nehemia stopped, befuddled. Geula then quietly pressed into Shimon's hand a cheap spare ring, whispering to him, "It's my gift to you. Use it to marry your bride." Geula glanced over at her husband with patient disapproval for forgetting about the ring, as Nehemia began his last blessings.

Geula had a lechayim waiting on a side table. As they downed their glass of wine together, Shaineh already called Shimon an *alter kocher;* he complained loudly about the *oisvulf* from Warsaw.

Geula quietly told Nehemia that she couldn't have another woman in her home. The chicken house had an unused upstairs area for storing hay. She would lend the furniture; with a little effort, they should have a very good home there for themselves.

The wedding night would have been peaceful; however, while Nehemia was in Warsaw, several eggs had been broken and eaten, leaving only pieces of shell smeared with yolk in the brooding box. Nehemia was furious with Shimon. If Shimon had put the hens out in the yard for the right length of time, they would never have had another cannibal chicken. A hen will eat another hen's eggs only out of boredom.

Nehemia's displeasure so upset Shimon that he skipped supper to clean out the entire chicken house, ignoring his bride entirely. As Shaineh went to bed alone, Shimon lay down in the chicken house, an army scout on patrol, watching for the culprit chicken.

That evening in the house, the three girls all resented the new woman in the family. Gita felt pushed out of her refuge in the chicken house, and Feigeleh aligned herself with her mother in her concern over the arrival of a strange woman, younger than herself. Esther was particularly disturbed; Nehemia had kissed Shaineh a shade too warmly after the chuppah, in a manner more intimate than was appropriate toward a servant. Watchful as she was, Geula had missed it; only Esther sensed the possible involvement. Without knowing how it happened, Esther knew something had closed off in her father. She felt a twinge of abandonment.

That evening, Esther sat down at the harpsichord and began playing dance tunes. With an edge of aggressive spite, she played Polish songs and every vulgar melody she could think of, singing loud and off-key, throwing everybody off-balance. When Nehemia strode out to escape her, she only banged the louder, until her tunes filled the house.

Banging the harpsichord, Esther rolled her eyes at Shaya. She didn't know why life should be so difficult. Her home was going dead on her; a home was all an Orthodox girl had to count on. She had about as much choice in her life as a worker ant. Her father had cut her off; her brother was an Orthodox saint. She couldn't stand it.

Shaya sensed the pressure. He abruptly got up, followed Nehemia into the kitchen, and tugged his pants until Nehemia picked him up.

"What?"

"I want to start Yeshiva."

"I'll start making arrangements."

Meanwhile, Shimon, lying immobile in the chicken house for two hours, spotted a hen pecking at an egg in the brooding box. He flailed forward, shrieking and grabbing for it. The hen fluttered out of reach, squawking and flapping its wings. Shimon hopped around the chicken house until he caught it and wrung its neck.

A moment later, he realized he should have saved it for ritual slaughter. Now they would be unable to eat its meat.

Chagrined, Shimon climbed in silence to his bridal chamber. Carefully, he crawled into bed with Shaineh, who made room, expecting nothing from her *alter kocher*.

An hour later, it dawned on Shimon that he was married, after years of bitter isolation. Immediately aroused, he woke Shaineh up.

She shrank back in amazement. "If you were still capable, why did you wait for so long?"

Shaineh lay back patiently and gave him his pleasure, her

blind hands feeling for Nehemia, who was a gentleman and Aharon Dovid's son. If she waited around long enough, maybe he would end up hers. Stranger things have happened. Her aunt Hinda adored Aharon Dovid until the day she died; she would do the same for Nehemia.

The next day, Nehemia helped Shimon clear out the hayloft. They sawed a square hole over the platform and built a second stairway to the next floor. They lifted up furniture, some of it dismantled. As they windproofed the walls, and put in a heater, Shimon broke into a sporadic lecture on how to build barracks. As the men worked, Shaineh walked around the chicken house with a fitful smile, palms out, sniffing. She touched the various foods, cracking grain between her nails to smell it. She felt around the water pan, the grain sack, the lye, and chalk, along and under the perches. She found the brooding boxes, the floor pophole, the poles surrounding their platform. She was constructing a world inside her head the exact replica of the chicken house. Once it was in place, she would inhabit it as if she could see. She made no approach to Geula. She knew without asking; her life was in the chicken house.

Geula came by several times and watched her from the door, finally coming grudgingly to admire her. She never trusted Shimon. Shaineh was too young, but she seemed to make her peace with him. She was a sane woman and automatically avoided trouble. Geula watched Shaineh and Nehemia, but she detected nothing there. Finally she decided that Shaineh was a very private woman.

Before Shimon and Nehemia finished arranging the hayloft, Shaineh already was in charge of the chicken house. By the end of her first month, she took over more and more; Shimon began to excuse himself from the daily chores—sitting idle for hours, and then starting up to go out on another long hike to scout out the territory.

In fits and starts, Shimon grasped that he was a husband, the head of a family. Embarrassed at his ignorance, he asked Feigeleh, the Bible reader among the girls, to translate from the Bible the parts about the patriarchs. He smiled when he heard how Abraham had a child in his old age. Nobody believed it possible; but people are always underestimating old men. In Joshua and Judges, he listened in rapt silence to the wars, grunting with satisfaction over Gideon's campaigns.

Geula was always watchful of her children, but she trusted Feigeleh to take care of herself. Had Shimon spoken too much to Gita, her mother would have driven him off the farm. Yet however secure she felt with Feigeleh, she always kept herself within screaming distance.

One day, as Nehemia came in the courtyard, Geula told him that Shimon had gone off for good. Nehemia remembered his own sporadic wandering, even after his marriage. If Shimon was headed out, he would pass through Melon. The next shtetl was Kabol.

Nehemia smiled. "I think I can find him."

Geula shook her head. "Let him go. Shaineh does all the work. Trust me, she wouldn't mind never seeing him again. He left? Let it end here."

Nehemia refused to hear it. He took his carriage to Kabol. As he entered their inn, Shimon rose and stood at attention. "There's a village where a boy named Cohen was given to the Czar. I have to report what happened to him. They keep a record of their children."

"You have time later. Come back; you're on duty."

The two men climbed into the carriage and returned to Radich.

Upon his next return to Warsaw, Nehemia entered the chicken house and Shimon rose from the floor and saluted, staggering, bits of grime and chicken droppings falling off his body. Shaineh was cleaning the dropping board into a bucket of fertilizer. Nehemia felt under the chickens.

Shaineh smiled. "My aunt Hinda kept a cow in a shed that I looked after. Get a cow, I'll care for it, and get milk for the whole house."

Nehemia trusted Shaineh. "I'll see if it can be done." Leaving, he thought how Geula was right; he should have let Shimon run off.

Chapter Nineteen

IN THE STILL BEFORE DAWN on the next market day, as a dry wind scudded the night clouds invisibly overhead, Nehemia and Shimon loaded the wagon with boxes of eggs and cages of chickens, and tied down the cages with string.

Inside the house, Geula woke Shaya and dressed him in his best clothes. He fell asleep again as she fitted on his shoes. Finished, she carried him outside and across the yard to the wagon, holding him to her bosom like a baby: giving up her son to school meant her childbearing years were finished, that she was entering middle age. She wished Gita were married already; she wouldn't mind having a baby around.

Geula looked up at the wagon. "You should have waited; he needs his sleep."

Nehemia reached down from the wagon and swung Shaya onto the wagon bench. "He'll sleep on the road."

Behind Geula, Gita and Feigeleh shyly stepped out together, Feigeleh with a jar of honey—she wasn't sure it fitted, but she had to give something—Gita fidgeting not to be left out. Esther lugged Shaya's suitcase, with his clothes, a slab of home-corned beef, a raisin kugel, and six rolls. Walking, Esther repeatedly pushed Shaineh away as she tried to take the suitcase away from her.

Nehemia loaded the suitcase, climbed on the wagon bench, and cracked the whip, already restless for Shaya to wake up. The wagon slowly pulled out of the yard.

Shaya woke up as they reached the Budapest road. Nehemia stopped by a pond so his son could wash his hands. Shaya quietly said his prayers, and ate one of Esther's rolls, dipping it in Feigeleh's honey jar.

The sun rose. The road kept joining with other roads and widening into a stream of traffic into the city. They continued beyond the Warsaw market. At the gate of the Belzer Yeshiva, Nehamia took out his tallis, swung it around Shaya, and carried him inside like a Torah scroll, with Shaya's suitcase in his other hand.

The dormitory supervisor looked at Shaya; his suitcase was fuller than usual for an incoming student. "A new boy's things sometimes disappear."

Nehemia grinned proudly. "My son is not a fool. Just give him a room with honest boys. Shaya, if you spot a thief, you'll tell the supervisor, won't you?"

Shaya solemnly nodded.

"I'll come by in the morning on my way back."

Shaya quickly adjusted to Yeshiva life. He got a window bed in a good room with ten boys. It helped not being a charity case. He came willingly to study but he missed home. During his first year, he went home every Thursday night, worked with his father on Friday, and studied on Saturday. He never mentioned the Yeshiva, nor did his father ask him.

Shaya was an innocent, but he had his father's instincts and trusted no one. His joyous, tranquil spirit had absorbed Nehemia's berserk force and compulsive solitude, his frustration and pious despair. There was a shell around Shaya that left him not blind to the world but indifferent. He didn't need it. Shaya knew already he was more talented than his father. As the first year melted into the second, and the studies took hold, his estrangement eased. He began spending Shabbes in the Yeshiva, but he was careful to go home at least once a month.

Gershuni made a point of visiting once or twice when Shaya was home. He marveled over Shaya's schoolboy reserve; the boy was a young Rothschild; with his presence, he could do business all over Europe. Shaya listened in silence and retired as soon as he could courteously escape.

The Yeshiva was an ocean of surplus boys. Parents unloaded their sons in the Yeshiva dormitory as more offspring came than they could house; they put up a *pushke* in the kitchen, a little blue box to put coins for school support. Some boys were abandoned to the dormitory by parents divorced or moved elsewhere. Many were simply orphans. They were all afloat in the sea of Talmud.

Shaya quickly aligned himself with the boys who grasped and retained their lessons. More distant boys were like the disoriented residents of a retirement home. They dressed, they prayed; they sat together in the study hall. But the material was too alien and difficult, and nobody helped them through it. As the years of wasted study passed, they sat in groups on Friday night, silken young men with pale faces, listless bodies, and black side curls, relieved that they had little to do. Eventually a shadchan would arrange a wife who would support them and raise their children as they passed their time in synagogue.

All the boys were religious. Every morning, they opened rolls of tefillin by the hundreds. On Friday night the dormitory rooms became like chapels, as each boy lit his own two Sabbath candles by his bed. But the boys also swapped dormitory beds, ignoring the supervisor. Sharing books and secret newspapers, the boys got an underground education. Those interested in politics collected in one dormitory room; the mathematics brains congregated in another. The religious rebels slept close together so as to cover for each other, as they took off their skullcaps, dived into bed, and spent the night bareheaded.

And Shaya made a friend, Nathan Finesilver, the most relaxed boy in the class, a beautiful boy with a patient despair, the son of a wholesale liquor salesman; Nathan always wore a clean shirt and sat for an hour cocking his head at the stupidities the other boys uttered.

69

Once Shaya walked out on a holiday celebration that got too noisy. On the street, Nathan was waiting.

"You had enough of the nudnicks?"

Shaya winced and made a face. "I had enough."

"I was looking for you; let's take a walk."

They walked the ghetto streets for an hour without saying a word—and came back to the Yeshiva, friends for life.

Shaya's teachers were forever surprised by his knowledge. The class had sharper boys but none clearer. Since Shaya never spoke in class, the Yeshiva could not judge his potential, but he was grouped with their best boys. Shaya succeeded, yet the Talmud class jarred him—especially the way his classmates showed off by throwing their bodies around, chewing over difficult ideas, never getting control of them.

Shaya slept in the dormitory amid the forlorn piety of boys with one father in heaven and another at home, neither of whom they ever saw as they bedded and prayed together, and scrounged like orphans. Every holiday, in home after home, groups of Yeshiva boys danced in stomping circles; they excited the impoverished street for a few minutes. After circulating for awhile in a charge of excitement, they returned to the dormitory to sleep.

Periodically, Shaya felt revolted by the brainless piety of boys around him. Refusing to melt into Yeshiva life, Shaya would take a coach home, finally walking from Melon to the Flying Goose, restless to be with his father, who was a man, as none of this band of students was. Then he would change to his working clothes and join his father in whatever he was doing. They worked together for several hours, and Shaya's spirits became serene again.

One evening, he rode with Nehemia to a neighboring dairy farmer and paid five rubles for a mild cow. Shaya attached it in back of their carriage as Nehemia got a few instructions. The two then returned to the chicken farm, the carriage rolling very slowly, pulling the cow behind.

The Yeshiva served breakfast and lunch in a kitchen basement. For dinner, the boys were farmed out among households in walking distance, in an elaborate system called *tisch* that absorbed the dormitory into the surrounding community. Poorer households offered a meal a week, more comfortable families a meal a night. With *tisch,* mothers with marriageable daughters managed to make a chaperoned acquaintance without a shadchan. Mothers instructed their sons whom to invite and which boys to keep away. Boys quickly discovered which meals were best and where to avoid bores. The Yeshiva moral director kept a list of addresses to which he could send a misfit. Nobody went without a meal.

As Shaya widened his Warsaw acquaintance, his home ties thinned until he could never stay for more than a short visit. He arranged his meals casually, carrying himself with enormous quiet dignity at *tisch*. If a household felt sticky, he got himself invited elsewhere. At table, his pale, depressed eyes, his strong body, and lazy gestures registered; like his father, Shaya was big for his age, and people refused to believe how young he was. His silence gave him a reputation for profundity.

An all-day school, the Yeshiva had a few basic secular classes. Once the math class proposed to change over from basic math to bookkeeping, so boys inclined that way should have a trade. The teacher rejected the proposal out of hand. A class delegation immediately met with the secular principal, who said flatly that a Yeshiva was not a trade school; the students responded that the Yeshiva should stop graduating unemployables.

When the students boycotted their math class, Reb Shloimeh Katz, the moral director, called the students into his office and accused them of arrogance; the curriculum wasn't their decision. They listened in silence, then went out and issued a manifesto with the slogan: "To live as a bookkeeper, you have to study bookkeeping." Smelling a worthy cause, the circle of Yeshiva literati moved in on the math class and took over the strike. A handbill was issued in Hebrew. A hymn to bookkeeping was written in the style of the Golden Age.

The Yeshiva board, fearing the Czarist authorities would grab at the strike as an excuse to take over their curriculum, tried to isolate the school. A rumor spread that Reb Shloimeh was withholding mail. A general strike was immediately called. In retaliation, the Yeshiva closed the kitchen. Boys sent out emissaries to the local households.

For three days, boys milled in the halls. Finally the Yeshiva agreed on a compromise. Bookkeeping belonged in a trade school, but they would teach mathematics as preparation for bookkeeping. The strike was called off, and the kitchen was reopened. The teacher continued exactly as he taught before; but calling it a preparation in math for bookkeeping, it was now somehow acceptable.

At loose ends during the strike, Shaya became troubled that he had no plans for his future. By now, he could no longer live in a shtetl. He needed guidance, but Nehemia's experience was too limited to help him, and Shaya would take advice from no one else. His occasional meetings with Gershuni poisoned any inclination he might have had for a career in business. Fishing in the dark, Shaya decided to be a cantor. He knew he was good. Keeping his serenity meant more to him than any ordinary career. He loved his own voice. He didn't want a real career; he just wanted to be happy. So he would become a cantor.

Shaya made a sudden trip home for his Bar Mitzvah, bringing his friend, Nathan Finesilver. Esther looked over Nathan as the family had a festive meal together; she felt a sting of jealous admiration for her brother, who knew how to find beautiful friends. There was something very casual, adult, and civilized about Nathan. She felt again that old quiver of annoyance that Shaya wasn't older than she. It would make her life a lot simpler if the shtetl had boys like Nathan in it.

The next morning at the Melon synagogue, Shaya read the Torah scroll for Thursday. The men beamed at Shaya's voice, which already smacked of authority. At home, Geula had a spread of wine, herring, and kuchen. Afterward, Nehemia loaded his wagon and took the two boys back to the Yeshiva.

Chapter Twenty

AFTER HIS BAR MITZVAH, Shaya involved himself more in the social life around the Yeshiva. Women liked Shaya. He was reserved, yet extraordinarily pleasant. He dressed well; in his own way, he was a Yeshiva sport. Absorbing his father's sense of abandonment, he refused to plan for the future. He appeared all things to all people. In his own sly, peasant way, he let it be. With Shaya, nothing caught, nothing took hold.

Before long, Shaya began to attend weddings. The Yeshiva boys married at sixteen, going immediately to work, or to live with their parents-in-law while they finished their studies. Such Warsaw weddings were vast productions, with elaborate dinners and introductions to strangers. But Shaya thought the way his father did when he was Shaya's age—that he had one life he would share with one partner. Until that happened, he was not to be had.

Nehemia kept trying to visit. He hungered for Shaya's religious quiet; Shaya felt like an extension of his soul. He sensed that Shaya had outgrown him and felt baffled, stranded, unable to move. Unable to force himself on his children, he would drop something off for Shaya with the dormitory supervisor every week—clean socks, a sweater, a jar of preserves; he would stand for a moment, available, and then continue to the market. He felt he had connected, even if he didn't see Shaya.

Shaya knew that Nehemia wanted to discuss his sisters. Most of the shtetl girls their age were already married. Sensing the pressure, they had stopped coming to synagogue. But Gita and Feigeleh both bored him; Shaya thought only about Esther. She controlled the whole house from that lookout of hers. Shaya reveled in his air of maturity, and yet he felt it was a sham; only Esther treated him for what he was, a little boy. He visited home to stay close to her.

The Jewish community at Melon by now welcomed Nehemia in their midst. If they looked askance at his daughters, it was without hostility. They were simply strange, or standoffish, in their own world; but those who talked, quickly assured themselves that when the girls finally married everything would straighten itself out. And yet the Melon Jews held off. The girls were too proud for their few connections, too ardent; they didn't know their place.

Of the three, only Esther was considered at all. She was blue-eyed, with trim ankles, a generous streak and little monkey nose, quick-witted and smiling, always reaching out, playing musical instruments. But she finally scared off the local Belzer. She moved too fast, and said wild things. They were never sure what her words meant.

A local tradesman's son fell in love with Esther and had his father speak to Nehemia. After one meal in the man's house Esther had it broken off. In the house of another young man, Esther got herself dead drunk and the family broke it off. Defying her luck, Esther made a song of it: she would be nothing but a scamp.

Esther was quick like her mother, but Geula knew the limits. Esther's world recognized no limits. She understood tradition, but had no patience. Theatrically she got rid of people by drinking, laughing too much, or saying silly things. She had a way of knocking her knees together like a pair of ladles. At a Melon wedding she hopped around all afternoon, making up songs and skits in her head. At home, she lolled around, bored.

When her second engagement was broken, Esther grasped the hopelessness of the family's situation. Feigeleh was too sane, too deep-feeling and dedicated; Gita was distant and a snob. No shtetl boy would marry a starry-eyed dreamer, not her, not Feige-leh, not Gita. But she didn't care; the shtetl was a bore. If the Queen of Sheba finally left King Solomon, it was probably be-cause she was bored—and how fast would a local grocer bore her? But in Yiddish Poland, only a husband will get a girl out the front door. For Esther there remained only the back window.

In Kabol, Esther saw a broadside of an amateur folk-review called *Oich Mir a Folk,* organized by Shmuel Pinsky, a wedding entertainer who visited in Italy, to educate the young to the grisly and unspeakable Jewish situation. Pinsky's fingers snapped to the Morse code, sending messages to the world de-manding help—teach your child the Morse code in Yiddish; his messages will be a revelation. And the three Zalman sisters would sing the secrets of every Jewish heart.

Esther was already composing in her head the song, "Spinster by the Fireside." Her future was settled; she would go onstage. But this was an amateur folk-review, which meant nobody got paid anything—only Pinsky, the manager; and even if she found a professional Yiddish musical stage, if it was in reach of her father's carriage he would be in the first row opening night, ready to drag her home.

To escape Nehemia, she had to die to her family. Since he adored her, that wouldn't be easy. She had to marry a gentile, but that would only trap her in housekeeping, except that the dishes she would wash would no longer be kosher. Maybe she could get out of housekeeping if she married a criminal, but she doubted it. Legal or illegal, a man was still a man. Better a terrorist who spent his day throwing bombs; in fact, him she wouldn't have to marry, he would be such a maniac, and a maniac was easier to handle than an experienced thief. Besides, her father was a Shabbatean, and to her a terrorist was a politi-cal Shabbatean. A terrorist would therefore be in the family tradition. But where does the daughter of an Orthodox chicken-farmer in a shtetl meet a terrorist? It was very simple. She knew him in Radich; his name was Jan Kris.

Jan was a vagabond who slept in the attic of the Catholic school. Beardless, pugnacious, with tangled curls, he did odd jobs in the area. His arrival coincided with an outbreak of thiev-ery and barn burning in the area. Stories spread of his seducing several local girls. Only Esther had the brains to tie the barn burning to Jan; burning barns, that was terror.

One afternoon, Esther saw Jan in the yard, making a delivery. She slowly strolled across the yard to the chicken house, then

74

slowly strolled back, taking care not to be observed by her mother. Jan paid no attention so she repeated the walk, equally slowly, to bring the milk. The next day Jan made another delivery. Esther was outside walking in the yard within five minutes. Afterward she ran to her room and threw herself on the bed, laughing hysterically. But why did life have to be so difficult?

Esther knew it didn't make much sense, but she could figure out no other way to escape. She decided to sign out on her body. It would do what it had to do. She would keep her spirit untouched.

On one of his visits, Shaya noticed Esther's strange behavior, and spotted Jan hanging around the yard. Jan was a shegetz and a pig, but Shaya didn't intervene. Some rich Yeshiva friends had talked about the world of music; he shared Esther's turbulent dreams of freedom, wanting to go to Germany to study music. He would not intervene.

So she wouldn't be looked for, Esther left a note in her room the night she disappeared with Jan. Downstairs, Gershuni droned, "The Polish Jew is in business for blood. Zfania Binstock and his three sons move like a swarm of locusts. When he listens to me he sucks in air between his teeth so I never know if the talk goes in his ears or down his throat. I make a contact; he goes down by coach, buys direct, and gives me no commission. So I give my contracts to his competition. I tell him plain, we'll freeze you out. On the spot, I get my commission. I give him a better contract; he's back in Bessarabia and on his own again."

The night Esther ran away was the biggest wedding of the winter in Warsaw, when the Brest Litovsk *illui* married the daughter of the head of the Warsaw rabbinic court. Bedding was so tight that a Lublin rabbi slept in one bed with his grown daughter so both could attend; to such a man, any woman but his wife was a stick of wood. One doesn't ask questions of a saint like that. At the wedding, Shaya had a strange sense of light-headed happiness. He took Nathan on his shoulders, singing as he danced, "And it shall be heard in the towns of Judah, the markets of Jerusalem, a voice of happiness, of joy, a voice of a groom, a voice of a bride," fitting the words to his father's Cossack song. A circle gathered around him. Then suddenly, as he danced near one of the tables of the wealthy, two huge eyes stopped him in his tracks. He returned the look; for a moment, he shared his soul with his future bride. He kicked his heels, looked again, and continued dancing.

Early the next morning, he got an emergency message and

came back home immediately. Esther was gone. By now, the family knew about Jan Kris.

That night, a warehouse safe was blasted open and looted, a professional job such as the village never saw before. Shaya smiled ruefully; he never guessed Jan was so good a thief.

Nehemia observed seven days of mourning over Esther, covering the mirrors. He sat on the ground and wept, unconsolable. Shaya refused to join in. He saw nothing to mourn. Esther was still alive, and she was too lazy and attached to home to travel very far. They would meet again in Warsaw.

After the seven days of mourning, Shaya cautiously approached his father. "If I find Esther and bring her back, will you take her in?"

"With her shegetz husband?"

"I mean Esther, with nobody else."

Nehemia burst into tears. "Only bring my baby back to me."

Chapter Twenty-one

ON A BRISK MARCH DAY, the family took off to attend a wedding in Melon, leaving Shaineh and Shimon to take care of the farm. Esther's disappearance had broken the family spirit, but the outing touched them to a juvenescence. The March rain had passed, and the spring seeding was completed. Fleeces of cloud drifted across the sky. Every turn of the wheel produced a fresh smell. The family traveled in the wagon so the three women could spread out on cushions in all their wedding finery. Nehemia had the palings up, with curtains hung over them, to hide the women with all their beauty from any passing Pole.

Sitting on the driver's bench in his best suit, Nehemia drove slowly, a little off the road so as not to stir too much dust. At such a gathering, he wanted his daughters at their ease and looking their best. The air had a soft radiance. Puddles were on the ground. They were a family on a wagon again. On such a day, seven years earlier, they all took off from Galicia for their migration north.

In Melon, Ovadiah Schultz, a shopkeeper who manufactured glass bottles and sold them to farmers and home canners, was in seventh heaven; he was marrying off his youngest daughter, and his responsibilities as a father were finally coming to an end. All five of his daughters had found husbands and, within his capacity for a dowry, had made good marriages to shtetl boys; no son of his would shame him.

When Ovadiah himself was first married, he put aside all his wedding gifts as possible dowry money. When his wife produced only daughters, he bargained over every *shiddach*. Now that his last daughter was going under the chuppah, he would expend his remaining wedding money to the last penny. His baby would have a wedding.

The chuppah was going up in his backyard between two of his apple trees, with his four sons-in-law holding up the poles. His parents were there, with their five grandchildren and his two surviving grandmothers. Boxes of flowers and baskets of apples from his orchard were everyhwere. The table held trays of kugel. There were kegs of raisin wine for the ladies, and bottles of vishnik; several men, already high, were pointing to the apple trees and making stupid jokes about the apple tree and the snake.

Three musicians circulated in the crowd. A badchen livened them up with riddles, stories, and ballads, on which he endlessly improvised, including everything from Elijah's chariot to Ovadiah's mustache, and to everyone's amazement, capping every stanza with a rhyme. A flautist and an accordion player accompanied the fiddler, who madly played the folk song about the rejoicing father marrying off his youngest daughter. People nudged each other and looked to see how Ovadiah took it.

It had taken years for the local Polish Jews to accept Nehemia, but by now he was a pillar of the community. When his wagon stopped in the yard, Ovadiah pulled him aside and asked him to give the last of the seven blessings; it would give his daughter such pleasure, he said. Nehemia accepted it as an honor.

As he stepped away, Nehemia heard two men gossip:

"Ovadiah looks worried."

"A Pole just opened a bottle shop; the Polish farmers will buy there. There isn't enough Jewish business. He's moving to Lodz."

"He'll want the money he's throwing away today."

"He's lucky he married off his daughters when he did. In five years, he would have more trouble."

"Melon hummed for a while, but a shtetl is too scattered. The Poles don't really want us. Jews need a city."

Three synagogue elders took Nehemia aside and pointed to a stranger who wanted a job teaching Hebrew. He knew his material but he used the new Hebrew. He had a strange flavor. They wanted Nehemia's opinion.

Nehemia was not learned, and had never before been consulted on a new teacher. He stroked his beard. "Why is it you ask me?"

The elder smiled. "He's a Kramer; we thought he might be family."

A stranger burst into the group. "It's a scandal, dancing at a wedding with the pogrom in Odessa."

The three elders instantly got excited:

"God help us! In Odessa?"

"The Czar would never allow it. What starts as a pogrom ends as a revolution. But it's not Ukrainians or Russians. The local Italian traders don't like Jews taking away their business."

"So! The wedding!"

The three musicians broke into a Chasidic march, for a fresh-air ceremony, under the apple orchard. The four brothers-in-law lifted high the chuppah poles. Everyone surged around the chuppah, making sure to keep a place for the two great-grandmothers.

Those in charge crackled through the service in a mixture of Hebrew and Aramaic, practiced and in record time. These were the first babies of the shtetl. At each stop, for the ring, the sip of wine, the contract, a sigh of satisfaction came from the shtetl throng. Nehemia delivered his last blessing with bravura, swinging into a familiar waltz at "*Kol sason vekol simcha, kol chasan vekol kallah*": "A sound of bliss, a sound of joy, the voice of a groom, the voice of a bride"; the entire crowd burst into song with him out in the fresh air.

Nehemia finished; breaths were held. The groom broke the glass with a loud smack. The crowd pressed forward with an explosive "Mazel tov!"; family on both sides inundated the couple with kisses, envelopes of money, and cries of satisfaction as they pushed out for *yichud,* their ritual union when they spend a moment together.

In their absence, the fiddler broke into a zestful "Joy, Song, Bliss, Sharing." To the accordionist's drumlike rhythm the crowd began a double circle dance, the local *shereleh,* the men holding hands around the women, all singing together until the couple returned.

Feigeleh felt a fresh wind blowing, a sense that her life was mysteriously changing. Her eyes were now on the stranger.

They had not as yet exchanged a word; yet in her soul, she had already given herself to him. All he needed now was to ask.

A flirtatious neighbor stopped and fanned herself alongside Nehemia. "And why so early a wedding?"

"Out of compassion for the bride and groom. They fast until the ceremony; let their fast be a short one."

"Mine was eleven at night, after five hours of speeches."

"It's a cruelty. You had the patience of a saint."

"Nobody asked me; and when was your wedding?"

"I had mine at five in the morning."

"What a liar you are!" Fanning herself, she gulped down a glass of vishnik. "But I like men who lie to women; they're men with style. At least they know what they're doing."

The couple returned to a noisy welcome and another dance.

The woman pressed Nehemia's arm. "Where were they? At yichud? When they're alone together as husband and wife? The room wouldn't even need a bed, as long as they're alone. But they came back fast, nobody should have thoughts about them. They're such innocents."

"They came back fast because they fasted all day; they can't wait to get to the strudel."

The woman slapped his arm. "You say such things! I don't understand you. You say nothing, and yet it sounds so wicked."

Nehemia noticed Geula, smiling patiently and shaking her head. He discreetly stepped away as the groom cut into a long twist loaf of bread with a loud blessing. Everybody sat down to eat and gossip.

A shopkeeper stepped alongside Nehemia. "I was sorry to hear about your daughter, Esther."

Nehemia blinked at him. "I have no daughter, Esther."

"Still it must hurt to see Ovadiah marry off his youngest daughter in his own yard."

"He's a fine man, Ovadiah; I wish him well. But I don't like what's happening in Odessa. They're Italians, the pogromchiks; but when a torch is lit, the flame has an itch to travel."

The crowd began a grandparents' dance. As the old bodies swung this way and that, Nehemia stepped alongside the stranger. "They say your name is Raphael Kramer. Did you ever know an Aharon Dovid Kramer?"

"I met my uncle once or twice. He passed away. Why do you ask?"

Nehemia smiled in gruff embarrassment. "He was my father."

Raphael broke into a coarse, genial smile. "From the father, it's not a bastard. You're a kosher Kramer."

Nehemia burst into a roar of laughter. "I have a chicken farm in Radich. Have dinner with us tomorrow night. I enjoy meeting family."

Nehemia noticed a handsome son of a dairy farmer. He stepped alongside his father and asked if his son was promised. The father smiled: not yet. Nehemia said they should talk. The man walked away with an enigmatic smile. Nehemia broke into a loud laugh, refusing to be depressed.

Meanwhile Feigeleh stood at the side, And if it was Raphael's home territory, she couldn't help that. She heard him sigh, "Breaking the glass is a memorial to the Temple torn down to the ground, and everybody cries 'Mazel tov!' And that's the Jew in exile."

Feigeleh shook her head. "I think people say mazel tov to the wedding, and not to the destroyed Temple."

"We need a new path, a blue flag of hope, a Messiah with the language of today, a new Zion of the fields, of a blade of grass."

His outburst left Feigeleh feeling motherly. "You don't dance?"

Raphael had a clumsy grin, showing two huge dimples. "I'm a stranger here; whom should I dance with?"

"If you're a stranger, it's because you make yourself a stranger; stop making yourself a stranger, and you won't be a stranger."

"And who are you?"

Feigeleh pointed shyly to her father. "I'm his daughter."

"Then you're my cousin!"

"You see? You start as a stranger, and end up as family. Come, let me give you some strudel, from the end piece with all the honey."

The two pushed in to the refreshment table, as Nehemia moved past them, bringing Gita a glass of wine, so she wouldn't feel lonely.

After the wedding, the family came home at dusk in the wagon, weary, stuffed with kugel and raisin wine, and a rich sense of fulfillment. As the wagon pulled into the yard, Nehemia noticed Gershuni's carriage waiting; once again a pall settled on his spirits.

Chapter Twenty-two

A MONTH LATER, Nehemia sold out early, and immediately packed hoping to reach Radich before dark. His heart was too turbulent to let him sleep over in a hotel. On the road, the urgency was still with him. Since he had begun his weekly wagon trip to Warsaw, the road south had been widened for an increasing stream of carriages. A unit of cavalry passed, riding toward Warsaw. In a field far to the left, a crew of thirty Poles, stripped to the waist, unloaded wagons of sand in a freshly dug trench, to extend a stretch of railroad. Hundreds of yards in front, other men leveled an orchard to make way for the track bed.

Warsaw was expanding but also becoming even more of a ghetto; the Jews were pouring in, off the shtetl, off the farm. It was not for him. Nehemia had started out fleeing settlement Jews who needed a tenth for a minyan; he would end his life with shtetl Jews, hanging on to a minyan in Melon. There was no help for it. In Warsaw, he could only join the old-age home. He knew that Shaya would never come home to live, so wherever he ended up he would be alone. It couldn't be helped. You're a father? You throw seed in the wind and pray that it lands on fertile soil.

Esther, his baby, was lost—Feigeleh also, during the last month. When he was Raphael's age, Nehemia was also a dreamer, but he had made work his way of life. On Raphael's first visit, he talked so much about health, labor, soil, and the meaning of animal life that he hardly ate and had no time to visit the chicken house.

Raphael reminded Nehemia of the crazy Messianic visionaries in Galicia. He wanted that first visit to end it; he started to tell Raphael, "You want soil, you collect a bucket of chicken droppings, step out in the middle of unseeded land, and . . ." Geula gestured him silent.

Nehemia looked up, startled. Feigeleh was hanging onto Raphael like a Chasid on the lip of the rebbe. Nehemia felt his heart breaking; it was too late to stop it without destroying her. Nehemia smiled helplessly and invited Raphael for the following night.

The night after his third visit, Feigeleh disappeared. During the night, Nehemia felt a violent shudder. In his bones, he witnessed their wedding night on his sliver of soil among the outdoor swings, as the sign of the Flying Goose flapped back and forth between the full moon and a pale reservoir of stars; and a thousand breezes wafted one behind the other over two vagabonds on a blanket.

Nehemia didn't sit in mourning over Feigeleh. Raphael might be empty but he had no cruelty in him. Let him stay loyal; Nehemia would harbor no grudges. What could Nehemia do? He wished they hadn't disappeared. Raphael could have taken an upstairs room—the inn had plenty—and discussed the soil for the next twenty years. Nehemia would gladly have supported them and all their children, just to have his daughter around. What did he have now? A big emptiness. But nobody asked him.

Driving his wagon, Nehemia chafed with fatherly guilt. He had loved his daughters too much, treated them as women, as his jewels. He should simply have given them jobs and ignored them. But how could he ignore them? They were his jewels, all three of them.

The setting sun just touched the horizon as Nehemia passed through Kabol. By Melon, the darkness poured westward thick as a black bean soup. Beyond Melon, Nehemia spotted a familiar figure jumping from side to side and hopping forward gleefully. It was Shimon, in his wagon driver's hat and heavy workman's coat, swinging a bag with all his belongings.

Nehemia stopped the wagon and waited, but Shimon passed him by, heaving wildly forward, not looking at him. Nehemia sat silent. If Shimon said nothing he said nothing. Nehemia broke into a bitter smile. This time he wasn't bringing him back.

Minutes later, as Nehemia reached home, he saw Gershuni's black carriage swing out of the yard, veer around, and head south.

In a sudden panic, Nehemia turned his wagon heavily into the yard, stumbled to the door and threw it open. Geula stood there alone, waiting.

Nehemia squinted at her. "What?"

"Shimon had our Gita in the body. And finally he's run away. Gershuni's taking Gita to Yitzik."

Nehemia swung back and grabbed for the door. "He can't! I'll catch up! I'll stop him! I won't let him take her!"

Geula gripped his hand. "She wandered outside while you were away, talking about Feigeleh. I couldn't catch her. We found her an hour ago. After what was done to her, it's this or nothing for our baby. What do you want her to end up, a *churvah*?"

Nehemia ran out to the horses, saddled the one he trusted

most, took his whip in his hand, and galloped toward Melon under a heavy night wind.

Just beyond Melon, he spotted Shimon on the road, heaving his whole body as he stumbled forward. Nehemia pulled the horse up short and swung out of the saddle.

"Shimon!"

Shimon pulled himself to attention, dropping his bag.

"Take off your shirt!"

Piece by piece, Shimon stripped himself to the waist. Nehemia cracked his whip full across his face, raising a bloody furrow. Shimon flinched, gasped, and twitched upright, like a soldier. Nehemia then laid the whip full force across his right shoulder and across his back. Shimon flinched and wriggled with pain. Unable to control himself, Nehemia laid his whip across Shimon's other shoulder and down his back. Shimon twitched all over, his body bleeding as though wounded in battle, not moving or saying a word, ready to die at attention.

Nehemia shuddered himself to a stop, unable to continue whipping a helpless man.

"What did you do? What are you running away from?"

His aged body twitching from the whiplash, Shimon drew himself up even straighter. "My name is Cohen. I was given to the Czarist army over forty years ago. I've lost the name of my village. I want somebody to tell me where it is so I can go home. I have a report to give about what happened to the boy they gave to the Czar."

Nehemia waved his hand in release. "You're doing the right thing. Don't ever give up; you'll finally find your village."

As Shimon disappeared up the road, his long body bleeding from two cross-welts on his back, Nehemia sank on his knees, praying that his son Shaya should have a real life.

PART TWO

Chapter Twenty-three

IN THE EARLY AFTERNOON, threads of cigarette smoke rose here and there in the high-ceilinged study hall of the senior division that also served as the Yeshiva synagogue. Having staked out a table, Shaya Kramer opened a folio of *Nedarim* opposite Nathan Finesilver, his long-term study partner. The sons of a chicken farmer and a supplier of army liquor, the two had hung on in the junior study hall below that was noisy and crowded and full of cigarette smoke, inundated by talk of jobs and precocious marriages, until it felt like a foundering ship. Shaya and Nathan held back from all this, and now had their own table in senior division.

Shaya was a habitual floater, without pace or direction, singing occasionally, watching for possibilities that he never picked up. Nathan was a dilettante, collecting mementos of the Shabbatean movement. At the Yeshiva he viewed his own doings and the doings of others with the same detached irony and bent for gossip. The Shabbatean stories charmed him; he was always digging up fresh tidbits.

Their new teacher, Shmaryahu Wolfson, was a Litvak and a graduate of Volozhin Yeshiva. The Lithuanians were aristocrats among Talmudists—dry, skeptical, self-reliant. They produced the Vilna edition and had the most exacting Yeshivas. The Gaon of Vilna was the highest Talmudic authority. If the Pale had a government, Volozhin would be its capital. Now just a province, the Litvaks had a crabbed frustration, a sense of their own aborted political power. Their Kahal stopped the Chasidic movement in its tracks, that itself had rebelled against Lithuanian coldness and authority. Wolfson refused a *shiddach* into a strong Talmudic dynasty, and then left Lithuania. The strongest Talmudist in the Yeshiva, he sensed a certain softness in the Chasidic brain. A Galitzianer in origin, Shaya would be trebly

87

anathema to a Litvak. Yet Shaya sensed already that Wolfson knew his student's worth. It gave him an exhilaration in his studies.

The downstairs class had sixty boys. Their present class, called first Mesivta, had about twenty-five boys, divided between serious rabbinic students and the more Orthodox among comfortable Warsaw families. Shaya hovered between the two groups. His trained mind, on top of his father's nihilism and alien wandering, gave him religious authority; yet the wealthy Warsaw boys attracted him, to whom finance came like the black Kabbalah—raw, immediate, full of symbols and powers from beyond the ghetto. Binstock was ruthless, but of an older generation, and followed ghetto procedures. These boys practiced a finance with alien rules, chasing money in a sudden investment, a windfall, a bluff, a connection that held. They moved at their pleasure; nobody pushed them into anything.

Nathan was engaged to his cousin, Miriam Ribalow, but the dowry negotiations dragged. Ribalow consigned a large crockery shop, but he felt them too young to live alone. Finesilver insisted that old enough to marry was old enough to keep a home. Ribalow balked; a shop and also a home would pinch the inheritance of his son.

Miriam was smarter than Nathan, forceful and level-headed. She visited the crockery shop, and then told her father his plates were too small; to expand, he should start making platters. Ribalow slapped her so hard he knocked her down. Refusing to be upset, Miriam returned to the shop and spotted a worker asleep behind his bench. She came home and told her father. He took off his belt and whipped her. Miriam kept herself agreeable. Stories about the businesswomen of Germany gripped her mind. It was time Warsaw got started. But could she manage it? How far could she go? She would find out by trial and error.

Miriam's blind pressure on Nathan had an edge of insecurity— he was the catch of that Yeshiva class—but it was more than that. Nathan had a shrewd sense of his situation; she was the businesswoman he would never be. His dilettante temperament despaired of arriving at anything. Miriam seemed solid as the universe, all business, but she kept herself limply acquiescent. He kept dreaming up ways to degrade himself, and as one of the Warsaw rich he acted out their dreams.

Nathan staggered slightly when he walked, as though unsure where his feet would land. Miriam felt him sexually aggressive, as if at any moment he could fall on her. Her fascination with business blinded her to his constant aggression. She was blindly ready to pay any price to make it, but was unsure what the price might be. Calm endurance was her way of standing up to Nathan's body and her father's beatings.

Orthodox Warsaw boys met their brides in the company of chaperones, but the rich made their own rules. Nathan and Miriam visited the same aunt. As soon as they arrived his aunt left the room and closed the door. Her impropriety only paralyzed Miriam into obedience. Nathan kissed and fondled her freely, cuddling her and touching her breasts; she kept pointing to their aunt in the next room.

Miriam offered to marry him secretly, but Nathan refused; her father then would give them nothing. She chewed her nails, committed to Nathan but unable to move.

"That crockery makes no profit," Nathan grumbled. "He's not unloading dead property on me and calling it a dowry."

"Take it; I'll manage and make a lot of money."

"That's got nothing to do with it; nobody makes a fool out of me." And Nathan walked out with his irregular, teasing walk. Idly improvising, a little cocky, Nathan ordered his aunt to go downstairs altogether when he was there with Miriam, not just to the next room. She breathed in silence for a moment, and then bowed her head.

Nathan was there early for Miriam's next visit. She gave a little frightened gasp of pretended surprise to see him there. He gestured his aunt out, and then explored how far he could go with Miriam, knowing beforehand that he would stop at nothing. He was amazed at how acquiescent she was when she realized that her aunt was gone for the afternoon, how easily she allowed him to enjoy her body to the full.

Early one evening as the two boys began a fresh page of Talmud, the Yeshiva moral director, Reb Shloimeh Katz, gestured to Shaya. Several curious glances followed him as he warily left the study hall. Nathan raised his fist in mock support; Shaya gestured for him not to clown. Sitting down in Reb Shloimeh's narrow office, Shaya masked his nervousness and depression under enormous reserve. Reb Shloimeh had a strange smile. "Shaya, you're in Mesivta now; and as our rabbis say, 'Eighteen, under the chuppah.' I have in mind a *shiddach*. I've been approached. Are you open to a discussion?"

Shaya shifted cautiously. "It isn't a thing on my mind."

"This is a distinguished man, with a treasure in this world, and another in the world to come. You know of Zfania Binstock?"

Shay's eyes glittered. "Lumber."

"A wholesaler, a giant. Border guards jump at his approach. His Rachel will bring a handsome dowry and a year of support at his home."

"The class has worthier boys."

"Zfania doesn't want a 'worthy boy'; he wants Shaya Kramer."

"My father has been spoken to?"

"He has, and is agreeable. You'll meet Binstock in this office in three day's time. It's agreed?"

Shaya blinked at him without answering, knowing that silence is legal consent. He returned to the study hall, where a table of graduate rabbis just had a stir of excitement. Word was in that a Lvov religious judge just had a stroke. They weighed approaches for an interview.

Nathan looked up. "What?"

Shaya waved the question aside. "It's not important."

Zfania was a short, skinny man who bathed constantly against a body smell. Originally Litvak, he had a goat beard, a pursed mouth, a brick-red face with no eyebrows; he sat facing Shaya in a black caftan and black-brimmed ghetto cap, with both hands on his cane, and he sucked through his teeth as he spoke about the hazardous roads in Turkey. He knew Gershuni and the Kramer family; yet he asked no polite questions, extended no regards. Obviously he was concerned only with Shaya. Shaya thought the old man disliked him and so gave no opening for intimate conversation. After a brief exchange, Binstock jumped up, shook Shaya's hand, and strode out. Shaya was relieved. Given Binstock's unpleasant manner with him, it should be all over.

Five minutes later, to Shaya's astonishment, Reb Shloimeh gestured him again out of the study hall. All smiles, he called their meeting a success, and informed him that the wedding would be in a month's time. Reb Shloimeh congratulated him, shaking both hands. Shaya tore away, wondering in annoyance what the rabbi's commission would be.

Nathan smiled impatiently as Shaya rejoined him. "What?"

"It's a shiddach."

"It's finished?"

"In a month, with Zfania Binstock's daughter."

"Binstock's a potz, but why look so unhappy?"

"Look, he doesn't like me; so why does he want me? Nothing people do in Warsaw makes sense so I'm unhappy. All right?"

"Miriam and Rachel are good friends. I'll find out through her."

The two boys had studied together for years, and clung together so the Yeshiva wouldn't see them as misfits. Days later, visitors from another Yeshiva brought word of the Musar movement, a system of severe discipline, self-examination, and moral self-help. They brought a few musar books, with stages of self-scrutiny and successive tasks for the cleansing of the soul. Soon a senior man was interrogating members and assigning necessary tasks.

Shaya and Nathan both refused to join the Musar movement. Even afloat in the sea of the Talmud, they felt something called the nineteenth century, something else called Polish anti-Semitism, something else called survival, all different from mere moral discipline. Feeling alienated in the Yeshiva and the city, they supported each other, each hoping to draw on the other's strength. Nathan had access to tips and gossip, a knowledge of how Warsaw was managed; Shaya believed totally and serenely in himself and God.

Chapter Twenty-four

A GENERATION OF NEW-RICH WARSAW JEWS, Nathan's circle, wanted out of the ghetto, but there was no particular place they wanted to go. At gatherings, they fingered over situations, fished for foreign news, and proposed riddles mixing a shrewd investment with a suicidal entrapment. Obsessed with the Rothschilds, they kept compulsively testing for openings in the ghetto walls. They wanted the West without altogether respecting it. They wanted to make a lot of money, but the game was developing new rules. They were never sure what contact they could trust, or where a threat became physical, or where sharp business simply became embezzlement. Old Simcha Garelik, for instance, had built up a business bottling kosher wine. His son Dudie, who bought Polish jewelry wholesale from pawnbrokers, had an unexpected connection and became supplier of Scotch whisky for an entire army headquarters at an enormous profit. His younger brother then brought a carriage of women to headquarters, and was beaten up so savagely that he was never normal again.

Nathan knew money, yet he kept his air of evasive secrecy. He planned eventually to study law, but Shaya suspected he would never make it. His dilettante mind was never altogether on what he did. Shaya suspected that once Nathan exposed himself he

91

would turn very small and drab. Loving him as a friend, Shaya was in no hurry to expose him.

He wouldn't leave Shaya alone. He enjoyed Shaya's life about as much as his own. In a dazed, half-alcoholic way, he kept stumbling after Shaya, whose sudden engagement obsessed him. After a year of marking time, his own engagement had started to bore him.

Shortly after Shaya's engagement became public knowledge Nathan stopped Shaya on a street corner. "Gazlen, you're going under the chuppah; look happy!"

"The whole thing is crazy. My Talmud exam is coming up in two weeks. And what does Binstock want? I have no money, and he's strictly business. He doesn't need me for my grandfather's lumber connections. It's crazy!"

"Maybe he likes the shape of your nose."

"If Binstock saw the shape of a nose, he'd look in a mirror and eat poison."

"I'm still checking Binstock through Miriam; but did you hear about this Bucharest Sabbatarian who repented before the rabbi of Amsterdam?"

"What have you got, another Shabbatean story?"

"For two days, he confessed everything. The rabbi's hair stood on end. There was not a commandment he had missed. And now he wanted to repent. He had a public humiliation inside the great synagogue and was called to the Torah. He then returned to Bucharest, the same sinner he always was."

"I figured it."

"He wrote a letter of thanks to the Amsterdam rabbi. He noticed on his check list one last unviolated command, the commandment to repent. The Bucharest rabbis had too much experience with him; in Amsterdam, he found a rabbi who was a naive fool. Thanks to him his list was now complete."

Shaya sighed. "Did you ever meet a real Shabbatean?"

"Where would I meet one? He wouldn't go to this Yeshiva."

"If he did, he wouldn't tell you."

"Did you ever meet one?"

"I sometimes suspect my father is one."

"That's fantastic! Would he tell me any stories?"

"He's got the real thing, so what does he need with stories?"

Shaya frowned as Nathan stepped away with a giggle. Why would Binstock give away his daughter like this? He didn't even like him. Shaya had an impulse to join the Musar movement, but their moral rigor was relentless; it lacked a sense of humor. It wasn't for him.

Nathan kept pouncing on Shaya. "You're worried about the wrong things. A shiddach is a matter of blind luck. You marry and take your chances. You don't know what to worry about."

"And what should I worry about?"

"Moving into Binstock's house. He sucks; he doesn't breathe out. You'll never get out of that place alive."

"So I'll stay until I die, and your thing isn't dragging?"

Nathan broke into a happy smile. "I'm making my aunt go out on the street. Miriam's so dignified and well-behaved, she doesn't know how to stop me. I can't get enough of her, she's so delicious."

Shaya's hair quivered. "You're sleeping with her?"

"I tell her I'm no good; it makes no difference. I tell her she's too good for this world; she needs to be brought down to earth to start living. Oh, don't worry; I'll get my house with the business."

Shaya gave him a pointed smile and walked away. "Good luck."

Shaya's engagement made him seem suddenly calculating to the boys in his class; he was moving among the families with real money. Several boys' sisters had taken his being agreeable on the Sabbath as a sign of interest, and felt slighted. One classmate bitterly congratulated Shaya for playing his cards right for a rich shiddach.

The mistrust weighed on Shaya. On impulse, he made a trip to see his father. Geula was spending a lot of time in Galicia, helping Gita with her children. Shaineh cooked in her absence. The assault on Gita and her departure had perceptibly widened the gap between Nehemia and Geula, but they were careful not to make things worse. They were each partially to blame. Difficult as things were, they still respected each other.

Coming home, Shaya felt just from Nehemia's manner what his engagement meant to him. Now, whatever happened, Nehemia had a son advancing in the world. Shaya no longer had the knack, but he worked a little in carpentry with Nehemia. He started one of Nehemia's melodies. Nehemia picked up the melody with the voice of an aging lion. Shaya then sang harmony to his singing. They felt very close.

On his return, Shaya took a long walk to Binstock's house. He kept looking around for Rachel. It was just before Passover and every yard held an oven making matzoh. Jewish workers passed with their tools, crying out their trade in a singsong—to fix furniture, clean chimneys, sharpen knives. Bearded street-gossips darted about. Shaya finally had a long look: Binstock's house reminded him of the Flying Goose. Shaya wondered if after entering it, he would ever get out alive.

Back at the Yeshiva, Nathan stepped up to Shaya with a huge smile. "I have information on your shiddach."

"What?"

"Rachel forced Binstock's hand. She saw you dance at the Bialystoker wedding. Since then, she had Miriam asking about your dress in class, your status, and your behavior at people's tables. I didn't think it meant anything, but she was passing it all on to Rachel. She finally told Binstock to get you for her; she would take nobody else."

The news shook Shaya out of his depression. At their next meeting, he grabbed Nathan's shirt. "Why should I take a shiddach on blind faith, when she took nothing on blind faith, and checked everything? Listen, does she have eyebrows? Binstock doesn't. What happens when she looks into a mirror?"

Nathan snickered. "You're talking silly."

"Well, I want to know what she looks like."

"What shall I tell you? You know the Song of Songs: 'Let him kiss me with the kisses of his mouth; thy breasts are sweeter than wine. ' And that's what she looks like."

Shaya pinched his nose hard and walked away, happy for no particular reason. He knew what her eyes looked like; what did the rest matter? And wasn't Binstock a rich man? Then why not travel to Germany after the wedding and study music there? His father was a wanderer. Only when could he bring it up? And to whom?

On impulse, in a tiny shop called Memories, Shaya bought a bouquet of blue china bits for flower petals mounted on wires wrapped in limp leather, and give it to Nathan as a go-between with a note attached: "Love, joy, peace, friendship. Shaya."

In the months before Shaya's wedding, the Belzer community had a spiritual event that touched off eddies for years afterward. A note of Warsaw's first Rebbe was found on parchment, promising the arrival of the Messiah when seven thousand lost seven. A crowd of number mystics set out to crack the message.

Four days later, Shaya received an ornamental bottle of raisin wine by the same route, with a note: "Friendship, peace, joy, love. Rachel."

Shaya smiled ruefully; love exploded in his head. Haunted by two eyes at a wealthy table, he could put his mind on nothing

94

else. Those eyes had stopped him in his tracks at the illui's wedding, opening with an enormous passivity over the body of a peasant. So Binstock disliked him; after a year, he would be on his own. And if not, he still had Rachel.

Seeing him so pensive, Nathan nudged him. "You want to meet Rachel? I can fix it. Just come along to my aunt, and she'll be there."

Shaya bit his knuckle. "I'll meet her under the chuppah."

Nathan smiled affectionately. Shaya made a blind stab. "Sometimes I feel you don't want to settle down with Miriam. I think you like all this confusion, with everything going on." Nathan said nothing.

Shaya suddenly squinted at him. "What is it, *gazlen*?"

"You'll get married first, but I'll be a father first."

Shaya gasped. "You can't mean that."

Nathan chuckled and kicked his heels. "And you agreed to live with Binstock, *meshuggener*?" And he headed off, his feet weaving forward.

Shaya shook his head. Ribalow was enormously decent, but he drank and had a foul temper. Sour and violent, he deeply mistrusted the younger Jewish businessmen, and his own marriage was as bitter; Miriam was the one pure thing in his life. Nathan was dancing on a pit of burning coals, too giddy to notice that his feet were growing scorched.

Chapter Twenty-five

RACHEL SPENT THE LAST WEEKS before her wedding with Miriam. The most conservative of their circle of religious girls, family relations and keeping a home satisfied Rachel completely. Miriam teased that Rachel would end up married to a rabbi; Rachel responded that Miriam would support a husband who would cook and keep house for her. In their case, being opposites made them friends for life.

Even after she became engaged, Rachel was a little jealous of Miriam's drama with her cousin, their secret meeting place and endless intrigues. All she could expect was her coming marriage. Miriam kept telling her dazedly how her holy body was being violated, how Nathan was changing her into a different person. Her father drank, but she fought the inclination; and now she felt herself in a balloon, slowly losing air and descending to earth.

Rachel's family always alienated her. Now she withdrew even more. Zfania was Orthodox in the wrong way, completely under the influence of rules and superstitions. He buttoned the left flap of his jacket over the right because the Poles buttoned the right over the left. On Saturdays, he folded his handkerchief in a scarf around his neck, making it legal to carry it on the Sabbath.

Binstock's constant calculations oppressed Rachel. Dreaming of a father she could respect, she fled to Miriam, but none of Miriam's experiences made any sense to Rachel. Miriam was the sanest, most practical woman she knew. How could she do these things? But Rachel had her own fears — that her friends would drop her, that Shaya would not be a companion, that she would trade in her girlhood for a gold ring and a set of pots to clean. Miriam seemed to know things about the body. She had an air of experience, an ability to surrender herself, where Rachel never dared anything. It was not that Rachel had any intention of changing, but she absorbed Miriam's courage by osmosis.

Rachel was forlorn and curious about Geula. Her own mother was dead many years. She got her mother's nightgowns after she died; they had an opening in that certain spot. Then her mother kept her nightgown on to make love! And the fabric was heavy, opaque. With her closed collar and sleeves to the wrist, she had never held Zfania in her bare arms. And the opening was so tiny! Was Zfania so tiny a man? And through that opening popped the family? It was ridiculous!

Geula visited the Binstock home before the wedding, bringing gifts. She wore gray cotton gloves and a bushy flower hat, and saw Rachel for half an hour. They approved of each other's out-fits—rich, solid fabrics covering them to the wrist and throat. Rachel was better educated, but she never allowed it to show. She listened, relaxed, as Geula chatted amusingly about the farm and invited Rachel to visit at any time. Geula asked if Rachel had made arrangements to visit the Belzer mikvah. Rachel had in fact made other arrangements, but she immediately asked Geula's company in preference to any of her sisters-in-law.

When she left, Geula gave Rachel several silk and linen *tichels,* or kerchiefs to cover the head after the wedding. Rachel picked the most expensive and tried it on. She felt as if she looked very young, with her mouth hanging slightly open and her lip dangling. The women parted cordially. They each knew where the other stood on religious observance. Privately Geula thought Rachel rather cowlike; Rachel thought Geula bossy and manipulative.

The next day, the two took a private entrance into the Belzer mikvah, adjoining a Russian steam bath and the old-age home, two other examples of institutional Jewry. On Friday, the bathhouse was exclusively for men; they arrived from early morning to purify themselves for the Sabbath. The crowd kept getting thicker until twenty minutes before sunset, when all the steam was let out of the bath through a loud whistle that sounded all over the area. The Sabbath was minutes away. The market emptied itself out fast.

For the street, Rachel wore pale pink gloves and the same *tichel,* and traditional long wrappings to support her bosom. It was such an earthy ritual, the mikvah. As an attendant gave Rachel a big towel and led them to a cubicle, she felt like a dumpling shoved into a potful of cooking water. A married woman her age was entering the next cubicle with a bath attendant. On her first visit, she probably also had her mother-in-law to inspect her for final approval, like a chef examining the platter before it goes out of the kitchen.

Inside the cubicle, Rachel felt Geula watching her. Stripping, she was exposing the torso and bosom she was bringing into the family. And yet she believed in herself and kept her serenity. As she unbuttoned her blouse and lowered her body wrapping, steam from the nearby Russian bath trickled under the door, carrying the smell of bathing male bodies.

Rachel glanced at Geula with sudden revulsion. She had asked her along, and yet once Geula had inquired about her arrangements, Rachel had no choice except to bring her. It was just slightly degrading. Geula's father was Binstock's spotter. And Rachel didn't mind exposing herself for comparison. Yet her brothers would never suffer this. Rachel's father was a wealthy, established man; and here was his daughter being examined for how much milk she could give a strange woman's grandchildren.

Stripped, Rachel refused to hurry. She glanced securely at her breasts, her fingernails, took a careful breath, and then stepped down the stone steps into the water that lapped up on her body with each step she took. She saw the moon rising in the reflected light, smiled, and jumped out into the pieces of moon.

At the bottom, Rachel immersed herself, angling up her arms and crouching so water touched all her skin. While underwater, she twisted around and glanced up. Geula had a smile of satisfaction on her lips. Then she wasn't imagining things. From the next cubicle came the primitive voice of a regular attendant, rising over the young woman she just saw, crying, "Koooooo-oooooosher!"

Having performed the ritual, Rachel wrapped and dried herself, and then slowly dressed. She was becoming a married woman, Geula's equal, with her sane skepticism, her practicality, and sense of being quality. Both were on the *zaftig* side, and of the same height. Both yearned for a noble male soul to fold around her; Rachel in particular felt revulsion against Binstock, who was so small, so precise and brainy, and never stopped moving. She yearned for something huge and male, an image of God the Father.

Rachel picked Shaya more than he picked her, and she worried about Shaya's attitude to her. She wouldn't be an image of his mother. Geula had a hard edge. She discussed practical things, and arranged them to move her way. Geula's manipulation made Rachel impatient; but from what she heard, Nehemia was a primitive man with a stir of violence. Geula would have to manipulate, just to live with such a man.

The two women stepped outside and parted with a kiss. Overcome with feeling, Rachel hurried to Miriam's house to find out more about Nehemia.

That evening, Nehemia was visiting Zfania to pay his respects. All afternoon, her father irritated Rachel. His voice always took on that religious tone when he was arranging a crooked business deal. Just his irritated wait of five hours between a meat and a milk meal was enough to make her a Shabbatean. Zfania was a Litvak fanatic, but he took warm baths on the Sabbath. It was forbidden, but his body smelled, and cold baths made him sick. He rationalized it on health grounds. But Miriam had called Nehemia a secret Shabbatean. From her talk, the Kramers had family secrets. Things happened to them; some children disappeared and some came to a bad end.

That evening, Rachel sat on the stairs to the second floor, watching over the banister. Nehemia finally came in the door, his greatcoat over his shoulders, and disappeared immediately into Zfania's room. Rachel hadn't gotten a good look. She rested her chin on the banister and waited a half hour, her mind blank.

Suddenly she stiffened. Nehemia was coming out to leave. She leaned far over. He seemed burned out inside, a walking ghost; a father who lived only for his children. A man that primitive was like a force of nature. Geula manipulated too much to understand a man like that.

Rachel sighed; Nehemia was too good for Geula.

Chapter Twenty-six

FASTING, IN WHITE COTTON ROBES, Shaya and Rachel stood in the vestibule of a Warsaw wedding hall with scribes and witnesses, as Binstock made over to Nehemia a substantial dowry. A tin box containing the cash settlement changed hands. Nehemia opened it, counted it, locked it again, and put it in the hall safe to take home after his next visit to Warsaw.

A scribe opened the parchment wedding contract, each section with calligraphic flourishes. The beadle filled in the date. The couple signed it, in the company of two witnesses. The hunchback Yerucham began a Belzer quadrille on his fiddle. Shaya and Nathan crossed hands and danced. Other Yeshiva boys joined them as a circle of Orthodox girls watched.

Two classmates in black coats escorted Shaya into a side room with six rows of tables under a very low ceiling, packed with Talmudists, to show off his learning at his wedding. Shaya took as his text a law of holiness. He explained minutiae of the profanations of the holy, its intricacies and connections, with primary and secondary impurities, as rows of black-bearded scholars wriggled to follow his argument.

His legal presentation finished, Shaya shifted to Midrash. He located the essence of holiness and impurity as a hair apart, like two sides of a mirror. Both seek the one God; good and evil ways converge on His body; but only holiness arrives there. Evil is the twisted path to God, trapped in its own devices, a path that cannot be followed to its end. If one approaches holiness too fast, one breaks through the mirror to the other side. But in an open confrontation, holiness is victorious, because evil is a *klipeh,* a shell, an outer coating, finally a nothing; but holiness is an essence, life, the body of God. Wrestling with a shadow, Jacob became Israel, being a life; but the shadow remained a nothing, being a *klipeh,* without name or blessing.

Shaya finished to a roar of applause and wails of pleasure. Scholars waved goblets of wine, crying, "Yisroel! Yisroel!" An old man shouted, "He has a golden spoon in his mouth."

Shaya led a grand march up the stairs, with his father at his side, Gershuni and the Horowitz family close behind, his Talmud class marching together before a throng of visitors, to veil his bride. Yerucham danced up and back along the wall, playing his fiddle.

Shaya leaned aside to whisper to Nehemia. "Zfania didn't

99

want me for a son-in-law; Rachel forced his hand. He kept holding back Gershuni's commission. My friend Nathan says he'll never give me anything."

"He signed the contract."

"The money you got is the last we'll ever see."

"The dowry will sit in a box in the ground, if you should ever need it. I won't touch a penny." Shaya pressed his father's hand in thanks.

At the top of the stairs, Shaya, Nehemia, Gershuni, and all the guests approached three carved oak chairs placed in the middle of the hall under a crystal chandelier filled with fresh-lit candles. Rachel wore the family wedding gown of blue silk. To her left sat her grandmother, who was married in the same gown. To her right stood an empty chair that represented her mother's soul.

Shaya lowered the veil over Rachel's face, his eyes fixed on the strange woman who had taken on his life. Yerucham made the students do an intricate troika, chanting like Cossacks: "God. God! God is thee. World! World! World is me!"

Carried away, Shaya kicked his heels in a drag step, until Nehemia pulled him to a halt. "You're fasting; have pity on yourself."

Rachel felt herself bumped and carried along, and traveled joyously intaking little breaths. Shaya was childlike, but his generosity had no limits. His face hid fear—of Polish Warsaw, her father, of life itself. He demanded mothering. She didn't care. His huge, brooding soul reached the edges of a sea of terror, white and mysterious; and over him hung Nehemia. She was finally entering a family of giants. Her coming life had no limits and no tradition she could cling to with certainty.

As they descended, Nathan tugged Shaya's arm. "You know, bigamy was first made illegal in the eleventh century. In the Bible, they all were bigamists. Even Adam had Lilith as a trial wife before Eve. I wonder if any of Lilith's children are still alive—they're Litvaks probably. I bet Binstock is descended from Lilith. He has that face."

Shaya gave him a radiant smile, not hearing a word. Nathan sighed and took a seat for the brisk ceremony, the wine, the contract, the seven blessings, each from a different rabbi. Shaya broke the glass to a great cry of "Mazel tov!" He then kissed Rachel while greedy relatives fought to pull them apart for their turn before the bride, and then the two of them stepped into an adjoining room for *yichud*.

Dazed by the wedding, the couple held hands, smiling sheepishly and making little gestures to each other not to worry, as impatient noises came from the wedding hall. Stepping out, they were lifted on teetering chairs for a march around the hall. Shaya gave Rachel his handkerchief, holding one end. She sighed in relief that he was so moral. Perched there, leading the march, Shaya spotted Binstock and his sons standing apart in fur-trimmed robes. A chill grew in Shaya's soul. In still despair, he entrusted his life to Rachel's hands.

Placed at the head table, Shaya cut a table-long loaf of challeh with a saw-edged blade, making a loud blessing. A boy sliced a piece of bread for each person in the hall, passing the bread on trays. As the banquet began, an endless line of people passed behind the head table, shaking hands and slipping envelopes into Shaya's palm.

A girl in muffled street garb aroused Shaya's curiosity. He held her hand as she slipped him an envelope. There was a single name on it: Esther.

Shaya tugged her sleeve. "Tell my sister I didn't sit in mourning. Tell her, to me she's still alive. I want her back in the family."

As the stranger nodded and left, Shaya opened the envelope and read a message: "Mazel tov! lokshen-face. She's kosher meat; I hope she's your choice and not Poppa Momma's. Season her right, and she'll stay on your platter." Shaya slipped the note into his pocket with a smile.

Nathan leaned over. "The rebbe's oldest son has a solution to the riddle. Ten is the number for Yud, the initial of God; seventeen is the number for chait or sin. The Messiah will come when seventeen subtracts seven, leaving ten, when God replaces sin."

"The reading will have a take?"

"It's too complicated; it will hurt him."

Shaya nodded and sipped his wine. There was something dreamlike about his wedding, as if it could pass away like smoke.

While Shaya hesitated, Yeshiva boys in the hall looked up toward him with barely concealed awe. Shaya hung over them like a prince, the man of Torah marrying a beauty. Refusing to surrender to their jealousy, they jumped up from their seats began a Cossak dance, sinking to their haunches in a *kazatskeh,* as Shaya watched in patient silence.

Shaya told Rachel of his three sisters and their mishaps. She refrained from telling him the gossip she had heard, wanting not

101

to upset him. She sensed her husband's bond to Esther and resolved to pursue it further.

The Binstocks leaned their heads together at their table. "A Yeshiva boy was asked if it was kosher to chew gum. He answered, what do you want to do, imitate a cow?"

"The image of God starts to moo!"

"You know why the groom gives the bride wine under the chuppah? To make sure she's the girl he put the veil on upstairs, and not like the farmer whose neighbor slipped the groom a veiled donkey."

"When Jacob married Leah, thinking it was Rachel, Rachel lay all night under the bed, whispering, 'Jacob, I love you,' while they made love, so he should hear her voice and think he had Rachel in bed."

The Binstocks roared and slapped each other's thighs.

Gita and her grandmother sat at the crowded Horowitz table like a witch and her assistant, wearing heavy jewelry, their heads shaven, beneath their wigs. Always slight, Gita had lost weight since marrying Yitzik. Her oldest son came seven months after the chuppah, but no one would put a stigma on the family. She lived adjacent to Gershuni, in the cottage Nehemia and Geula had before they came north. They jarred Rachel, with their red silk dresses, the loose flowing material suggesting transparency and skin. They should reserve their exposure for their husbands.

The Binstocks knocked their heads together, groaning, snickering, and wagging their fists: "King Solomon was a bastard; his mother Bathsheba was still married to Uriah when King David slept with her."

"The smartest man in the world was a bastard?"

"It's not a problem; in a king, you're allowed."

Bursts of singing peppered the banquet. The badchen moved sinuously in a black suit, the jacket flapping open as he dramatized a tale of an ancient rabbi who found on the road an exquisite woman wrapped only in a thin sheet. She said she was the daughter of a jewel merchant, just married; a Bedouin band had fallen on her wedding party, killing everyone but her, whom they enjoyed at their leisure and then abandoned on the highway. She begged the judge to give her a night's shelter and help her on the road to her family in peace the next day. As the rabbi brought her to his home; she seemed to him to float like a spirit. Her ashen hair blew behind her; her feet left no footprints. The rabbi wondered what she was, woman or spirit.

102

Night came on. In his home, he ordered her to climb to his second floor. He then took his ax and chopped up the stairs to make contact between them impossible: but during the night, a rage of lust overcame the rabbi. He dragged inside the orchard ladder and began to climb. Halfway up, he saw the image of his father over him. He grabbed the ladder in his arms and prayed to God to protect his soul from sin. When he finished his prayer, the ladder disappeared; but his lust held him hanging in midair.

The crowd was intrigued. The rabbis tapped the table and pretended not to hear, when a messenger burst through the door and pushed through the crowd to Zfania: "A blood accusation in Constantinople; a Jewish family was thrown into prison. They said the matzoh was blood flour, a curse."

A rabbi wailed. "Rothschild won't allow it."

Zfania swung over his sons. "We buy now, and get our own price."

Shaya tugged Rachel's arm, tipsy. "Do you repent, Rachel?"

"For what should I repent?"

"For being born a Litvak."

"I'll repent being born a Litvak, if you repent asking me to."

"I repent with all my heart."

"And for being born a Galitzianer, that's a worse blemish."

"I repent that also."

"Then I repent being a Litvak, not that I can help it."

"Only a Litvak would put down such conditions for repentance."

Both smiled—Shaya because he had the last word, Rachel because she read his thoughts so easily. Already it promised to become a happy marriage. Geula cupped her mouth to Gershuni's ear. Restless, Nehemia caught Rachel's eye. Choked with a sudden spasm of loneliness, he blinked at her, his eyes brimming with all his frustrated passion for his daughters. Even though she was occupied with her father, Geula caught the exchange, and remembered her mother's comments when she married Nehemia. She felt a twinge of guilt, a pang of jealousy, an even-handed justice. The hall rose to dance the *shereleh.*

Binstock arched a finger. "What was Esther really to Mordecai?"

"What do you mean? Uncle and niece; he fathered the girl."

"He uncled her, and uncles can marry nieces. I bet he married her, and then gave her to Ahasuerus to protect the Jewish people, the way Abraham gave Sarah to Pharaoh."

"Esther stewed in a perfume vat for six months to get in condition."

"Mordecai didn't give Esther to the court as a queen; he gave her as a concubine. Then Mordecai was a pimp."

Zfania quieted him with a satisfied smile. "You go too far."

All over the hall, men knotted up, drinking, gossiping, talking politics, telling stories. As for the table of unmarried girls, some of them were so preoccupied with the men that they sat almost in a trance. The other girls didn't exist for them. They kept organizing their feelings to give a man support. Nothing else existed in their lives.

Shaya and Rachel left the hall for their wedding night in the wing of Binstock's home. They climbed, opened their door, and found a storage area piled with furniture. Zfania hadn't bothered to convert his attic into rooms for them to live in. Shaya and Rachel had to climb over furniture to reach their beds. Rachel made Shaya crawl first, so he wouldn't see under her clothes. She wanted to undress in private—she would die undressing before a man—but furniture packed the room, so Rachel untied and unbuttoned her clothes as she crawled, like a snake shedding an old skin. She had doused herself with a love cologne; she moved as lightly as possible not to rub it off. She arrived in bed naked, a trail of clothes behind her and a love scent as a spoor.

Rachel lay back and watched Shaya emerge, big-chested and hairy. That big a man called for a harder mattress. Then he lay back; she started toward him, unable to stop herself.

"Are you sorry it's me and not Miriam Ribalow?"

"I love you, Rachel."

"I think your father is such a wonderful man."

All night in the pit of a down mattress, Rachel felt Kramer spirits all around her in the room. Shaya rode her like a raft afloat on turbulent waters, his eyes immense with starvation. Appalled at his silence and love, she felt her way into the landscape of his soul that she would inhabit for the rest of her life.

Chapter Twenty-seven

YESHIVA CLASSES WERE OPTIONAL the week before Passover, so many boys went home for the holiday. Shaya took time off and worked with Rachel setting up their rooms. They kept the more handsome pieces and Rachel's mother's things, the only womanly pieces in the house. The rest of the furniture they shifted to another storage area. Rachel didn't like her mother's possessions all that much, but she liked adapting and rearranging things. She cleared off an inlaid table and put a lamp on it, then cleaned out her mother's perfume casket. It gave her a catch in the throat to be the woman in the family, no longer her mother's shadow.

To interest Shaya and entice him from his studies, she kept trying on things from her mother's chest. Shaya didn't seem that interested. Frustrated, she continued for her own pleasure. But some of her mother's dresses were still medieval. When she put them on she felt herself a delicious lie. She was utterly honest, but that only made the lie delicious.

Rachel tried on her mother's nightgown with the hole, and asked Shaya's opinion. Shaya had none. She put it away in silence. He didn't understand what the nightdress signified. Then she was satisfied to keep him an innocent.

Rachel asked why Shaya avoided talking about Geula. Her husband said he didn't know; he didn't feel his mother was part of the family. She was loyal to Nehemia, but she kept herself somehow a Horowitz.

After an early supper, Rachel put on a heavy jacket and babushka, Shaya a fur-trimmed skullcap. They went to services at the Belzer synagogue. Reb Reuven Dressler stopped Shaya at the door, exactly as he had stopped his father. "Kramer, take the table."

Shaya stepped up to the table and began a moody melody in a minor key. The crowd half knew it and began snapping their fingers in rhythm. Shaya then did cantorial variations to their finger percussion. Standing in the women's section behind the curtain, listening, Rachel caught the music in his voice, haunting, wordless, charged with fulfillment. She grasped his secret desire to study music, but it would never happen. What was impractical, she let be.

After services, Rachel hurried off to urge Miriam to stop postponing things and just get married. She was married for two days, and Miriam was a fool not to get married herself. Miriam drank wine. She needed controls; she couldn't control herself.

As Rachel was with Miriam, Shaya entered the anteroom where the Belzer gabbai, or representative, was meeting with local shopkeepers, teachers, workers, and housewives. A Hebraist family had moved in their neighborhood. What should be their attitude? The gabbai called the use of Hebrew except in prayer a desecration. Hebrew was a holy language. They should guard their children against them, and not let them be recruited into a profane practice.

An abandoned wife had located her husband elsewhere in the city. She demanded either his return or a divorce, she no longer cared which. She couldn't live as a married widow. The gabbai undertook to bring it to a head.

A shopkeeper complained that the Labor Socialists preached universal peace, labor, and abundance—then they were a cult to be fought root and branch like the Shabbateans. The gabbai said that since the Socialists did not believe in God, they were atheists, not Messianics, and therefore should be left alone. Any action against them would bring trouble with the government.

The local cemetery-director asked about burying the bodies of lifelong sinners side by side with pillars of the Jewish community. He now had a body that was never circumcised and refused to bury it. Circumcision was the covenant; the body was outside the covenant, and so its Jewishness was questionable. The gabbai answered that a dead body is not given punishment. The soul would stand up for judgment at the heavenly court, but a Jewish body is Jewish from birth and deserves a Jewish burial.

A Hebrew teacher complained that the Belzer wedding melody was originally a Napoleonic army song. The gabbai replied that the melody in fact was older than Napoleon, and since Napoleon was a friend of the Jews, he should allow the song. The meeting closed as the group made a collection of Passover baskets for the poor.

The next morning, Nathan came to help move furniture for Shaya and Rachel. He brought with him word of a new scandal in his circle: at an all-night drinking party, Dudie Garelik had showed off his Jewish knowledge by holding a mock wedding with a thirteen-year-old girl, hilariously singing the marriage service. Then he slept with her, crying to his friends, "The Black Mass! The Black Mass!" The next day, the girl was on his doorstep with both parents, expecting to join her husband. The gabbai supported her, insisting that Garelik had married and slept with his wife. Dudie offered her a large bribe to accept a divorce. Her father demanded treble the money. A rabbinic court was taking up the case.

Toward noon, Miriam visited. Bland in manner, with pale blue eyes and sandy braids, her expressionless face, steady sadness, and soft, high-pitched whine finally became hypnotic to those around her. A born businesswoman, shrewd with money

106

and quick with numbers, she could pull an entire family behind her, change direction, and keep lurching forward.

The four shared fish cakes and crackers, careful not to spread crumbs before Passover. Nathan and Shaya began discussing leaving Warsaw—not that either wanted to leave, but their roots were thinner than those of their parents. Odessa was a rich city, free and open—but a friend who visited Western Europe was talking about New York.

That Miriam and Nathan met so freely surprised Rachel. Their aunt's home offered them privacy, but to meet outside without a chaperone was really asking for trouble. Then after their snack together, Nathen escorted Miriam out of the house. Something in Miriam's walk, an unsteadiness at the door, made Rachel suddenly look at her belly.

"If it were any other woman, I could swear Miriam is with child."

Shaya grinned dryly. "She is."

"Ribalow will throw her out of the house for a thing like that!"

Rachel was scandalized. Nathan became a small man in her eyes, reducing his bride to real estate so as to collect a dowry. He was a fool to think it would work. Miriam had ten times his brain; she had no business agreeing to it. But perhaps there were mysteries here of which Rachel had no inkling. But she was most furious at their aunt. What was she running, a bawdy house? A bell should be hung around her neck.

Since the time they were little girls, Rachel and Miriam had argued over who would have the first baby. Miriam was a pig, getting pregnant like that, but a baby born out of wedlock didn't count. She was still having the first baby. But to go so far! It was . . . it was unthinkable!

Shaya felt revulsion at the thought of spending Passover with the Binstocks, and insisted they visit the chicken farm. Rachel strongly supported him. Her father's house was no longer a home. She intended to work her way into Shaya's family; Passover seemed like a good time to begin. She couldn't get Nehemia out of her head; he had been the only peasant in the wedding hall, with nobody to talk to. That look he threw her unleashed her imagination, like a call for help. Gita avoided her father; the other two daughters had run off with strange men. It must hurt. He had relatives in Warsaw but he never made contact with them. If they were her relatives, every one of them would have been at the wedding.

Shaya mentioned that Nehemia had put away the dowry money, to have it ready when his son needed it. That bit of information made Nehemia's generosity, his deep truth, his commitment to his children seem irresistible to Rachel. Shaya had some of his father's despair, and he was something of a drifter. They were very similar. Both had a skeptical disbelief that anything important ever happened. Nehemia was a born outcast, an alien, but Rachel refused to reject him.

Zfania was surprisingly agreeable to their spending Passover in Radich. A door had snapped shut in his head during the wedding. His brain turned on legalisms; he made calculations in order to avoid having any thoughts. His three daughters-in-law had been Binstocks; but Rachel was now a Kramer, equivalent to a hotel guest in his home. The wedding rearranged the family in his head, but he wasn't cruel about it. Amid his own holiday preparations he gave them his carriage for the ride south.

Chapter Twenty-eight

ON THE ROAD TO RADICH, the couple passed an occasional farm, but the countryside wasn't really developing. Poland was an occupied country. There were abandoned stretches, closed mills and villages steeped in poverty, hillsides with their soil gutted, where nobody bothered to seed or plant saplings.

As he drove the carriage Shaya told Rachel of his old irritations with Reb Shloimeh Katz, the moral director. The Yeshiva had charity cases but it catered to the rich. The Yiddish labor unions were taking hold, developing their own organizations— and they were all Socialists. The Jewish religion was losing its hold on the workingman.

Rachel nodded and agreed, but since her father's house was opaque to ideas they made her uneasy; it frightened her that Shaya had them.

They passed wagons with Chasidim on holiday pilgrimage, carriages with closed curtains, identical to those of the Polish nobility. The Polish peasants working in the fields eyed the carriages, scratching their heads, unsure if they should salute or spit. A Pole signaled for Shaya to pull over and stop. He waved back as though exchanging a hello and kept moving.

Shaya explained to Rachel further developments in the riddle of the Messiah and seven thousand minus seven. The Rebbe's second son had insisted that to bring the time of the Messiah, you must go back to beginnings; seven taken from the beginning of seven thousand would leave 0000. The Messiah would come when seven thousand Jews reduced themselves to the four nothings. This independent thinking stirred a furor in the Belzer community. Was the Rebbe's son trying to take the succession away from his older brother? Was he trying to build his own movement? Was he simply an original? What were the four nothings? More was coming for him to unfold.

Rachel had listened fitfully. The news about Miriam bothered her too much to listen. If Nathan really loved Miriam, how could he make her pregnant like that? Yet Miriam adored him; she hung on to everything he said. And Shaya's references to the Socialists in Warsaw jarred her. Too many married women held two jobs and raised their children while their men studied and prayed all day. Shaya had some of that sweet passivity; but he did throw himself into setting up their new home. Rachel was uncertain about Shaya, but she counted on some talent, an ambition that would unfold itself.

Suddenly Rachel pressed Shaya's hand to stop. She leaned out and threw up on the road. As she wiped her lips, she and Shaya looked at each other with sheepish grins.

"You'll deliver a few months after Miriam."

"She and I are doing completely different things."

"I never meant to compare you."

Shaya's mention of Miriam shook Rachel. Was Miriam on his mind? You start out being compared and end up hearing the ways in which you are inadequate. For all her mildness, Miriam was a fanatic who forced her way into a man's world, even though she would never be at home there. Her father's beatings had leveled somthing inside her. She would do whatever Nathan asked—steal, lie, get pregnant.

As they continued south, Rachel felt a huge satisfaction at how totally she read Shaya's thoughts. But for all her savvy in understanding her husband; her willpower eluded her. She staggered along under a strange man's flag. Single, she did things; married, she just lived. Shaya was happy with her tagging along after him, an echo to his own thoughts. It was not a bad way to start a marriage.

Rachel glanced up. "You'll finish in the Yeshiva?"

"It'll let lie all those things in your father's contract."

"Just don't come out a batlan."

Rachel's mood darkened when she thought about Miriam. Everything Miriam did was by way of apology. Even her courage was a nothing, because she was forever apologizing. She had nothing to apologize for, but her very existence, as a woman, in her family, her city, her life called for apology. Her helplessness only finalized it—that lassitude, that sane, delicious whine. Just getting pregnant had an apologetic whine about it: whatever went wrong in her life, she would at least have a baby.

Rachel sighed. She would wait out whatever was bothering Shaya. It would not be so bad with Shaya in the Yeshiva: she would have a few precious years with her children before the storm broke and all their troubles began. The air was balmy, the ride relaxing. Rachel dozed, leaning against Shaya's shoulder.

After an hour, she was jolted awake. They were in the yard. Shaya's eyes were full of mischief. He gestured Rachel to climb off and follow him to a shed adjoining the chicken house, where a blind woman was milking a cow, her face alive with happiness, her hands strongly bearing in and down, sending a stream of warm milk into a pail between her legs.

Rachel followed Shaya into the house, where over dinner Nehemia began talking of his wanderings as a boy in Galicia. Rachel took his talk as a sign that he accepted her. Then the blind woman came in and crouched in a corner. Nehemia felt to Rachel like a male presence gone adrift, there to be picked up and had.

Rachel quickly fell into life on a Jewish farm. The Flying Goose felt like Noah's ark before its launching. As she walked through the farmyard, she soon distinguished dog droppings, chicken droppings, and horse droppings, not to speak of the outhouse, where she soon joined the ranks of the producers of fertilizer. Smells came by the bucketful and no substance was wasted. Something felt right about her visiting here at the beginning of pregnancy.

Shaineh was impressive, handling the chicken house all by herself. Hurrying back and forth from the inn, vibrating a wand before her, she looked like one of the touched, the holy wanderers Rachel had sometimes seen on the road, but Shaineh was always half-unbuttoned, her skirt loosely tied. Rachel wondered if she slept with Nehemia when Geula was in the south. She felt a surging resentment that Shaineh might have moved in on another woman's husband, but Geula should have detected it. Something was wrong in that marriage. Geula wasn't around that much and her mind was always elsewhere. Gita's departure had thrown her. She now kept two homes, tending to Nehemia and also her father. Geula never really got married.

Rachel marveled at the many unused rooms in the house. Geula should have had at least one child here to make the house hers. In the attic, an old flagpole leaned on the wall, still carrying its red flag. Rachel ran downstairs, dragged Shaya up, and gestured in awkward curiosity.

"This was a house of the red flag?"

"It's the sign of a tannery in Bucharest."

Rachel shot him a skeptical glance. Shaya blinked at her helplessly. Rachel fought her impatience. "Have patience, Shaya. You know women expecting their first baby, they want the moon."

Downstairs, Rachel found Nehemia in the kitchen. She filled a large bowl with borscht and put the jar away. Watching him eat, Rachel pressed her bosom to control her excitement at giving him a meal.

Shaya took her on exploratory walks over the grounds. Several times, Rachel leaned against a tree, suddenly nauseous.

On their sliver of lawn, Rachel noticed the tub Shaya's sisters had used. "Who brought this out here?"

Shaya shrugged. "Esther. She lugged the water and took baths here, and she made her sisters come out too. Afterward they danced together."

Rachel broke into a thin smile. "And Nehemia allowed all this?"

"It's the Shabbatean in him; he liked seeing his girls in their underwear."

"I think that drove all three girls out of the house."

"Warsaw has much worse, believe me."

Rachel read his face. "You spied on them here, didn't you? You and Esther were very close."

For an answer, Shaya reached in his pocket and held out Esther's wedding card. Rachel read it over and flushed deeply, unable to stand being called kosher meat, but loving it and feeling exactly right. Shaya folded her in his arms for a long kiss. Rachel allowed it, and then shrugged. "All the same, your sister Esther likes you a lot more than is good for her."

"It's my father she's in love with."

"Your father, your father, your father. It's impossible to escape him in this family. But where is Esther now? She's in Warsaw, isn't she? Why haven't you found her? You're just like your father; he never looks for his Warsaw relatives either."

Shaya's jaw fell. "The family sat shivah, seven days of mourning. We love her, but now she has to come back."

111

"So she sailed out of the house. People do things, but you don't lose a sister like that. I want you to find her."

"I'll see what I can do."

That night, as they undressed for bed, they heard an anxious shout. Everybody ran downstairs, where Shaineh stood shawled, waving her wand helplessly. "The yard door was open; twenty chickens have gotten out."

They all ran out where a heavy moon hung in the orchard foliage, and stomped in the wild grass, kicking up swarms of insects. When a chicken jumped, somebody snatched it. Nehemia pinched its wings in back and forced it through the pophole into the chicken house.

Rachel stumbled over one. Shrieking, she fell on it, nearly killing it. It scuffed in the dirt, fluttering its wings, squawking, and bit her finger so hard she let out a scream, as Nehemia reached over his shoulder and grabbed it by both wings. Rachel felt him looking at her with a grin of pleasure. She was bare-armed and in her body wrap. She stood up, demure as a peony, drinking in his eyes. She was a Kramer now, part of the farming family.

That night Rachel could not get enough of Shaya. Some floodgate opened inside her. She kissed him endlessly, and Shaya responded with his whole being, marveling that the Flying Goose did this to her. He would have to bring her home regularly.

The next morning a messenger brought news from Galicia. After Shaya's wedding, Yael had developed an insatiable hunger. She ate a plate of meat gone rotten in the kitchen and died of food poisoning. Geula wanted to return with the messenger and sit seven days of mourning with her family. Nehemia insisted that she be at his seder. She worried about Gita, living there without her grandmother. Nehemia looked at Rachel. She gently nodded. Nehemia allowed Geula to leave for Galicia with the messenger.

Rachel served as hostess at the seder. She marveled at how Oriental Nehemia was, leaning back on an embroidered pillow like a Bedouin monarch. By her third glass of wine, she wondered if she would ever join Nehemia's harem. She sang the Haggadah with her whole being. Tears came to her eyes. She unbuttoned her collar to relax at the feast, something she never did at home.

Nehemia let Rachel find the last matzoh, since she was the youngest person there. He asked what she wanted in exchange for it; she said she wanted just the pleasure of serving him food.

But Nehemia's own existence had grown bleaker in spite of Rachel, with Yael's sudden poisoning and Geula's withdrawal. He lounged in his greatcoat, hiking stick in hand, singing the Haggadah in a series of marching melodies. He saw the Angel of Death outside his window.

The next morning at dawn, Rachel slipped outside into the woods. Overhead, the pine trees webbed their needles under a pale moon. Approaching alone, Rachel felt the secret lawn sacred somehow, with the woods so still, and the moon fading fast. Feeling an impulse to dance naked, Rachel started to unbutton her blouse. And then she felt a twinge in her belly. She stood up and giggled; she was having a baby. She turned and lightly skipped back to the house.

Chapter Twenty-nine

AFTER PASSOVER, the couple went back to Warsaw and Shaya resumed his Yeshiva studies. A half hour after his first class began, Rabbi Wolfson knew Shaya wasn't really there. The rabbi thought this could be temporary, but Shaya now had a rich wife and might join the talented dilettantes passing time in school. No one else was worried. Single, Shaya had the same barrier around himself; married, he stayed as quiet and perceptive as ever.

Wolfson bided his time. They were entering difficult material. Either Shaya pulled back on track, or the study itself would throw him off. He respected Shaya's reserve, his subtlety and clarity, how he avoided gossip. He was worth working with and waiting for.

On Shaya's second day back, Reb Shloimeh called him into his office for a conference. Shaya told him he would continue at the Yeshiva until ordination. Reb Shloimeh lifted an eyebrow; Binstock would support him for several more years? Shaya was sure he would. The house was there anyway; food was not expensive. The arrangement would cost him very little.

Shaya's dreamy withdrawal again made Rachel a little impatient, but she adored her husband's reserve. Nehemia already fitted into an empty space in her life as both a husband and a father. She was slipping deeper into the web of a strange family.

That night she told Shaya she wanted to deliver in Radich, under Nehemia's roof. Shaya said Geula was an experienced midwife. Rachel said she wanted Shaya's mother to deliver her, and dozed off with a happy smile.

Shaya looked wistfully at his happy little girl, already asleep. He sensed that she guessed his ambition for music. It would take her mind off uglier, more personal things. But the look of blind rejection on Geula's face haunted him. His mother had returned to Galicia at her own insistence, yet she looked as though thrown out of the house.

The Belzer's second son issued a book of meditation. *The Four Nothings: Steps to the Messiah,* a spiritual pilgrimage from the nothing of property to the nothing of humanity, then to the nothing of self, and finally to the nothing of love, arriving finally at the absolute in a sea of total emptiness. The book was in every dormitory room. Boys hummed a chant over it in the study hall. The Rebbe's second son already gave amulets; several wealthy Chasidim did his bidding, in charities and political maneuvering.

After a month, several groups of four boys flaked away from the student body and became nothings to each other. The Musar movement was too rational to allow them mystical illumination. The Four Nothings went around with looks of radiant joy on their faces. And yet no serious Yeshiva student became involved, and most had an intangible mistrust of the Rebbe's second son. The Four Nothings alienated Shaya. Ghetto orphans, each trailing his will-of-the-wisp, and blindly out of it, they would end up trapped in another nothing-ghetto courtyard.

Warsaw was darkening into winter. The soft coal cast soot over the city. The warehouse laid in extra supplies. Flights of birds winged south. Blankets were thrown over the horses' backs. Children looked out their windows every morning, watching for snow.

Nathan began visiting more often. He could still not visit Miriam's home and was too tense to remain alone. It was a period of waiting for both men. Nathan insisted Ribalow knew by now of his daughter's pregnancy but was playing some sort of Russian roulette, to force a marriage on his own terms. Shaya disagreed. Many Orthodox men wore horse blinkers, pulling their wagon. But the later Ribalow found out about his daughter, the more violent his reaction would be.

In the interim, the Four Nothings increased Nathan's irritation. Having made Miriam pregnant, he was suddenly full of

Ruth and the Song of Songs. The Four Nothings were somehow monastic; they didn't even feel Jewish. And that idiot joy on their faces, those empty minds made in the image of an empty God. A Belzer employer who made uniforms gave each a beaver *shtreimel* hat a good inch taller than the foxtail of the other Belzer. Wearing it made them seem stately when there was absolutely nothing to them.

Shaya had his own misgivings. The Four Nothings were becoming isolated in the Yeshiva. Mystics of waiting, without the stiffening backbone of a tough Talmudist or any real program, the circle was becoming vague and increasingly lacked coherence. Shaya doubted if they would stay in the Yeshiva; they would just be forced out. None of them seemed to want to marry. The Yeshiva had its own delicate web of prospect lists, encounters at weddings, Sabbath visits, the calculations of aunts and shadchonim, but the Four Nothings viewed all this as the third nothing of marriage. Squared off in groups of four, their isolation was not to be cracked.

As the Four Nothings became familiar in the community, several groups of young women formed their own groups of four, dressing plainly and observing each other. With the boys, the parents didn't mind—there they were not in a hurry—but the parents didn't want their daughters to be spinsters. There were flare-ups—a *shiddach* falling through, a girl refusing to attend a wedding, demands from an impatient shadchan for extra money, a girl who refused to marry altogether. The confrontations were grim. Their fathers called the girls selfish hypocrites who were seeking an excuse not to bear children. Several girls were savagely beaten and ordered to marry by the power of the Fifth Commandment.

Amid all the turbulence, a second book of meditations appeared, entitled *The Sukkah of the Spirit.* A sukkah was a loose wooden hut with an open roof full of sweet-smelling branches, to make the spirit porous with all dead coating eliminated. The book confused the Four Nothings. They wanted not poetry but a code to live by. Several boys went barefoot. Then one got a nail in his foot he ignored; it began to gangrene. Several musar students in the dormitory complained that the feet of the Four Nothings smelled. The Four Nothings finally got a room to themselves on the top floor of the dormitory.

Restless, Shaya sporadically explored Warsaw. He pushed through closed courtyards of six-story tenements, each with a fixed passageway to the next courtyard, thoroughfares where

115

wagoners drove teams of horses, cracking whips. A Yiddish newspaper adjoined an antique shop of old contracts; then came a writers' café. Rashi's wedding contract for his daughter was on display below the headquarters of a Socialist labor union. Every shop had its list of customers, every newspaper its circle of readers.

Shaya wrung his hands in confusion. After eight years, Warsaw was still a strange city. But his forceful walk and openness attracted attention. Strong, big-bodied, with the bushy beard of a peasant, yet dressed as an elegant Jewish gentleman, he was a vital presence on the street.

In a flower market, a streetwalker sidled over and spoke to Shaya. "Esther wants to see you." She began swaying and moving away, looking back provocatively. Seeing him hesitate, she laughed and ran off.

Shaya was jarred, but he was also lonely for his sister. To send a streetwalker as a go-between was just Esther's way of teasing.

A moment later, another streetwalker brushed him. Shaya spun around expecting to see his sister appear and disappear beside him. It baffled him that he had never seen the streetwalkers before. They smiled provocatively at him. One bared her shoulder, daring him to follow her.

On his next exploratory walk, Shaya noticed a Yiddish entertainment. He entered the old building, looking for Esther, and was assured with amused cordiality by the proprietor that there was no indecent exposure or vulgar speeches inside. The show, *Grüneh Felder, Green Fields,* turned out to be a Messianic pageant of Yiddish labor. He was the only Orthodox Jew in a packed hall, surrounded by men in worn jackets and open-collar shirts and women bundled in shawls. The program included skits about settling on the land, with endless arguments among the workers about where to build their library. This was followed by a series of encounters between a man and a woman, each scene with its point of view about society and love and ending in a marriage duet. The cast then lined up side by side, put their hoes on their shoulders like rifles, stepped up to a field wall made of pillows painted to resemble bricks—Shaya wanted to yell not to kick it accidentally and send the blocks sailing out over the audience—and began a Socialist song about beating their rifles into hoes. The entire audience joined in, singing of labor, hope, and universal peace—all but Shaya, who never heard the song in his life before.

That night in bed, Shaya told Rachel about his wanderings,

the streetwalkers, Esther's message, and the Socialist program. Rachel told him to follow the streetwalkers; no path was shameful if it led to his sister. If Shabbetai Zevi could enter a mosque after the spark of God's presence that had strayed there, Shaya could enter a salon with ladies of entertainment. She trusted him; she knew how innocent he was.

"Stop already; I'll find Esther," Shaya grumbled.

Hearing his promise, Rachel happily fell asleep. Shaya looked at her little hands with ten perfect fingernails, and smelled her carefully applied cologne, a scent she managed never to be without. Love gripped him. So few Yeshiva boys knew what a woman was. Rachel's little vanities were so fragile they scarcely existed, but she clung to them the more stubbornly; they were her feather of distinction, her key to his heart.

One night, Shaya and Nathan got into an intense argument about moving to New York. Nathan grinned triumphantly. "The shipping companies are behind it all. New York is the farthest; they can charge the most to get there."

"It's not the companies; people want to get out of Warsaw."

"You're not a Warshaver; you're a Galitzianer drifter and can't stay put; but the crockery factory I'm getting will set me up for life."

Shaya shook his head in exasperation. He knew Nathan's factory was lost already.

Rachel heard familiar steps on the stairs. She tore open the door and ran outside. Moments later, she helped Miriam inside, gasping and staggering, half-dressed, heavy with pregnancy, bearing lash marks.

Shaya and Rachel helped Miriam into a chair.

"He knows?" Nathan burst in with a scream.

"He knows," Miriam echoed in a dreamy quiet.

Shaya and Rachel discovered she was marked all over her body. Ribalow had stripped and beaten her. Rachel spread a screen, took out her lotions, bathed and bandaged her, and gave Miriam her robe to wear.

Rachel squinted hard at Miriam, shuddering. She leaned over her. "It's coming?"

Miriam nodded patiently. "It started while he whipped me."

"I'll get a midwife fast!" Rachel shouted, flying across the room. Rachel glanced at Shaya as she stepped out. "Get my brother for a witness. Use my mother's bed with the overhang for a chuppah."

Nathan went rigid. His face started working but he was unable to speak. His mouth settled into a smile of disbelief. "He's not making a fool out of me! I'll take Miriam right back there! We're not married? Then she's still his responsibility."

Shaya slapped him across the face, knocking him over, paused, and then picked him up off the floor. "Mamzer, you made her pregnant? She's your responsibility."

Nathan nodded helplessly, working his fingers. They helped Miriam into Rachel's mother's tiny antique four-poster bed with the embroidered cover.

"Stay with her; I'll get what's necessary."

Shaya ran downstairs for wine, a spare ring, the marriage service, and one of Rachel's brothers to serve as second witness. He had misgivings about the marriage, but the baby needed a father, a home, and a place in the universe.

Moments later, with a weak smile, Nathan sat on the bed by Miriam, and fitted a ring on her finger, saying *"Harai at . . ."*: "Behold thou art consecrated unto me . . ." Shaya finished the last blessing as Rachel hurried in the door with a midwife and a basin of wet towels. Twenty minutes later Miriam gave birth to her first child. Overwrought, Shaya and Rachel went to Radich for the Sabbath. Nehemia told them that Gershuni had suffered a stroke and was partially paralyzed. A weak man, he was growing morbid, convinced that Yael's spirit was struggling to possess him and Nehemia's curse had made him helpless. He depended completely on Geula, who spent more and more time in Galicia in an effort to keep her father from falling apart. Shaya arranged that a messenger should bring Geula home to the Flying Goose when Rachel's ninth month began, so she could ready herself for the delivery.

Chapter Thirty

NATHAN TRIED TO STAY ON at the Yeshiva, but the atmosphere was unhealthy. There had been suspicions about Miriam; now the story spread from floor to floor like wildfire, with nothing omitted—Nathan's maneuvers for more dowry, the pregnancy, how Nathan tried to bluff his father-in-law. The story was so obvious and so shameful that nobody in the study hall could crack jokes about it, but the repressed grins as Nathan passed were enough. Unable to bear the ridicule, he began attending intermittently.

Nathan got living quarters for Miriam and the baby in his

father's home. Finesilver wanted a learned son and would have kept Nathan going to the Yeshiva at his expense, but as he sat over the Talmud Nathan's mind kept coming to a standstill. He had a fast mind and a lawyer's temperament, but morally he knew he had no business being ordained as a rabbi.

When Nathan stopped regular attendance, his father made him a delivery man for liquor to army units and irregular spots in the city. To distract thieves, Nathan wore a worn field jacket and a driver's cap; the bottles were buried under old rags. His father told him to talk to no one, and make friends with no one—just travel alone, make his deliveries, get his pay, and leave fast; he should remember the younger Garelik boy who never recovered from his beating.

Finesilver's advice was sound, but Nathan sensed that his father didn't trust him. His life was headed nowhere; giving him this blind alley was his father's way of putting him on his own.

The winter was grim. Once Nathan turned back on the road and barely escaped a blizzard. Passing horses kicked mud that froze in his beard. In a final frustration, he once continued into a blizzard, defying it to kill him. His horse lost all sense of the road. As a chill set in his body, his limbs started to freeze, and everywhere the falling snow sifted down. Nathan made it a game of Russian roulette. And he won it after all; a flickering light led him to a Polish farm. He banged on the door like someone escaping Siberia. Thawed out, he lost only a finger to frostbite.

The Warsaw Jews felt an intense malaise that winter. A decline on the Bourse spread insecurity about jobs. Another blood accusation was reported from Galicia. It got out that a street-walker had become pregnant and died in an abortion; rumors spread of secret abortion mills.

Miriam was very quiet in Nathan's home. She nursed his son and gave him her full attention, but her eyes flicked about, waiting for something to happen. Bad reports kept coming in about Ribalow. After throwing her out of the house, he had a three-day drunken binge, and beat up a foreman, sending him to the hospital. Her mother was having convulsions and was unable to retain food. Then Ribalow had a heart attack and was advised to ease up on his work. Miriam waited, keeping occupied with her baby.

On the first warm day in spring, Nathan finished a delivery in the city, changed to better clothes, and wandered through the streets, biting his lip and swinging his hands, carrying a flask of schnapps in his pocket; he now had a trim, close-cropped beard.

119

He had time on his hands. Instead of connecting with his rich friends for another job, he was visiting cafés and starting to drink. Passersby always glanced at him curiously; men that well-dressed weren't usually at such loose ends.

Everything Nathan saw aggravated his desire to leave Warsaw. Too many people knew about him. He craved anonymity the way a tortured man craves sleep. His Yeshiva class was starting its last preparations for its orals. He should be going into law; instead he had become a wagon driver.

Nathan smiled bitterly into a crowded Hebrew school yard. The Warsaw Jews never stopped producing babies—they were fruitful and multiplied. The day they stopped, they would go into shock over how empty their lives were. Nathan leaned aside and took a long swallow from his flask. Religion was like alcohol—a stimulant, an addiction. You can't have one, you take the other. Out in the world, he got his stimulant raw.

A bearded courier ran past Nathan, wearing a visored cap, his prayer fringes flying. The courier worked for the older Garelik. Nathan should have quit the Yeshiva with Dudie and Shrilik Garelik; in another ten years, those boys would be running Warsaw. Even the Rebbe would come to them for support.

Nathan squinted about helplessly. Shaya had gotten under his skin. He wanted to violate Shaya as he violated Miriam; this chuppah had changed nothing. Fatherhood was all right; he just didn't see that much in children. As Miriam's husband, he still violated her, enjoying her body and refusing to support her, but Shaya haunted him—his brooding eyes, his rhapsodic tenor voice, the immense godliness inside him. Religion was an itch in Nathan's skin.

Nathan approached a small church. Two Jews walking in front of him automatically crossed the street and spat. The Warsaw Jews were an army on garrison duty between skirmishes for survival. But with the passage of years, all their strategy had shriveled up. The city had more and more religious runaways; now Nathan was rapidly becoming one.

Tomorrow came another delivery to the army base. His skin was getting coarse from the outdoors, like a fieldworker; he had the squint of a permanent traveler. His deliveries had already cost him a finger. Miriam made no demands, and yet between deliveries he knew he should be pursuing business connections. He knew enough people. but something in him rejected a permanent, respectable job. Miriam said nothing about his waste of time, but he could feel the excitement and even the stir of

120

danger in her body. He was a creature of sin. When they met in secret in their aunt's room before the wedding, a creature of sin was what she embraced.

Nathan shook his head. Shaya should do very well at that oral exam. He had acute instincts in the Talmud, and he was Wolfson's protégé, the best of the current crop. As a practicing lawyer, Shaya would be helpless, but the Talmud was an antique mix of law, history, anecdote, and revelation, a dinosaur who refused to die after the community had long disappeared.

Nathan rubbed the stump of his missing finger. His father hated him, but he supported him and gave his family a home. Miriam might not love him, but he was the animal she couldn't shake off. When his father had enough, she would finally support him.

Nathan looked at his watch. Shrilik Garelik was opening a money exchange. Nathan traveled freely and could smuggle money. It was a natural partnership; he would end up as Shrilik's runner. Where was he headed anyway? Yes, to Shrilik, to discuss the terms of his work. But his wasn't Shrilik's neighborhood. He was approaching a streetwalker. Somebody had told him of a new parlor in this neighborhood.

Feeling zestful, Nathan turned aside and took another swallow from the flask. He saw a doorway with a red knob over it, entered, and started up the stairs, as a tiny streetwalker tripped down them in a yellow, knitted, body-stocking dress, bow lips, and thin etched cheekbones.

Nathan stopped her. "You're with the parlor upstairs?"

"You want a little pleasure? It's thirty kopeks before."

Nathan broke into a raunchy laugh. It was Miriam's very voice, a soft, high-pitched whine. He nodded. Pleased at getting a customer so fast, she ran upstairs, with Nathan following, into a chamber with plum walls and plush upholstery; there were three tiny bedrooms in back, a bar, and a baby grand. Two women were straightening up the room. One was Jewish, named Aphrodita, and had been part of this establishment for a long time.

With a bang on the piano, the madame stood up, frail and airy in a pale silver gown with black lace. She poured two glasses of wine and came toward him with a devilishly familiar face.

"You're Nathan, Shaya's study partner."

Nathan started. "Esther Kramer!"

"I'm Esther, but don't tell Shaya. He'll see when it's time. He studies very hard. You were closest to him of all the Yeshiva."

Nathan brushed her face, unable to restrain himself. "You're so beautiful, I don't know what to say."

Esther smiled evasively. "This is my parlor; I have girls."

Nathan crinkled his nose. "I don't want girls when you're in the room. It's strange the way more and more becomes kosher."

Esther overflowed with laughter. He was four years younger than she. Were he four years older, they might be married by now. She sensed he was dead inside. Violating her deepest rule, she took him into one of the bedrooms.

Making love to Esther, Nathan felt something open within him. His soul had unsnagged. He had finally found a way to violate Shaya. He would soon leave Warsaw for New York.

Chapter Thirty-one

REB SHLOIMEH KATZ CONFERRED with Rabbi Wolfson. Rabbi Wolfson felt that Shaya had established himself and should be encouraged in every way, so Reb Shloimeh then shifted Shaya to second Mesivta, a class well into preparations for rabbinic examinations, and thus saved him a year.

Shaya got as a new study partner, Azriel Tomashevsky, a veteran musarnik and a tough, well-trained scholar. Shaya began to study more seriously. Rachel pressed him to find Esther but he was absorbed elsewhere. Second Mesivta didn't know him; the boys had established study habits before the rabbinic examination. He was again a loner.

Study with Azriel was bracing. Nathan was a compulsive bon vivant, but not a superfluous word passed Azriel's lips. He had a lean, swarthy face and a leathery torso; he had grown up a street orphan, stealing and scavenging; a chance encounter with a rebbe made him enter the Yeshiva. Now he never suffered from a depression, never wasted a moment, and never accepted help from anybody. Several front teeth were missing from earlier beatings; two years after his ordination, he planned to have saved enough for a completely new set of teeth.

Each day, as Shaya sat down and opened his folio, Azriel's eyes shone with a swift hello. They immediately got to work. Mastering material in partnership required mental acrobatics. Shaya was more subtle and intuitive; Azriel had a better method of simplifying and consolidating material. Azriel thought confusion the source of all evil. By the time Shaya met him, he had cut all confusion out of his life. Studying, Azriel could feel a complete set of teeth in the making.

A boy off the street, without political connections, his chances for a rabbinic post would be slender. To Shaya's surprise, Azriel came to Radich on a visit. Nehemia taught him the ritual of slaughter of fowl. An orphan, he adopted Shaya's family for lack of another.

As the winter deepened, a sense of drift and decay filled the city. The Belzer Yeshiva organized a parade to boost morale. Several hundred boys quietly shuffled through the streets, singing religious hymns against the cries of peddlers, the grind of passing wagons.

A rumor spread in the Yeshiva that the Four Nothings movement harbored homosexuals. Their constant, compulsive involvement with one another and their own unsupervised room on the top floor suddenly took a sinister cast. The mention of mystical experience now drew uneasy giggles. The Four Nothings accused the Musar people of spreading the story, but however it started, it refused to die. Hearing the report, the Rebbe's second son, who by now had a large personal following, decreed that the Four Nothings should marry and have children. A manufacturer of uniforms, who had donated their beaver *shtreimels,* owned a courtyard with living quarters. Paired off and living there, they would stay close and have permanent jobs working for him. Frightened, loyal, but fumbling, uneasy for an out, they moved pell-mell from the Yeshiva into the courtyard. A shadchan found women willing to marry them. In twenty-four hours, their every Yeshiva bed was occupied by other students. Dispersed, with no institution to give them bed and breakfast, their movement was rapidly forgotten.

At the beginning of Rachel's eighth month, Shaya took her to Radich in Binstock's carriage and returned immediately to join the fifteen remaining students who were organizing themselves for senior examinations toward the degree of *Yoreh-Yoreh, Yadin-Yadin,* teacher and a judge. Upon Rachel's ninth month, a messenger went to bring Geula from Galicia. Shaya returned home for the delivery. He sensed in Rachel a strong, new feeling of place and belonging, as if a lifelong hunger for a family and a home had finally been met in Radich. This was her place. It shook Shaya a bit.

Three days later, Rachel went into labor. Shaya sat in a spread of towels, compresses, and basins of water. Gripping the bedpost with one hand and Shaya's hand with the other, Rachel cursed, squeezed, shrieked, and grunted. An hour later, a hairy little animal squirmed at Rachel's side, bawling to be fed. So Chatzkel was born.

To Shaya, the birth was an interlude in his studies. He got back to the Yeshiva the next day, climbed the stairs to his study hall, and sat down opposite Azriel.

Azriel's eyes flicked up. "It was?"

"A son."

"You missed four days. Back to work, *bruder.*"

Shaya's orals lasted three hours, before a panel of four; the questions came like bullets—abrupt, impersonal, without a break. Shaya gave as good as he got, then sat in the waiting room while they conferred. Neither boy who preceded him had passed. One was told to study another year, the other to leave and do something else.

Beyond the windows of the waiting room, the city mood was somber. A sudden April warmth brought with it the threat of pogroms. A report came that Ukrainians had pillaged the Jewish section of a shtetl; an adjoining police station waited a full day before breaking up the mob. Binstock dismissed it; the local villagers were Greek Orthodox, and Polish Roman Catholics would not get out of hand like that; but Shaya was uneasy. Perhaps the police were testing that mob.

Shaya frowned, flexing his fingers nervously. This was the end of his road in the Yeshiva. By now all the rich boys had dropped out, leaving a core of serious, mature students. His work was brilliant, yet his father's primitive nihilism was a stronger force inside him than any discipline he learned in the Yeshiva.

Shaya glanced uneasily at the examination room door. What was taking them so long? He knew the material so cold; the conference afterward should have been a mere formality. So long a conference meant there was a serious chance he would be rejected. But it was himself he should be coming to terms with, not the examining board. And on the eve of his ordination, a hairy demon in the pit of his stomach insisted he was an atheist and an ignoramus. He felt on the verge of obliteration.

Shaya leaned back with a hapless smile. He refused to fall apart. His last examination was over, and with it ended all his years in school. In a few minutes he would know whether he had passed or failed, and either way he would move from school into the working world.

The door opened. Reb Shloimeh appeared in the doorway and

called him back inside. Once Shaya entered, each examiner shook his hand in congratulations. Rabbi Wolfson threw his arms around his shoulders. After the two previous failed examinations, they were in a very good mood; their conference was so long because they were exchanging jokes and deciding what sort of future was best for Shaya. Early in the examination he had caught Rabbi Wolfson on a point: That happened very rarely. They wanted Shaya to stay on as a senior tutor, work with a younger class, or do advanced work on his own that would lead to an eventual teaching post.

Shaya thanked them all and stepped outside. Ever suspicious, he refrained from asking if the money for the tutorship came from Binstock personally. Had he gotten the wrong answer, he would have turned the offer down. Evasive as he was, he did want the teaching post badly, but to receive it because of the influence of his father-in-law would cheapen him. By now, Rachel was again pregnant. She seemed to demand nothing more out of life. Preparing for *smicha*, he had avoided all problems. Now he would never come near a problem until the grave.

Out in the hall, Shaya spotted Azriel, waiting by the door. He had been standing there for over an hour, waiting for the news.

Azriel looked up. "It was?"

"It was."

"How long was the conference after?"

"Twenty minutes."

"That long and they said yes? You're lucky."

"They asked me to stay on and teach."

"If they wanted that, they should have told you sooner."

"They were relaxing."

"Barbarians. You'll take the job?"

"I think. You want to eat something?"

"I'm late to the slaughterhouse. I stayed only to hear."

Azriel embraced Shaya, kissed him on both cheeks, and plunged off.

Back home, Shaya found a note: "*Chevraman*, Warsaw is dead. My father has turned his back on me. When you see this letter, I'll be on a boat to New York, where nobody knows me. Come also. Nathan."

Shaya immediately stepped over to the Finesilver home, but Miriam was gone. A house servant told him she was pregnant again and had returned to her father's house. With Nathan permanently away, Ribalow took her back.

Chapter Thirty-two

THE NEXT AFTERNOON, Reb Shloimeh Katz called in the successful graduates for his last conference. Eight young rabbis crowded his narrow office, five sitting around his table, the other three leaning against the wall between his glass-covered bookshelves. Three wore business suits; four had long black caftans. Azriel wore a slaughterer's smock. All had full beards; only Shaya wore no glasses.

Reb Shloimeh viewed his circle of graduates with a devious smile: "Boys, I worked with you for twelve years. I was at your weddings, the births of your children. I gave you moral lessons, made plans while you slept, watched you grow into rabbis in Israel. The walls finally said, *dayenu,* enough. So now we'll ordain you, give you *smicha,* send you out a new generation in the chain of Jewish leadership. We'll call you rabbis, scholars, judges, teachers we trust. Believe me, those whom we didn't trust we found ways to get rid of years ago.

"Yet somebody asked me in private, Shloimeh Katz, is there one boy you totally trust in the whole bunch, I'd have to tell him I trust not one graduate in this room. Oh, you're very fit, very zealous. You know how far you can walk on Saturday. But the years come, the years go. Ideas spread like a disease in an ocean of sick human beings. In five years, you can turn criminal, lie, steal, destroy your children, throw bombs, become bitter anti-Semites, snatch at pleasures whatever the cost. They say Torquemada was a converted Jew; a born gentile would not have butchered so many. But one thing I guarantee you: you may violate the entire Ten Commandments, but you won't enjoy it. It will give you no pleasure.

"In the Yeshiva, you became men of the Talmud. You ate text as Ezekiel ate the scroll of God. You swallowed it; it was sweet to your stomachs. You digested it now. I am not your teacher anymore. I have nothing more to give you. You are now the teachers."

Reb Shloimeh mopped his brow. The other boys shook his hand and left, but Shaya was listless and moody. He took Rachel and Chatzkel by coach to Radich and sprawled in his father's yard for days, refusing to move. The spring winds, good food, and an abundance of family love finally brought him back. He arranged for Geula to handle Rachel's next delivery and returned with his family to Warsaw.

Shaya chose to do independent study. He had calculated that

the later he started to teach the more advanced a class he would get. At his own lectern on the east wall of the study room, he began a program in Jewish mysticism. Days dissolved into weeks; Shaya studied constantly.

Leaving on a brisk fall day, Shaya saw a street preacher, Reb Chaim Gericht, talking to idlers on the steps. "The fires are lit; Gog and Magog have started to scratch themselves. There is no escape. When the Angel of Death starts from sleep, he'll satisfy himself with Jewish blood, not the firstborn of Egypt. But all this is a great sign. The pogrom knives will usher in the days of the Messiah when . . ."

Shaya nudged the next Jew. "What's Reb Chaim talking about?"

"A lot of millworkers were fired from their jobs south of the river. There's talk of a pogrom."

On his way home, Shaya saw that business was listless, but one crockery shop had about a dozen customers inside.

Shaya leaned into the doorway. "Things are moving, Asher?"

The shopkeeper looked across the counter. "She has a head, Miriam. Since she became manager, Ribalow's plates have been moving."

At the corner, a large new clothing store had its windows shuttered and siding nailed across its door. Shaya leaned into the doorway. "Cohen is closed down already?"

"He thought a big Vienna store would work here, but Warshavers like a store where they know the salesman. He's joining his brother in Vienna. A few people are leaving."

Back home, Shaya saw a letter from Nathan; he opened it with a smile.

Chevraman:

Where are you? Why aren't you here already? I hate writing letters.

I have a job in the garment industry. I'm saving money to bring over Miriam and the children. When they're here, I'll buy a sewing machine and go into business for myself. If you and Rachel aren't here by then, maybe I'll buy a machine after I bring both our families over.

New York is a city, you have no idea. The streets are invitations to start moving. Yiddish from all over the world, Yekke, Hungar, Galitz. Nobody lives here with family, not like in Warsaw. Your janitor insults you? You move to the next block.

Did you ever find your sister Esther? I bet you didn't even look.

127

Find her and bring her over too. I'll pay for her ticket. In New York, you can start a new life.

Your friend, Nathan.

Rachel poked her head in from the kitchen. "He's all right?" Shaya held out the letter. Rachel skimmed through it, as Chatzkel crawled across the floor toward his father's feet. Shaya hoisted him up for a big hug and a kiss.

"I made gefilte fish and some stuffed prunes. Sit down."

Shaya blessed bread and started to eat. Rachel sat down opposite him and started to feed Chatzkel, smiling at Nathan's letter. "What's the garment industry? I bet he's on somebody else's sewing machine."

"Maybe he's a salesman."

"Trust me; if he sold, he'd talk about opening a store. If it's buying a machine, then he's on a machine. And he'll bring over Miriam, us, and the children? And Esther too? He's a fool, and that's worse than being a bad man. On a sewing machine, he'll be lucky to have food from day to day. I don't know why you stay in touch, he's so unreliable."

Shaya squinted at her. "Something is bothering you. Tell me."

"There's something about the way this letter talks about Esther. He finishes with her, not you. And he'll buy her ticket? A single man doesn't buy a ticket just like that to bring over a woman."

Shaya smiled in embarrassment. "I talked a lot about finding Esther, and bringing her over."

"And why not find Esther? Here, take five rubles. Promise them to a streetwalker; she'll take you to your sister."

Shaya frowned. "If there's something between Nathan and Esther, why do you want her? I thought you were Miriam's friend."

Rachel smiled cheerfully. "Miriam's doing very well; she's practically running the business. But she's fooling herself; this isn't what she really wants. Don't ask too many questions; just find Esther."

"Five rubles is too much."

"That's why it'll bring results. Give just enough, and you'll get nothing. Go, find Esther; she's my sister and I want her."

Shaya stepped out, brooding over Chaim Gericht's words on the Yeshiva steps. If he thought lives were in danger, he should have said, in plain language, to find a safe cellar and wait out the pogrom. But he had nothing in mind; he was just producing

128

spiritual music. The pogromchik raised his smoky torch like a conductor's baton and Chaim Gericht started playing death and the Messiah. The irony was bitter. All around, Jews made music in forty keys, on every corner, in every conversation—the Rebbe on the Chasidic violin, the shadchan on his organ. The problem was that Jewish music was heartache, a human voice, the cry of pain the world ignores. So the Jew kills himself to have his music heard, and the gentile kills the Jew for making so much noise.

Distracted, Shaya walked by three streetwalkers in a row, all weaving with the same bland smile. Maybe his body saw them, but in his mind he knew himself to be a bearded, dignified scholar, an initiate into Lurianic Kabbalah, and he didn't like the way they showed their bodies through their clothes. But a tiny woman leaned against a church wall, in a yellow knitted dress as tight as a body stocking. She smiled hopefully, then her smile broadened in relief. Shaya had noticed she was there.

Seeing his hesitant smile, she walked up to him. "Want a little pleasure? It's thirty kopeks before."

Shaya smiled, charmed. "I look for my sister, Esther Kramer. She plays the harpsichord, and maybe six instruments by now. Five years ago, maybe more, she disappeared from our farm in Radich, near Melon, by the Bucharest road. She ran away with a Pole, Jan Kris."

She broke into a wary smile. "Jan is feeding termites. They blamed the secret police, but he cheated on the gang."

"He was a very vain man."

"You're Esther's brother?"

"She's in Warsaw. She was sending me messages to find her. She even sent a friend to my wedding. Was it . . . was it you?"

She grinned inscrutably. "Why not?"

"Take me to her, and I'll put five rubles in your hand."

Shaya showed her the money. The streetwalker glanced up and down the street. "Wait here; I got to find out something."

As Shaya waited, he noticed the two stores opposite were boarded up. From the river came a sound like loose, choppy water, but scary, human and violent. Shaya wanted to leave, but already the streetwalker was back.

"It's good you made it; there's going to be a pogrom."

"A brother of mine is organizing it."

"What is he, a maniac?"

"Just average."

They entered a doorway by a stable, under a red knob, and

129

climbed upstairs into a salon with drapes, plush lounges, upholstered chairs, and a baby grand. A Westernized Jew behind the bar smirked aggressively. Two women in dressing gowns marveled at a Polish bank clerk for taking time off from work—it was such an aristocratic thing to do.

A fourth woman at the piano played "*Oifn Pribetchok*" with a restless lilt. Esther was bidding him welcome. She tinkled a flurry of high notes by way of greeting. She had glossy curls to her shoulders, like a woman in a picture book, and her fingernails were chartreuse. The entire scene was a show—Esther had delayed so as to set the scene right. She was still in awe of him.

Shaya reached in his pocket and passed five rubles to the messenger; she slipped them in her bosom and started to leave just as a sudden explosion shook the panes in the glass. She stepped to the window and looked out.

Shaya ignored the sound and sat down awkwardly alongside Esther. Still playing, she smiled at the keys. "You have a son."

"Rachel is expecting again."

"And how's Nehemia?"

He's bitter; you were his darling. Gita married a Horowitz. Feigeleh ran off with a Zionist dreamer; Geula visits in Galicia more and more. Gershuni had a stroke. But Nehemia never got over losing you."

Esther laughed with sudden pleasure, tossing her curls luxuriously. Her abandonment felt vindicated. The slate was clean; Nehemia was bitter and unfulfilled. But she felt soulless.

Esther began a lilting tune on the piano. Shaya gave her a quick glance. "Nathan Finesilver writes from New York that I should bring you."

Esther took a long breath. "You're going?"

Shaya shook his head. "They're taking me on at the Yeshiva to teach."

Esther smiled at the wall. "You're going; it's a settled thing. Just don't leave me behind. I'm in a trap; I have to leave Warsaw."

They looked up, startled. An angry street noise had suddenly become louder. The streetwalker stepped over and whispered in Esther's ear. She banged a discordant note and rose to her feet. "Marcella, take the good pan into the first room; we're so crowded here. Aphrodita, make Mr. Silverberg comfortable. Put his money in a safe place where nobody can find it."

The streetwalker pressed the five rubles into Shaya's hand. "Give it to me again afterward. Esther will protect you."

130

At a sound of breaking glass and smashing wood, Esther pulled Shaya into the last bedroom and made him crawl under the bed. A moment later, the doors flew open. Shaya saw a pair of men's shoes.

"Mr. Liebowitz, what a pleasure!"

"I barely made it upstairs! There are thirty of them! Knives and clubs, and stuffed sacks. I . . . I . . . what do they want? Money? Blood? It's hard to know. How are you Esther? I never see you."

"Come into my room; I was so cruel before. Don't be afraid. They're so lazy they'd rather go next door than climb a set of stairs."

Esther got him into her bedroom and undressed him, too shaky with fear to know what was happening. She gestured to Shaya to stay out of sight.

"Why are you frightened? Come, let me make you comfortable."

Esther bubbled over with radiant theatrical laughter. Shaya turned his back and hugged the wall—as fifteen or twenty men burst inside the door with sacks, axes, and knives.

A thin, high-pitched voice sang out. "I'm Pavel Donila's sister. Where is my brother?"

"Pinching geese," came an instant reply.

An ax came down on the piano, followed by noisy movement, screams, moans, breaking glass, grunts, and lusty guffaws. Shaya clung to the wall, refusing to hear anything, until there was silence, and then crawled out to find two naked Jewish corpses, repeatedly stabbed, a Polack with both arms broken, a gutted interior, all upholstery ripped open, and four women repeatedly raped.

Shaya breathed a song of deliverance. "Though I walk through the valley of the shadow of death, I fear no evil; for Thou art with me."

Esther was lying in bed crying. She raised both hands to Shaya. "I saved your life. I . . . I don't have men; I took Liebowitz to bed so that they shouldn't look for you hiding underneath! Pity me, Shaya! I only put on these curls because I had to! I'm clean! Don't turn your back on me!"

Shaya shut her lips with his fingers. He slipped the five rubles back to the raped streetwalker where she lay on the carpet, breathing deeply, bruised and naked. Her finger clenched around the money. Shaya wrapped Esther in a sheet, carried her outside, and hired a coach to drive them back to Radich.

Four hours later, the coach drove into the inn yard. Shaya carried Esther to the door, shouting for Nehemia.

Nehemia opened and took a long look. "She comes alone?"

"The Polack is in the grave."

Nehemia swung the door open.

Chapter Thirty-three

BRUISED, PENNILESS, AND UNABLE TO CARE for herself, Esther moved back into her room. The doctor visited that night. After an examination and a few questions, he prescribed rest, warm food, and a minimum of strain. Shaya immediately took the coach back to Warsaw, promising to visit soon. It was dark already; Rachel would be sick with worry.

As Shaya left, Shaineh Nissel fumbled up the stairs, waving her wand before her. She sniffed hard in Esther's room, sniffed again, and then clapped her hands. "Esther is become a lady!" She sat down on the bed and held Esther to her bosom, crooning a melody. Esther began weeping; weeping, she fell asleep.

Esther woke the next afternoon. She blinked about her, drinking it all in, and her spirit reentered her body. Her room had been left untouched through her absence. It was as if some wrinkle in time had smoothed over and left her as before. After an hour, she took a leisurely bath and came downstairs.

As Esther entered the kitchen, Nehemia slipped out the door without a word. Esther sighed. If her father refused to talk to her, then she had no home here. There was nothing she could do. Nehemia was a jail door she could not slip around a second time. But Shaineh stayed away; Geula was in Galicia. Then it was her kitchen. She fried half a chicken with some tsimmes. When Nehemia came in, she had his table ready.

Nehemia ate and then went out again. He did not seem angry, but he had nothing to say to her. Esther went back upstairs and collapsed into bed. As she fell asleep, all her family feeling flowed back toward Shaya, who accepted her without question. Esther had a misgiving that she might never bear children. She entrusted Shaya with her soul. Her last thought before she slipped into sleep was a forlorn prayer to Shaya never to abandon her.

Before a week was out, Esther slipped into moral despondency. She felt she had no home here and kept scrubbing the kitchen floor to earn the right to stay. She wore long dresses with a closed neck and full sleeves and became exact about kosher food. Her life felt like a hair shirt. Nehemia's silence at meals made her listless and unable to plan anything.

On Shaya's next visit, Esther dragged him to their secret lawn, where the sign of the Flying Goose still hung, its paint flaky, the wood beginning to crack. Sitting on a log, Esther recounted some of what happened to her since she ran away from Radich.

In Warsaw, half of Jan Kris's gang were Jewish, with an ideology as crazy as the Frankists. They shared everything. Every night, another member told of an important experience of the day, and was examined for bourgeois tendencies. The meetings bored her to death. She tried feverishly to locate the Warsaw Yiddish theater, but wherever she went the performers were volunteers.

The group demanded a robbery as an initiation rite. Esther kept making excuses. Knowing that they would put her into a parlor, she told Jan to make her manager of a parlor; if she ran the place, she needn't sleep with the customers. Three days later, Jan put her in a parlor with a piano, where she sang songs and managed the place for a small salary. There, she met Aphrodita—her real name was Sarah Cohen—who was raising money to follow her husband to New York. Aphrodita was a Socialist and a proud woman. She told Esther Jan Kris was farming her out and putting half her real pay in her pocket. Feeling used, Esther told his radical group in detail of Jan's robbery in Melon. They searched his belongings in his absence and then shot him dead.

Shaya groaned over her story. What she needed was a stiff dose of Yeshiva Musar. And why didn't she ask him for help? Esther insisted she could not inflict her petty problems on her brother. Besides, it was God's responsibility to have a Yiddish theater waiting when she arrived in Warsaw. Aphrodita had helped her. She told Aphrodita to hide Liebowitz's money. It would get her to New York. Shaya was aggravating her, and the doctor prescribed total tranquility.

Before he left, Shaya promised to visit her salon room in Warsaw. He brought back everything there. Esther then cut off the last two inches of her curls. She left her nails plain, but moon-shaped, clipped and tidy, and found in the bag a pair of bloomers that Aphrodita made for her. She smiled to herself; Nathan would appreciate clothes like that. Soon she was making up skits in her head, tapping her foot in rhythm as she scrubbed a pot.

Shaya visited when he could. He asked about the strange prongs on her dresser and the tinted jars. Esther laughed and explained her curls. Before his wondering eyes, she put one on to show him, and then all of them. Shaya touched one, half expecting to burn his hand.

That night, Esther started awake in a panic. She looked out her window, aghast at the full moon flooding the earth with silver light. Caught in a trance, she wrapped a flimsy robe around her and stole outside. Everywhere the leaves were brushed with white light. She pushed to her secret lair. She lay down on the grass beneath the sign of the Flying Goose and looked up, trying to communicate with the moon, but the moon wouldn't speak to her. She lay back, listless and moody. She needed a haven; none was in reach.

Esther sighed. Nehemia was a secret Shabbatean, in a bleak lifelong quest for God in his labor. She was his daughter, running off with Jan Kris. It was what Shabbetai Zevi looked for, praying to Mecca. She wanted a new way for a woman, God's body laughing in strange clothes. She had schemed, jumped, and maneuvered not to end up as a prostitute; yet at any time she might meet a man who saw her in the parlor. Her life had been like loose clothing that threatened to fall off and expose a stained body. God should wash the stains off her flesh.

Esther started awake. The grass was cold. How long had she lain here? The moon was down; the trees exhaled a wet wind. Shivering with the night chill, she hurried back barefoot, wrapping her flimsy robe around her, stole upstairs, and crawled back into bed.

On Shaya's next visit, Esther took him into the woods again, moving from spot to spot, following bird calls. Where the sunlight vibrated through prickles and pins of pine, Esther pointed about her:

"The lark has a different call in Radich, because all its paths intersect here. Radich is the crossroads. One flies to Italy; another wings to the Crimea. A third brings news from Lithuania. They all want to go to Austria, then change their minds, and they are free because both their bodies and wills are free. You don't know where you will go, do you, brother?"

Shaya patiently shook his head. "No, I don't, sister."

Esther laughed. "You're going to New York, and you'll take me with you. And there nobody will know me. The ocean wind will wash me clean; I'll have a new life."

"You're a wise woman, sister; it may be as you say."

134

Geula often returned to Galicia for brief visits. She trusted Esther as she did Shaineh, and she felt guilty toward Nehemia who was so isolated, so estranged from people; but she was torn between her father and her husband.

On his visits, Shaya distracted Esther with Jewish mysticism, the Lurianic emptiness that God made within Himself like a celestial womb, to allow creation. The sexuality of Lurianic creation startled Esther, creation coming as seeds of divine force shot into the emptiness and tearing the emptiness to bits. She protested to Shaya that God started off as male and added a female in Himself when He created the world.

"That's big of Him," Esther added with a tart smile.

Shaya shook his head. "God is the One, the Boundless; when division came, the female in God existed before the male entering her."

Esther then grumbled about her own situation, her difficulty in making a life for herself. She kept thinking moodily about Nathan, that beautiful cripple, that torn leaf. Miriam was blindly devoted to him, but Nathan needed to be known in ways that Miriam would never know a man. Not having a baby, Esther saw Nathan as a lost, dignified child. Her gift of herself freed him to sail for America. He was now sinking roots in a strange city.

As the months slipped away, Esther's estrangement from Nehemia faded. He was like a burned-out furnace, distant from everybody. He had no personal score to settle with her. When she was ill, in need of clothing, supplies, a ride to Warsaw, he was there before she could ask.

Chapter Thirty-four

As SHAYA'S FAMILY GREW, Azriel regularly dropped by after work. He would eventually marry—he wanted a family—but the price of teeth was going up. If he married first, he would never get his teeth; but if he got his teeth first, he would have both teeth and wife.

Azriel visited for half an hour before supper. He knew his conversation was limited, so he smiled and waited for Shaya to start talking. He was ready to discuss the workings of the slaughterhouse, but no one asked him. He would accompany someone anywhere or hear any opinion about Warsaw Jewry. He knew the Belzer market, but the subject never came up. After an hour of smiling here, angling there, making himself available, but staying out of the way, he went home, having had a delightful visit.

Through Miriam, Shaya kept in touch with Nathan's old circle of friends, those who were his Yeshiva classmates when they all were boys. Several lived in Paris, Vienna, Berlin, even New York, and had cut their Warsaw roots. Their brains worked internationally, and Warsaw was a provincial center.

After a year of independent study, Shaya was given a middle-level class, sixty-five boys whom he conducted through *Gittin,* a folio page a day. His Yeshiva appointment was for life, but Shaya's commitment to Warsaw was paper-thin. Esther's prediction sat in his head as a truth. She would never marry in Poland; she didn't feel clean in Poland. She waited for him to take her to New York.

Nehemia now corresponded with his uncle in Vienna, Tevya Kramer, who had a clothing store, hiring a scribe to write his letters. Tevya invited Shaya several times to move to Vienna, but his letters were so ornate in style that Shaya didn't trust the invitation as being sincere.

By now, Shaya knew from Nathan's circle of something called grand opera. Had he gone to Germany, he might have tried to become an opera tenor. Now that he was a family man, it wasn't to be talked about. Fitting into the Yeshiva, he began serving as its cantor. He never got a penny; it even hurt his reputation, because there was that old prejudice, *"Chazzonim, naronim,"* "A cantor, a fool," that those jealous of him repeated. Shaya didn't care; he needed the outlet.

Before Shaya knew it, Chatzkel was four, a child with his own personality. He stayed apart from his baby sister and insisted on coming along whenever Shaya visited Radich. Chatzkel was closer to Nehemia in spirit than Shaya, who was wrapped in his rabbinic learning; yet down to earth as Chatzkel was, he thoroughly enjoyed his father's company. They walked a lot, Shaya talking about Jewish life, as Chatzkel steered them where there was shade, and made sure they got back in time for supper.

One day Shaya came home at noon from the Yeshiva. He blessed bread and started to eat. Rachel sat down opposite him and started to nurse Rivka, when Chatzkel squirmed onto Shaya's lap and started to dig at his chest. Shaya was about to teach Chatzkel some Hebrew letters as he ate, but he sensed something bothering Rachel.

Shaya turned with a sharp look. "What's wrong?"

136

Rachel shifted Rivka to her other breast. "Zfania wants to take Chatzkel south with him on one of his trips."

"What's wrong with that? The south is where we come from."

"I know my father. He has it in his head to take Chatzkel away from you. He's talking about you in a way I don't like."

Shaya smiled in amazement. "I gave up music. I'm a Rosh Yeshiva. I didn't fight him about the dowry. What else does he want?"

Rachel shook her head, sighing at Shaya's innocence. "He wants Chatzkel. He's a maniac, but not a fool. Chatzkel is his smartest grandson. If he starts him in the business, we'll lose him. He'll make it happen too. We have to leave this house."

Shaya's eyes narrowed. That evening, he mentioned to Binstock that he was sailing to America.

With the news, the Binstock household became precipitously hostile. Hardware became spotty; food came in short supply from the kitchen, so Shaya had to make his own purchases. When Shaya came in the door, Zfania whirled around and glared until he disappeared up the stairs. When things started to disappear from their rooms, Shaya stopped going out together with Rachel. One of them was always at home to guard the children.

Shaya checked with Nehemia. The dowry money would buy only three tickets; they were now a family of five. Rachel told Shaya to go ahead with Chatzkel, and take Esther on the third ticket; she would stay in Radich with the little ones, her baby boy and girl, and come over when she could.

As Shaya refused to capitulate, Binstock and his sons began to call Shaya a parasite around the neighborhood. When somebody disagreed, they fell silent, then started in again. Binstock could pressure and intimidate the simple storekeepers. He then started complaining in the Yeshiva itself. With the first announcement that Shaya intended to leave, his Yeshiva class was given to another rabbi. The Yeshiva kept only permanent staff.

Binstock wouldn't stop; he kept churning out fresh demands. He wanted Shaya thrown out of the Yeshiva altogether. The Belzer *gabbai* called a trip to America an abandonment of faith. Here the Yeshiva balked; the gabbai had his position, but they moved by Jewish law. There nowhere New York was forbidden. He was kept on as ordained rabbi and senior tutor.

The relentless pressure took its toll. Helpless to respond for fear of the consequences to Rachel, Shaya began to feel himself living on charity. He felt grateful to be continued as Sabbath

137

cantor; he kept his dignity, and yet the shock of his coming voyage added a quaver of pain to his voice—the accent of life in exile.

The Belzer had a synagogue meeting with a new gabbai, a burly administrator with a spreading red beard. There Binstock complained that his son-in-law lived off him and wandered the city—a parasite, a confirmed parasite. Binstock would finally throw him out of the house for buying a ticket to New York. Here, the gabbai jumped to his feet, slamming the table in outrage. Binstock's family should observe seven days of mourning. Too many foolish, innocent Jewish families were under some American delusion, leaving behind them broken homes, abandoned wives, violating every commandment and making Warsaw a vast spiritual cemetery.

Shaya maintained a stoic indifference under the pressure. Then one day, Binstock pushed between him and Chatzkel on the staircase. He seemed ready to kidnap his son. Shaya determined to leave for New York immediately, and take Chatzkel with him.

Walking on the street, Shaya saw a revival announced of the Bund musical, *Grüneh Felder* that he had seen when he was looking for Esther. He stepped inside and bought two tickets, for himself and Chatzkel; Chatzkel should get used to being with him when Rachel was away.

The performance was exactly the same as on his last visit, with the same props, the wall of pillows threatening to fly into the audience, and the same cry for universal peace. When the cast lined up, put their hoes to their shoulders, and started their song about beating their rifles into hoes, the entire audience joined in a single voice. Shaya sang along heartily.

As they were leaving, Shaya murmured, "America will be our green fields." Chatzkel grinned up at him and took his hand.

The next morning, Rachel packed a small suitcase for Chatzkel. Shaya took him to the Belzer market. Nehemia saw them pushing through the throng and climbed off the wagon.

"What?"

"I'm taking Chatzkel, and also Esther. I want the next boat. Rachel will stay with you, and come later with the children."

"Maybe Chatzkel should stay with Rachel; it's a hard trip."

"Binstock will steal him, he knows how. You keep Chatzkel until we leave. It can't be helped. Once we leave, I'll watch him with my life."

"This is all the money; you'll have three more tickets to buy."

138

"God will turn His face to me with a blessing."

Nehemia embraced his son. "I'll not come after; when you leave, we'll never meet again."

"It has to happen."

Nehemia picked up Chatzkel with a dry smile. "So come home with me; I'll show you how to watch for bedbugs. You'll be your father's right-hand man." Chatzkel nodded solemnly.

Nehemiah put Chatzkel on the driver's bench for the ride south. He passed the remaining eggs and chickens to another wagon to sell for him. Then he climbed on and leaned out with a piece of paper. "This is Tevya's address in Vienna. Had I not been so suspicious, we would all be in Vienna today. Stay in touch with him; you don't lose family."

"I will."

"New York has a Belzer Society. Yakov Rivers is the secretary. We'll write you there. Ask. He'll have our letters."

As the wagon pulled out of the market with Nehemia and Chatzkel, Azriel stepped out of the throng in his slaughterhouse apron. He had spotted Shaya and waited until he was alone.

"You're going? Let me accompany you home. I can take an hour off. You have so many errands. Everybody is full of your trip. Perhaps I'll bring some rope tonight; it might help tie your suitcases. Yes. I shall do that tonight."

Azriel walked off, feeling very tranquil. At last he had figured out something helpful to do.

Chapter Thirty-five

As Shaya entered Binstock's house, Zfania grabbed his arm and yanked him aside. His son Habbakuk locked the door and was at his side with an open briefcase. Shaya was so surprised that he was unable to fight them off.

Zfania pulled out a parchment document. "I had a scribe write out this divorce."

Shaya smiled helplessly. "How can I divorce my wife?"

Zfania's nails sank into Shaya's arm. "In the old days, a God-fearing merchant gave his wife a divorce before every long trip. Without a witness, if there's a shipwreck, a massacre, a deadly accident, the woman is cut off until the day she dies. A divorce is her protection. Sign it. Tomorrow morning, you'll give it to her at the train station."

Shaya wrung his hands helplessly. "I'm going to America to bring her after me, not to leave her here in Warsaw."

Zfania waved the thought away, suddenly cheerful. "This is a protection, not a divorce. You won't even remarry. You get together? You just tear it up and you're man and wife again. Only a selfish man would refuse. Come, sign it now."

As Shaya hesitated, two other sons, Haggai and Malachi, strode through the hall, one behind the other, eyeing him. Did they intend to lock him up somewhere if he refused, and hold him as hostage for his son Chatzkel? He knew very well, that once he signed that divorce paper Zfania would take it as final and press Rachel to remarry. Yet it did protect the woman against a misfortune.

"Sign it already," Zfania hissed, pulling Shaya to a side table.

Habbakuk pushed a quill and a bottle of ink into his hand. Shaya signed the divorce with a heavy heart. Zfania snatched it away in a triumph, slipped it into the briefcase, and strode out with Habbakuk.

Upstairs, Rachel served Shaya some flanken soup with a *knaydl*. She sat down opposite him and took the baby on her lap.

"Chatzkel got off?"

"Like a worker."

"Esther is going with you?"

"There's money for only three tickets, and we're five in the family. I owe it to her; she saved my life."

"Stop already; it was my idea. But do something for me in New York. There's something between Esther and Nathan. Watch them and write whatever happens between them. I want to light a little fire under Miriam."

"Maybe she should stay here? She's doing very well without him."

"She's started to drink. Besides, I want her there. She's my friend. Exaggerate a little; it'll bring husband and wife together."

"And what will it do to Esther?"

"Don't ask so much; don't think so much. You want Esther to get married? Just get a shadchan to find her a husband. You're such a family of children; somebody always has to tell you what to do."

Shaya gestured. "Downstairs, Zfania had me sign a divorce to give you at the train station, to protect you if anything happens to me."

Rachel's eyes flashed. "Thanks for the news; I'll be ready for the happy experience."

She crossed the room and brought Shaya an elegant shawl with a daffodil pattern. "Give this to Nehemia to give to Esther and wish her a good crossing. He has to encourage her to find herself a man."

The next morning in the market, Nehemia had a sealed dirty urn and Shaya had Rachel's shawl. "Here, give this to Esther for a safe crossing. But you mustn't mention me; it has to be your gift to her."

In the office of a Jewish ticket agent, Nehemia broke the seal and tumbled the money on the scratchy counter. The agent counted it, and made out three sets of tickets. He explained the crossing, how there were contacts in Bremen that would help them reach their ship. Shaya entrusted Nehemia with the tickets and went home.

Upstairs, Rachel sat with her hands between her knees as at a funeral. She looked up with a fleeting smile. "You're going?"

"Tomorrow."

She folded him in her arms, unable to talk. Shaya kept smiling at her as the tears streamed down her cheeks.

Rachel shuddered, and then twitched upright. "The Bremen Express leaves at ten. Spend the night with Chatzkel. At nine-thirty, I'll be at the station with all your things ready. When you leave, I'll move to Radich. With Nehemia, I won't be altogether away from you. With my father I wouldn't last a day. Here's some strudel for Chatzkel. Go already!"

Shaya embraced her and shambled out of the room.

The next morning, Shaya led Chatzkel into the Warsaw train station. The boy squinted about warily looking for pickpockets. Esther came behind him, wrapped in Rachel's shawl. Nehemia carried Esther's suitcase and Shaineh Nissel's satchel of food. Rachel waited with Azriel, bearing a huge suitcase tied with rope and another containing food.

Esther gripped Rachel. "Take my ticket; it's your place."

Rachel smiled distantly. "Let Shaya make a place for me. If I go, we'll be the blind leading the blind."

Esther blinked up, confused and disbelieving. Then a smile of pleasant satisfaction crossed her lips.

"If you give, I take," she murmured.

Rachel turned to Shaya. "How was Chatzkel at the Flying Goose?"

"Strong as a side of lumber."

Rachel swept Chatzkel up for a kiss. "You're my man."

Shaya felt treacherous, leaving Warsaw, the city he was ordained to serve as a rabbi; then he saw Binstock stride across the station with his three sons. Binstock held out the divorce; Rachel snatched it away, took a sewing knife from her pocket, and cut it in little pieces.

Frustrated and furious, Binstock lashed himself upright, inhaled hard, and spat Shaya full in the face. The three brothers stepped up to Shaya, one behind the other, but Rachel interposed her body and slapped the first full in the face. The three spun around indignantly, and rushed out after their father.

Rachel snatched Shaya and Chatzkel aside and told them to watch the suitcase, not to bang it apart on the trip. The two bags held all the kosher food they would have until Ellis Island.

Rachel gripped Shaya's arm. "Pay Chatzkel close attention; he scares me. He sees everything. He . . . he's a genius." She turned away and gripped Nehemia's arm to leave. Nehemia bowed over her protectively.

Seeing them leave, Esther felt a tremor of uneasiness for her mother. Distant as Geula was, Esther kept her place in Radich intact, as did Shaineh. They were all Rachel's responsibility now.

Chapter Thirty-six

THERE WAS A MOOD of turbulent defiance, a brooding grief and repressed rage, in both Nehemia and Rachel as they turned to leave the station. They had brought about their own willful abandonment, but it only galled them the more. Nehemia had started a family in the Flying Goose; when he finally left the old inn, all he had made there would vanish. Rachel had thrown off her father to save her oldest son, only to give him to her sister-in-law. Their sense of being cheated in life only strengthened their determination not to let life crush them. What they had, they had; and they still had plenty. Nehemia had lost all three of his daughters; his wife was scarcely there. He now had a jewel to replace them all; Rachel had thrown off her whole family to become a Kramer, and now she had the patriarch himself.

Rachel had left her two younger children in the waiting room with a nurse, not to strain the family's parting beyond endurance. Pushing into the anteroom, Nehemia and Rachel both kept glancing behind them, not wanting to be surprised by Zfania and his three sons. Rachel held her infant son against her bosom. His name, Simcha, or Joy, was her choice. Nehemia picked up Rivka with a gusty satisfaction and held her close as they walked outside to the street. He was used to carrying his daughters, and let Rivka shift and fidget until she finally accepted his shoulder; Rachel's children were his real grandchildren; he had no other. Gita's offspring would always be Horowitzes and strangers. All the family women had dodged and escaped him. But Rachel's decision to stay with him was his vindication as a father.

As Rachel approached Nehemia's wagon with a bleak smile, her impatience with Shaya surged to life inside her. He should have found a way to get them out of her father's house; Nehemia was the man in the Kramer family. Rachel was now the mother of the house at Radich.

Rachel suddenly gripped Nehemia's arm with both her own as they approached his wagon.

Nehemia started. "You're packed at home?"

"Everything. I can be out in ten minutes."

"The children also?"

Rachel flashed him a scornful look and didn't answer.

Nehemia cracked the whip and the horses heaved into motion. "Zfania will try to stop us?"

"He might."

"It's not a worry."

Twenty minutes later, the wagon pulled into the carriageway at Zfania's home. All four got out together. Only servants were at home. They got the bags out fast. Half an hour later, the loaded wagon pulled out of the Warsaw city limits.

As they passed a long field of alfalfa, Rachel bared her bosom and lifted up Simcha, turning toward Nehemia as she nursed, remembering her trip with Geula to the mikvah just before the wedding. Let Nehemia also see the body that had come into the Kramer family. Nehemia took a huge breath and continued driving.

That night, Binstock came home and found his daughter gone with her children and all their things. He rushed to the Belzer gabbai in a fury, and accused the Kramers of stealing his children.

The gabbai stroked his beard. "This is Kramer, the chicken farmer?"

"That devil, the *oisvulf*. What should I do?"

"What should you do? Do nothing, Zfania."

"Nothing? Nothing? I'll die, doing nothing."

"Do nothing, Zfania."

The next week, Nehemia returned from Warsaw and saw Zfania's coach in the yard. Like Gershuni he had come on a night Nehemia was away. Rage gripped him. He had lost Geula, but nobody was taking Rachel away from him.

Nehemia strode inside, picked Zfania up bodily, carried him outside, and spilled him on the floor of his carriage. He released the horse and lashed it with his Cossack whip. It reared back, kicking the air. He lashed it again, and Zfania's carriage disappeared at a wild gallop.

PART THREE

Chapter Thirty-seven

CHATZKEL KRAMER WAS EIGHT when he climbed on the train with his father and Aunt Esther, leaving his mother, sister, and brother behind. Sturdy, mistrustful, of average height, with eyes that made special demands and a voice edged with ghetto awareness, his forelocks tucked behind his ears, he clung to Shaya as the train pulled out of Warsaw.

The year was 1884 but the Kramers counted time from the creation of the universe. A family with broad earthy bodies and an air of confidence, who shared a satchel of kosher food and refused to be pushed, they sat down on the Bremen Express opposite a German businessman who brushed his mustache and read a financial journal. A Polish mother had a daughter Chatzkel's age sitting by the window. The family group was Jewish, Orthodox, people of the Pale, yet sat on the train with their own style of distinction. Shaya and Esther kept Chatzkel sandwiched between them; the torn family would not fall apart any further.

As the Bremen Express pulled out of the Warsaw station and yard, and rolled west and north, pushing ever faster, the daughter and Chatzkel ignored each other. Chatzkel saw the cathedral towers through the window and instantly looked away to avoid the evil eye. The Polish girl was viewing him as under glass. Shaya gave her a sudden grin. She shifted her eyes to the scenery. He squinted at the train corridor, watchful against thieves.

The train was picking up speed too fast. Chatzkel felt a clap of fear, feeling as if he were on some raft or piece of floating wreckage. A sudden wind could blow them into Siberia. This was a gentile world, full of uniforms, porters, police, train officials, Russian army officers. Even the wealthy Germans had a kind of uniform. Gentiles wore uniforms; Jews wore clothes.

147

Was another Jew on the train? Jews traveled by wagon. Why weren't they on a wagon? Did Shaya know what he was doing? This trip wasn't all that safe.

Chatzkel glanced up. Esther's curls dangled over his mother's shawl. How did she get it? Rachel would never give it up. Maybe God gave it to Nehemia the way Moses got a second Ten Commandments after the first set was smashed, to give Chatzkel something to cling to during their crossing. But Esther with a double of Rachel's shawl? Sometimes God just didn't think.

Chatzkel looked up at his father, a Belzer rabbi and cantor with the knuckles of a farmer, a Russian greatcoat, and an uncombed bushy beard, a holy man and a happy scholar. God was close to Shaya, but not to him. When Chatzkel prayed, God didn't answer. That was that. But businessmen weren't all that religious. They made out, businessmen; but this trip, he had to sense what his father wanted and make it happen.

Chatzkel sighed. Seeing Rivka in Rachel's arms in the train station, snuggling, pissing, maneuvering for another nursing, Chatzkel grinned from ear to ear because it hurt so much. And there was the baby too. At least he'd never change a diaper again, not until his own children. By the time Rachel got over, his brother and sister would wear ordinary underwear.

Chatzkel closed his eyes and thought about his mother. She was of Lithuanian stock, shrewder and more knowing than his father. Chatzkel had her awareness but also his father's calm passivity. Back in the train station, Rachel had called him her man. Nehemia was the one who should be taking them to Ellis Island; he handled the chicken house, and the Belzer market, and blind Shaineh Nissel. But Shaya was a religious giant. This was some titanic family: Shaya, then Nehemia, all the way back to Abraham, Isaac, and Jacob—all giants. What was Chatzkel doing in that succession?

He tugged Shaya's sleeve. Shaya escorted him down the aisle past sections of seats, knobs, and brass rails, then opened the door next to the drinking water tank and waited outside. Chatzkel laboriously opened his pants, lifted the seat, and aimed at the hole at the bottom of the drain where the cold air breathed up. In the dead of winter, if he pissed too slowly he could freeze his doodoo. But Chatzkel pissed fast like a real killer; it would never happen to him. A pogromchik should lie on the tracks, waiting for a Jew. He would let him have it right in the eye.

Chatzkel aimed well. The drops bounced off the stones in the roadbed below. He buttoned up, smiling with satisfaction. Shaya then escorted him back to their seats. Sitting down again between Shaya and Esther, he noticed the Polish girl looking at him again. He returned the glance with icy scorn. She giggled and looked out the window.

Sitting back, Chatzkel remembered that if he recited the *Shma* with perfect pronunciation, he would be guaranteed a seat in heaven after he died. A guarantee like that was pretty good. Then he would ask God why He didn't answer his prayers. The trouble was that God would see the question coming and not let him into heaven to begin with. Who needs aggravation?

The businessman left the car. A younger German with a signet ring on his forefinger noticed Shaya. He let himself in the sliding glass door, and sat down in the empty seat, turning his whole body toward them.

"I see you are of the House of Jacob. My name is Yakov Hertz. I live in Frankfurt. Moses Mendelssohn, my teacher, said, 'A Jew at home, a man on the street.' "

Shaya leaned forward and shook his hand. "You honor me with your noble company. My name is Shaya Kramer; I come from Warsaw."

"What was that sudden unpleasantness, a blood accusation in the Ukraine? A pogrom in Warsaw? What is going on?"

"The Russians make some of us uneasy. Once the Jew was protected to push off a revolution, now the mob is turned onto the Jew in a pogrom."

The man waved his hand. "The barbarian mind! Thank God, we live in a civilized country! But tell me, have you family in Germany?"

"My uncle Tevya Kramer sells clothes in Vienna."

The man's eyes warmed. "We have dealings. Tevya Kramer is a fine man, a prince. You're joining him, of course."

Shaya shook his head. "No, we're going to America."

The man's eyes savored the joke. "You're related to Tevya Kramer, and you're going to America?" Shaking his head, his lips pursed in a smile at Shaya's barbarism, the man got up and left the car.

The Bremen Express now moved at high speeed. The Kramers passed through a series of passport checks, car changes, and border crossings. Chatzkel dozed to the whistle and roll of the engine, the steady flicker of farming villages passing by. He half awoke, and began softly repeating the *Shma* as Shaya and Esther shared glances and broke into smiles, remembering their

149

childhood. Their old dream of freedom and escape stirred awake as they left Poland, drawing them very close.

They crossed the German border with a great checking of certificates. Chatzkel awoke beneath a blanket in Esther's lap. He snuggled closer and started to cry. Weeping, he was overcome with shame. He twisted around. The Polish girl had long left the car. He cuddled up more quietly in Esther's lap. He had a job now—to look after Shaya. He dozed off again, as the train pulled into the Berlin station to change passengers before continuing to Bremen.

Chapter Thirty-eight

THE DANISH *Neustadt* SLIPPED AWAY from its dock and nosed out of the berth for ocean vessels. It passed a line of smokestacks, released its pilot, and continued out of Bremen. Immigration was still being organized in 1884. A cavernous hold in steerage contained close rows of iron cots; a bare dozen passengers were in steerage on a ship that could carry a thousand at a crossing.

A few dozen ships were the narrows through which several million Jews of the Pale would eventually pass into New York Harbor. Agents throughout the Pale were at work outside the Jewish communal machinery—one was the agent Nehemia spoke to—selling tickets, giving detailed information in plain Yiddish, eliminating kinks and roadblocks as fast as they came up, to keep the crossing clear. In steerage were not simple workmen but people already displaced and in transit, the footloose middle class, dissatisfied individuals who would bring to New York a constructive energy but also a restlessness, the uncertainties that came with immigration. Their fathers repaired what they had; they would improvise with whatever lay at hand.

First- and second-class passengers occasionally looked over the rail of the steerage deck at the immigrant Jews. The liner offered a primitive kosher kitchen, but the passengers were wary of the ship's kitchen and shared their small supplies of food. Lacking a minyan the men prayed in private, each with his tallis and tefillin. Shaya prayed facing westward toward New York. His exile was coming to an end; this was now the direction of his life—toward self-respect, a family, green fields.

Near Shaya's bed, a young tailor with a Vandyke, shallow rectangular steel glasses, and elastic garters on his sleeves ac-

150

companied his bride, who sported ruffles. Newlyweds, they found Lodz housing difficult. Full of themselves, having enough wedding money, they took the plunge. Nightly, she moaned quietly and made noises in his arms, dreaming of arriving pregnant in Ellis Island to deliver in a new world. From Nathan's letters, Shaya guessed the groom would spend his life bent over a sewing machine; the bride would sew all day at home.

A somber bearded man of fifty stayed severely to himself. He seemed isolated by misfortune. His name on a baggage stub gave him away—Shmarya Nisselson. In Warsaw, he had been an editor for a prayer-book publisher and had written a fiery column called "Young Israel." After many barren years, his wife died in childbirth. A Jonah, he was fleeing his work in Warsaw. Shaya prayed that God bring no storm in judgment of him. Nobody would throw Shmarya Nisselson overboard to save the ship.

Two women in their thirties, Frumah Katz and Chedvah Bronstein, met on the gangplank and became fast friends. Frumah had a five-year-old son. Both intense labor Socialists, they were joining their husbands who were finally bringing them over after years of separation. They felt isolated and estranged in a steerage full of patriarchal Jewish men.

A wholesale clothing man, Aaron Binder, had a wife with a big blond sheitel that she kept shifting uncomfortably on her head. Chatzkel spotted their daughter on deck, crawling toward the rail, and snatched her up. As a result, he was appointed baby-sitter for the trip. It might as well be his sister Rivka. Each time he changed her diaper, he asked himself, would Nehemia submit to this? The answer was no. Would Shaya submit to this? The answer was again no. His family had an Abraham and an Isaac, but when it came to their Jacob, something was clearly missing.

Shaya's group soon began to draw attention. Shaya was tall, stately, very strong, and with his Russian greatcoat and uncombed beard he had a natural refinement to his gestures. Raised as a peasant, in steerage he had an air of holiness and a measured distance that had people circling around him. Was Esther really his sister? Was she his mistress? But they were fanatically Orthodox. The other passengers could arrive at no conclusions.

Chatzkel kept to the rail a lot. Sometimes he stayed all day in bed, not wanting to have to meet people or help anybody do anything. By his calculation, the men in his family were happy every second generation. He was born in the wrong generation. He lay, wishing people would leave him alone. He didn't get on the ship to baby-sit.

Esther cared for Chatzkel, but he resisted her. His brother and sister in Warsaw had their real mother—why should he accept a substitute? He showed respect to Esther but his eyes flashed with a stubborn honesty. He woke up sobbing, full of dreams of his mother, afraid to fall asleep again. Esther understood and refused to push him.

The departure was on a Thursday. The following night was the Sabbath. With Esther's jar of gefilte fish and a bottle of homemade wine, Shaya made kiddush under a smokestack, between a still moon and the slapping waves, for a cluster of shawls, babushkas, beards, and yarmulkes, giving each passenger a sip of wine and a slice of gefilte fish on a piece of matzoh, for a Warsaw Sabbath in the belly of the sea. Afterward, Shaya sat on deck near the rail, singing Sabbath hymns to the spread of steel-gray water.

Several passengers spread blankets on the deck and slept under the stars in the late summer's warmth. Each night, Shaya lay down and held Chatzkel close until he fell asleep, singing softly as the boat moved, *"Lekhah Dodi" "Hineni," "Ovinu Shebashamayin."* Hearing his father, Chatzkel rocked with the boat and smiled. They were both dreamers.

On a night of doldrums, Esther lay awake, idly thinking about Nathan. Restless, she wrapped herself in a thin robe, walked to the rail, and stared down into the black gurgle and suck of the water.

Suddenly a hand gripped her arm. She looked up, startled. Aaron Binder stood very close. "Don't."

"I wasn't going to," she answered simply, allowed him to escort her back to the hold, tapped his nose in thanks, and went to sleep.

Frumah Katz watched their group suspiciously. She finally stopped Esther, pointing with a skeptical smile. "Where's his wife?"

Esther was taken aback. "We have yet to get her a ticket."

"He left her pregnant, didn't he? The bastard!"

Esther faltered. "I really . . . don't speak of such things."

"My man took six years off my life, but he had his pleasure."

"You're a Socialist, aren't you?"

"We were organizers. I learned always to check the exits when I entered a hall or a building, where the second door was, and if the bathroom had a window."

"I'm sure you'll find in America a whole new life."

Aaron joined Shaya by the rail. "I don't mean to impose, but to get through Ellis Island, you need a craft, a job invitation, a sponsor."

Shaya hesitated. "I have *smicha* from the Belzer Yeshiva."

"A rabbi needs an invitation from a congregation to pass."

"My father is a chicken farmer."

Aaron smiled. "That's good. When they ask what you plan to do, say you plan to work on a chicken farm."

Shaya broke into an enormous smile. "I appreciate your kindness."

"My brother started a Belzer *shteibel*. Would you join us? New York has no real rabbis. I'll give you Jonathan's address."

"I would enjoy being with you in the city."

Shaya smiled as he stepped away. Aaron was drawn to Esther, but he behaved himself. Aaron would make a useful friend in New York. As Aaron talked to Shaya, Frumah pulled Chedvah aside, watching Shaya suspiciously. "There's something not kosher about that family. They look too good; only swindlers show that much love. They're always working on somebody, she especially. I can't figure out what she is."

Chedvah shrugged. "Forget it; they won't swindle either of us."

That night, the sky darkened precipitously. With a clap of thunder, the rain began slamming into the sea. As the ship heaved and pitched, Shaya strode on deck to sing under the drenching downpour with Chatzkel hanging on to him; "Thou didst cast me into the deep. Floods compassed me about; thy billows passed over me, even unto my soul. The depths closed me about; water wrapped my head. I cried from my affliction unto the Lord; and He heard me. Out of the belly of hell, cried I; and Thou heardest my voice."

Two days later, the twelve Jews lined up by the steerage rail as land came in sight. As the Statue of Liberty rose over the horizon, Aaron Binder's wife threw her sheitel overboard and shook her hair free. Shaya and Chatzkel gazed at the approaching skyline. Esther peered back at the water, fascinated, watching the knot of hair disappear among the waves, a piece of ocean garbage as they glided toward Ellis Island.

Chapter Thirty-nine

SHAYA, CHATZKEL, AND ESTHER backed against row after row of chemical barrels just shipped from Germany. On the next dock, a Dutch steamer was unloading passengers, including some Jews from steerage. On the Hudson, a pleasure boat was sailing upstream.

As he got off the boat, Shmarya Nisselson told Shaya an election was coming. The last president, James Garfield, was assassinated.

Shaya wrung his hands. "You mean America has anarchists?" Shmarya smiled dryly. "Only maniacs."

"What's the difference between an anarchist and a maniac?"

"A maniac does it just for pleasure."

Esther wore Rachel's shawl for protection, keeping her suitcase behind her against the barrel as strangers banged against them in passing. Shaineh Nissel's food bag was long discarded; their remaining food was in Rachel's bag. Refusing to move, Shaya and Chatzkel kept Rachel's huge suitcase on the planking between them.

Their boatload was already scattered. The tailor and his wife were still on Ellis Island; he didn't know where to go next. Shmarya Nisselson got through without difficulty; people made room in line for him. With his experience in Yiddish journalism, he was sure to find employment. His record carried no suggestion that he was a radical. Aaron Binder also had his answers ready before the questions were asked. His wife stayed close, minding the baby now that Chatzkel was gone.

Chedvah Bronstein's husband waited for her at the gangplank, already a burly American workman who helped her through customs. There was a desperate scream from two tables away; Frumah Katz clutched her frightened son, gesturing to Chedvah to support her as Chedvah stubbornly pushed away from her through the crowd: "What do you mean, I got a disease? My husband spent six years of savings to buy our tickets! Now I suddenly got a disease! I was faithful to the bastard! What are you trying to fix me with? Where would I get a disease?"

Shaya looked away. A lie had sunk its teeth into Frumah's soul and refused to let go. He knew by now she had poisoned the crossing for Esther, with all her talk about Rachel. Six years of separation were enough to ruin anybody. He had to get Rachel over fast. His Chatzkel was only six weeks away from his mother and already troubled.

The sky overhead was a grainy blue. The liner loomed over them, bigger than a bank. Stevedores kept leaning over the rail, sliding boxes down a chute as teams of men heaved them on a wagon. All over the dock was the suck of harbor noises, brine, and a bruising smell of chemicals and dust. A team of six dray horses, more powerful than any horses in Poland, pulled off the dock a wagon loaded with mahogany furniture.

Shaya smiled. He presented papers for the three of them, gesturing Chatzkel and Esther to stay close.

The clerk checked Shaya's items with a pencil. He then looked up. "What do you plan to do in America?"

Shaya grinned. "Work on a chicken farm."

"If a palace was wrecked, would you use the lumber for a hatchery?"

"None of it. All used lumber is diseased."

The clerk grinned and waved them by. "Good luck to you."

Shaya gave Aaron a grin and nod. Waiting by the door, Aaron waved congratulations and pushed outside with his family.

Across the dock, harbor police kept a cordon, as a hundred men in blue military uniforms marched onto a ship painted steel gray, followed by another hundred men; on Ellis Island Shaya had heard excited talk about a war, but there was always fighting somewhere—Russia pushing into the Balkans, America fighting across the continent. America was fighting the Indians? Shaya had no time for it. Chatzkel and Esther needed beds for the night.

Shaya sighed patiently on the dock, trying to savor a new country. He had expected freedom, but this freedom was quiet, basic, in the nature of things, a sheer openness, a letting go. The very air was looser. The dock, slightly larger than docks in Europe, thrust a long way into the water. There were passages in back, but no wall. A passing policeman didn't automatically establish himself. Nobody bothered with him except those who had business with him. He was just an immigrant; he was no longer a *zhid.*

A Litvak with a thin, agitated beard dashed up, limping slightly. He snapped his fingers in a pantomime of piety. "Make a blessing over a new fruit! It's America! A new fruit! God insists you do it right away!"

Shaya smiled patiently. "God is not such a *meshuggener.*"

The Litvak threw up his hands. "What are you telling me? God in heaven, the arrogance!" And he dashed off to another dock.

Shaya brushed his nose; the man made him ashamed.

A young clerk stepped over, obviously Jewish, though he was bareheaded, shaven, and dressed American.

"You just left the ship?" He spoke an American Yiddish.

Shaya pointed behind him. "I, my sister, and my son."

"Your speech is Warsaw."

"We come from Warsaw."

"Family is meeting you?"

"We still have our family to bring over."

"You have nobody? I'll help you through customs, then see if anybody is on the next dock. You're with friends."

"God be thanked."

Chatzkel tugged Shaya's sleeve. Shaya stopped the guide with an apologetic smile. He frowned, and then pointed to a comfort station. Shaya took Chatzkel inside and waited. Their little party moved through customs and their guide went to the next dock.

Esther sighed. "Rachel should see all this; I took her place."

Shaya frowned. "This is Frumah Katz talking: she was too crazy with bitterness to know anything. We had money for only three tickets. Rachel could never come and leave a child behind for the wolves."

"I finished your money; now you need three tickets."

Shaya embraced her. "God sent you in Rachel's place, to sing a little and look after Chatzkel, so that we shouldn't be so lonely."

Esther pressed Shaya to be quiet as their escort led them and two other sets of immigrants from the Dutch steamer to a waiting wagon. As they rode to the Lower East Side, a woman changed their money into American bills and coins. Shaya and Chatzkel rode quietly, worn out. Esther, never still, sat glancing from side to side, a dreamy patience in her eyes.

By nightfall, they had a two-room, cold-water walk-up on Rivington Street. Shaya and Chatzkel shared a straw mattress that consisted of two shallow troughs with a straw ridge down the middle worn in a succession of users. Esther had a single in the other room.

Chapter Forty

ESTHER DUG HER CURLERS and chemicals out of her suitcase. The ocean air had made her hair frizzy. She put on her curlers, tied a towel over them, curled up under her blanket, and fell instantly asleep.

The next morning, she started awake, irritated by the trough of dried straw she lay on. With all its use, by now it should have bugs. Grumbling, Esther took off her nightgown and curlers. She checked the stove for fuel and kindling. Satisfied, she wrapped herself in a Chinese mandarin robe and stepped down the hall with a towel and a bar of soap. The door to the bath was locked. Esther gave one knock and leaned back, listless and moody. Had she known about the wait, she would have kept her nightgown on.

After a ten-minute wait, an old woman came out in a gray robe. She gave Esther's robe a long look and walked off with a stony face. Esther stepped inside, irritated by the look. Why did old women get up so early?

The tub had one faucet; that meant cold water. Esther hung up her robe, gritted her teeth, climbed inside, and squatted. The tub was big enough, but she refused to lie down. She turned on the water, soaped and splashed herself, shivering with cold. She dried off, returned to the room and dressed in Rachel's shawl over a peasant skirt and blouse.

The old woman's look stuck in her head. New York was supposed to be worldly, but Warshavers ignored well-dressed women. These were slum people, superstitious as shtetl Jews. Esther glanced in the mirror and smiled mischievously. Rachel's shawl suited her, and her curls had all grown back.

Esther wanted to apply her chartreuse nail polish but the slum attitude toward adornment intimidated her. Esther tapped her foot impatiently. She gave a sudden sweeping turn, and then glanced in the mirror. Her curls dangled almost to her shoulders. She looked cautiously at her nails. They still had their perfect moon shape. She shrugged and put on her chartreuse polish.

Esther felt troubled as she went down the stairs to the outside. She needed to work, save a little each week, and give Shaya the price of a steamship ticket. By that time she would know what she wanted for herself. But she enjoyed her present confusion. She was an entertainer trapped in a traditional family; the trap left her confused and helpless, but she didn't mind. Shaya accepted her; he judged no one.

Esther stumbled and nearly fell on a stair; an old woman leaned out her door at the sound. Esther stopped and panted, pressing her breasts to calm herself. Why was she so eager? Why was she so urgent to look her best? Shaya was stone-blind to all women except Rachel. Chatzkel at eight knew more than his father about women. She had seen that little Polish aristocrat on the Bremen Express; Chatzkel had her eating out of his hand. But it was Nathan she was preparing for, in case he showed up for dinner.

Esther smiled ruefully. Shaya was too religious. It wasn't just observances—Esther could keep them—but Shaya had too much God in him. To Esther, the human sea was life enough, and her share of holiness.

Esther reached the outside door and pushed it open. The street was shadowed with row after row of tenements, each with identical concrete steps leading to identical doors. Such a tide of concrete gave her no sense of solidity.

On the street were girls in long dresses, boys in Polish caps, long-sleeved shirts, and pants with suspenders. They played stickball and jacks, grudgingly allowing a wagon to pass among them. They seemed unsupervised. Some boys with yarmulkes played with Irish and Polish children. The boys' Yiddish was full of strange words. A wall remained a *vant;* but a *fenster* became a windeh. In Warsaw, *yinglach* played with *mödlach*. In New York, girls stayed *mödlach;* but the *yinglach* became boyes. Even gentile children used a few Yiddish words, but when a gang of Polish boys approached, these children carefully made room to let them pass.

Three or four women squatted on the stoop in gray-black dresses whose sleeves barely exposed their fingers. They eyed Esther's curls with strong disapproval. Their hair was pulled back severely straight and tied in a bun. What was New York, their city, that they were moral judges? Esther decided they were all immigrants, just like her, immigrants who should go back where they came from.

Esther walked to the corner of Attorney Street, where push-carts maneuvered around jammed pushcarts, the peddlers hawking their wares—fish, candles, shoestrings, used clothes. Seven of them cursed a passing carriage in seven varieties of Yiddish.

Esther bought six potatoes, five pounds of sea bass, six eggs, two pounds of kishke, a bunch of spinach, a sausage end, a honey jar, cinnamon, sour salt, horseradish, and a pumpernickel, and started back to prepare their supper, having bought a little extra in case Nathan came. She already expected him. He had treated her with respect in that Warsaw parlor. Still, she would restrain him. He was a womanizer, but if he thought he could do anything to her, he had a screw loose somewhere.

Esther passed a couple just landed. In front marched the husband, a portly Hungarian with a bleak, ferocious beard and a tall felt hat banged up en route. In one hand he carried an embroidered tallis bag of blue silk; with the other, he pressed a scroll of Ecclesiastes against his heart. Behind him strode his wife, carrying a huge suitcase in one hand, a satchel with food in the other, all their linen in a giant net on her back, held in place by a strap across her forehead. Behind marched seven children, one behind the other, in descending age, size, and resemblance to the father.

Upstairs, Esther loaded the Primus stove. She then scrubbed their two floors, using a pail, a hard scrubbing brush, and a bar of soap she had found in the hall closet. When she was a girl, she dreamed of marriage to Nehemia. Now Rachel had Nehemia and she had Shaya. Shaya was too princely. She knew him through and through. He was made in the image of God, but he still had grown up on a farm. And in whose image was she made? Nobody's, only Nehemia's. She was approaching thirty; she wanted a husband. She was a farm girl and could handle successfully only so much movement. City people were different. They never had to dig an outhouse or sing their own music. Services and bathrooms were always available.

Not wanting to get depressed as she scrubbed the floor, Esther composed a song in her head called "Jews Do a Thorough Job"—touching on law, savings, talk, and explaining in its finale why Jewish women are so *zaftig,* because Jews do a thorough job. The song got her so excited that she danced on her knees as she scrubbed, pushing the brush this way then that way, tapping at the wall for emphasis, getting the words exactly right in her head, just in case the occasion should arise to sing it for others.

Chapter Forty-one

ON THE STREET, Shaya wore his long black coat and a high Cossack hat that felt somehow more American. He left his *shtreimel* in his suitcase, remembering the words of the German Jew on the Bremen Express: "A Jew at home, a man on the street." Looking around, he saw how on other bodies the long Polish coat thinned out to a Prince Albert, a cutaway. Shaya sensed that the shift to a short jacket marked the beginning of a freethinker.

Walking close to his father, Chatzkel looked over the four- and five-year-olds on the street and pushed his side curls behind his ears, not wanting to look a freak. He still dressed Polish, in short pants with a high, three-button waist, the underwear showing down the thigh, with navy socks over the knees, a blue-check shirt buttoned to the neck, and thin pointed shoes. American shoes were snub-nosed and heavy. How cold was the winter?

Walking, Chatzkel muttered, "I thank Thee, King alive and enduring, that thou hast returned my soul to me, faithful, with Thy great mercy."

Shaya was startled. "What's that?"

Chatzkel poked out his lower lip. "I forgot my *Modeh Ani* when I woke up this morning. Mother used to say it with me."

"You're a big boy."

"The trip over mixed me up."

"Don't make excuses; just do it."

"I'll try to be more careful."

Shaya showed Nathan's address to people, who smiled at the greenhorn who didn't know Hester Street. Chatzkel was on the verge of humiliated tears, his shoulders up stiff, hanging on to Shaya's jacket with both hands.

Shaya suddenly stopped. "I'll say *Modeh Ani* with you in the morning.

"You don't have to."

"I'm sorry I was sharp before."

Chatzkel reached up and took Shaya's hand.

The blocks grew congested and dirty. Fire escapes zigzagged down the fronts of each tenement. Everywhere were beggars, grit, hunger, and a frantic urgency, as the ghetto sullied its inhabitants.

The pushcarts made way for a wagon, its big noisy bell clanging, among upright signs of cowboys and Indians, and American flags. A bearded Litvak in a kapote was yelling left and right to vote for James Blaine, *der mensh fun Maine.* It was crazy, Shaya thought. Where would immigrant Jews go to vote? Besides, he had a Litvak accent. Who wanted a Litvak for President?

He finally found the Hester Street address, and stepped up to the man sweeping in front. "Nathan Finesilver. I have family regards."

The man gave him a long look. "You just landed?"

160

"I have a room on Rivington Street."

"How much do you pay?"

"A dollar a room a week. We have two rooms, one for my sister."

"It's too much. I'll give you a room with a double and a single, and a partition for your sister. You'll pay one dollar instead of two."

Shaya thought for a moment, and then smiled. "I'll ask Nathan."

Chatzkel tugged Shaya's sleeve. Shaya bent over as Chatzkel knotted up, cupping his hand. "What are you, crazy? That's a much better deal. Tell him we want to see the room."

Shaya nodded. "Let me see the vacancy."

The janitor gave Chatzkel a sour look, but the boy hung on to Shaya's jacket with both hands and glared right back. They climbed to the third floor and walked down a long hall. The janitor opened a door to a small room with no window, containing a double and a single bed, with a partition between them. A corner platform held a storage space under it, and in one corner stood a walk-in closet with a glass door.

Chatzkel squinted around suspiciously. He lifted the straw mattress and ran his finger along the sew line, pressed down on the chairs to see if they wobbled, and then ran down the hall to look at the toilets. He hurried back and tapped the closet door for termites. He tugged Shaya's arm from behind him, refusing to look at the janitor.

Shaya bent over. "What?"

Chatzkel cupped his hand next to Shaya's ear. "Ask for one with a window, over the street, so we can look out."

Shaya turned. "Have you got a front room with a street window?"

The janitor gestured impatiently. "This is the room."

Chatzkel shook his head. The two started to leave, but the janitor stopped them. "You want to look at a vacancy on the second floor?"

The janitor led them down a flight of stairs and into a room double the size of the first, with two big street windows. "This is a dollar and a half a week, but you'll still save half a dollar a week."

Chatzkel looked around suspiciously and then nodded. Shaya put a dollar and a half on the table. As he removed the key from his key ring, the janitor gave Chatzkel another long look. Chatzkel clung to Shaya's jacket, refusing to return his look.

"The building inspector doesn't look over a room the way your son does."

"He doesn't have to live there."

"Nathan Finesilver works for Acme Pants, two blocks to the right and a right-hand turn. I'll write the address."

He wrote the address and the two disappeared down the street.

Chapter Forty-two

SHAYA HEADED DOWN THE STREET, with Chatzkel hanging on tight, but the boy grasped the street and exulted in it. The God who kept escaping him in Warsaw was coming to him in America; he felt him all around. Chatzkel's poverty no longer mattered.

On Hester Street, Jews buying eggs held each egg up to the sun and squinted for blood spots. A wagon peddled stale bread, a penny for a loaf. Another vendor hung rows of mangy chickens, two and three tied together by the neck, wildly kicking their legs. A man walked with a thousand suspenders hanging over his shoulders and around his neck. Emaciated little girls begged in frayed shawls, holding up a cup with strange dignity.

At the corner, a pushcart pulled away and left an opening on the street. An accordion immediately appeared, playing a mournful ghetto song. Seeing the empty space, eight little girls began to dance the *shereleh,* clapping hands, their bodies alive to the music. Then a pushcart of apples shoved in among them. The children dispersed, and old men began feeling the apples as the peddlers watched them patiently.

Chatzkel gripped a bridle post as Shaya stepped down three steps and knocked at a basement shop with a row of windows under heavy mesh. In a moment, a swarthy Rumanian, in his undershirt, bareheaded, his eyes watery, opened the door. Behind him, six immigrants sat in a row in a long, narrow, low-ceilinged room, each bent over a sewing machine, the window their only light. Each had a yardstick, scissors, spools of thread, and a box for waste. They worked with the steady concentration of pieceworkers—another side of cloth, another nickel's wage. A small stack of finished pants stood by each machine. In back, a seventh worker crayoned patterns onto a roll of fabric to be cut and sewn. Behind him, an old woman ironed the pants and put them into a box for delivery.

162

"I have regards for Nathan Finesilver from his family."

The foreman leaned back. "They're from the old country, Finesilver. Take an hour; make it up tonight before quitting."

"Just pay me for one piece less, and don't worry about it."

As the other workers smiled, Nathan covered the third machine under the window, stretched and wiggled his fingers. He was bare-headed now, with garter sleeves, a trim beard, and silver-frame glasses; driving the liquor wagon in Warsaw had left him with a gambler's cool.

The two men embraced with a minimum of fuss. Nathan patted Chatzkel, then put on a Panama straw and hurried them off down the street. An eyeglass shop exhibited a copy of Nathan's frames on the counter. He exchanged a friendly wave with the counterwoman and checked the cut of his beard in the mirror window, as she waited patiently in case he wanted to come in.

"The boss didn't like your answer about staying out late."

"He's a small potato—saves half a penny a pair of pants by working the men without a lamp. A Delancey Street pants maker gives him pants on a rush order. How many Jews were in steerage? An empty steerage makes it a worker's pick on jobs."

"Twelve, but a Dutch ship was also unloading, also with steerage."

Nathan had a wry grin. "Two ships in one day? They're stepping it up. Full ships make it another story. The bosses are organizing the exodus from Poland so that a mob of workingmen will fight for every job. I got to find a shop where I'm paid by the hour, so I won't sweat out my guts working."

They passed an eight-year-old girl on a tenement step, leaning back, holding a baby sister in her arms, blinking at the street, motionless, guarding the child while the mother worked.

Nathan led them into a spa, where he ordered three glasses of a chocolate drink. Chatzkel sat listlessly, his hand on Shaya's thigh. Shaya began to see Nathan differently now, as basically a courteous man who needed room not to bang against people, and as a salesman, a connections man.

"Miriam went home as soon as you left. She manages Ribalow's business now, and making a success at it. The stores buy her ideas."

"Yeah, she writes."

"Your daughter is a big girl now, and your son. You've been here for two years. When are you bringing them over?"

"Listen, Miriam makes a lot. She writes that when she feels like coming, she'll bring herself over."

"I think Rachel will be lighting a fire under her."

A nearby shopkeeper nudged his friend. "So I told him, no, we go to your bank; and you'll pay me in cash. Cash never bounces."

"Yeah, I like that."

Nathan looked up. "You passed your exams, didn't you? Only Wolfson I trusted in that pack of wolves. But a *smicha* is an old skin you can't throw off. I'm lucky I got out. You . . . brought Esther?"

"She's right now setting up our rooms."

"Did she talk at all about me?"

"She knows I'm seeing you. You'll have supper with us. We're on Rivington Street, but we're moving into your building."

"Maram's a Bulgar, Sephardic, a real Turk, but the halls are clean. We have a bathtub on every floor; the next block has only one cold-water faucet for a floor. But Hester Street is alive, not like Rivington Street and its Hungarian Jews. You can even leave your door open; just don't make it a habit."

Shaya smiled dryly. "I never leave a door open."

"I'm on the third floor; I told him to put you there."

"He offered a back room with no windows. We took one on the second floor over the street, but the three of us are in it."

"Things are moving that way, people putting in an extra bed for a lodger. Up the backstairs, Maram is putting in eight, ten beds in a room and charging by the bed."

"I heard in Ellis Island."

"The Odessa Café has some interesting people. I told the manager about Esther; he'll give her a waitress job."

"Do you know an Aaron Binder? We met on the boat."

"He's joining his brother. What's he doing, men's clothes? There's a killing to be made there in blue serge, the Wall Street uniform. The East Side Jew wants the feel of a uniform."

"Suggest it to him; you'll work as a salesman, and not over a machine."

"Yeah, have to think about it."

"Aaron wants me in the *shteibel*."

Nathan flicked a smile. "You're mad at me, aren't you? For not being on the dock. It's the truth, isn't it, *gazlen*?"

"Why? We're expecting you for dinner; Esther is preparing now."

"So, I'm not reliable. I still made something for you, a map of all these streets, with Yiddish names so you won't get lost."

Shaya studied it. Overcome with relief and gratitude, he

stepped around and embraced Nathan. "You're well again, aren't you? Coming to America was good for you."

Nathan jabbed the air. "Esther did it for me. What's there to talk about? You see this stump of a finger? It was frozen on the road, and then I saw Esther and it didn't matter anymore. I adore your sister; she's an angel. The . . ."

Shaya pressed his hand. "Enough, no more."

Outside, the word was hissed along a row of peddlers that the Health Inspector was coming. A dozen peddlers disappeared into shops and entrances, one dragging a barrel of fish, another chickens infested with lice. They slammed and locked the doors as a cart approached escorted by police. The Health Inspector examined the pushcarts. The police dumped stale vegetables, moldy baked goods, and rotten fish into a wagon in the cart, as curses rained down on the police from the windows.

Nathan waved it aside. "Shabbes, we'll walk by the water; I'll show you where the barges dock and the banana boats unload."

They entered a stable stacked with merchandise on a back platform. Three large wagons were making wholesale deliveries by a pile of broken pushcarts, their handles poking up. Nathan pushed through to the manager.

"Kutch? Shaya Kramer just arrived. He'll start tomorrow. Give him something that sells, will you? I'll appreciate it."

Shaya put his name down for the next morning. Stepping out, he found a locksmith and made a duplicate key to their new room for Esther; his mind was so full of his next letter to Rachel that it never occurred to him to worry what Nathan's visit might do to Esther.

Chapter Forty-three

SHAYA SQUINTED: a row of empty pushcarts was rolling into the warehouse, returning for another load. In America things moved, but with idiot Litvaks selling blessings on the dock, the country seemed full of spiritual lightweights, and there was looseness all around; people moved in randomly, all noise and chatter. Shaya had been overhasty, when he faced westward on the boat to pray. In Poland, he was just a bright Yeshiva boy who was ordained; but here, he enjoined himself, "In a place where there are no men, be thou the man."

It was crazy, what Nathan said—that Esther had saved his life. Nathan was a taster, a fixer, a middleman; he made bonds that were not bonds but just arrangements; he had always been an American. What was he adoring Esther for? A grown man adores his mother. To adore an unmarried woman only confuses her. He would never marry Esther, so he should leave her alone.

Back home, Rachel told him to find Esther a shadchan. In Warsaw, Esther had managed a house of ill fame, but that was over now. As far as Shaya was concerned, a Jew made a fresh start. You do what you can do. But what shadchan can you ever trust? He'll arrange any union, just to collect his fee. Shaya needed to consult a serious Belzer. He took out Aaron Binder's note on which he had written his brother's address, spread out Nathan's map, traced street directions, and took off. Chatzkel held his hand, committing himself to his father, yet mistrusting everything his father did.

Half an hour later, Shaya entered a tiny entrance in a row of clothing shops stacked with durable dry goods, towels, sheets, blankets, and tablecloths, everything in reach, with boxes piled in back. A customer was examining pillowcases, another the weave of a tablecloth. The storekeeper stood in back, bearded and paunchy; he looked more settled than Aaron, with that black velvet yarmulke that covered his bald spot. A black kapote open in front showed a solid-gold watch chain across his chest.

Shaya walked over. "Jonathan Binder?"

"I have the pleasure?"

"Shaya Kramer. I was on the *Neustadt* with Aaron."

"Blessed are they who arrive."

"Aaron is well?"

"God be thanked, and working hard. And this is Chatzkel?" Jonathan reached in a drawer and slipped a cookie into Chatzkel's hand. "Aaron was saying what a help he was."

"Children should keep busy; he's starting school tomorrow."

"Regular school?"

"To learn English. Our family teaches *Yiddishkeit* at home."

"I'm not sure that's possible in America. You're ordained from the Belzer Yeshiva? You're our first here in America."

"I taught a class. Shmarya Wolfson trained me. He taught a plain text; but his mind was a knife, a Litvak, but a true Belzer."

"And the Rebbe softened his attitude to us in America?"

Shaya broke into a wry smile. "His gabbai told my father-in-law to sit in mourning for the dead if I came to America."

Jonathan shook his head. "We have wives held back to keep their children in Warsaw. We keep writing, to the Rebbe, to our families. But what do we need letters? Let the gabbai come over and see for himself. Yet people come over more and more. Poland is death."

Shaya nodded. "I felt it; that's why I came over."

"Perhaps you can help us. Our *shteibel* has argued sunset for over a year. We have members who walk the streets looking for stars to end the Sabbath; but the air is so dirty, an hour after sunset you see nothing. And we get ocean fogs. How shall we mark the end of the Sabbath?"

Shaya smiled dryly. "The question already came up in Poland. It's not just dirty air. A cloud will blanket out the stars for days. And it's not just the Sabbath. When does New Year start? What marks the start of a pilgrim holiday? But we no longer look for stars; we know how the firmament moves. In Safed, the stars first appeared eighteen minutes after sunset. If you wait twenty-two minutes after sunset, according to law, you can regard the Sabbath as over."

"Twenty-two minutes after sunset; that's very soon."

Shaya instantly smiled. "But to be comfortable, and because additional Sabbath is a blessing, you should wait one hour after sunset."

"That's very nice to know. And has anything brought you into my store?"

"I'm actually looking for a shadchan for a woman relative. I want an experienced man I can trust completely. I thought you could help me."

"There is some special problem? I ask with respect."

"If you ask if she is pregnant, divorced, with a sickness, a cripple, venereal, nothing like that. What's there to say? Esther has a soul. She lives in Jewish music. My only worry is that an unworthy man will interest her too soon. Esther needs a noble man who will give her joy."

Jonathan closed his kapote and tied a black twist belt around his waist, so pleased he gave Chatzkel another cookie.

"Avigdor? Handle the store. I'm going out with this gentleman. Come. The bookseller is two doors up the road. This is your sister from the boat? From Aaron's description, I'm sorry I'm not a single man."

Jonathan caressed Chatzkel's head as he munched his cookie, hanging on to Shaya's coat, refusing to listen to idiots.

"When you ask for a reliable shadchan, I thought you had a

smaller relative in mind. Once Chatzkel started looking after Aaron's little Ellen, she was quiet the whole trip."

"To change a diaper is a strange way to start a *shiddach*."

"In America, anything can happen. I think if you agreed, Aaron would write a contract now with a dowry. Never laugh at a determined man."

"I see you're a *chevraman*."

"I'm still a Belzer."

"I'm not interrupting your work?"

"To match a good Jewish woman in search of joy, it's worth giving Avigdor the store for an hour. And from Aaron's description, your sister is a real Jewish woman. If a choice *shiddach* is available, then surely the secretary of the Belzer Society will know about it."

Shaya looked up sharply. "His name is Yakov Rivers?"

"A man of silk. He grew up in the Warsaw orphanage. He was in your Yeshiva, but was too poor to continue to *smicha*."

"My father mentioned him before we left."

Chatzkel grimly hung on to his father's sleeve. His father was too simple, even something of a child. Maybe it was because he grew up on a farm with animals. And, because he didn't see through anybody, people trusted him.

Chatzkel peered suspiciously at three boys on a stoop, gorging on slices of pumpernickel and a jar of sour pickles, as Shaya and Jonathan entered Yakov's shop as old friends.

Chapter Forty-four

PEDDLERS KEPT BANGING against Chatzkel on their way home. Dodging a ball, he slipped and fell. At each mother's scream for her son from an overhead tenement, he grabbed Shaya's coat in both hands.

Back on Rivington Street, Chatzkel pulled Shaya's sleeve. Shaya carried him up five flights past supper noises seeping through every door. Shaya knocked, and they entered into a heavy smell of schav, gefilte fish, and frying sausages. Esther had stopped to wash herself and dress for supper. Her curls hung very full over her peasant skirt and Rachel's shawl.

As Shaya took off his coat, Esther glanced over from the Primus. "You should have brought Chatzkel sooner; he was on the street too long. People here are just rude. I could take it for only an hour."

Shaya gestured her to calm herself. "You get used to it; to-morrow should go easier. I signed up for a pushcart; I'll start tomorrow. I also talked to Jonathan Binder, Aaron's brother. I think the Belzer will want me as their rabbi. They can't pay now but finally it'll be a job."

"So it'll take time, but we're getting started."

"I also got us a big room on Hester Street, with a partition. We'll save half a dollar a week. It has a view, and only one flight up. Chatzkel said to take it."

Esther picked Chatzkel up, kissed his cheek, and put him down. Chatzkel made a face, but accepted it as his due.

"Chatzkel's right. This block has real shtetl people; they looked at me not in a good way."

"We're moving to Nathan's building."

Esther's ladle fell with a clatter. "That's interesting."

Shaya opened Chatzkel's Hebrew book, but Chatzkel yawned and looked away. Shaya closed the book again. Chatzkel wasn't a student; tired or not, Shaya himself would have plunged right in.

"Nathan had a room set up for us on his floor, but it was too small. Chatzkel said not to take it."

Esther stepped over and kissed Chatzkel again. Shaya murmured, "Nathan said that in his building, people leave their doors open. I told him I never leave my door open. This is a fine schav."

"I had time to prepare."

"It's good; I invited Nathan."

"I thought you might."

"Nathan has a job for you, in an interesting café. He'll take you there after supper. He's straightened out a lot, becoming American. He knows everybody around. He dresses like a shegetz."

Esther suddenly looked at him. "Why are you telling me all this?"

"Because I found you a *shiddach*."

Esther clutched at her shawl. "You wasted no time, did you?"

Shaya looked at her. "You do want your own children. The man has a bookstore near Aaron Binder's brother."

"He's also a Belzer?"

"Their social secretary. He'll take you without a dowry, save you a lot of headache."

"Yeah? What's wrong with him? Not that I'm interested."

"Nothing. He's a shadchan, knows everybody around. When I told him about you, he closed the *shadchones* file."

"What did you tell him?"

"The truth—that you're a wise woman and have a beautiful soul, that you love music, that a man should bring you joy."

"But I'm a nothing."

"I even interested Jonathan Binder, and he's married."

"So was Aaron. The Belzer sound like a flock of innocent babies. I have a feeling I'll help you get the job with the Belzer."

"Yakov is a *soyfer,* a scribe; he writes mezuzahs, marriage contracts. He's smart as a whip. You have to see a *soyfer*'s hands. His brother, Ariel Rivers, is another *soyfer* in Newark."

Esther smiled wistfully. "You told him I have a beautiful soul?"

"I spoke only the truth."

"Did you tell him I once managed a parlor?"

"No, I didn't."

"It's necessary."

"I don't see why."

"Tell him. If he's still interested, then I'll marry him; otherwise I don't want ever to see him. What's his name anyway? He sounds intelligent, and a *mensh.*"

"Yakov Rivers. I told him to come to the Odessa tonight."

Esther flashed a sudden look. "Nathan is a fool, isn't he?"

Shaya smiled helplessly. "He talks too much. He said you saved his life, made him stop feeling like a cripple. He adores you."

"Yes? And when is Miriam coming over?"

"As soon as I write to Rachel how nice he is to you."

Esther stopped dead and gave him a sharp look. "Rachel arranged all this, didn't she?"

Esther smiled sardonically. So she was here to bring Nathan and Miriam together. Not that she would be foolish, but she might try to give Nathan an idea of what a real companion was.

Esther picked up Chatzkel with a kiss, sat him down at the table and began feeding him, one spoon at a time, controlling her excitement.

Esther waved her hand. "I'll put Chatzkel to bed right after his supper. I'll pack to move to Nathan's building after I get back from the café. You tie the suitcases in the morning. The luggage isn't that strong."

Feeding Chatzkel, Esther looked up. "You know, we're the only peasants who made it. New York Jews are city people; they'll eat us up alive."

Shaya looked up. "You frighten too easily, Esther."

Chatzkel got bored being fed and took the spoon. Shaya sharpened his quill with a chafing stone and began a letter to his wife, but a knock on the door interrupted him.

As Shaya put aside the manuscript, Esther wiped Chatzkel's mouth and carried him to bed murmuring, "Chatzkel, do you know how beautiful your body will be? The women will die for you, and you have so much soul."

Chatzkel made a face. Shaya opened the door to Nathan Finesilver who was carrying a bottle of wine in honor of the reunion of old friends.

Chapter Forty-five

EMPTY SCHAV BOWLS filled the iron basin, with dishes leaning against them. A vapor of fried sausage and steamed fish glowed around the table's two candles. The door was ajar to the adjoining room, so Esther could hear if Chatzkel's sleep was disturbed.

Nathan gestured in feeble protest. "Enough! It's not necessary!"

Esther tapped the table with her knuckles in frustration. "And throw good food in the garbage? Don't balk at me, Nathan."

Nathan sprawled back, flushed, sweating under his shirt, a strand of spinach caught in his beard, his knees apart, his collar loose, as Esther descended on his platter with a ladle and the deep frying pan. She had intended a make-believe romance with Nathan, to swim demurely in the heady waters of love, full of the bittersweet wine of frustration and futility. Now Shaya's proposed *shiddach,* together with the news about Rachel and Miriam, altered everything. Drunk on wine, she forced the last hard-boiled egg onto Nathan's platter, brown-red with sausage juices and strings of spinach.

Unable to relax, Esther stepped behind Chatzkel's bed and loosened her clothing. Wisps of hair broke loose between her careful curls. A *shiddach* in the making forbade even a demure, distant romance, but she was a stubborn woman and would have it in one form or another. She would marry the bookseller; she was helpless to frustrate Shaya's arrangements. She would make plain the woman she was, show Nathan what a companion was, Chatzkel how a mother loved. They both needed a little womanly company.

Esther returned and sat down again. Nathan looked like a shegetz in a short jacket, his beard so close it hardly counted.

171

But the way he ignored her, talking only to Shaya, glancing at her like the apple wobbling on top of a Purim stick, and then talking to Shaya again, made her feel unstable. She hadn't met the bookseller yet, and felt in her bones she should delay and dangle herself for a while, keep things in suspense, if Shaya was to get his job in the bargain.

"How does that detachable collar get washed?" she asked weakly.

Nathan looked over with disdain. "Me wash this collar? It's made of paper; dirty, I throw it away."

"If you throw clothing away, what do the children get?"

Nathan turned to Shaya, talking loudly. "The Jewish woman lives on pure frustration; and when I say frustration, I mean to its furthest reaches. That's why the New York Jewish woman is completely different, because she has different things to frustrate herself with, different rules of the game to lose by."

Esther gestured. "Please, I don't understand."

Nathan downed his last section of egg. He washed it down with a swallow of wine, then opened and closed his fingers.

"In Poland, the Jewish woman always lost to the Rebbe. Before Passover, a man's choice was to stay with the wife or visit the Rebbe; so he visited the Rebbe of course. Whose face was in his billfold? Hers might be there, but it was his Rebbe's face he took out to look at. What do you think of all this, Esther?" He flashed her a glance.

Esther started, then she snorted triumphantly. "You're the one who's living in frustration, Nathan."

Nathan broke into an idiot grin. "Don't count on it, Esther."

Esther poured herself a drop of wine. "What frustrates Jewish women in New York, Nathan?"

Nathan spun around. "Shiksehs!"

Esther's jaw dropped. "On Hester Street he meets shiksehs?"

"The Jewish shikseh is a thousand times worse. You want to know why the Jewish woman fights for the truth? Because the truth is Mount Sinai, and the man has it. She reads all the time, building up her education."

Esther pressed her bosom. "The shikseh never gets frustrated?"

Nathan snorted. "Yes, but by the shegetz, who's a sport, a gambler, an officer. He fences and wears a uniform, so she keeps her poise, wears her elegant clothes and learns her dancing steps. She demands nothing; she aspires to nothing. There's nothing to her, so she'll win every time. It puts the American

172

Jewish woman in a rage. Losing to a shikseh isn't part of Jewish tradition."

Hearing a soft moan through the door, Esther stepped in to Chatzkel, cautioning the men with her hand to be quiet.

Nathan leaned close to Shaya. "The Belzer *shteibel* interests you? Let me give you a piece of advice."

Shaya's eyes narrowed. "What?"

"Go as their chazan, not their rabbi. They all know you have *smicha;* so whatever is in that, you'll get anyway. To be a cantor hurt you in Warsaw. Here a cantor's appreciated, but a Polish rabbi has no security. The streets are too free. Ignoramuses with loud voices pass as experts. The German Reform rabbi uptown, he has the power."

"America-turn-on-its-head," Shaya breathed.

"Here you make it by being a *shvitzer,* irritating, grabbing, never stopping, taking money out of pockets, always *kvetching* for more, and feeling cheated if there's not more to take."

"The Binders want me for my *smicha,* to push the Warsaw Rebbe into letting more of his people come to America."

Nathan shook his head. "The East Side is a little Warsaw, full of ignoramuses who make it. You think you can give them something? You're too honest, chaver. Go in as their rabbi, and I guarantee you, in a year, you will be looking for another job."

Upset, Shaya stroked his beard, unaccountably sleepy, as Esther entered, smiling, her face washed, her clothes straightened, ready for the excursion. One look at Shaya, and she saw that Nathan had shaken him badly. Esther felt abandoned. A slow anger kindled inside her. Didn't Shaya see that Nathan was after her? She should have shut Nathan up. But maybe Shaya was blinding himself, getting ready for his message to Rachel and Miriam. Shaya was using her; she had to fend for herself. It was a good thing she was meeting Yakov Rivers; he would counter Nathan.

Esther gestured to Shaya and pointed to his stationery; Nathan rose, put on his jacket, and escorted her out, leaving Shaya moody and quiet.

Chapter Forty-six

NATHAN AND ESTHER STROLLED down the Bowery toward Canal Street, Nathan in a gray waistcoat, a sack coat, and a soft felt hat with a deep-rolled brim; Esther in a mustard-yellow bodice with a long skirt, full at the back, her curls dangling to Rachel's shawl.

Nathan leaned close and smiled agreeably. "Each time we meet is in another life—Radich, Warsaw, and now this wilderness."

Esther nodded, drinking him in, cautiously playing, only half-listening. "We're creatures of exile."

"You gave me life, Esther, that day in Warsaw. I was headed for the grave. Whatever I was guilty of, it was strangling me. You did what no other woman could do. You touched me, and all my guilt disappeared. I . . . I think you're not a human being. I think you're an angel."

Esther smiled patiently. "I touched you, Nathan?"

"We touched each other. I dare not ask you to forgive what I did."

Esther breathed deeply and pressed his hand. "You must speak no more of that. I have to tell you the truth. Shaya has arranged a *shiddach* for me, with Yakov Rivers, the scribe. That's why I permitted myself to come with you tonight, because I belong to another man, and . . . and you to another woman. If I gave you life, Nathan, don't take advantage. You're very dear to me. Make my life easier, not harder."

Esther wrung her hands uncertainly, feeling him slide away. They passed an occasional pushcart, covered with tarpaulin. A night guard with a coat and derby leaned over each. The atmosphere lightened on Canal Street. They passed cafés, where an editor, a poet, an anarchist thinker, sought a place where he could be with comfortable companions.

Esther followed as Nathan entered the Odessa at the corner of Mott Street. One look told her Nathan was a fool to bring her here for a job. It made her feel compassionate toward him, knowing how out of touch with café life he was. The café was austere and literary, with tiny round tables and lyre-shaped chair backs. Every second table held a lit candle. The men scattered about all wore their hats. Nathan left Esther to speak to the café manager.

Two habitués in the corner noted her immediately. Minna Schwanger, whose Yiddish novel, *The Stepfather,* appeared when she was seventeen, was established as a woman of letters. She now translated Goethe into Yiddish and contributed to literary weeklies. Batsheva Kalb, a Vilna woman trained as a dentist in Germany, was now a scientific journalist who subscribed to journals from around the world and spoke six languages. Both women registered Esther's curls with disdain.

Minna then peered over to Batsheva, her hair severely brushed up under a gray bonnet with a veil. "You have a secret you're not sharing. What is it?"

Her companion smiled slyly, her gray-black hair swept up into a crown. "Have you ever heard of the French biologist, Louis Pasteur? A Heidelberg newsletter put me on his trail. If my source is correct, he has found a way to prevent disease. Can you imagine?"

"Well you must write an article on him. It would be a coup."

"I've already started one, but the French journals slight him. I've written to a doctor I trust in London, asking for information by return mail. I want to know exactly what he does."

Minna stirred her tea. "Have you met Abraham Cahan yet?"

Batsheva smoothed her long-sleeved blouse with its throat bow. "That Socialist leader who writes sketches? I understand he's very good."

"He addressed the Socialist Society. He's a beautiful man, but those Yiddish Socialist writers, with all their realism, are just musicians who can read an honest score. But Tolstoy wrote the music they play. Everything after Tolstoy is plagiarism."

"So she bores you, gentle, eager Flisseleh, who comes up from the shtetl and is betrayed."

"Oh, she does suffer; I just don't get the smell of her underwear in all her suffering."

"The smell of her underwear. Really, Minna, I think a writer can leave that to your imagination."

A young man sitting bareheaded in a threadbare jacket waved at Esther. She sat down.

"How long are you over?" he asked in a dry, careful voice.

"Two days. And you?"

He frowned painfully at his fingertips. "Too long, believe me. What can I do? I have nowhere to go, so I sit."

"Do you write for the anarchist monthlies?"

He cocked his head and blinked at her. "What do they preach, anarchism? They dream of the Messiah, but they're tired of singing in synagogue. So they sit in cafés and listen to each other plan the free society. The Jew works on his sincerity because his brain is empty of anything else."

A strange woman entered, in a gray-white gown, older and thinner than Esther, and walked slowly by. Minna and Batsheva dismissed her with the same disdainful glance. Esther's companion gestured to her to sit down. She obeyed, barely. He gestured a shade more brusquely, and she slumped in her chair, joining them.

175

Esther licked her lips. "In Warsaw, did you know a Shaya Kramer?"

"Shaya is in New York? He was two years ahead of me."

"We just landed. I'm sure he wishes you well."

Nathan touched Esther's shoulder. "Rivers was here, but he left."

"He was probably uncomfortable here. Come, let's leave."

Nathan smiled as they stepped outside. "Shaya said Aaron Binder is going into clothing. I told him what to sell to make a fortune."

Esther blinked suspiciously. "Information like that can get you a partnership."

Nathan tipped his Panama forward. "Maybe I'll talk it over with the woman who runs the eyeglass store. She's a real Jewish shikseh."

Esther felt shaken. She took a huge breath and got control of herself.

Nathan took her arm. "Would you visit me? It's on the way home."

Esther smiled radiantly. "It would be so nice, but I have to pack our things tonight, so Shaya can move them in the morning. Perhaps you can visit the woman with the eyeglass store. A man as nice as you shouldn't have to be alone. And don't think your mentioning her upset me. It was stupid; but usually you have better manners, so I forgive you."

Nathan nodded evenly, and escorted Esther to Rivington Street.

Chapter Forty-seven

IN THE HUSH BEFORE DAWN, the straw in his mattress crackled softly bringing Shaya wide awake. Chatzkel huddled next to him, his fist in his mouth, snorting. Shaya murmured *Modeh Ani,* and washed his hands from a floor pot near the bed to cleanse himself of the night spirits. He put on work clothes, then his tallis and tefillin, and said his morning prayers. Finished, he began tying up the suitcases that Esther had left packed.

By now, a pearly light was whitening the wall. The street sounded with movement. Shaya squinted out the window. A first pushcart peddler offered hot rolls at a penny a roll; another sold whitefish, cod, and weakfish from the night catch. The New York morning felt hard and cold. Men hurried down the street on business; a few aged carried tallis bags. Shaya could hear no one take time to say hello.

Seeing Chatzkel stir in bed, Shaya bent over and kissed him. He said *Modeh Ani,* holding his father's hand. Chatzkel quickly dressed. The two ate salad and slices of pumpernickel.

Shaya banged on Esther's door. "Esther? Are you awake?" After a moment, came a sleepy, "I'll be in a minute."

Esther came in, wearing a robe over her cotton nightgown and a towel over her curlers. Shaya handed her a key and a slip of paper with their new address. She looked jarred somehow.

"You didn't like Rivers?"

Esther tossed her head. "I never met him. The Odessa made him uncomfortable, so he left early. Talk to him today. Apologize for our sending him there. Maybe we should meet tonight. Maybe he can find me a waitress job in a café. The Odessa isn't for me."

Shaya made a face. "Was Nathan unpleasant?"

"No, just sticky."

Shaya hoisted the two suitcases, in his work clothes and tall Cossack hat, grunting at the weight.

"The place is a distance; porters are downstairs."

"We have to start saving money. We'll see you there tonight. You have the address? It's the very front room on the second floor."

Chatzkel fought for a suitcase, and finally settled for holding one with Shaya. As they stumbled downstairs, Esther went back to sleep.

On the street, Shaya looked at Chatzkel. "We'll take these to the new rooms, then you'll start school. I'll hang around while you're inside, so you can join me when school lets out."

Hester Street had a raw sea smell. Children hurried to school. Here and there, street Arabs hustled for leftovers from early-morning sales, and housewives arranged food for supper before going to work on their sewing machines.

Shaya and Chatzkel put the suitcases away and headed for the supply warehouse. Kutch gave Shaya a load of children's clothing and explained in a drone his prices, what numbers fitted what child, and cautioned them not to let customers forage in the cart.

Pushing together, Shaya and Chatzkel got out the entrance. Chatzkel immediately began calling out: "Children's clothes, all new, pants, socks, shirts," beckoning Shaya to join him.

Shaya hesitated, then the two cried together. Soon they were scrambling about, checking numbers with sizes, maintaining the price schedule, keeping the pieces where they belonged.

After six sales, Chatzkel stepped into the school a veteran businessman. Seeing a strange boy in the hall in Polish clothing, the passing students directed Chatzkel in Yiddish to the assistant principal. They smiled and imitated the newest greenhorn among them.

The assistant principal, John C. Franklin, received Chatzkel in his office. Seeing that he understood no English, he opened the door and called out: "Rose?! Miss Rubin! Translation from the Yiddish!"

Rose Rubin entered and got to work. Chatzkel had no papers, not even a birth certificate. He lived somewhere on Hester Street. He didn't even know his whole name, just Chatzkel. He thought he was eight, but time in Poland might be different from time in New York. His mother couldn't fill out a form. She was still in Warsaw, waiting to come over.

Chatzkel answered one and two words to each question, and then slumped over, looking down. Mr. Franklin cupped his hands. "His name is Isaac. That's what Chatzkel is, isn't it? Isaac."

Mr. Franklin brooded. He looked at Chatzkel. Finally, he started up again. "This applicant is very elusive. Perhaps he's retarded; he looks retarded. Tell him to go home and come back with his father tomorrow. We need something on paper to justify his presence at school."

Miss Rubin repeated Mr. Franklin's word in Yiddish. She got a long answer. When Chatzkel finished, she said to Mr. Franklin: "The boy says you haven't a thing to worry about. His father was a professor at the Warsaw Rabbinic Academy. His grandfather is a Warsaw merchant for Bessarabian lumber. There is nothing at this school he can't handle. He would leave now, but it's his father's first day on a pushcart. It would upset him to see his son out of school. He sent him in for a day of school, and he should get a day of school. He assures you that you have nothing to worry about. He's here to learn English; that's what he'll do, learn English."

Mr. Franklin broke into a strange smile. "He said that?"

"You have a close translation."

"Do you suppose the boy is after my job?"

"Not immediately, but one never knows."

"I wonder what the father is selling on the pushcart."

"Something very simple, I'm sure, shoes or pots and pans."

"At least we've established that he's not retarded. Put him in with Miss Smith's first-grade class on a temporary basis; let him learn a little English."

"If I can presume a suggestion, put him in with Miss Hemenway in the second grade, and don't worry about his English."

"Let her check if his neck is clean; this is on a temporary basis."

"Oh, of course, only on a temporary basis."

Miss Rubin took Chatzkel out. Her Yiddish was German, but Chatzkel thought she was nice for a Yekke. In Miss Hemenway's room, he sat looking out the window, absorbing the sounds of the class, not understanding a word. The instant class ended, before anyone could stop him, he ran out and down the street, where Shaya stood with the pushcart, waiting.

Chatzkel climbed on and burrowed under the clothes, as Shaya cried, "Chatzkel, the clothes are for sale! *Gevald!* What are you doing?"

Moments later, Chatzkel emerged from under the clothes, dressed American.

Shaya took a long look. "The shirt's too big; try a seven."

Chapter Forty-eight

As SHAYA PUSHED THE CART, Chatzkel darted ahead, looking at the goods in disgust. "We sold more just coming to school!"

"People are out in the morning."

"I can't trust you in anything; you weren't reading, were you?"

Shaya lifted his hand helplessly. "No, I wasn't reading."

"I don't want ever to catch you reading: we got to bring *Imah* over."

"Let's go by Yakov Rivers'; I have to make peace for Esther."

Calling and making sales, they pushed past a basement window of an Italian tenement, where a family of fourteen, from a great-grandmother to a five-year-old girl, all sat around a big table, all making ties in exactly the same pattern. At the corner, a farm wagon was unloading barrels of pickles onto pushcarts that pulled away to peddle them, at a penny a pickle.

At the bookstore, Chatzkel watched the wagon; Shaya stepped through the curtain to where Yakov sat at the counter between piles of books—thirty-five, lean, pale, a little anemic, with a thin blond beard, a shock of faded hair, sensitive fingers, and a pointed nose.

Yakov lifted his pinkie in greeting, his face rigid.

Shaya sighed. "You didn't like the Odessa? Esther didn't stay either. You go where you feel comfortable."

Yakov reached over a pile of books for a *tshuves,* a book of responsa on legal questions. "This just came in; what do you think?"

"I studied with Bunim Landau for a year." Shaya opened it and flipped pages, reading here and there. "It's worthless."

"The man doesn't know?"

"Reb Bunim reads everything, he remembers everything, he knows everything, and he lectures seven hours without a break. It's all dancing ideas."

Yakov smiled. "I'll read it for the learning."

An old woman in a babushka entered, touching the mezuzah and kissing her fingers. "A Jewish calendar?"

Yakov pointed to a barrel. She picked one up and examined it.

"How much?"

"A nickel."

"It's too much."

She put down three pennies, touched the mezuzah, and shuffled out.

"Nathan Finesilver arranged the Odessa meeting. We were in the Yeshiva together. He said Esther could get a waitress job there."

The mention of the Yeshiva stirred Yakov's memory. "What's with Azriel Tomashevsky? Of the really poor boys, only he stayed, a fighter."

"Azriel was my study partner; he works now as a shochet."

Sensing that Yakov was relaxing, Shaya spoke more directly. "The minute she stepped inside the café, Esther felt the mistake. You're a good man, Yakov. You need a woman who can look after a man, give him food, leave him alone. Esther meant no harm, sending you there. Nathan called it a good place. He's a fool, Nathan."

Yakov sat still, but he relaxed several shades. A porter pushed inside, asking for prayer books for the Talmud Torah. Yakov pointed.

He relaxed in the barrel. "How much for forty?"

"Seven dollars."

"Essex Street has for six."

"Give me five."

The porter counted out forty into a sack, deposited four single dollars and change, and strode out. Still a bit formal, Yakov reached into his file.

"This letter is from a Warshaver. His brother died childless; the brother's wife needs a special divorce to remarry. I wrote for the Belzer Society; he answered, saying nothing but blaming her for his brother's coming to America."

"That's no answer."

"No answer is an answer of no."

Shaya stroked his beard. "Send a copy of the brother's letter to the new Belzer gabbai, and say, if the brother denies her a release, and in despair she remarries anyway, the sin of adultery and the illegitimate children are on his head for not intervening."

Yakov looked up. "It'll work? The gabbai doesn't answer our letters. We beg him for instructions, and we receive not a line in return. The members feel cut off."

"Write a legal letter about adultery. Request nothing; demand an answer in Jewish law. I would write myself, but Avrom Aaron told my father-in-law to sit in mourning over me. When he apologizes, I'll write to him."

"I'll write the letter."

Shaya stepped closer. "And something else. Get Esther a job in a good café. She shouldn't be behind a sewing machine. You know café people. Make Esther happy. Don't harbor a grudge. She respects you, Esther."

"Why does the Rebbe hate us? And this city is full of idiots worse than in Warsaw, idiot Jews. It's so empty, America; you have no idea. You just have no idea. What is there to say? Exile."

"Yakov, work, marry, give God joy, and there is no emptiness."

Shaya reached out. Yakov reached up hesitantly. Suddenly he took Shaya's hand and kissed it. Shaya stood patiently.

"Come by tonight. You'll take Esther to a café where she might get a job. She asked that you come by for her. And harbor no grudges."

Shaya stepped outside. The pushcart was stripped bare; Shaya clutched his breast in panic. Chatzkel held out a small bundle of money.

Shaya's eyes widened. "You sold all that?"

"I told some mothers their kids looked like greenhorns."

181

"You shouldn't frighten people."

"Should we go back to Kutch for another load?"

"It's enough for the day. We'll go home. I'll give you a Bible lesson."

Shaya pushed the cart toward Hester Street, as Chatzkel danced restlessly around him. "How do you like New York?" he asked Chatzkel.

"We should be on a farm."

"This is better than nothing."

"If I had a choice, I'd pick nothing."

"Your mother will come over, and you'll feel better."

They passed a shawled woman sitting on the street, holding a bundle of clothes, three children clinging to her, and a plate before her on the ground.

Shaya stopped a man standing in the doorway behind them. "How much was her rent?"

The man gave him a hard look. "Two dollars."

Shaya counted out two dollars. "Get her back inside."

Shaya started down the street with Chatzkel clutching his coat, his eyes burning with indignation. Shaya was giving away the money he earned to bring his mother over, she should come before strange women. His father was a holy idiot. Shaya caressed his son's head as they walked. He knew what was bothering him and had no explanation, but he couldn't leave a woman abandoned on the street, and with children. He just couldn't do it.

Chapter Forty-nine

As Esther washed, dried, and stacked their supper dishes in the glass cabinet over the sink on Hester Street, Shaya nailed Nehemia's mezuzah, shaped like a medieval tower, on the doorpost. When he finished, Chatzkel dragged him to the backstairs to rooms organized like barracks, with rows of hammocks, where lodgers paid by the bed for a night's lodging. Both were disturbed; a Warsaw home lasted for a lifetime, and here lodging was no more permanent than a train station. Shaya insisted their door never be left open.

As her two men explored the building, Esther, behind her screen, dressed for the evening. Her day's chores were over; she had served a good supper. Shaya had made fresh contact with Yakov; she could work in a café after all. She felt a giddy pitch of excitement, the more joyous since she was soon meeting Yakov, her destined groom.

Her voice sang out. "Chartreuse on my nails, Shaya?"

"Why is that a problem?"

"Rivington Street didn't like it."

"Hungarian Jews."

"I can?"

"Give yourself pleasure, Esther."

Chatzkel heard Esther's little giggle of pleasure behind her screen. He gave Shaya a dissatisfied look and returned to his Bible.

"Shaya, remember Aphrodita's bloomers?"

"Her what?"

"Her bloomers, from her London fashion newsletter. You brought a pair from the parlor to Radich. Could I wear them tonight?"

"They're clothes?"

"They're underwear."

"Your underwear is your own business."

Chatzkel heard another squeal of pleasure. Esther swept from behind her screen in her bloomers and stays, slim, flexible leather shoes with three-quarter heels over the ankle, and a petticoat top. Her eyes danced. She felt the future taking shape inside her.

Esther thrust her fingers at Shaya. "Tell me they're beautiful!" She angled up her ankle. "And these shoes too." She danced over to Chatzkel, kissed him on top of his head as he waved her off with a grudging smile, and swept back behind her screen.

Shaya looked up. "I'm not sure about the bloomers."

"You said I could wear them."

"They're pants. A woman wearing pants is like a man wearing a dress."

"They don't feel like pants to me; they feel like bloomers."

"But they are pants. Women are different; they should dress differently. Otherwise people get confused; it can lead to trouble."

"But bloomers are underwear; nobody sees them under a skirt."

"Knowing they're there can give Yakov ideas."

"I wouldn't dream of telling him."

"Just wearing them can give you ideas."

"Any ideas I can get from a pair of bloomers, I have already."

Shaya fell silent. Chatzkel gave him a look of absolute disgust. Satisfied with the bloomers, Esther began to wrap extra layers of fabric under her breasts to raise them. "So Yakov is getting me a job?"

"He knows the café people."

"Oh, I love him already! But a bookseller?! They're so papery. Will he come alive for me, Shaya?"

"It's up to you, Esther."

"You're not sure?"

"No, I'm not sure."

"He needs a Yiddishe mameh?"

"He's starved for one, but don't overdo it. He's very smart."

"Being starved for a mother has nothing to do with brains."

Esther lifted the fabric higher under her breasts. She turned this way and that, looking at herself, and began looking for the right gown.

"How tall is he?"

He smiled up. "He's just your height."

"You're taller than he is," Chatzkel murmured.

"What's his beard like?"

"Thin, sandy brown, the color of straw."

"It's not a goat beard, is it?"

"Not really. He's very skinny, very pale."

"It is a goat beard," Chatzkel squealed.

"He sounds a little anemic."

"He'll come to life faster than a good dowry."

"I suppose."

"You have a good meeting with Aaron's brother?"

"The Belzer have a loan fund for new arrivals, enough to buy me a new pushcart. These Belzer have a starvation for Kedusha, a hunger for holiness. When I left, Yakov kissed my hand."

Esther frowned. Shaya sounded oddly complacent. He was becoming a rabbi too fast, without having really thought about it. She pulled out a pale silver gown with black lace sewed over one hip.

There was a knock. As she slipped the gown over her head and began going at the snaps, Shaya opened the door and Yakov entered, wearing a Western suit with a high collar, his hair rising in front under his derby. He looked pale, uncomfortable, shy, pessimistic, and very wary.

Shaya poured a glass of wine. "Esther will be a minute."

"I was just with the sick committee. Goldfeld is getting worse.

His wife wants a *kvitel* for his bedroom, but where will we get one here?"

Shaya drew him closer. "You're a scribe, Yakov. The store has old *kvitels*. Copy one out on fresh parchment with Gold-feld's name."

Yakov's eyes widened. "You have power to sign it?"

"If it brings hope to the family."

"I'll copy it out in the morning. The family will pay, of course."

"We'll divide the money between us."

Yakov gasped and rose to his feet. Esther had entered in all her radiance. Shaya gestured her not to overpower him, to keep it casual. She smiled back at him, telling him not to worry; she wanted him overpowered, in fact overwhelmed. Then suddenly she realized she was wearing the dress she had always worn at the Warsaw parlor. She must really want Yakov to give her babies, she thought.

Smiling with womanly pleasure, Esther approached her groom.

Chapter Fifty

MIST THICKENED along the gutters, swam against the tenement windows, trickled along the walks, carrying coal dust and the smell of fish. Three twelve-year-olds curled in a cellarway, ragged scarfs around their necks, caps pulled over their ears.

Walking down Hester Street with Yakov, Esther asked her angel to hover a little closer and breathe a blessing. They were on a first walk together, overdressed and unsure of what was supposed to happen, moving like two whole matzohs leaning together in a box. An orphan, Yakov had little grace. He was so skinny; if a storm wind shook him, Esther thought, he would clank. Could he shift around and keep on his feet? The street felt derelict; the evening would be a disaster.

People stared as Esther passed. This was the hour for street-walkers. Wearing this dress, she felt she might as well carry a sign. Yakov was too inexperienced to notice, but she shuddered to think about what would happen when she entered the café. At least Yakov was her escort; women in his hands stayed innocent.

At that hour, advanced women visited the cafés, women who were editors, sketch-writers, intellectuals. Their clothes were individual, quieter, more subtle. Should she have dressed like this? But she wasn't advanced or quietly subtle. All she needed was to sit down in a café in an opaque silver-gray gown. A man would lean over and say something witty about Tolstoy. She would look at him. She was the balloon rented out to children. She wrote songs, so did the badchan at Shaya's wedding. She had talent, but what does talent have to do with being advanced? Nothing. Was Tolstoy advanced? Probably not. She was just an ordinary Jewish girl who got into trouble. Not that anybody really cared, but she cared.

Esther fought hard not to burst into tears; she swung her free hand in frustration, growling out loud.

Yakov looked up, suspicious. "You all right?"

"Not really."

"Yeah, I know."

Esther frowned. Why was America so difficult? In Warsaw, your father made a *shiddach*. The contract was signed, and you got acquainted. First came a hard thing, the contract, then a soft thing, getting acquainted, which was always accomplished with a sense of security and *tachlis*. Here you waste your time running around in circles getting acquainted, and to get acquainted with no sense of *tachlis* was crazy.

Esther suddenly looked down and realized she had worn this dress when Nathan visited the parlor, with its snaps loose so she could relax. It had practically fallen off when she brought Nathan a glass of wine. She wished she could loosen the snaps now. If she had worn Rachel's shawl to cover, maybe she could have.

Esther squinted guardedly at Yakov. Chatzkel was right, of course. She was taller than Yakov, and he had a goat beard. She probably weighed more, and she was no Warsaw wet-nurse. His skin was dry; he would need a lotion after he washed himself. But Shaya was right; those were beautiful hands. She could practically feel them. If Yakov kept that wary presence, he probably wanted a child-woman. He was at that age. He wasn't making a move. There was no help for it; making acquaintance was up to her.

"Shaya tells me you grew up in the Warsaw home."

Yakov flashed her a guarded look but Esther ignored it and took his arm. "At least you had a home. My father wandered all over Galicia from the time of his Bar Mitzvah. He was a real vagabond. Then he married my mother, and his wanderings were over."

Yakov winced. "Every morning, we had a slice of day-old

186

bread. The beadle spread butter and then scraped it all off with a knife. We got what was left after the scraping was over."

Esther sighed. "Nothing like that will happen to a child of mine."

"He took home our leftovers, and he made sure he always had leftovers. He used bread hard as a rock, and scraped until nothing was left but what was in the little air holes."

"What a cruel man."

"Mrs. Gavrilovitch was a nightmare; she called us dirty, sneaky, sly. She kept going over our linen. She once accused me of doing it in bed when she mixed up my linen with Yasha Korn's."

"Well, did you tell her?"

"And make trouble for Yosh?"

"And what was before the house?"

"My *abah* had a dairy, and brought milk to Warsaw on his wagon. My mother ran off. He died. They sold the cow and put me in a house."

"I lived on a chicken farm; my father sold in the Warsaw market too."

Yakov nodded. "We're going to the Pinchas Strauss. I told Feder about you. He was interested—in the job, I mean."

"Shaya was saying what a good man you are, how he relies on you."

Yakov hunched up, resisting the compliment as he drank it up. As they turned onto Canal Street, three editors passed them, arguing strenuously if Yiddish was a language. Esther smiled happily; she had made contact with Yakov.

Esther licked her lips. "It's so strange, the way people come to America—what they want, what they expect to happen. They have no idea what will happen to them, only that they need to get out. Poland is a pollution. They escape it, and suddenly they're in America. But what's America? That's the question we finally have to ask: what's America?"

"Yakov Rivers?! You sport! And you have company."

A vigorous man strode across the street, his hands slashing the air as he walked, his raccoon coat flapping open. Red-eyed, his gaunt, knobby cheeks were dotted with acne. His beard had a point that matched the ends of his mustache.

Yakov broke into a helpless giggle. "Esther? This is Wolfe Abramov. He's assistant principal of the Yiddish Folk Schule."

Wolfe corrected with decision. "Associate, not assistant. I told the last board meeting: I assist nobody. But the Newark folk-schule wants me as principal. You must join your brother as their communal organizer."

Yakov tapped his foot. "Well I'm thinking about it."

Wolfe banged his head. "You're thinking? Thinking is the Jewish curse. They thought in Jerusalem while the Romans scattered salt on the ruins. They thought in Spain as the Inquisition burned them alive. They thought in Poland as Napoleon marched across Europe. The Jew has been thinking for the last two thousand years. It gets to be a bore after a while."

Esther turned to look at Yakov and suddenly gasped. Yakov had disappeared on her. He couldn't stand Wolfe and simply ran off.

Wolfe gestured all around. "These Jews frustrate me; they never show their money. They fear an evil eye. You never know who is starving and who has a nest egg under his mattress as a down payment on a store. They all live like paupers. Come, I'll take you to the Pinchas Strauss. You need somebody who knows his way around."

Esther had misgivings, but she needed a job. Yakov had already spoken to the manager. He was interested. She was going in.

Chapter Fifty-one

AFTER THE ODESSA, the Pinchas Strauss seemed big, noisy, and crowded with riffraff intelligentsia, but Esther felt right at home. It had lamps instead of candles and a sawdust floor. The tables were too close, the ceiling too low, the parties too pushy. A piano hugged the wall. Guests mixed and let go, hunting for a connection or some new political line, or just wanting to shake off a parasite.

Nathan was against the far wall with a woman with eyeglasses identical to his. This must be his Jewish shikseh, one of those women who demanded nothing, aspired to nothing, and won every time. Nathan gestured hello, then leaned over and whispered. The woman gave Esther a long amused stare, but only to satisfy Nathan; Esther didn't interest her at all. She got up without a word. Esther sensed he had told her to leave.

She felt sluggish and uncomfortable. For all his vanity, Wolfe didn't know his way about a café; he hesitated to take an empty table. She would dump him soon. Nathan studied her with his usual suave amusement. Did he recognize her dress? His mind was impossible to read.

188

The café manager, Feder Strauss, was Yakov's age, and probably had known him in Warsaw. He had a black suit, a German cap, a flat shaved face with deep trenches above his bearded jowls.

Esther waved. Feder strode slowly over.

"You're Feder Strauss?"

"I have the pleasure?"

"I'm Esther Kramer; Yakov Rivers mentioned you."

"Yakov is a very agreeable man; you wanted some kind of work?"

"I can be a waitress, a cook, even an assistant manager. Just give me an honest wage. I managed my own place in Warsaw."

"Yakov said you sing."

"Your piano is in tune?"

"Take a table with Wolfe; I'll come back."

As they sat down, Esther noticed Feder watching her. She wished she had come in with better company. Wolfe took out a pipe and tobacco pouch and began pounding in tobacco. Someone at the next table slid back into his chair. Wolfe looked furious and refused to make room.

He made a face. "Yakov's problem is that he's a *shmatte;* wherever you put him, he'll wipe the table. The Torah is Yakov's curse; he lives his life to God's formula. This is life in a balloon, with no human contact. The law is the hunch on the Jewish back. We Yiddish educators give your children a real philosophy of life, a people, a language, a soil. If Nietzsche spoke Yiddish, I'd introduce him to our senior class."

A voice sang out: "She never heard of William Shakespeare, and she's talking. Can you imagine?"

Esther smiled warily. "You're going to Newark?"

"Newark is the Paris of Yiddish culture, a jewel, a living jewel."

Esther cocked her head. "Newark may be the Paris of Yiddish culture; the question is, is Paris the Newark of French culture?"

Wolfe exploded in laughter. "That I call a *shtoch!* I'll introduce you to our senior class."

Wolfe's chair got banged again. He refused to move. At the next table, a writer was pushing an article on public health onto a Socialist editor of a monthly.

The editor resisted. "Batsheva Kalb has that column for herself; she's a very fine journalist, very conscientious. She has a following."

The writer clapped his brow in dismay. "And you call yourself a Socialist? Batsheva Kalb is an elitist, without touch with the people. Her theory of germs is a luxury for the rich who don't have to work for a living. I have a scandal that will tear the ghetto apart, if you're interested."

"And what's the scandal?"

"You know where used clothing comes from? A man stops breathing; the family strips him of his clothes to pay the funeral costs. No ghetto man or woman sells a rag they can still wear. And you know what ghetto Jews die of? Typhus, smallpox, tuberculosis, whooping cough. The next day, his clothing goes on a pushcart, the blood not yet washed out of it. There's talk that the Health Inspector . . ."

"Enough. Write a news story on public health; I'll publish it."

"And then we'll have another conversation on Batsheva's column; I haven't given up on that."

Glancing back, Esther noticed Aphrodita at the table behind her laughing attentively with two wealthy clothing men. She kept talking, cool and distant, waiting for Esther to make the first move. Then she was a kept woman, Esther thought. She had believed that coming to America would make Aphrodita go straight.

Esther leaned back, nudged her, and whispered. "Are you still Aphrodita?"

"I'm Sarah Cohen again."

Wolfe saw Esther getting involved with another table. His chair nudged from a fresh direction, he rose and waited for Esther to tell him to sit down again. She ignored him. He walked right out of the café.

Esther half turned. "What happened to Marcella?" Aphrodita asked. "My brother got me out of the country before I could hear anything."

"Well after the pogrom, she was in the hospital and started seeing devils; nobody could come near her. They finally put her in a home."

"And Donila, our street scout?"

"Her brother heard that his men had her; he killed her in a rage."

"So only you and I made it out alive."

"Silverberg's money got me to New York, but my husband insisted he never laid eyes on me. After twenty minutes over a sewing machine, I got back to my Warsaw ways."

"Are you angry at him?"

"Why waste my time? Let him stew in his own juices."

190

Esther patted her hand. "You look terrific; you got where to live?"

Aphrodita nudged the man next to her. "Harry keeps me; he pays all my food bills and gives me little surprises. You want to know Max, the man he's with? I already know he likes you."

Harry stepped over, turned Esther's chair around, and pushed her into the table. "Sure, join the party. I like that; I really like that."

As Esther and Aphrodita sat side by side, not understanding a word, patiently waiting to be noticed, Harry resumed his conversation with the other man in English, gesturing strenuously, showing bulky rings:

"Why do you suppose we came down here? We can talk figures in your office. You stay too locked up in channels. You don't know what these people can do; you don't talk their language."

"I trust channels."

"America is too big for channels; it overflows them every time."

Harry swung around hard and spoke Yiddish. "Your name, *bubeleh?*"

Esther clasped her hands. "Esther Kramer."

"That's nice; yeah, it's good. Did you hear that, Max? Esther Kramer. *Ketzeleh,* sit over by Max and make him relax. He's giving me a hard time, this *bandeet.*"

Esther smiled and nodded without moving, suddenly brainless, a girl waiting, on call. When the man turned on, she responded; when the man turned off, she shut up again. She felt afloat, effortlessly moving. Yakov was first in her evening, then Wolfe, and now Harry Kahane. She didn't mind; it was a free country.

Harry turned to Max. "When I say these immigrants work, I don't just mean a full day, fourteen hours under the sun like a Kansas farmhand. These people are around-the-clock fanatics. It's time to eat? One hand keeps working the scissors. The baby's hungry? The breast comes out over the sewing machine. I swear they work in their sleep."

"The Broadway shops are too organized to crack."

"Well, this neighborhood will crack them. Look, Max, all I want out of you is a fifteen-grand investment. You throw money like that on the tracks. This is a new population. You don't know what Jews and Italians can do. Look at the body on this one. You won't even have to talk to her; she won't understand you anyway. You'll use sign language."

Harry swung back to Esther. "How long are you over, *faygeleh?*"

Esther clasped her hands again. "A couple of days."

"How do you like that, Max; two days, and she's already on the job. Show him your teeth like pearls, *zisseleh,* and your eyes like stars."

Harry snapped his fingers as Esther grinned hard. "What did I tell you, Max? These girls know how to get down to elementals."

He swung back again. "You and Sarah worked together in Warsaw?"

Esther tossed her head. "Who remembers Warsaw?"

"That's good; I like that, yeah. You heard what she said, Max? Who remembers Warsaw? Forget the past; this a new world. Oh, they're darling people! Where did you grow up, *bubeleh?*"

"On a chicken farm."

"What do you think of that, Max? She grew up on a chicken farm. Get Esther a room, nickels for food, a cotton blouse. Work out a language, and she'll be your contact. You'll get real service."

Max worked his ring. "The Broadway outfits will slap on six injunctions from child labor to public health."

"They'll stop America? First tell the ocean not to flow."

"What does that mean?"

"It means these people take work home. No injunction can stop you on child labor or anything else. You got six women on machines? After ten hours, each one takes a bundle on her head to finish at home. Her six kids work through the night. By morning, your order is ready to ship, with zero overhead. And these people can live on twenty-five cents a day."

Max twisted his ring so the stone faced his palm. "Labor is never a problem. Every farm girl knows how to put in a day's work."

"Not like these people. And more come in all the time from Riga and Lodz and Warsaw. Forget the Broadway shops. You open on Essex Street, where the labor is. In five years, the Broadway shops will be finished."

Max shook his head. "You forget the Warsaw unions. You build an industry with Socialist labor. You start out big; in three years, they'll organize and you'll wish you were on Broadway."

"In Warsaw, they had nothing to do with their time, so they talked Socialism. Here they're too busy taking night courses in English. What'll the unions organize? The tenement Jews? We'll give the help subcontracts with their relatives and that's the end of the union. Besides, we can bust any organization they'll set up. You just fire the lot of them and take fresh help off the next boat. My connections tell me this can go on for another fifty years. You got a pocket of Calcutta right here in New York. Where will they go? There's no way back to Warsaw and the shtetl through Ellis Island."

Esther felt at loose ends. Unsure what to do, she stepped around the table, gave Max a warm kiss, and then slipped around the café to Nathan's table; but Feder Strauss beckoned her behind the counter.

"O.K. Your job is on. The dreck Abramov soured me on you, but you dumped him fast, and those two rich men at the back table. I like a woman who knows how to move. Dress quieter next time. I'll pay two dollars a night. I owe Yakov the favor, but tell him I don't want the society to meet here on a Thursday night. Two other societies come in on Thursday. He changes his benefit to a Sunday night, or the deal is off."

"I'll tell him."

"You could sing tonight, but this crowd likes to talk. You sing, everybody listens, and then they all go home. I've seen that happen. You're here to work, but you'll sing when the crowd is right. Then you'll get an extra dollar. But arrange the Sunday night with Yakov."

As Esther sat down nearer to Nathan, she could feel a huge, lazy pleasure in Nathan's body as he lolled in his chair, preparing to try to seduce her. She stiffened herself, wanting to avoid any trouble.

"You got the job?"

"I start tomorrow night."

"I just got fired. I took too much time off for Shaya."

Esther followed Nathan out in a daze, but suddenly he was ignoring her. It threw her off balance.

"That was your eyeglass woman you were with. What did you do, tell her to leave?"

Nathan's face had a coarse grin. "Yeah, she never gets sticky."

He began fingering the black lace on her dress. Esther felt a little relieved. She smiled ruefully, preparing to fend him off. "You remember the dress, don't you?"

Nathan grinned broadly and didn't answer, but then at her door he simply said good night and continued up the stairs. It irritated her. What was he talking about Jewish shiksehs? There

193

are no Jewish shiksehs; Jewish women are loyal. It was he that was a Jewish shegetz. He was a nothing. Esther nodded with satisfaction at the thought and went right to sleep.

Chapter Fifty-two

IN THE MORNING, Esther woke hearing Shaya and Chatzkel behind the partition as they finished praying. She tied the robe around herself and stepped around the partition, glancing at Chatzkel suspiciously. She yanked him under the window and bent down his collar. Determined that no gentile teacher find her child dirty, she threw him on the bed, stripped and washed him in the iron basin with a bar of soap as he screamed against the cold water.

As Chatzkel dressed, Esther told Shaya how Yakov disappeared on the street when Wolfe showed up. Her job depended on his shifting the theater benefit to a Sunday night.

Shaya broke into a moody smile. "He liked you?"

"He disappeared on me, but first he told me about his childhood."

"Then it's a *shiddach*."

"I think so."

Esther gave them breakfast and went back to sleep. It threw her off-balance, how Nathan said good night casually and didn't try anything. She had braced herself and felt like a fool. She was furious.

Shaya hurried out with Chatzkel. It seemed early, but once they got to the stable, Kutch was irritated at their coming late. He had pushcarts on the street already. He liked a peddler who started early and sold three loads a day. If Shaya couldn't hustle children's clothing, he should sell something simple like suspenders.

Shaya glanced at the long row of waiting pushcarts. So Kutch was another *shvitzer*. They got the cart out and pushed it for an hour, crying out their goods, Chatzkel jumping from side to side and spotting potential customers.

Shaya was patient, but the crowded streets gave him no pleasure. To keep up his spirits, he practiced cantorial pieces under his breath. Hearing him, Chatzkel tried an accompaniment, though he had no voice. Shaya silenced him with a look, and the street smells enveloped the boy—stale meat, skewered chickens, leavings of herring, and horse droppings.

Chatzkel resented Shaya's weakness in business. Both knew Shaya would have no chance of seeing Rachel again without Chatzkel's help; he might even starve to death. Yet Shaya felt only compassion for his son. The boy would never be a scholar, read a book with wisdom or explore an idea. Business had captured his soul.

After an hour of peddling, the breakfast shoppers were gone; children swarmed on all sides to school, their knapsacks on their backs, the straps crossed on their chests. Chatzkel instructed Shaya to avoid side streets and not to read. And Shaya should be there when school let out. He wished he could step out at recess and see how Shaya was doing.

Practicing the *Kol Nidre* under his breath, Shaya headed off alone for Yakov's shop to sign the *kvitel* and see to Esther's business about changing the theater night. He also wanted information on the Belzer building fund; until the building was up, he would get no salary.

As Shaya disappeared down the street, Chatzkel found his way to Felicity Hemenway's class. Felicity was tall, with flaxen hair, and very advanced in her thinking. She was politically aware, and supported candidates, even though she had no right to vote. She wore a Yankee tweed suit, read a steady stream of women's books, and had a warmth about as personal as a stove; yet she was wise enough to let Chatzkel work at his own pace.

Cleanliness was a school problem. To address it, all the children started the day by reciting together:

> *We keep clean bodies,*
> *And we soap our hands.*
> *We breathe clean air*
> *In a beautiful land.*

Miss Hemenway looked hard at Chatzkel. Moving in front of his desk, she managed to lift back his collar and look underneath. Then she continued her rounds.

The day before, Chatzkel ran out so fast that he eluded her, but this time Miss Hemenway stopped him in his tracks at the recess bell. "I'm Quaker, but you Jews are a Biblical people. We have so much to teach each other." Understanding her tone but not her words, Chatzkel nodded respectfully, as Miss Hemenway crossed the hall to Miss Rubin's desk to share her impressions of the unusual child.

Out in the yard, Chatzkel stayed aloof from the play. A fat,

195

motherly, overdressed girl named Leah Rabinowitz, with pig-tails and frizzy eyebrows, began pointing to things and telling him their English names. She reached in her bag, took out a piece of strudel wrapped in paper, and held it out. Chatzkel gave her a long look, and then ate it. She said she would bring him some *tagel*. She showed Chatzkel a letter she kept from her father in Warsaw, demanding a ticket to America.

Leah told Chatzkel that a shop manager kept her mother. She allowed it and also worked for him because she was so desperate to bring over her husband. Leah was sent down to the street whenever he paid a visit. Chatzkel didn't approve of such talk, but he listened patiently and said nothing. Leah ate a lot; she was very motherly.

A few blocks away, Shaya stepped into Yakov's shop. As he approached the counter, Yakov held out a letter. Shaya opened it and read:

To my saintly and beloved husband, whom this letter should find arrived safely and in peace. The children are well and strong. Simcha is growing into a beautiful child, and with your eyes. I now realize that his name is Simcha to foreshadow our coming joy.

We learned that Uncle Tevya's son in Vienna was accepted for training by a leading voice teacher. My heart bleeds for your great talent stillborn, like so many in the ghetto.

Your sister Feigeleh, whom we thought never to see again, appeared with a daughter, Chaneleh. She is frightfully thin, a fanatic Zionist and a Socialist who thinks everything we do is evil. She thinks Jewish life in exile has made us all parasites. I certainly hope no anti-Semite talks to her and gets ideas. I have enough trouble now staying alive. She came with two friends, both members of her Zionist group. They are constantly together, as if solitude is a form of pride.

Her Zionist movement is starting a farm somewhere in Palestine, so as to live off the land. Raphael, who brought her into the movement, has no sense of responsibility. When he saw where they were going, he quit the movement and now teaches Hebrew in a Warsaw school.

Nehemia went to Warsaw and forced Raphael to give Feigeleh a Jewish divorce. She now blames Nehemia for everything that has happened to her. She says nothing, but the atmosphere is frightening. Thank God I am here with the children to remind him that he still has a family.

Feigeleh left with her group yesterday, leaving Chaneleh with me. There is smallpox and other diseases where they are going.

Feigeleh got on the train with the mark of death on her face. Chaneleh is now our child. Raphael will never have her. I will bring her.

Shaya broke into a wail, the tears streaming down his cheeks. Yakov looked up. "It's bad news?"

"I have one more ticket to buy; I'll never see my wife again."

Chapter Fifty-three

ESTHER ROSE LATE and then shopped, planning an early supper so she could visit Yakov's store on her way to work. She made extra—not that Nathan belonged at her table, but if he came she couldn't turn him away. Esther had noticed how Shaya was starting to roll his eyes up and out of sight when he meditated, and as she walked the street it bothered her; yet she enjoyed keeping the family going, and she felt no pressure to bring Rachel over, not with Chatzkel becoming her son.

Nathan came to dinner as a matter of course it seemed, and the men shared personal news. Shaya got from Yakov his first *kvitel* to sign, and bought a pushcart from him for half a dollar; a Belzer peddler had died. Nathan talked endlessly about their various classmates scattered across Europe. Miriam's letters kept him in contact. He ignored Esther completely. After supper, he mentioned the way families took single men on as boarders. He was now without a job; if Shaya agreed, he would pay a few cents a night for a bed and also contribute for the food.

Esther fought for self-control. "He sleeps with me, you, or Chatzkel?"

Nathan looked up with amused disdain. "I'll move in my own bed."

Esther felt vaguely ashamed for being selfish. But it occurred to her that Nathan could get another job. If he was moving in, it was to sleep with her. He wouldn't have to lift a finger; he would just position himself there, and sooner or later he thought she would come to him.

Esther changed her clothes behind the partition and stepped out an advanced woman. If someone at the Pinchas Strauss mentioned Tolstoy, she would slowly smile, and then say, "Tolstoy is very interesting"—because if Tolstoy had one thing in

197

common with Napoleon, Herzl, Mozart, the Bible, and Nehemia's chicken farm, it was that they were all interesting.

Esther's shoes were too heavy, but she didn't care. She dressed advanced so Nathan should notice her outfit, not that anything would happen—he obviously preferred the Jewish shikseh. Shaya was too much the presumptuous patriarch, making her available to Nathan like that. She didn't even know why he did it—to keep his household comfortable, or to have evidence when he wrote to Rachel. She was preparing to marry Yakov, but after all the frustration Nathan was causing her, her dressing advanced might just frustrate him.

Esther left the house, walked five blocks, and stepped into Yakov's shop; Yakov was in his kapote, a big yarmulke on his head, leaning on the counter, unmoving.

"What is it?" Esther asked with a hushed voice.

"I arrived with a *kvitel,* and found Goldfeld dead."

"They'll still pay for your *kvitel.* They ordered it; you wrote it and delivered it. It's their responsibility."

"To press it would hurt the society. But we have another problem. The building fund was toward a synagogue, but the Goldfelds now want a cemetery lot to rest their father on Belzer ground. An emergency meeting is called for tonight. I don't think it can be stopped."

"No synagogue, no job for Shaya?"

"It'll come, but more slowly; he's still our rabbi."

"And what happened the last time you left a woman stranded on the street, the way you left me last night?"

"I was never on the street with a woman before. People talked *shiddachs* for years, but you're the first woman who wasn't an idiot."

"Well, don't do it to me again."

Esther looked around at the musty stacks of books and elaborate society records, the unmade cot, the water pump, the single change of clothing, the few dishes. Yakov belonged among his records; he was an institutional man. Other things were bleached out of his mind. To marry him was a step backward, but she still wanted to have her own baby.

Esther had a tart smile. "Wolfe can *hack a chainik* about schools."

Yakov grinned dryly. "In Warsaw he had dignity. A lot of people turn into fools on Ellis Island. In Poland, they worked and prayed. Here they don't know what to pray for; it turns them into idiots."

"Feder offered me a job. I start tonight, on condition you change the theater benefit from Thursday to Sunday."

"I'll announce it at tonight's meeting."

Esther gave him a moody look. "Shaya didn't tell you, did he? I have a past. You should know if we're to be serious about each other."

"You were never married?"

"Never."

Yakov bowed over his hands. "Esther, a long time ago I knew no woman would ever love me. Maybe my brother Ariel loved me. My aunt wanted to raise one of us, and she picked Ariel; I got put in the home. Real love doesn't come in an orphanage. Marriage wasn't made for an orphan like me. You're a noble woman from a real family, born to love; so you loved. Tell me nothing; I don't want to know. Just sharing your life is a gift from the Almighty."

Esther felt flooded with warmth. "Yakov, start taking me to the theater. When I come by, I'll bring you things you'll enjoy."

Esther stepped out, shaken by Yakov's decency. He fooled himself in nothing. He was the father she wanted for her children.

Esther went to work at the Pinchas Strauss. She got a sense of Feder's desperate poverty, how he sent every spare penny back to Warsaw to bring over his family. He wore a shirt with a false front that opened down the back, and a single celluloid collar for shirt after shirt that he wiped clean with a damp cloth. He kept in constant touch with his café.

Her first night was Socialist party benefit night. Their journalists were worked up about the *Tageblatt,* the established daily, whose Germanic Yiddish demeaned the ghetto reader. Their only *Arbeiter Zeitung* used a Polish Yiddish, Warsaw *mamaloshen,* but it was a weekly. The new *Jewish Daily Forward* was too communal, and so would betray Socialism. Only a daily had an impact, but a real Socialist daily would get no readers.

Abraham Cahan stepped in with five associates. Feder immediately pushed two tables together and told Esther to give them close attention. His visit was worth fifty customers.

Minutes later, a Yiddish theater crowd swarmed in, after seeing Shakespeare on Second Avenue; who ever heard of such a thing, *Romeo and Juliet* on the Lower East Side? Beggars, charity collectors, political activists slipped in off the street, many in rags, circulating from table to table, asking clothing for a cripple, support for an orphanage, adherence to Zionist labor. Feder allowed them as long as they didn't make pests of themselves.

Coming home late that night, Esther unlocked the door quietly and entered. Nathan had a bed on her side of the partition. Esther undressed quietly with her back turned. Exhausted, she fell asleep immediately, enveloped by Shaya's spirit, with her marriage and children before her.

Chapter Fifty-four

SHAYA KNEW that business was not for him and resented his son for being a natural at it. Maneuvering his pushcart over the cobbled streets, he stitched a wedding waltz onto a Chasidic march; the Napoleonic kick brought tears to his eyes, and he was oblivious to customers as they shouted for service and waved to his passing pushcart.

Jarred by the crowded avenues, Shaya took deserted alleyways, past blocks being emptied out and subdivided for tenements. By now, Shaya recognized a new arrival on sight and had a list of instructions ready. Warsaw was a network of passageways, but New York streets continued until they disappeared, and everywhere herds of Jews sank roots and struggled to get away to a better life. Shaya knew the Lower East Side wouldn't support a Polish rabbi, but he wheeled his pushcart with vigor, his mind on higher things. Occasionally he was stopped on the street for a word or a piece of advice. If it was a crank or a nudnik, he listened patiently, scratching under his Cossack hat, and then walked on, imperturbable as before.

At the Belzer storefront south of Houston Street, they sometimes stood in the street, grabbing at passersby for a tenth for a minyan. At prayers, groans of loneliness rose for their families in Poland. Over the back table, the batlanim spent hours devising strategies for their letters home. Regularly they sent the Rebbe group letters, asking the gabbai to visit; their letters were uniformly ignored.

One influential fanatic didn't like what he saw in America—grown women with their heads uncovered, when it is written "Women's hair is venereal." He trusted neither the kosher butchers nor the mikvahs. The separating curtain in the synagogue was too thin. He took the next boat back to Poland. Feeling his departure like a curse, the batlanim clung together, holding on in memory to a lost mother, a fading way of life.

Shaya's life was loose, his thoughts despairing; still, he tasted

New York with an exhilaration. Pushing his cart, Shaya had a haunting memory of his father Nehemia's wanderings before his marriage, the lost-family child who had grown up as an orphan. Shaya felt like a piece of wood torn from the flame; his every spare penny went into the bank. Peddling, he wore his old fleece coat and his Cossack hat, now grown ragged, his knobby gloves, boots like canal barges, and his beard grown wild. The bourgeois frustration he saw all around him made him a Socialist; the Socialist herd made him a Chasid. Chatzkel's eyes made him a failure; the absence of Rachel made him weep. Exalted and a little crazy, he sang under his breath, a total failure and the only happy Polish Jew in New York, who could unfold a *"Lekhah Dodi"* so beautiful that angels hung down from heaven and waved their wings in accompaniment.

At night, Shaya eased his body into his room's only comfortable chair. Chatzkel pulled off his boots one by one and brought his two slippers made of old rugging. They took turns walking to the tub to wash for supper—the big and the little bear, each in his robe.

Chatzkel couldn't let Shaya alone; he was always with him in his own torn and frayed coat. Those were Rachel's instructions—to watch over Shaya and bring her across soon. The streets swarmed with children, but when anyone drew too near, he pressed automatically back to Shaya. Shaya became dependent on him. Chatzkel knew their merchandise better and always bawled Shaya out for selling so little while he was in school. Whenever he dared, Chatzkel played hookey to sell out and do a double load before going home for supper. Chatzkel exulted in his father's closeness, his handsome public presence; as for him, he was the family throwaway.

They lunched on a two-penny roll and ate an early supper like peasants so Esther could get off to work. All of them were forever preparing. Esther was endlessly organizing herself to marry Yakov; Shaya marked time for the Belzer synagogue to open; Chatzkel kept struggling to bring Rachel over. Their lives danced in circles, and all their relationships floundered. All the while Nathan sat nightly at table in a broadcloth shirt with garters on the sleeves, white collar and cuffs, finding fault with his latest employer.

A Polish boy banged into Chatzkel in the hall and tore his shirt. After school, he backed him into a wall and stole a penny. Chatzkel found Shaya and led him to where the boy lived; Shaya hurried, pushing the cart. Chatzkel spotted the boy on the steps. Seeing them coming, the boy backed against the door and returned the penny with a grin. Shaya slapped him hard. He wanted to talk to the boy's mother, but it was a Polish block. They got on the next block fast.

For the next month, Shaya led Chatzkel to school every day and was always at the steps when he got out. It cut down his movements but Shaya couldn't help that. He had to protect his son.

In the winter, as darkness rolled in on the vacant lots, before bonfires of ship planking, rotten barrels, and broken boxes, the shadows of orphans and runaways like that Polish boy jumped in the bitter cold, older boys forced out when the family needed another bed, their growths permanently stunted. They slept in news-office basements, to be shipped west at sixteen on a one-way ticket by a ghetto charity.

As the months dragged on, Shaya began to lose heart. Nothing defined itself for him. Even though he put every spare penny in the bank, he barely had money for a single ticket. He would have joined the synagogue ballanim, but Chatzkel wouldn't leave him alone. And Chatzkel became chipper, impatient, sarcastic. Speaking English, he was the family boss. He blamed Shaya for the divided family. More and more patients hung Shaya's *kvitel* in their sickrooms. Shaya wanted to complain to God—his life wasn't to be endured—but he could no more complain than peddle. He had a street community, even if he made no living. He had the finest wife in the world, even if she was on the other side of the world. Blessings rained down from heaven, even if none of them landed on his head.

Shaya wished he had a horse cart; it would make his life easier. His father had a horse and wagon in Poland; in New York, he was the horse to his own wagon. After a while, he began to complain to the horse he didn't have: "Why did *Tateh* have to open a chicken farm? Can I raise chickens on Orchard Street? If he had joined his uncle in Vienna, maybe I'd be singing today in the Vienna Opera. If I had learned to fix watches, I would have a trade I could use. Think only of yourself, and your children end up with nothing."

Grumbling to the nonexistent horse, Shaya maneuvered his pushcart around and up the next block, crying: "Children's clothes, all new, pants, socks, shirts." He was a Jew making a living.

Chapter Fifty-five

IN NEW YORK, Esther's life got its second wind. While Shaya kept track of Jewish history, Esther traced her own life. In Poland she had waded through crisis after crisis with every strategy arising out of desperation. Now penniless in a strange land, she was out of moral indebtedness. She was no longer running; she had choices to make.

With a family still to bring over, Feder manuevered endlessly to attract ghetto personalities with a following. He had the facilities and worked for a broad and varied clientele. One night, his tables had a Litvak accent; the next night the tables were Galitzianer. In either accent, they said the same vulgarities about each other.

When the café fell quiet, Esther struck a few notes on the piano. The room hushed. She then delivered, "I'm an Ordinary Jewish Girl," "You're in a New World, Brother," or "What Do the Goyim Want?" Her singing—hoarse, articulate, infectious—registered a fresh personality, but she was too brainy and ironic to develop a strong personal following. Listeners didn't rush into the café to hear her, but once they were there they stayed to listen.

Several producers dropped by, fishing for talent, but nobody took her on. In France, she would have a career, but a Yiddish chanteuse needed a following. So her songs hung fire; as Esther cooked, served, and played the piano, she was simply the beautiful Jewess off a Polish shtetl, laden with experience, who never made a disturbance. Every night, some patron insisted on getting personal. Someone from a clientele more suave than Feder's might have won her, but by the time Esther got propositioned she had seen all the preparations from an hour before. In the café, no Jewish male ever took her by surprise. During the week, men fulfilled the injunction, "Six days shalt thou labor"; on the Sabbath they resolved to "Be fruitful and multiply." Orthodox women made a mystique of conceiving on Friday night, when they had a double soul. The Socialists also believed in productivity. Play seemed somehow childish; it had no *tachlis*.

A week after Esther started, Aphrodita took a back table alone. Esther sat down by her with two glasses of wine.

Aphrodita leaned forward. "Feder has enemies; they're having him deported. It can't be stopped. He was in jail in Warsaw. Had the police known his record, he would have been stopped

cold. Do you have a finger on a dollar? The café is yours when
he gets arrested."

Esther took a long sip. "You want a partnership."

"I'll settle for a decent job; I have to break out of this."

"You come clean or dirty?"

"I come clean."

"We'll do it." Esther said, erasing what she knew from her
mind.

At home, Esther related to Nathan with few inhibitions, but
she belonged to Yakov. When she came in, he was asleep or out
for the night. He lay in bed as she got up to look after Shaya
and Chatzkel and then went back to sleep. He then rose and
left, before she woke again for the day.

By now, Esther knew that Nathan found her attractive. She
even suspected that he loved her, seeing him jump when he
heard her unexpectedly. When she came in at night, he sometimes lay facing her bed, breathing lightly. She turned her back
and stood in a dark corner to undress; anything more complicated than that was too much bother. And he seemed to her as
innocent and unreal as a wood nymph; exposing herself to him
seemed not to matter. Besides, she didn't trust herself further
than this.

Living with him in such close quarters, Esther saw Nathan
with enormous clarity. He didn't refuse to work; work just
didn't matter to him. Between jobs, the eyeglass woman maintained him. Others helped also, Esther was sure; he was basically a kept man, but felt in debt to no one. Miriam would come
on her own because she wanted him, to support him through
life, and on his terms.

No longer on the run, Esther was now able to fall in love. She
lit the Sabbath candles in a meditative mood. Sometimes she lay
awake all night, remembering over and over how her dress fell
off as she approached Nathan in the Warsaw parlor. It was sad
to fall in love with the wrong man, but it was a very beautiful
feeling. And Nathan's love gave his indifference an edge of
exquisite consideration. He was not a destructive man; Esther
would not let him violate Shaya's home.

But Esther finally broke. She had not shaken off altogether
her father's farm. To postpone things indefinitely with Yakov,
she told him she came to America on Rachel's ticket and had
sworn an oath not to marry until Rachel came over too. Yakov
seemed relieved. Growing up in an orphanage, he had no sense

of social pace. He was now somehow committed; his life continued as before.

Esther now started washing Nathan's clothes and putting them on his bed. She washed his sheet almost every day. He began visiting the café regularly, though he always left early and pretended to be asleep when she got home. And yet with all her ambivalent feelings, Esther carefully cultivated Yakov. Yakov was her future, not Nathan. A fatalist, she endlessly discussed making a home, visiting Newark, attending the theater. She began to relish Yakov's dry, pessimistic spirit, so similar to her own. His hands were very beautiful. Orthodoxy kept them apart until their chuppah; they made their peace with it. Thorough pessimists and realists, they grew intimate over the lack of any intimacy between them.

One night, Esther noticed that Nathan lay facing her bed, breathing very gently. She stepped by him and caught her foot. She touched his bed to steady herself, and caressed his face. Then she undressed, not bothering to turn her back. As she bared her torso, she thought she saw the faintest of smiles on his face. Obedient as a wife at a signal, she crawled into his bed. Nathan turned and crushed her in his arms.

Their afternoon of love in Warsaw flooded around them. His body was an agony of familiar pleasure; his hands were knowing, experienced, subtly flattering. All night they made love like an old married couple. Esther didn't mind. She might as well have him while she could; her heart would be breaking soon enough.

The next night was unbearably hot. Everybody climbed to the roof where half the tenement slept; others slept on mattresses on every fire escape. Esther and Nathan found a spot behind the chimney. Esther remembered how she had struggled to sleep on deck, how Chatzkel kept kicking her in his sleep. She finally shifted over and crawled against Nathan.

From then on, Shaya and Chatzkel climbed upstairs to the roof; Esther and Nathan stayed below. They made love all night. When one sheet was wringing wet with sweat, they shifted to the other. Esther kept wondering who would get seasick first.

After that, they slept together, now in Esther's bed, now in Nathan's. Chatzkel kept waking up, hearing their heavy breath in the dark. He decided this meant nothing. He was Esther's real boyfriend.

Chapter Fifty-six

THE PENITENTIAL NINE DAYS led to the Fast of Ab. Shaya chanted the Book of Lamentations to a large *shteibel* crowd. The fast, combined with the summer heat and rumors of the hideous Black Hundreds in Russia, produced a somber ghetto mood. One suicide touched off another.

The next Sunday Aaron Binder rented a big rowboat at the Delancey Street pier to visit Coney Island. Coney Island rang on Hester Street like the words "Statue of Liberty" in Warsaw. After jumping from Warsaw to Hester Street, the next arrival was at Coney Island.

Early Sunday morning, Aaron shouted up to their window. Shaya, Esther, Chatzkel, and Nathan came downstairs and joined Aaron, his wife Bess, and their daughter, recently renamed Ellen. Esther and Bess each had a big basket of food. On the way, they picked up Yakov at his bookstore. Three men wore derbies; Nathan wore a straw boater.

As they descended Delancey Street to the dock, Bess nagged her husband about the trip. Did Aaron want a little rest? Was this Monte Carlo, where you go out on a boat to rest? What did he want, wind? You stand on a roof and you get wind. Suddenly he needed water? What was Coney Island, the Salzburg Baths? Why this trip? Aaron walked hunched forward, his eyes glittering from time to time at Esther, listening enough not to be rude, but not absorbing a single word.

Esther had brought extra umbrellas. Hearing Bess talk, she gave her one. Bess opened it and shut up. Aaron gave Esther a look of appreciation. Esther suddenly realized that he organized the whole trip as an excuse to spend the day with her. Esther died inside; only this she needed, on top of the stress of Nathan and Yakov traveling together.

Walking, Shaya rehearsed with Chatzkel the names of the three sons of Noah, who fathered the three races of man, and the twelve tribes that moved into Canaan, and the prophets, beginning with Moses, who received the law. Chatzkel solemnly participated.

The pier serviced smaller commercial fishing boats, several going out for a day's catch with three-man crews. One just in was unloading fish directly onto a row of three pushcarts, the captain throwing them by the tail as an assistant checked the count. By the pier, there was some excitement. A man had jumped off. Two men jumped after but the current sucked him under.

Aaron's family climbed under the front awning, the Kramers in the rear. Yakov and Nathan manned the long oars from the middle bench. They cast off and drifted south and east on the East River, but the boat began to slip to the north. Two men in striped blazers sped past in a narrow canoe. Esther and Bess both opened their baskets of food.

Sitting in back, Esther and Chatzkel both mistrusted the whole expedition. Esther remembered Aaron's attention in steerage. He controlled himself but she was still uncomfortable. She had to give something to secure Shaya's job, but she would go only so far. And Esther shuddered at Yakov and Nathan rowing together. She hoped they didn't carry knives. Chatzkel for his part was sure Bess organized the whole expedition for him to baby-sit Ellen in preparation for the *shiddach*. That look she gave him when she opened Esther's umbrella gave it away.

Sitting sideways, Shaya began a discourse on the dangers of the sea. The Jews were a landed people, old-line farmers. Water was not the Jewish element. The exodus was over the desert, and even there only a miracle saved the Hebrews from drowning in the Red Sea. Noah survived the flood in the ark only to turn into a drunken fool. God knows what his three daughters-in-law would have done to him, rocking with the elements, had his three sons not been there. Lot's two daughters developed incestuous appetites fleeing the rain of fire on Sodom. Their father was never the same again. And Jonah's trip by water was a total disaster.

"He ended up in the belly of a whale," Chatzkel solemnly intoned.

"The Torah says a large fish," Shaya corrected him. "The leviathan itself rose from the belly of the sea to swallow up Jonah."

Bess squinted at Aaron. "Which way is Coney Island?"

Aaron gestured airily. "Boats are out to ask; we won't get lost."

"We're lost already." Bess rolled up her eyes.

Shaya nodded sagely. "They say Columbus had a Marrano crew, escaping the Inquisition. Then the Jews discovered America."

This outing wasn't going anywhere. Esther shrugged. She put an umbrella in a hole in the back panel and took out her food.

Bess looked up and gestured. "Chatzkel, would you come over and help with Ellen? You were so good on the boat."

Chatzkel obeyed as heavily as he could, taking Ellen on his lap.

Ellen brushed against Chatzkel. Bess cuddled his head. Aaron shifted over to give Chatzkel room, took off his shirt, and slipped between the two oarsmen to take Chatzkel's place by Esther.

As Chatzkel and Esther exchanged bleak looks of understanding, Nathan turned to Shaya with a smile. "Oscar Wilde is in New York, lecturing."

"Who is Oscar Wilde?" Shaya asked patiently.

"He's a London playwright who carries a lily in his hand and thinks we're all ugly."

"He sounds like an anti-Semite to me."

"He never mentions the Jews!"

"They're all anti-Semites."

Several boats were on the water. Bess pointed to one close by, where two bearded Jews fished. "Let's ask where is Coney Island?"

Nathan and Yakov began rowing closer. Yakov heaved the oar out of the water with a flick back, splashing Aaron with every stroke.

"Stop that!" Aaron shouted.

"Sit in back, and you get splashed."

Yakov gave Esther a cunning look; she gave him a ravishing smile of gratitude.

Shaya leaned far out. "Do you know which way is Coney Island?"

The two Jews let out a laugh, one louder than the other. "You want to know where is Coney Island?"

They had a Litvak Yiddish. Shaya could scarcely contain his rage. "Yes, we want to go to Coney Island."

They hooted to one another. "He wants to go to Coney Island!"

"Litvak *paskudnyaks*! Can't you answer in *mama-loshen*?"

Esther pressed Shaya's hand. "We'll have Coney Island on the boat, and then you and Aaron can row us back to the pier. You're so much stronger than the crew we got now."

Esther gave Aaron a delighted look, but she gave Yakov the biggest sausage sandwich, with a double piece of strudel to fatten him up.

Feeling rejected, Nathan gave Bess his profile. Frightened, she gave Chatzkel's head another cuddle.

Chapter Fifty-seven

THE NEXT DAY, Esther stepped over to Yakov's counter and stood waiting. Yakov looked up. "It's something?"

"Feder is being deported to Warsaw."

"He told you?"

"He doesn't know it. His enemies are telling Immigration. I heard it from a friend."

"He was in jail; if his enemies are telling Immigration, then he's finished."

"I want the café."

Yakov squinted at her. "You'll give me children?"

"I'll give you."

"I'll get you the café; I know the building owner."

Yakov bent over the scroll, exultant. His marriage was a notch closer. He felt a dry trust and loyalty to Esther, but because he had the breath of the orphanage and could take just so much of a human being, having Esther manage the café would free him more to do communal business.

Esther fumbled for the right balance for her life. Yakov was too old-fashioned for her, but the idea of children haunted her. After thirty, her chances for children were limited, and Yakov had a sharp, evasive intelligence that kept surprising her. He knew how to leave her alone. He was generous enough to make a good father. Whatever her worldliness, she trusted him more and more. Her singing enriched the café, but it hadn't caught fire to the point of a theater career and some human compromise was called for.

Esther still kept house for Shaya, sleeping behind the partition. She mothered Chatzkel with enormous love. Yakov was by now Shaya's secretary. Shaya sometimes performed a wedding on the street under the stars. The services brought in very little but it drew a community around them.

It was crucial to Esther that Yakov attend theater. Once Esther got him started, Yakov enjoyed the theater thoroughly. On Friday night, they attended after an early service, paying in advance. Yakov thought the plays unbelievably stupid, but he received thorough satisfaction in seeing a play and then knocking it to pieces. The Belzer Society had given him a sharp social eye. He so disregarded the local Jews that his comments gave Esther nothing but pleasure.

One Friday night, during the *Dnieper Othello*, Iago paused

and lit a cigarette. Twenty people stood up in the audience, demanding that he respect the Sabbath. Startled, he put it out. Yakov then shouted that it was equally illegal to put a fire out. On the Sabbath, you let it burn.

This touched off an explosion:

"If the cigarette burns, we all burn!"

"Human life takes precedence! Human life takes precedence!"

"Send the fanatic back to Vilna!"

To quiet the audience, the Dnieper Othello stepped forward and began to recite, "To be or not to be" in a loud Yiddish. The experts shouted in outrage that that was from *Hamlet;* he had the wrong play. He rejoined that the Dnieper Othello knew his *Hamlet* as they did. That quieted them and the play continued.

Nathan sensed that he was losing Esther. That night he came in late and crawled humbly into his own bed. Esther knew how he felt and joined him in his bed. They made love with a wise despair. He felt more and more to her like a backward child she hesitated to abandon. She wished Miriam would come over soon.

Impatient to get married, Yakov checked in the society for ways to bring Rachel over. The cemetery was cleared and bringing in a slight income. The building fund was again preparing to build a synagogue. Shaya would get a salary in the new synagogue, but bringing over Rachel and three dependents required a substantial lump sum. It might be advanced as a loan; but when word spread of his engagement to Esther, Yakov could be accused of diverting Society money to his own family. Everybody else had relatives to bring over; opening that door could tear the society apart.

Yakov finally told Esther that the society could do nothing about Rachel. To branch out as a cantor, Shaya inquired among shopkeepers and was directed to a concert hall for cantorial music, but the secretary insisted they handled only experienced cantors. Experience meant a job with pay. The Belzer paid him nothing, so he had no experience.

Undaunted, Shaya visited Aaron's shop and asked for a canceled check to give the secretary. Intrigued, Aaron made out a twenty-dollar check to Cantor Shaya Kramer. Shaya cashed it at Aaron's bank. Aaron redeposited it and gave Shaya the canceled check.

They bumped into Feder Strauss as they left the bank. Fishing for a good word, Feder and Aaron began to argue why the Jew survived. Aaron called it plain resourcefulness, how the Jew shifted from country to country. Feder called it stupidity; if the Jew ever honestly saw his situation, he would drop dead in despair. Only his ignorance of the gentile mind kept him alive.

Shaya lifted his hand. The two men fell silent. Shaya then recalled a lengthy responsa on a question of holiness that stopped abruptly with these words: "The reader must forgive me for stopping short. I began writing this while fleeing a pogrom; and leaving my house, I neglected to take along enough paper for a full discussion."

Shaya lifted his finger. "He fled a pogrom, but Torah filled his mind. And that's how the Jew survived."

Aaron and Feder both smiled with pleasure. Neither understood him, but they liked such stories. They discussed the projected Belzer synagogue—rough-cut, Romanesque, with two concrete lions in front.

Shaya took his canceled check to the secretary of the hall. She turned it this way and that. Twenty dollars was a lot of money for a cantor.

"There's a Belzer synagogue?"

"Aaron Binder is the president; you can ask him."

She shrugged and put Shaya on the concert schedule. He had a check; she wasn't interested in problems.

Shaya prepared a concert. Then, working his pushcart one day, he saw the cantor's hall being wrecked to make way for a stable. The organization was gone, and his concert with it. He couldn't even complain; everything in America was built on water.

That night, in the Pinchas Strauss, two burly, well-dressed gentiles in derbies and navy coats stepped in. Esther knew them on sight as Immigration, and stepped away to take an order. She turned at a muffled shout, and saw Feder being rushed to the door, gesturing frantically to her. She took a huge breath and continued the service as before.

Late that night, Esther locked up. The next morning she told Yakov. By the next night, Aphrodita was the assistant in Esther's café.

PART FOUR

Chapter Fifty-eight

CHATZKEL REACHED PUBERTY EARLY. His tough little body was a part of the pushcart world; he was a street boy with calloused hands and mental scars, but his father's spirit ate inside him like vinegar. Everywhere around him was blind power, a punishment without justice, but Shaya's God haunted him. Unable to endure it, he handled his penis at night the way he handled his wares during the day.

Making free with his flesh as he dreamed of children, a wife, a home, he felt his dreams dissolve into memories of the great crossing, when the ocean spread in a waste and void over which Shaya walked the deck. Sexual eruptions shook in small earthquakes as the waters above parted from the waters below and fertile shallows evaporated to leave dry land.

Puberty drew Chatzkel toward Esther. With all her nutty poses, her fantasies of the Yiddish stage, Esther scrambled and had her own café; she was a survivor. With one half-crazy sister, and another who had probably died on a kibbutz, she went out every day in tough leather shoes that buttoned over the ankle, a long skirt and a blouse with starched cuffs, her hair rolled in a bun in back, and she survived because she was brave.

Chatzkel had a yen for raw milk. He bought a panful on the street and carried it upstairs. The sound as he drank glass after glass stirred an uncontrollable motherly feeling in Esther. She poured a glass of milk and held it to Chatzkel's lips, pushing with a teasing, hesitant laugh until he drank it down, then held out another glass. He blinked at her in confusion and drank it. They then moved to different rooms, feeling they had done something immoral but deeply satisfying.

The immigrant ships kept arriving from Hungary, Lithuania, Poland. Each dislocated family had bits of news, and reports of

215

pogroms, a brief breath of the Pale. The arrivals flowed massively through to Brownsville, in Brooklyn, the West Side, Chicago, and Boston; yet New York became steadily more crowded. Rows of hammocks hung in basements for eight-hour shifts of sleepers around the clock; eight and ten boarders slept in one room with a family of five. Feeling guilty, the immigrants wore too many clothes, mistrusting the New York winter and keeping their bodies in hiding. Nothing was betrayed—not family secrets, nor the money in the mattress.

With Nathan more often away, Yakov now joined them nightly for dinner, patient and colorless, following Shaya's lead at table with unquestioning respect. Chatzkel refused to accept him, seeing him still as something out of an orphanage. He also viewed his father with fresh mistrust. Didn't Shaya need a woman? But maybe saints were different. Chatzkel knew he himself was not a saint. Managing the pushcart, he made the family livelihood, and what he did with his stubborn, piggish body was his own business. He refused to feel guilty.

Chatzkel hung on in school, while boys and girls in his class pitched into their books to escape the Lower East Side. He was headed nowhere. He got truancy warnings and shrugged them off. He would finally have his own family, but he didn't see happiness in the cards. But he knew when he had a son he would do better by him than Shaya did by him.

Esther still made sure Chatzkel's neck was clean for school. She knew Chatzkel was smarter than his father. By now she sensed that he knew of her affair with Nathan and kept quiet to protect her. She washed Chatzkel's sheets and understood the areas stiff with dried semen. She fumbled for ways to help him, but Chatzkel held back. She felt him entering the male wilderness that she was making her peace with, and wanted him healthy there. She gave him honest companionship in her private strategy for family survival. Feeling his starvation for a mother, she held him close before leaving for the café, kissing his head and calling him loving names, telling him how much women would love him. Her flirtatious giggle flew out to hide her embarrassment, and she always left fast. To Chatzkel, Esther's embarrassment meant there was something to hide. He refused to unfold his further thoughts to himself and yet he walked the street with her eyes hanging before him and dreaming. Each time Esther started off for work, Chatzkel felt aghast at the teeming Hester Street she would enter, where a dozen Yiddish accents flew together helter-skelter. The workers were penniless property-holders, who hungered for something solid of their own. Ghetto women slipped cash into their mattresses as the schools took over their children and the job system absorbed their husbands. Fearing to be dismissed as foreigners, they entrenched themselves in their homes and piled on the poundage, jewelry, talcum powder, flesh, underwear, each giving her husband an anchor he could cling to.

Esther was a creature apart. Still caught up in her dreams of the Yiddish stage, she kept her petite figure, occasionally playing the piano in her café. To Chatzkel, she had her own brand of holiness. Esther filled an emptiness. They trusted each other, the two of them underground diggers, as Americanized as they dared be. He adored her and used her however he could; Esther didn't seem to mind.

Chapter Fifty-nine

SOMETIMES, PEDDLING, CHATZKEL IGNORED A LOOSE BRICK, stumbled, and fell on his face. He got up shaken, with a look of defiant foolishness. So he stumbled—let his father answer for it, the man who brought him into the world. He was pissing out his life behind the pushcart. When the Belzer synagogue was finished, Shaya would get a salary and give up peddling; and his son would end up another junk heap, uneducated, emptied out, left with a pushcart.

Sometimes Chatzkel pushed out of the ghetto, south into Irish blocks and east among the Italians. Walking empty streets alongside the ghetto, Chatzkel defied the churches to destroy him and gentile gangs to beat him up. He was called a kike. He refused to flinch. This was his city.

Once a month, Shaya conducted a squirm session. Did Chatzkel wait five hours after meat to drink milk? Did he pin on his yarmulke at night? Did he bless the new moon? Then, in a penitential mood, the two wrote to Rachel in Poland together. Chatzkel chafed at it, but he participated. This was a family team. He handled the business, Esther kept them both alive, but religion was Shaya's department.

At school, Leah Rabinowitz still sometimes showed Chatzkel her body, with all its bumps and odd parts. Chatzkel stayed on his guard. She had a patient, questioning silence, passively available for things she scarcely knew. Chatzkel continued to take her strudel. She dragged him behind the building and asked to see his body. He refused. She was hurt but he ignored it. Chatzkel asked for her copybook; she gave it and was marked down for not having done her work. When he skipped school, she did an extra page of homework and passed it to him as he came in the next day.

Leah's mother Zippie lost her protector. Desperate to bring over her husband, she quit the sewing machine and began receiving men in her room. Staying at home, she supervised Leah in earnest, screaming at her and calling her crazy, compulsively pushing her steel-rimmed glasses up her nose as though it were immoral for the frames to sit still. She kept telling her neighbors how hard she worked to bring over her husband. Once, missing Leah and fearing her lost, she jumped off the dock, but they fished her out in time.

Zippie's block refused to take the respectable *churvah*. People avoided her; isolated, she felt compulsive knots of joy, sure they knew nothing. Sometimes she gave Leah a quick meal before sending her downstairs to the landing, and then fed her another after the men left. Leah ate both meals in silence, wanting not to shame her mother. If she heard a remark about her, she refused to think about it. Chatzkel thought they made a funny pair—Zippie pushy, hysterical, the scream in her throat, Leah flattened out and indifferent to anything.

With Leah he didn't have to be shy—somehow her mother's livelihood made her available—but he didn't do anything. Sometimes after school, he spotted Leah hiding in her doorway. He solemnly waved. She waved back, grateful that he didn't try to talk to her.

Zippie once stopped Shaya's cart and dragged him into a doorway, as Chatzkel tagged after. "Reb Shaya, holy man, my filthy life is only to get my husband out of Poland. I have no other way."

"You should go to your death first."

"He's my man, my husband; I'll never get another."

"Your daughter is enough. Let me get you a divorce from a Warsaw rabbi. Make a decent living. Show Leah a mother in Israel."

"It's hard, so hard." She tore out compulsively without the answer she wanted, but at least she spoke to somebody.

Chatzkel blinked up after she had stumbled away. "Why not help her get him out of Poland?"

"I know him from Warsaw; he should never reach New York."

The next Thursday morning at six o'clock, the family trailed out to Chatzkel's Bar Mitzvah. Leah spotted them on the street and waved Chatzkel a silent mazel tov. A school buddy working by his father's pushcart took one look; grinning from ear to ear, he drew his finger across his throat as Chatzkel gestured him to be serious.

Chatzkel noticed a peddler in the storefront with a new Polish hat. The man smiled in excitement. "It's nice, eh? It took three years, but I brought my wife over. She brought the hat as a present."

Chatzkel bit his lip. "My mother is still on the other side."

The man leaned closer. "Your father plays games. You want to make money peddling, you put a pack on your back and climb floors. You get a curse? You move to the next door."

The early minyan was just starting. Shaya conducted fast, ringing prayers for thirty workers on their way to a job. Then Aaron Binder came in in a rich black coat, accompanied by Bess and Ellen. He was the new society president and Shaya's strong supporter, but he left his other children at home, bringing only Ellen, a bustling happy girl with a mousy body. Chatzkel didn't particularly like Ellen, but then nobody ever asked what he did like. There was no fighting destiny.

Chatzkel was in a near panic when Nissel Federbush called him up, giving his "*Ya'amod*" an extra kick for the occasion. It was Chatzkel's Bar Mitzvah, but as usual, other people were running it. Nobody would even notice if he disappeared after the last blessing. Then as everybody fell quiet, Shaya burst into tears, and instantly gripped Chatzkel's shoulder. Chatzkel bit his lip. He had blockages; Hebrew just wasn't his language. He had everything committed to memory, not trusting himself to read straight. Now out of control, he forgot his blessing.

And then Chatzkel connected. He delivered in a stiff, halting fashion, but everybody cried, "*Ya'asher koach!*" "*Ya'asher koach.*" Chatzkel wanted to walk up and tell the Binders that if they wanted somebody spiritual for Ellen they were making a ghastly mistake; he wasn't like his father at all. But they would only grin and be embarrassed, praise his modesty, and not understand a word. Ellen was already looking at him the way her father looked at Shaya, so what was the use?

When Chatzkel took his seat again, he turned around and stuck his tongue out at Ellen. She immediately stuck her tongue out at him. He did it again. She did it again. They both grinned; in a mysterious way, they had become engaged.

219

Chapter Sixty

Now THAT SHE WAS IN CHARGE of the Pinchas Strauss, Esther got acquainted with the smaller, more cloistered cafés in the Canal Street area. Some were difficult to find, with bare doors, their clientele a few enlightened ones, Jews broken loose, with dim projects on their minds. With living quarters so pinched and austere, they took their nightly seat to sip tea and chat by the hour about literary trends in Paris, about Balkan nationalism, about the nihilism they felt spreading throughout the world. Each table held a single candle. A stranger rarely intruded. Their managers, themselves European arrivals, often poor and reclusive, maintained themselves by a stringent budget, outside work, and the meager café returns.

The Pinchas Strauss was a larger café for people who worked, to whom an evening away from home was an event, not a way of life. The after-dinner crowd of the societies filled Esther's café, using its upright piano that was always going out of tune for a holiday song or to celebrate a national election. Its size, changing clientele, and lamps and gray walls gave it a frontier atmosphere. The cheerful vulgarity, camaraderie, and constant movement gave zest to their weekly night out and justified an occasional night without sleep.

To build up her clientele, Esther stayed close to the society secretaries. Outright money would backfire, but Esther gave personal service and holiday gifts, plying them with advice and connections. In return, they took a slack night at the Pinchas Strauss, assuring the house of a constant attendance. She steadily developed her own repertoire of café songs.

Having finally escaped a life of prostitution, Aphrodita was now cashier at the café, yet old habits die hard. When they nearly lost one of their societies, she started sleeping occasionally with its secretary, whose wife had never left Lithuania. Striking in appearance, in a full calico dress, Aphrodita had a tiny tenement closet on Henry Street and belonged to the Socialist party. She carried herself with a defiant honesty and independence, but she did whatever Esther told her. Aphrodita wanted back her old name of Sarah Cohen; Esther thought Aphrodita gave the Pinchas Strauss an air of the exotic, so she kept it.

They consulted constantly about their customers, going over each group to make sure they were satisfied. Esther had the Belzer through Yakov and Shaya. The Cloak Makers liked the

220

Pinchas Strauss because it welcomed outside guests. Aphrodita regularly attended meetings of the Socialist Society. As for the Anshei Vilna Society, when that came up, Esther would look up—"You're still seeing Mossman, the chairman?"—Aphrodita would then break into a low chuckle. "You haven't got a thing to worry about."

The serious Yiddish writers shrank from the constant arguments over brands of salami and access to the society cemetery, conducted each night in a different accent of Yiddish, but the journalists attended. And in back, one or two satirists always glanced about like bird watchers with a pencil stub, polishing phrases for a weekly piece. They nodded to well-wishers and looked away, wanting to be left alone.

Something was always afoot in the Pinchas Strauss—an unexpected meeting, a blatant vulgarity, a misunderstanding, a tidbit of fresh news, a report of the Warsaw literary clubs. The Socialist journalists knew the garment industry better than its employees, but they let things alone.

To celebrate Chatzkel's fifteenth birthday, Esther and Yakov took him to see a Yiddish play. The theater was packed, with block parties and ticket books at a discount. Workers brought their wives; there were parties from Shaya's school. Whole rows of workingwomen came to sit, weep, and be outraged at the melodrama of the fall of a working girl. The theater critics sat in the first five rows, bored and cynical, their notebooks already full of devastating flourishes to destroy the production before the curtain rose. One or two gentile guests obviously didn't understand a word. A rich lecher, thoroughly Americanized, was taking in a poor immigrant girl, his *greeneh korsineh,* clinching the seduction with a promise of marriage. As each actor appeared on stage, he was met with applause from his fans.

"Dolling, he has a wife already!" a woman yelled from in back, as the heroine removed her coat.

"It won't help her to know," a man growled.

"Why shouldn't it help?!"

"Because she's an idiot!"

"Yeah? Thanks for telling me what you are!"

"You always tell the woman her situation!"

"Yeah, let her decide what she wants to do!"

The audience shushed them, and the packed hall fell silent as the stage organized itself for the unspeakably tragic confrontation.

Afterward, at an adjoining café, as a critic at the next table sipped cognac and wrote his review, Esther told Chatzkel that she felt steadily more secure with Yakov. She now realized that a mistrust of men was the real cause of her delay; she had seen too many ghetto women who were adored without being respected. But time had quieted her misgivings and given her trust. The synagogue soon would open. Rachel and the three children would arrive, and she and Yakov were getting married.

Chatzkel sat back, heartsick; at the next table, a follower walked up to the critic, "Podolsky, what do you make of the Shakespeare in Yiddish?"

Podolsky squirmed up with an airy giggle. "If Shakespeare attended the performance I saw, he would find it amusing. He would only wonder which actor was playing Othello and which Iago." He paused for a moment, and then added, "It's no wonder he would be confused; I don't think the actors knew themselves!"

Chatzkel leaned forward. "You're starting a home? Let me live with you."

Esther gave a little resistant laugh, not at all displeased. "What do you say? Your dear mother is coming back."

Yakov shook his head. "Reb Shaya would never hear of it."

Chatzkel got up and walked out, more depressed than ever. It wasn't just Esther's home he wanted. After spending years on the street as a peddler, he was out of Polish rabbinic Orthodoxy. Esther's café had a little life. Talented people visited there, artists with ideas. He wanted to shift over to Esther's café and work there. He would somehow make it happen.

Chapter Sixty-one

AS SYNAGOGUE PLANS DEVELOPED, Shaya became more formal in his proprieties. Without spying, he sensed the intimacy between Esther and Nathan. He had ignored it before, but now he wrote to Rachel, explaining the housing difficulties in New York. Places simply weren't to be had. He described their present sleeping arrangements. It began simply because Nathan lost his job, but now Nathan was drifting. Miriam should come over without delay, or she could expect Shaya would send her a divorce. He wasn't allowing Esther to be used.

Shaya's letter went out at the beginning of summer. After several weeks, he got a short letter from Miriam. She had bought three tickets and was bringing over their children to join Nathan.

Always cool, whatever his feelings, Nathan luckily found a furnished room around the corner, and he crowded in two extra beds for the children.

Esther sensed Nathan's quiet courage, and her old love for him fitfully flared up. He was the most beautiful man she ever met. And yet he drained all her energy. She refused to wallow; she loved Nathan enough to be relieved that he was gone. In his own way, he loved his wife. Miriam allowed his womanizing; they had children. It was enough.

Nathan checked the dock and time of Miriam's arrival. Shaya accompanied him uptown. They went early, but East Side Jews already jammed the pier, ready to welcome family, and there was a veteran team present with a registered nurse on call. Tugboats eased the ship into dock among cries of recognition, shrieks to lower the gangplank already, gestures of marvel at the grown children, groans at the change in garb. Bulky ropes tied the boat fore and aft as the immigrants shouted down scraps of news and their American families shouted questions about family back in Poland.

The gangplank was swung and settled into place. The first to push her way off the ship was Miriam, carrying her daughter and leading her son. She was dressed as a Berlin businesswoman, in a suit with a long flaring skirt. Her porter carried three huge suitcases, followed by a tumultuous throng. Her short straight hair was tinted auburn and parted down the middle.

Shaya and Nathan exchanged awkward grins of satisfaction; the lioness had landed. A moment later, Miriam ran toward them with a shriek of discovery. Nathan and Shaya sprinted to help with the children. As Miriam and Nathan embraced, the air crackled with their perverse joy at reunion; her coming over uninvited added the ingredient of the forbidden their marriage fed on.

A practiced businesswoman, Miriam briefly gave Shaya the news that everyone in Warsaw was well, and immediately got down to Nathan's present situation. Why was he still on somebody's sewing machine? Without waiting for an answer, she demanded the price of a sewing machine and the terms of loan from the local banks. She would open with at least fifteen machines.

Shaya liked her brusque directness, but she now had the smell of the Warsaw speculators, angling a killing into shape. She brought regards from Rachel, and news of each of his children. But she knew too much about them; Shaya felt his privacy violated.

"Warsaw has a mood?"

"It's not good. There are too many political parties, and the Russians are loosening their controls. Once the Black Hundreds started, there was no stepping back. A few more people are beginning to think that the Zionists were correct."

"Let them come over here."

"The Socialists don't trust capitalist New York."

"And the Rebbe has a plan?"

"He has a following; what does he need a plan?"

Impatient as ever, Miriam darted off to a carriage for hire, lifting her skirts slightly so as not to trip, and got it just ahead of two other couples. Nathan followed her, carrying his screaming daughter. Shaya pulled the boy by the hand, as he fought to kick a dog. The porter followed, still carrying the three suitcases.

As they climbed into the carriage, a huge dark spot spread in the crotch of the boy's pants. Miriam spotted it instantly, and looked at Nathan in disgust. Shaya gave Nathan a compassionate smile.

In the carriage, Miriam peered out, drinking in the city as they rolled south. They passed a horse-drawn bus, crowded with people.

Miriam looked at Shaya. "It's got money, New York."

"It's a rich city."

"Everything's open; everything moves."

"It's so big that you have to be careful in all directions."

Suddenly Miriam faced Nathan. "What kind of a place did you get? Does it have your furniture or the landlord's?"

"It's the landlord's."

"Tomorrow I'll find us another place. You pay through the nose with the landlord's furniture. I won't live in a hotel."

Nathan and Miriam unpacked and brought their children to Shaya's room for supper. Coming in the door, Miriam saw Esther with Yakov, and closed her eyes in relief. Her situation had stabilized itself.

Esther served a hot flanken soup with spinach leaves, sections of cooked potato, and pieces of meat, and a tsimmes with honeyed prunes. The children ate off of suitcases on the wooden platform. Chatzkel supervised them, glumly missing his own mother. When they finished eating, Miriam gave Shaya regards from Zfania Binstock, his father-in-law. Shaya's one thought was that Poland certainly must be deteriorating; Zfania wanted a connection in New York.

Miriam gave Shaya a sharp look. "You say nothing."

"He's your friend, Zfania, isn't he?"

"What makes you say that?"

"But you are writing him a letter."

Miriam smiled in embarrassment. "Who told you this?"

"I knew it when I saw you on the dock."

"You see into people like water."

"When you write, tell Zfania to send over Rachel and the children. He can use the money he stole cheating on my wedding contract."

Miriam stopped smiling. "That's all?"

Shaya started to shudder. "Tell him my face still carries the spit he put there as I was leaving Warsaw."

Too agitated to be with people, Shaya grabbed Chatzkel by the hand. He fled downstairs and blindly pushed through the ghetto, humiliated that Nathan had his wife over and all he had was a pushcart.

Chapter Sixty-two

Unable to keep up, as Shaya strode blindly through the ghetto streets, Chatzkel finally grabbed hold of his coat, closed his eyes, and let himself be dragged blindly along. Shaya turned a corner and banged into a night watchman. The man stood indifferent in his greatcoat and derby, his hands crossed over his pushcart. When Shaya started again, Chatzkel began to wail out loud, yelling in his head to Miriam to go back to Poland. Shaya stopped, turned, and pressed his son against his breast. After a silent moment the two finally returned home.

The next morning, Miriam left Nathan to guard the children as she talked to superintendents and landlords. She stepped into a bank with branches in Germany and Poland and presented a letter of introduction; soon she was in conference with the bank manager.

That evening, in a ceremony of the Belzer Society, Shaya wrote the *tnayim*, the preliminary wedding contract, for Yakov and Esther.

After the *tnayim* were signed and witnessed, Aaron Binder unrolled for Shaya their plans for the Belzer synagogue. They discussed the arrangement of the interior and Chatzkel listened with jealous attention, unsure where he fitted in all this, when Aaron turned:

"Chatzkel, when your father works for us, would you like to help in my store after school?"

Chatzkel shrugged; this man was now his father's boss. "Sure, be nice."

That night, Chatzkel woke up, hearing somebody sobbing. He looked over. Shaya was lying in bed, the tears streaming down his cheeks. Chatzkel began asking what was wrong. He was unable to bear it.

Suddenly Shaya tore out of bed, lit a candle, and wrote a three-word message to his father in Radich: "*Tateh, hilf mir.*" "Daddy, help me." He didn't bother to explain. His father always understood him with a minimum of words.

Several weeks later, Shaya received a letter with a black border. He opened it with foreboding, and read this:

To my beloved husband, Shaya, in whose absence my life is a spread of emptiness. I share your life from afar, the good and the bad alike.

A letter came from Palestine that your beloved sister Feigeleh has entered the world of truth. She was born a dreamer; her dream is now ours. What can I tell you? It breaks our hearts, that young and beautiful soul is no longer with us. Malaria took her in a shtetl not yet on any map, Dagania, near the Sea of Galilee. From the woods of Radich, wild birds fly in all directions. Hers flew to the Galilean shore. The land loved her; it accepted her; it took her into its bosom forever.

Raphael has visited Chaneleh. Had he gone with Feigeleh, she might have fought to stay alive. They were both dreamers, but she made her dream her life. He stayed asleep, dreaming. He wasn't a husband to Feigeleh; he doesn't deserve her children. When we come to America, I won't tell him. I want her with us, and no trouble at the station.

A second death was of your grandfather Gershuni. Your mother cared for him to the end. In my opinion, she did wrong. The Horowitz family would have cared for him. Your mother was hardly in touch. Then, when Gershuni died, she came back with all her things, thinking to resume her life here. Nehemia ordered her back to Galicia. She refused. Nehemia beat her. She accepted it as justified. Nehemia had a divorce written. He forced it in her hand, forced her on a carriage, and told her to go back to the Horowitz family with his curse for denying him a wife.

Geula accused me of taking her place and forcing her out, an accusation that I reject entirely. Maybe if she did that to her mother, then what happened is God's justice; but Shaineh Nissel took your mother's place, not me. I heard her accusation in silence. Let her hate me; it won't kill her. In my judgment, the most unbearable thing to a bitter, rejected woman is the truth.

Nehemia was strong when Geula left, but he soon weakened. Your mother was wrong, but she meant him no harm. It was for him to protect his wife in her folly, not to punish her for being what she was. This was the woman he married; he will never really have another. Nehemia has grown absentminded and out of touch. He is suddenly old. Melon has lost its minyan. He now prays alone.

Shaya, each morning I pray that news will arrive that I will join you. My father wants me back in his house, but I refused. When he tried to have me divorced, I blotted him out of my life. Bear your losses with strength. The children are all well and strong. I don't think Nehemia will stay here much longer. The Kramers are now your family.

My love and greetings to my sister, Esther. All my love to my strong son, Chatzkel.

Your devoted wife, Rachel.

Esther read the letter after Shaya. When she finished, she shook her head. "Our mother is not a fool; if she said it, there is something there."

"She should not have stayed away from Nehemia for so long."

"Had I looked after Nehemia, he would have taken Geula back. This letter hides a lot of bitterness."

"The bitterness is my doing in not bringing her over. But I think my letter to Nehemia will bring her over soon. No more bitterness; we have to sit in mourning for my sister Feigeleh."

Shaya and Esther went about covering mirrors and turning up the chairs. Shaya then began reading Lamentations. Yakov brought them vegetable food and arranged for a minyan morning and evening so they could say the kaddish.

A few weeks after they finished shivah, a one-line letter came from Nehemia, telling Shaya what boat carried Rachel and the children. Shaya looked at the date. She would come in two days. Nehemia must have sold his chicken farm immediately upon receipt of his letter, to get the money to buy four tickets.

Shaya took the letter to Esther. She read it and clutched at her heart. "Shaya, all our years of savings are enough for one ticket. Send it to Mother, care of Gita. Tell her to buy a ticket and come to America. Tell her I need her. She helped Gita long enough. Her children are grown. Now I'm going to have children; it's time she helped me."

That night, Shaya, Yakov, and Esther began planning the wedding for the evening of Rachel's arrival. Yakov wanted to wait but Esther was haunted by undefined, spasmodic fears, and was in a hurry to have a baby before it was too late for her.

As they made their wedding plans, the first light was creeping across the plains in Poland. Nehemiah was on the road—his farm gone, his money gone, having sent his family overseas, with all his remaining belongings strapped onto the double wagon behind him, as he headed for the Belzer old-age home in Warsaw. Coming out of Galicia, he had an extra mule tied on the back of his wagon, carrying extra provisions; now he had his milk cow.

Nehemia started up. "I have a son. His name is Kramer; he's an orphan in Galicia."

Shaineh nodded, showing her teeth. "Sooner or later, he will find his way to Warsaw."

Nehemia suddenly rose erect. "I raised a fine family."

Shaineh broke into a strong growl. "Every child of yours is a prince."

Nehemia cracked his whip, but they moved slowly to allow for their milk cow, tied on in back. As they traveled, Shaineh turned from side to side with a strained smile, blindly drinking in the portion of earth they passed through.

Chapter Sixty-three

THE FAMILY ARRIVED early at the dock and waited for an hour as the clouds thinned and disappeared. A green scud was kicking off the water in a thinning delta behind two tugboats. Chatzkel looked around impatiently as the dock got steadily more crowded. Then as Rachel's boat eased in, the waves, heavy as lead, had a film of oily grit.

Chatzkel's nervous system couldn't take it as the huge ropes were flung down and the immigrants pressed to the rail before the jam of family shrieking regards. If he got any happier, God would let him have it in the throat.

Voices drifted over:

"So I told him, you put away a dollar a week for five years, and Feivel said nothing. He refuses to see the simplest things."

"You can only teach people what they know already."

"He doesn't need her anymore; he likes living alone."

Several housewives were chatting:

"You want the whitefish fresh? Carnoff on Orchard Street. A whole fish scaled for fifty cents, huge, and always fresh."

"His wife throws up at night. So she's on the dock buying at four in the morning."

"She can't sleep, so she has to do something."

Two older Jews talked obliquely:

"He'll eat American slaughter?"

"He's using the ticket we sent him? A vegetarian he's not."

"In Poland, I once saw two bearded farmers plowing, one on each side of the road, one a Jew, the other a Pole. So I asked myself, is there any difference between them? But there was. The Polack was praying, 'Dear God, give me rain; spare me locusts; let me have a good harvest and food for the winter.' And the Jew was praying, 'Dear God, let my plow turn up a box with enough money in it so I can leave this farm and get into the city with my family and open a business.' "

The crowd shifted, pushing forward. Leah Rabinowitz was with her mother, both wearing dark glasses and dressed with conservative elegance. Zippie's hands kept pushing together; on her face was a compulsive joy that her husband was coming over at last. She had gotten him a ticket on that same ship.

Chatzkel edged toward Leah, but Zippie snatched her away like the kosher clip on a dead chicken. Moaning under her breath, she dragged Leah toward the gangplank, yelling at her to push harder.

A crazy wind of happiness was in the air. The harbor was clear, the sky wispy blue with not a cloud anywhere. The ship was packed with immigrants. Chatzkel's stomach was quiet. Police were there to help; a Jew had a homemade wagon on wheels, with hand-polished apples on it. An institution representative was there to help immigrants. Everything felt right to him.

The crowd on the dock pressed against the ship, spotting relatives at the rail. The noise got louder. They began unpacking their kitchen idiocies, screaming to the others to talk louder, yelling things that belonged in the privacy of their rooms. A presser on the dock gave a kicking dance, shouting up in a taunt: "Avrom! You took time off in the shop in Bialystok to sing wedding songs with Yankel Kvatch? The singing is over, *bruderlein*! You'll learn in America what work is!"

Three hefty sisters leaned up from the dock toward a fourth, who leaned over the rail:

"Zisseh! Zisseh! They got the wagon driver!"

"They got! They got!"

"Feigeh's wagon driver!"

"Him! Who else?"

"God be thanked!"

"So what did the mamzer do?"

"Do? He married her!"

"God be thanked! God be thanked!"

"They have a roof?"

"They want to come with the baby!"

"We have to start saving for three more tickets?"

"What can you do?! I'll help. It'll go faster!"

Chatzkel's teachers at school talked differently—not just English, but laundered English. These women used *mama-loshen*. Shaya never had to talk at all; his face shone with the Word.

Chatzkel stiffened. Aaron Binder was pushing onto the dock with Bess and Ellen, and the girl was wearing a prosperous suit, a cloak, a bodice, and skirt. People automatically made room. He was starting to make Chatzkel uneasy. Binder had come to welcome the wife of his rabbi. Very nice, very nice. But there was Ellen again, and she had little breasts already. Chatzkel choked; he wanted time to breathe before he marched under the chuppah.

The two families joined together. As Binder told Shaya of a private carriage he had hired, Ellen pushed a box into Chatzkel's hand. "It's *teiglach;* give them to the little ones coming in."

Chatzkel flashed her a look of appreciation.

And then Chatzkel spotted her, Rachel, his mother, stepping on the gangplank with the three children pressed around so she could hardly move, all of them helping with bags, her babushka around her neck. It was exactly her step in the Warsaw station when she told him to look after his father. Chatzkel heard the laughing angels spreading everywhere through heaven. Shocked, he screamed, "It's momma!" And everybody pressed forward to welcome her.

Moments later, she was in their midst. Shaya embraced her. Aaron Binder had a porter take her bags. Esther and Rachel wept on each other's shoulders. And Chatzkel noticed his brother and sister side by side and close to his father, in new clothes for the landing, eyeing him like the Warsaw Binstocks—sharp, rich, on the make. With one look Chatzkel knew that neither had ever worked a day in their lives. He was not yet fully grown, and already he was a workingman, his hands calloused, wearing cheap glasses and a pair of worn shoes. He was already no longer a child, but they were not only children but *haute bourgeoisie*. Chatzkel wished he had a bed to crawl under. Everything he did, everything in his life, was forced, alien, crippling.

But Rachel was looking at him. Chatzkel couldn't get near her, and suddenly he was embarrassed. She was a piece of God's body but she was also a stranger from Poland, a place he was spending his life getting away from. How can anybody be warm and honest with a stranger? His own feelings left him exposed. He kept pushing to hide behind Shaya's back. Rachel dragged him out and kissed him, and told him how American he looked. What could he say? He had given his childhood to bring her over; now that she was here, she was a stranger.

Chapter Sixty-four

CHATZKEL SPUN AROUND. Leah's father was marching off in a wolfskin coat, dragging Leah by the hand through large families collecting their strays. He had a lean face, a vertical scar close along the ear that made his face look pasted on, and high-speed eyes already figuring up his wife's money. He kept flexing his knuckles, a man who thought with the back of his hand. Zippie tramped behind as fast as he moved, lugging his bags, her face insane with love. Even Chatzkel knew she should have moved to another building before her husband found out what she was.

Chatzkel glanced aside. A boy and a girl from his school stood close by; the boy pressed against her back, jiggling in rhythm, as she stood still, jiggling with him. At school, the nonreligious kids were touching, didn't swat each other, and were starting to pair off. He felt more mature, stronger, more effective. He didn't have to grow up; if he were more grown up, he would simply be ready to raise his own children.

Chatzkel grinned at his brother Simcha. "You wear no glasses? I'm surprised."

Simcha snapped up, on his guard. "I don't need glasses."

"You're a student and you don't wear glasses? It's funny."

Simcha angled off, groping for a killing answer.

They all started for Mr. Binder's carriage behind the dock. Simcha walked in front, shaking his fists like train pistons. Some women got out of his way. He climbed in first and took the far corner seat by the window. They all climbed in after him. Chatz-

231

kel sat on top of Simcha, then moved off fast, remarking that Simcha was so small he didn't notice him.

The carriage took off. Rivka, Chatzkel's sister, wore a little Dutch bonnet. Chaneleh his orphan cousin, sat opposite. She was frail, with a nut-shaped face, and two pigtails coming from under her prim cap. If he married Chaneleh he would escape Ellen Binder, who gave him a pain even if he liked her. And marrying an orphan cousin was such a kindness.

"You're my cousin, Chaneleh?"

She nodded on signal. "My mother died in Dagania; that's a settlement in Palestine."

"Your mother died in Dagania? Mazel tov!"

Chaneleh burst into tears. Rachel patted Chatzkel's head and whispered, "Be nice to your cousin, *bubeleh;* she's an orphan."

Chatzkel held out Ellen's box. "Take a *teigel* and don't mind me."

Chaneleh took one and became quiet. Rachel beamed from ear to ear. Chatzkel exchanged a rueful glance of satisfaction with Ellen.

Shaya sat up. "Where are you up to in learning?"

Simcha instantly answered. "Exodus. 'I shall destroy!' "

"How many mothers did Moses have?"

"Two. His real mother, and Pharaoh's daughter, who was his foster mother, and also Miriam who looked after him."

"When did Moses walk barefoot?"

"Before the burning bush, because he stood on holy ground."

"Why did Moses' father-in-law have so many names?"

"Because he had so many daughters. Their suitors kept demanding dowries, so he was always hiding."

The women in the carriage covered their faces and tittered.

Back on their block, Chatzkel ran away to Leah; he felt shamed by his brother's gunfire answers, but some old women were gathered in front of Leah's building, as if something was happening inside.

Chatzkel turned to an old woman. "What?"

"Rabinowitz just found out about his wife."

"She paid to bring him over!"

"With what, the money she made as a *churvah*?"

"How did he find out so fast?"

"What do you mean? He has to know his wife was a *churvah*."

A noise inside the building got steadily louder. Then the couple burst out onto the street, Zippie first, her matted hair strung together like a horse's mane after a run, her glasses miss-

232

ing, with only a bathrobe to cover her shame. Brutally beaten, her body quivered under her robe. Sobbing, appalled, desperate, the blood running down her face, a welt on her cheek, two more on her neck, she lost a slipper in the doorway, reached her foot back but couldn't find it as Rabinowitz pushed her, slashing with his belt like a cattleman driving an animal, his hand twitching back for another blow, screaming with a driven joy: "*Churvah! Paskudnika! Schmutz! Dreck!*"

Zippie kept reaching behind her. "That's my room! Don't shame me before my neighbors!"

Unable to control himself, he ripped her robe down the back. "Look at you! Your neighbors know what you are! The whole city knows you!"

"That's my home! Those are my clothes, my pots! Who will you give them to? Why are you destroying me? I worked like a slave to bring you over! I bought your ticket from Poland!"

Zippie started toward the dock in a nervous snaky dance with one bare foot; on her face was still that look of desperate happiness that her husband was back. Her robe came off one shoulder.

Leah slipped into the doorway, then smiled in relief as she spotted Chatzkel. Chatzkel grinned. If he married Leah, then he would be her savior, and he needn't marry Ellen or Chaneleh. Leah came over.

"He threw out your mother?"

"As soon as he got her key."

"There was money hidden?"

"He took it all. He wants me to stay. What shall I do?"

"Follow your mother and fast. She brought you up; she was good to you. You're her life. Get her before she kills herself. He's a bad man; he won't leave you alone."

"Maybe you're right; I . . ."

They were snatched up and shaken in the air, as Rabinowitz spat at Leah with a grinning snarl. "Taking after your mother already?"

Chatzkel gritted his teeth, speaking slowly and evenly: "You're a bad father; you're a bad man. You should have died in Poland, you . . ."

Rabinowitz threw him in the dirt, lashed him with his belt, and kicked him. Chatzkel twitched away with a stabbing pain. Bystanders closed in around him as Rabinowitz dragged Leah inside in triumph.

An old woman helped Chatzkel drag himself upright. Limping

and fighting for breath, he started home. His side hurt; he was filthy. It had been so beautiful on the dock, even if he didn't fit in. He was making this some homecoming. He risked his life to save Leah, but she didn't seem to mind his dragging her inside. And her mother was probably drowned. But his father would do the right thing as soon as they talked; Chatzkel knew he would.

Chapter Sixty-five

SHAYA'S NEW QUARTERS were low-ceilinged, with ridged paneling and wall hangings to keep out the cold. His room was larger than the room on Hester Street and closer to where his synagogue would be. Around the table were more people than there were chairs, all of them dressed American, but bearded and conservatively dressed for a visit to the rabbi. Binder sat at Shaya's side. Other Belzer stood and sat around, smoking cigars, talking, leaning forward for another word from the rabbi, all gathered for Rachel's arrival.

On the table, Esther had spread fricassee, gefilte fish, and tiny, very hard slices of kishke. The visiting children were perched on the platform, watched by their older sisters. A bunch of daisies stood in a glass vase, slightly wilted but still tied together with string. A handful of roasted walnuts lay in a plate, soggy with spilled wine. On the wall hung an image of an eternal light that Rachel had knitted on the boat. An upturned goblet spread a purple stain on the tablecloth. Two women spread flour on it and a third one spread salt.

They had just finished singing. The air in the room stirred with stilled music, nostalgia for Poland, tobacco, wine, the afterglow of family reunion. Rachel, who had been so lively in Poland, was smiling sedately—the rabbi's wife. In back, the women discussed tying bits of fur around their legs against the chill New York winters. Around the table, the men argued the officers of the coming Belzer congregation, and if cemetery money could be siphoned off to maintain the new building.

At the head of the table Shaya stroked his beard, his eyes fixed on Chatzkel, half-hidden in the doorway. He was very upset with his bad news, but he was unwilling to enter and upset the homecoming. Shaya gestured patience.

Gradually the table began following Shaya's gaze. When the room was quiet, Shaya lifted thumb and forefinger in invitation.

Chatzkel limped to his side, seeing nobody there. Shaya raised his hand against the general gasp at Chatzkel's appearance.

"It was?"

"Rabinowitz, who was on Momma's boat."

"He hit you?"

"He used his belt; he kicked me also. But people made him stop."

The table stirred with anger. Again Shaya gestured them quiet, shielding Chatzkel from their view.

"This was?"

"In front of his wife's building."

"You had what there?"

"I went to talk to his daughter Leah."

"You told her?"

"To stay with her mother who loved her and brought her up, and not go upstairs with her father. He dragged her inside anyway. She's in my school; she gives me food. He's a bad man; I smelled trouble."

"And the mother?"

"He got her key and then he beat her up and threw her out on the street without any clothes on. She had money inside; he took that also. He kept all her things."

"The daughter saw this?"

"Everything."

Shaya turned. "Reb Aaron, you knew Rabinowitz in Warsaw?"

"He was with Shaikeh Haverman, that the Polonsky watchman killed. He had a worse name than Shaikeh."

"Rabinowitz was arrested?"

"More than once; the police know him."

"Then he lied on Ellis Island. The wife sent him the ticket; it cost him nothing. She was crazy about him. She would give him the daughter to do with what he wanted, just to keep him."

Chatzkel nodded. "I told him he was a bad man and a bad father."

Shaya stroked his beard. "It should have shamed him. Nabal had a stroke and died of shame, but Pharaoh after the fifth plague stopped feeling shame. The Rabinowitz is a Pharaoh."

Aaron gestured. "We do something?"

"The wife is not our business unless she asks. She invited him to America? She paid for his ticket? What a woman chooses to live with is not for us to interfere. The daughter is another thing."

"He'll prostitute the daughter?" Yakov asked.

Shaya breathed heavily. "He'll do worse, believe me, much worse. Aie, such meshugaas. The wedding is tonight; we have no time for this. Yakov, the orphan money can put her somewhere? But the wife had money, if he didn't throw it all away."

Yakov gestured. "I can fill in the names on a divorce."

"He won't sign it, life means nothing to a son of Lilith."

"And if he signed it, would she accept it?"

"That's a very good question; a bad house is a nest of hornets."

Chatzkel looked up. "She won't take a divorce."

Shaya looked up sharply. "Why not?"

"She ran off to drown herself; and she had time, so she did it."

"She tried once before, but they fished her out. Then she had her own dear husband to bring over, and she worked all those years, and now he came over on her money, and he beat her and threw her out naked; now she's dead! I know she's dead!" And Chatzkel burst into tears.

Shaya took him in his arms. The table stirred again in anger. Shaya quieted them. "Reb Aaron, what do you think?"

"I'll call Immigration, also the police. Let him go back to Warsaw; they know him there."

"The police will listen?"

"I'll tell Cohen; he'll go with the stick."

"So another Jewish headache lands on Cohen's head."

"He's on the force? Let him do his job."

Shaya heaved on his feet. "My apologies to the guests. We have to put an orphan in a home. Esther, no worries; today they're forbidden. Chatzkel will hold a pole at your wedding tonight. Yakov, tell the house. We'll bring the girl."

Aaron Binder also rose. "I'll tell Cohen right away; don't go upstairs without him."

Chatzkel followed to the door, Ellen appeared out of nowhere with a piece of *teigel*. Startled, Chatzkel took it; unsure what to do, he popped it into his mouth and stumbled after Shaya out the door.

Downstairs, the news of Zippie's drowning was spreading along the street, somehow associated with the pogroms in Poland. Details kept spilling out—how two fishermen found her body naked under a pier, how there were bruises all over her body. She had taken off her bathrobe before jumping—so the world should see what had been done to her, or maybe so somebody else could use her bathrobe.

His judgment vindicated that she would kill herself, Chatzkel took hold of Shaya's coat. Shaya looked down at him:

"Chatzkel, you see a lot that goes on, maybe more than I do; but you know why I'm the rabbi? Because I know what I have to do. My life is straight and simple. You hear?"

Chatzkel blinked up. "What?"

"Leave Leah alone. Crooked things come out of torn people."

Chatzkel heard but resisted, wondering where this was leading.

Shaya gripped Chatzkel's shoulder. "We'll make a bargain. I'll save the girl, and get her to a decent home; but I want one promise in exchange—that you'll stay away from her. At your age, there is no friendship with a single woman. Either she becomes your wife or you become her heartache. This is too broken a family."

Chatzkel clung to Shaya's coat to hear his words better. "And our family isn't broken?"

Shaya slowly sighed. "Chatzkel, our family was apart, but we were faithful. Marriage made your mother and me one person. There was no criminal driving his wife to suicide and a drowning. You fool yourself; she doesn't share your soul, nor you hers."

Chatzkel bit his lip. "It would be so beautiful."

"Chatzkel, marriage is not a charity. You want a strong, healthy girl who likes children. I want your answer. I'll get Leah to a decent home, you'll stay away from her. Agreed?"

Chatzkel squinted up. "On one condition."

"What?"

"That I can live with Yakov and Esther."

There was a long pause. "Simcha is bothering you? He's a lot to take. You're a strange boy, with everything and always without. But you brought Rachel over more than I did. All right, live with Yakov and Esther; and when you want, you'll come home. Agreed?

Chatzkel grimaced that Shaya understood him so badly. They were very far apart. "I agree."

Shaya waved the question aside. "We have Esther's wedding to arrange, and what's to be afraid of? Come?"

Shaya strode up the stairs with Chatzkel scrambling behind him, and banged at a door. It opened a crack. "What?"

Shaya leaned into the doorway. "I'm Shaya Kramer; I bring

you sad news. Your wife is dead. They just found her drowned body in the water by the pier, with nothing on her."

"What else?"

Shaya leaned closer. "The police are on their way to arrest you. Your wife was badly beaten all over her body. You're reported as a wife beater. Immigration knows about your doings in Poland, the arrests and Shaikeh Haverman. You're going back on the next boat."

"There's more?"

Shaya forced the door open and dragged Chatzkel inside. Zippie's belongings, with all her clothes, spilled out of a sack, ready to be sold to a peddler. Leah sat in the corner in a body garment, patiently watching, her skin pale as the pigeon on her windowsill.

Shaya's whole face was working. "This is my son."

Rabinowitz gave him a smile. Chatzkel instantly spit at him. Rabinowitz flicked his eyes away. "Immigration knows?"

"Everything. You go from jail to the boat. I know your family back home. Your brothers will have no pleasure seeing you."

"Rabinowitz stirred like a sliver of flame. His eyes flicked around the room with a wily patience. Then he sprang for the door and stumbled down the stairs. Chatzkel shook

Leah dressed quickly. On the stairs, Chatzkel looked up. "I want to work with Esther in the café, not with Binder in the store."

"The family has an understanding."

"I know."

"You don't want Ellen? Ellen is yours; you know that."

"She's still a little girl."

"Work in the café, but the understanding is still there."

On the street, a tall police officer with massive shoulders stepped toward them in a jiggling walk, his hand on his stick. He had an Irish pug nose, slightly upturned. Chatzkel promptly decided the nose was what got him on the force.

"Rabinowitz is upstairs?"

Shaya grinned from ear to ear. "You're Cohen?"

He drew up at attention. "Sergeant Benjamin Cohen of the New York Police Force."

"My sister's chuppah is tonight at the Belzer *shteibel* by Canal Street. Would you honor us by coming?"

Cohen brushed Chatzkel's head. "Fine-looking boy. A wed-

238

ding? Yes. Contact with the people." And off he jiggled like an Irish tinker, his hand on his stick.

Chatzkel shook his head. "He doesn't look Jewish."

Shaya shruuged. "He's a policeman."

"Why does he walk so funny?"

"He wants somebody to run him for some office."

"He knows what he's doing?"

"What do you expect? A Jewish policeman."

Chapter Sixty-six

THE NIGHT OF ESTHER'S WEDDING, a north wind unbalanced a mess of shorebirds, brushing them against the water. Waves slapped around the docks. As the solitary intellectuals strolled to their cafés on Canal Street, a scatter of beggars followed the Kramer wedding party to a tiny square just west of Mott Street. There was no night traffic. Five homeless boys slept scattered on the floor in the basement of a press. A row of derelicts hunched one against the other in an adjoining hallway.

Chatzkel's usual mistrust of marriage was aggravated by the beating he got that afternoon. All the trouble was Zippie's fault for marrying Wolfe in the first place. Why did women get married anyway? But a chuppah was the blind leading the blind. Maybe his father could marry, a man who was a saint and blind to the world around him, and could marry someone like his mother, who was another saint. But marriage was a joke for people like Esther. And it was exactly the same with him.

A vast crowd of Belzer was gathered for the wedding, as word spread about building plans for the synagogue. After all these years, construction would soon get under way. For the Belzer crowd, it was a passage of the straits. The grim blot of immigrant life was getting some kind of shape. The curse was fading away; the boatloads of steerage passengers were becoming a community. The new arrivals stirred awake a nostalgia for Warsaw, its familiar courtyards and secure family ways, where all knew what they could make of their lives.

For the evening festivities, they unpacked their Polish finery. After years of the drab practicalities of the street, they wore black *shtreimel* hats, gleaming black cloaks, white stockings, and buckled shoes. The babushkas had their moth holes patched over; torn seams were held together with pins. Mingled with the

Polish outfits, other guests, clean-shaven and in American suits, circled serpentine before the chuppah and gave envelopes to Yakov for his *gutute* home.

Chatzkel watched the guests with a sense of waste. The glue had come loose among the Belzer. They were becoming tasters and joiners, with multiple membership in landsmanshaft, unions, even in other societies. The Polish costumes had a flavor of theater. Neither his mother helping Esther, nor his father with Yakov knew a thing that was going on; yet they had God, and he didn't. An ignoramus has it easier with God. He wished they would sin a little and meet him halfway; but they had a music inside them, he had none. They all met in Warsaw at a wedding just like this one. If he had met his own mother at a wedding, she would take a long look and keep walking.

Chatzkel felt estranged. He could feel the rift between Esther and his mother. He had never seen Esther so cold and distant. Something had happened in Poland to separate them. He felt torn apart inside. Rachel was his mother, but Esther was closer. Esther had brought him up and made him a mensch. Inside him, he knew he would never have a home.

Yakov was advancing on Esther to put the veil on her face, accompanied by Shaya and the other dignitaries. Chatzkel circled behind them, his eyes fixed on Esther. She was a Polish jewel decked in family lace, an heirloom, the Kramer treasure. As Yakov dropped the veil, Esther wore an eager, pacifying look that Chatzkel was long familiar with. It was the bargain of ghetto women, desperate for marriage, surrendering all independence for a few children, a little decency, and a promise not to be kicked.

Chatzkel turned away, heartsick. She was still a shtetl girl, with no willpower, no real decision. Chatzkel's side ached, but he refused to limp. In his family, a man showed neither pain nor doubt in public.

Chatzkel started up. Shimik Balaban, an orphan from Chatzkel's class, who left school to join a gang, was slipping behind Aaron Binder. As his hand reached for Aaron's wallet pocket, Chatzkel strode up and threw him around. Shimik flinched against his kick. He recognized Chatzkel.

"What?"

"This is my aunt's wedding."

"So? He's a relative?"

"This is my aunt's wedding; I don't have to say anymore."

"You want the whole wedding?! *Chazer!*"

240

"Let's not have trouble."

"I make something or I get a beating."

"Go to Canal Street."

"I need crowds; I got to live. What do you want from me?"

Chatzkel stood watching as he stole down the street, looking back at every step, cursing under his breath.

As Chatzkel slipped back into the wedding crowd, the word spread that Sergeant Cohen was coming. Nobody ever heard of such a thing as a Jewish policeman. There might as well be a Jewish president. Everybody laughed, though the joke escaped them. And yet to have a policeman in America dance at your wedding!

A contingent of twenty Chasidim from Newark came dancing up the street in full regalia, led by Yakov's brother Ariel. They had traveled for a whole day to show to the Lower East Side the Belzer of Newark. To Rivington Street, Newark was the Wild West. They kicked like reindeer as they danced their Belzer dance down Mott Street.

The locals made room with cries of welcome. They formed three circles, dancing one inside the other. At the narrow end of the square the unmarried girls formed their own dancing circle to fit into the room available.

Chatzkel glanced at Aphrodita, taller than he, with carefully plucked brows, a comfortable horseface, a long torso, and motherly bosom. She looked saner than the others, with a resigned strength that would pay any price for acceptance. Chatzkel edged alongside her.

"You don't dance with the girls?"

"Without men, dancing is a waste of time."

"You dance only with men?"

"Yeah, you can put it that way. I hear General Cohen is coming to the wedding. Binder must have told him. He's chasing after his daughter Ellen."

Chatzkel started up. "How do you know that?"

"Why else is he always there? To talk to his wife?"

"And what do you think of Esther getting married?"

Aphrodita clapped her hands with satisfaction. "What? Esther getting married? It's better than anything! I love getting married! I got married five times. It's so nice to stand under a chuppah and give yourself."

Chatzkel's hair quivered. "Five times?! What happened to your husbands? Did they all die?"

Aphrodita threw up her hands. "God in heaven, how should I

know? They disappeared on me, but they never did me any harm. The third one died of typhus. I'd give anything if he had just run off. Two were married already, so what can you do? The last one I really loved. I followed him to America, but he didn't want me. He has the right. I wish no man harm; I hope they wish me a little spot of happiness."

"Your husbands disappeared, and a rabbi let you marry again?"

"You don't think I was such an idiot as to tell him; he'd tie me hand and foot. But I love getting married."

"And if the last husband shows up on your next wedding night and said, 'Where's my supper?' What will you say to him?"

"I'd tell him to go to the nearest restaurant and get a good meal but he should try again, in case I got abandoned. More than one husband at a time, that's bigamy. Still there's no harm in having one on call."

Chatzkel slouched off, evasive as ever. Aphrodita followed him with her eyes. He interested her.

The crowd parted with excitement before Sergeant Cohen in full uniform. He advanced in his jiggling Irish walk until he reached Shaya, and stood at attention. "Sergeant Benjamin Cohen of the New York Police Force, here to give good wishes to the bride and groom. We want contact among people."

Esther curtseyed. Yakov shook his head. Aaron poured him a small goblet of schnapps. Chatzkel burned with jealousy, as Sergeant Cohen raised the goblet: "To the bride and groom! Long may they wave!"

"*Omein!*" everybody shouted, laughing hysterically as Sergeant Cohen downed the schnapps in a single gulp. He spotted Chatzkel, hoisted him on his shoulders, and danced an Irish jig as they sang: "And it shall be heard in the towns of Judah, the markets of Jerusalem, a voice of happiness, of joy, a voice of a groom, a voice of a bride."

Carried away in memory to the *illui*'s wedding, when Rachel saw him for the first time, had thought him an innocent man and resolved to have him for a husband, Shaya began to dance alone, kicking his heels and tossing his fingers.

Seeing his radiant joy, Rachel shuddered with a nervous smile, remembering that magic year, when she was Nehemia's woman, feeding her children half-dressed, singing songs of loneliness. A wild animal, Nehemia became her male shadow who quietly exulted and never lifted a finger in sin. But the strained balance became paper-thin when Geula was cast off. Shaya's call for help tore it to bits. She then prepared to come to America, and Nehemia prepared to die.

Rachel's tumult quieted; her love for Shaya gushed forth with all its old force. She sang with the others, clapping her hands, overcome that life brought her such blessing and such fulfillment.

When the dance finished, Sergeant Cohen lifted Chatzkel down. The Belzer opened an avenue, and Cohen left with his jiggling walk as the rumors buzzed left and right that he was running for Senator.

Chatzkel suddenly hurried back to Canal Street. He spotted Shimik and cornered him.

Shimik swung back with a defiant snarl. "What?"

"Rabinowitz, from today's drowning. I want him."

"It's worth?"

"A dollar."

"Make it five."

"Two is final."

"I'll find him for you."

As Chatzkel returned to the square, he spotted Nathan and Miriam hurrying before him, luxuriously dressed. How did Nathan dare come to Esther's wedding? Miriam was already a legend, the businesswoman who had just opened Universal Mills with Nathan as a sales manager.

Chatzkel stepped over to listen as she talked to Shaya:

"All the talaysim here are Polish-made. An American tallis maker has a guaranteed market. Let me use your name, and I'll give you a quarter for every tallis I sell. All the Belzer will buy it."

"Give the workers the Saturday off."

"Oh, the plant arranges its own work schedule."

"If you work them on Saturday, I'll make a public announcement that your tallis isn't kosher."

"It's not a problem. I give them piecework, to do whenever they like. I'll make it half a dollar a tallis. It's only right."

"Sh, it's time for the chuppah."

A celebration followed the wedding, but Yakov and Esther retired early to their new quarters. Chatzkel looked for Aphrodita, but she had left early. Estranged, he wandered alone down Canal Street, vaguely hoping for something new; nothing happened. He thought of opening a store where everybody is always crowding in and finding things.

An hour later, Chatzkel climbed the steps to Esther's new

apartment and lay down at her doorstep with his suitcase. There he fell asleep, his head on his arm, his packed suitcase against the door, not to disturb Esther's wedding night.

Chapter Sixty-seven

ESTHER WOKE UP to a scraping noise in the hall. She looked over and sighed at her husband's wispy beard and stringy neck. The gap was scarcely to be bridged yet his hands were exceedingly gentle and knowing.

A gray light crept along the wall. A pigeon waddled along the window ledge. Esther lay very still, pressing her hands against her belly, listening to feel if she was pregnant already. She shook her head; she heard nothing, felt nothing.

The noise came again, a dragging or scraping. Frowning suspiciously, she put on a robe and *tichel* over her hair, and opened the door a crack. Chatzkel lay in the hall in his heavy jacket, with the irregular breath of a runaway asleep in a tenement hall. She was not surprised. There was always a bit of the runaway in Chatzkel.

Up and down the hall, the tenement was awakening. A line of men and women waited for the hall latrine. Next door, cabbage was cooking. A schoolgirl carefully ignored Chatzkel, as she passed him in her robe.

Chatzkel was clearly moving in. Shaya must have agreed. There was no question that she would take him in; Shaya had brought her home the same way. She leaned over and shook Chatzkel awake. He crunched up in a ball, frightened, and then leaned back with a sleepy grin. He couldn't get over the *tichel;* Esther a married woman with her hair covered.

A woman climbed the stairs with a pan of milk from a wagon downstairs, another, two eggs. A cry of hot rolls floated up the stairs. Chatzkel got up and stretched, comfortable in Esther's company.

"You slept here? You could have knocked."

"I wouldn't bother you."

"Shaya is letting you? I didn't think he would."

"I gave him what in exchange."

"It must have been worth a lot, but don't tell me what. Yakov, look at the Elijah we had all night on our doorstep."

"Shaya allows?"

"Believe me, he does; otherwise Chatzkel wouldn't be here."

"I'll check later."

Chatzkel looked around at the Polish table, a substantial dresser and hautboy, and a couch with a wooden back. The pieces shone, looking very Old World, but all were refinished. Chatzkel washed his hands and said *Modeh Ani.* Being away from home had broken something loose inside him. Yakov put a spare tefillin sack on the table, then his own.

Esther beamed with pleasure as Chatzkel said his prayers; she began talking as soon as Chatzkel began putting away his tefillin:

"Rachel was never asked about your moving here, was she? But I brought you up more than she. I'm expecting—at least I'll have a baby soon—and perhaps I'm expecting already; but you're still my oldest. Imagine, all these years we slept across a partition, and now you and my baby. Isn't that funny! Of course when the baby grows up, there may be a problem, but you'll be married by then, won't you?"

"I'll help in the café."

"Peel potatoes, and clean tables, and give me tips about what's happening. Night work isn't day work. These aren't shtetl people, everybody starting work when the sun rises. The café is another world."

"I'll manage."

"Then you won't be with Binder in the store; and you can marry Ellen when you're ready, and not when Binder's ready. You'll quit school and sleep late, just like the rich in Paris."

"My morning prayers are before ten."

"Ten o'clock—what an idea! Nobody sleeps that late unless they're sick. But you couldn't be sick if you tried. The way you danced yesterday after Rabinowitz kicked you! Yakov, can you get a bed for Chatzkel?"

"I'll take care of it."

Chatzkel had a sudden clap of fear that it was too late; Esther had experienced too much. She would have no baby. If God existed, to deny Esther a baby was too cruel; but since He didn't exist, He could use the outer limits of cruelty.

A moment later, he had another spasm of awareness. If Esther had no child, sooner or later Yakov would divorce her. He was a fanatic, religiously bound to have children. Esther's marriage that absorbed her so much was an episode and a passing dream. She would be finally his.

"Nathan Finesilver should not have come to the wedding, and

neither should his wife who sucks the blood out of her workers. I hear stories. At the wedding, she was pushing business with Shaya."

Esther flashed Chatzkel a look of warning. He fell silent. He wished he had his own family already, instead of sharing a room with a nonexistent baby.

Esther served the two men a vegetable salad and slices of pumpernickel and butter, using institutional silverware from the customs warehouse. Cries of peddlers came up from the street. Men tramped down the hall on their way to work.

The wedding music was ringing in Esther's head. She wanted to talk about the wedding, the dancing, Yakov's brother from Newark, but she felt a little shy. The two men were clearly onto other things.

Esther sat down and pushed off the pumpernickel. "In Warsaw, we sometimes bought a French roll called croissant for breakfast."

Yakov and Chatzkel both looked up; their jaws fell.

"It's kosher?"

"It's a roll?"

"Made with butter, no animal fat."

Yakov had a thin smile. "Esther, I think you're expecting."

Esther was all smiles. "What makes you say that?"

"A croissant for breakfast? Only a woman that's expecting a baby would have such ideas."

Esther looked at Chatzkel. "You'd eat a croissant for breakfast?"

"I like a slice of pump."

"You're not a woman that's expecting a baby, are you?"

"God protect me!"

Esther looked as the two men rose. "What do you want for supper?"

"Anything you make."

"Whatever."

And the two men went out on the street, leaving Esther alone, impatient and anxious for her baby.

Chapter Sixty-eight

ON HIS FIRST NIGHT at the Pinchas Strauss, Esther had Chatzkel peeling and scraping potatoes, brewing coffee and tea, and frying latkes six at a time, sprinkling them with cinnamon and brown sugar. Chatzkel was good with his hands, and could cook with half a mind.

The society members didn't know what a delicacy was and grumbled constantly about the small latke, setting up Esther's against her neighbor's as proof of their discrimination. Chatzkel promptly swung into his sales pitch: the Pinchas Strauss was a café, not a restaurant. It served delicacies like latkes, not dinners. Two delicacies do not make a meal; for that, you go to a restaurant. They shut up, but the small latke still bothered them.

Esther enjoyed having Chatzkel around, but he was a little too inexperienced for her taste. She felt frustrated. She remembered seeing Chatzkel with Aphrodita at her wedding. Leaving that night, she smiled gently.

"You like Aphrodita, don't you? She's such a loyal woman. You don't know how rare loyalty is in a woman. You have to know how to use the loyalty in a woman."

"I suppose."

Certain that Esther would have no baby, Chatzkel stayed close and did little favors to distract her from the subject. When Esther finally mentioned the coming baby, he answered nothing. Old romantic rages lingered in his head. He sensed Esther resented him but also appreciated his nearness. They walked to the café together and back home in the early morning.

Meanwhile, every night another crowd exploded afresh in reaction to some new theater production. Melodrama, musicals, adapted world classics, all were staples of their Yiddish Renaissance. They smoked cigars, traded rumor and gossip, argued society politics, and cued each other on the job market. They showed solidarity with Vilna and with Belz, and squinted around the café, checking on attendance. Every absence was a betrayal of the group.

The society members liked bringing their wives. Their shapes, hair, jewelry, and lively color were their husband's best latke, a real delicacy. They teased the women, loudly bragging about their own sexual powers, yet with all their exhibitionism there was an enormous secretiveness about money and family matters.

At adjoining tables, garment industry executives sat with padded shoulders, signet rings, and yards of expensive serge, showing off the vitality of the area to their customers. Nathan came often, bringing customers and also company models that he loosely handled. Always the fatalist, he had slipped into his new life completely; he knew how to enjoy himself, whatever he did.

247

Single women visited the Pinchas Strauss, workingwomen dreaming of being kept in style. They took tables close to the garment executives and let their eyes linger on them. Voices were always heatedly raised, hands swept the air in theatrical excitement, and soon the spoken appraisals were mixed with vulgarities that were not received amiss. It was the place on Canal Street for bon vivants to spend an evening.

A sudden boom in business stepped up union activity. Strikes were called, one on top of the other, among the pressers, the fitters, the cloak makers. Factory shop boss became a dirty phrase but *store* felt somehow proletarian, like a place of free movement and democracy. Since Binder had a store, Chatzkel absorbed much of this talk, and he felt he could enjoy his money some day with a clean conscience.

The rash of strikes began to intrude into the Pinchas Strauss. The English press called the strikes acts against God. In the Pinchas Strauss, a strike leader sometimes gave his story to a reporter for a Socialist journal, speaking in a ghetto voice that carried across the room. One night, two pressers, exhausted from running, strode over to a writer for the *Arbeiter Zeitung,* sat down, and tumbled it all out:

"Strikebreakers broke both Moshe Feldstein's arms with clubs; he's in the hospital."

"Weinstein hires his strikebreakers off the gangplank."

Esther hurried across the room and gestured to the journalist. He immediately plunged out the door, followed by the two men, talking all the time. Esther smiled a helpless apology to the next table. Weinstein gestured back to forget it.

Esther stepped over to Aphrodita. "We've had too much of this lately. We need something to pull the people together or we'll end up with a riot."

"You have an idea?"

"I'm thinking about it."

Esther felt the unions competing with the societies for active members, and the unions spoke the language of Jewish conscience. The societies began to feel old-fashioned and out of touch. Retrenching, they began emphasizing family and the sense of community. They printed lists of Hebrew teachers, professional addresses in Warsaw, members in their cemetery.

Esther waited until a more traditional society, the Anshei Vilna, was out in force at her café. Then, upon request, she sat down at the piano and chimed a few notes. The hall fell quiet. She then sang in her guttural lisp, *"Vos Viel der Shegetz Fun*

248

Mir?" "What Does the Gentile Want from Me?" a song almost smug in its pouting insecurities.

The society began to applaud before Esther finished, with shrieks of agreement and satisfaction. Hearing their response, Esther was impatient for Geula's answer to Shaya's invitation to come to America and look after her children. It would never carry in Warsaw, to own a café and be a mother; but her instincts told her that New York was loose enough.

Esther walked home with Chatzkel without bothering with the *tichel* on her head; she had gotten Yakov to wear a Western suit to go to the theater with her, and that was something else she could do here that a woman couldn't do in Poland.

Esther glanced at Chatzkel with a half-smile. "You still have what with Ellen Binder?"

"We never get together, so there's no way to break it up."

"You'll finally go under the chuppah then?"

"I expect we will."

"I like Ellen; I like her very much."

They continued home very peacefully and in silence.

Chapter Sixty-nine

APHRODITA WAS A STRONG PRESENCE in the Pinchas Strauss, with her statuesque body over the cashbox, her long, thin Roman nose, and her frizzy halo of orange hair like a bonnet. Everybody liked Aphrodita. She took money with the serenity of an institution; she seated guests like a force of nature. Just her name, with no family connection, made her a celebrity. Her torso was a provocation. Men were forever positioning themselves in front of her and engaging her in conversation. She always responded in that dry, distant, irregular throaty voice, starched and crackling, never allowing a chair near her. Propositioned, she turned the man down with a knowing laugh. She knew every trick of the trade from Warsaw.

Aphrodita enjoyed her place on Canal Street. Men called her the musarnik and hinted at irregular liaisons—if she rejected them as lovers, then she must be in some way perverse—but they kept coming back to talk. And yet Aphrodita's image of invulnerability made her very vulnerable.

Aphrodita conducted her affair with Mossman off the back of her hand. A shop boss with authority over thirty-five machines, the secretary of the Vilna Society, tall, strong as a bull, and

249

fanatically Orthodox, with a long, full, black beard, he was forever sitting up hard in bed in helpless outrage. Aphrodita didn't care. She slept with him for the Pinchas Strauss, for Esther. Once, after sex, she began planning ways to bring Mossman's wife over. Another time, she began insisting on a chuppah; Mossman's wife in Vilna was just his cover for being a pig.

Aphrodita sensed early that Esther wanted to enjoy Chatzkel through her. They were old friends, but Esther was still her boss. Yet Aphrodita didn't resent it all that much. She saw Socialism as people working in cooperation for a shared goal. Esther couldn't handle her feelings about Chatzkel? Then she would take over in the old socialist spirit. And if it gave Mossman a *shtoch*, let him suffer. He deserved it.

On Chatzkel's first day at work, Aphrodita thought him too young for her to bother with; by nightfall, she felt relieved that he did his job and kept away. As he continued to work there, she felt perversely flattered that he still ignored her. He treated her like an ordinary human being. It added a breath of sanity to the place. His movements even had a certain gentility; she liked his relaxed slouch and physical strength.

Aphrodita stopped Esther by her table. "It's just a cousin; you should enjoy him a little."

"Take him off my hands, why don't you?" Esther murmured in her easy, high-pitched lisp.

"Ask me again and I'll think about it."

Leaving Aphrodita, Esther winked at Chatzkel. He looked down and continued his work. Esther felt strangely happy.

All that season, garment production boomed. With the prosperity, more women decided that a manufacturer was more enjoyable than work over a sewing machine. Like Esther, Aphrodita watched their clientele with a cagy alertness. Knowing everything that was going on, the sight of Chatzkel working all night and not coming near began to get under her skin.

She gestured Esther over. "He's alive?"

"It ties up your kishkes, doesn't it?"

"Never mind my kishkes. What is he, a mule? A *shlepper*? He never does anything."

"You think he ignores you? The opposite, he watches your every move and he knows your every thought. Why, you want him?"

"No."

That night, two prostitutes stepped into the café, each with long platinum hair and a plume around her neck. They took a table near three young manufacturers and began making loud clever remarks about the old-fashioned people in the café, as five journalists sitting behind them watched with sardonic satisfaction. Aphrodita motioned to Chatzkel to avoid their table, but they carried on without being waited on. Nothing bothered them.

A pimp in a luxurious sack coat stepped in the door and slouched back, watching. Aphrodita walked over and muttered in Polish, "Get the two *churvahs* out of here." The pimp gave her a long even look.

Aphrodita leaned back and murmured a message to Chatzkel. He hurried across to a side table and leaned over Mossman. Mossman listened, frowning, until he pointed to Aphrodita. Then his shovel face started to work. In a rage, he rushed over and grabbed the pimp with both hands.

The pimp reached for his pocket. Mossman threw him around, grabbed him collar and pants, and slammed his face first into the wall. "*Schmutz!*" he screamed, threw him sprawling on the street, sprang around, and began swinging his hands. "And where are the *churvahs*?"

Aphrodita strode over to the two prostitutes. "You want to leave with or without your clothes?"

The two rose and swayed out the door, one behind the other. Aphrodita leaned out into the street as they joined the pimp on either side. "Next time you come in here, you'll get a frying pan across the head!"

Aphrodita was worked up. She breathed hard, her eyelids fluttering, as Esther sidled over to calm her.

"You're right, he watches my every move, he reads all my thoughts. It drives me crazy, the way he stands off and does nothing."

"He's not standing off; he's waiting for a word from you."

"I know him already—Orthodox, but not crazy like Mossman."

"How long will you want him for?"

"I'll want him until I stop wanting him."

"Send him back when you're finished; I'll miss him."

Esther took a deep breath and stepped over to Chatzkel. "*Bubchick,* a lot of news."

Chatzkel blinked up at her guardedly. "What?"

"The Binder girl was around, asking about you."

Chatzkel shrugged. "What else?"

"Leah Rabinowitz, that Shaya put in a home? Her father stole her out with him. He took her." Esther spoke gently.

"You know where she is?"

"It doesn't matter anymore. She took gas."

Chatzkel closed his eyes in mourning.

Esther bent closer. She sensed what was going on inside him. "You'll go home with Aphrodita afterward?"

Chatzkel nodded and continued frying latkes. As Esther suspected, he knew everything that went on.

Chapter Seventy

AT TWO A.M., Chatzkel squinted up at a block-long tenement looming before him like an abandoned barracks. In a building that long, an air shaft behind every second entrance would service six floors below; two out of three rooms would be always in the dark, except for an occasional open door. The bottom of the air shaft would hold broken glass, wrappings, and rotting food, its vapors wafting up to the roof.

Aphrodita glanced restlessly. "What are you thinking about, with that crazy smile of yours?"

Chatzkel threw his shoulder forward evasively. "About the *Shechinah!*"

"That's nice."

Aphrodita fell silent. His father was a rabbi, so he thought about God, like the Warsaw ex-Yeshiva boys—lawyers, accountants, men with brains like a pickled herring.

As they passed a broken pushcart, a hand pushed out from under its flap. A derelict was begging in his sleep.

Aphrodita grinned teasingly, rubbing one of her breasts. "Still thinking about the *Shechinah?*"

Chatzkel shrugged. "I think about the *Shechinah* all the time."

"And not about women?"

"I never talk about that."

Aphrodita suddenly wagged her finger. "You know what's wrong with Jewish men? You're always practicing *mitsves*. It's in your kishkes, everything dead serious, over and over, eating, working, praying, every morning with the tefillin, every afternoon with the bank, every night with the wife, another mitzvah, obnoxious, loudmouth bores, all of you. I'm making love and the man is doing another mitzvah. It turns you into dybbuks."

252

"Problems."

Aphrodita relaxed; Chatzkel felt relieved. He liked how quickly she calmed down. Then he could be calm in her company.

The steps to Aphrodita's building were slippery. Climbing in the pitch-dark, Chatzkel gripped the banister and instantly let it go. Something soft was underfoot; he stepped aside fast. He grabbed Aphrodita for balance. She turned patiently and leaned her body against him.

They continued to the sixth floor. Aphrodita opened the door and lit a candle that cast more shadow than light. Her room was a closet, windowless but very clean. A mattress took nearly all the floor space. A one-shelf cast-iron cabinet on the wall held all her things.

Chatzkel heard a steady racking cough through the wall.

"Somebody's dying?"

"Tuberculosis."

"His room is like this one?"

"Smaller, also with no window. He came alone to bring his family from Warsaw, an expert tailor, put away every nickel. Then the sickness caught him. He's lain there for over a month, coughing blood. No visitors. The neighbor who brings food and candles stopped cleaning up after him. She can't stand the sight of him. He wears no clothes; his hair is matted to his body, his cough. He stopped caring. You won't hear the cough after a while."

They undressed for bed like an old married couple. Chatzkel settled against her big bosom, completely relaxed. Aphrodita felt his erection shoot up against her leg, gave a little gasping cough, and then broke into a smile of relief that there were no difficulties. There was a knock at the door.

"Who is it?" Aphrodita hissed hysterically.

"Clara Lebo," a vibrant voice sang through the door.

Aphrodita lunged out of bed, covering her bosom with a sheet, opened the door, and let in a girl of eighteen, one of the *farbrenteh*, the young fanatic women organizing the Lower East Side. She had short hair cut close to the head so a policeman couldn't grab it. A holy one, who tried never to sleep, she sat down in Aphrodita's only chair with a saucy chin and laughing, defiant eyes.

"I'm interrupting?"

"It's perfectly all right."

Clara grinned with sly pleasure. "Imagine, I met a presser at

Universal. I reached him during his lunch. He told me how fifty of them left his village in Rumania after Jassy, when they learned the pogrom was government-inspired. He was one of the *fusgeyer!* They were the best men in town, young, and with real skills, not what comes out of the old shtetl."

"How many women went with?" Aphrodita murmured.

"Five. They practiced for a month in khaki and marching shoes, and then everybody marched with a knapsack, waving a Rumanian flag and a blue-and-white. The farmers on the way gave them food."

"How many reached Bremen?"

"Ten; but it was still worth it."

"Did any women reach Bremen?"

"I had no time to ask; he was due on his machine."

"Always find time to ask about the women. You want to know how many women made it? I don't have to ask. None of them made it, because they gave their last food to the men. They should make it."

Clara gestured impatiently. "I told him never mind the past, Rumania, his family, the march to Bremen. His job now was to help organize a union at Universal. He said he made a living; it was enough. I told him his boss made gold out of his flesh and blood, and was he satisfied? He said he was."

"He sounds like a very nice man."

"I asked, did he believe in Moses, and he said yes. I told him, when Moses gave the order, the satisfied Jews started packing. He said a row of sewing machines are not a pyramid. I asked, did he know Hester Tamarin? Hester had a miscarriage at her machine. So she dropped a Jewish baby onto the pyramids of New York, like his march from Rumania dropped women into the pyramids of Europe. He said he would picket. You're a little crowded; maybe I should bother Shireleh Katz."

Clara eyed Chatzkel and then pointed at him. "Can I have him in the morning? Miriam Finesilver is sending for scabs from off the boat. We need bodies for the picket line."

"I'll send him."

Clara left pleased.

Aphrodita snuffed the candle end. As it guttered out, she lowered the blanket. All night, they made love in the pitch-dark. A touch, a laugh, a brush of skin made it happen one more time. Aphrodita remembered pleasures so extraordinary that she shuddered as she did them all for Chatzkel. Nothing bothered Chatzkel. If it was a choice between the Garden of

Eden and Aphrodita, a man would have to be a fool to pick the Garden of Eden.

In the morning, Chatzkel woke up to a strange stillness. The cough had stopped on the other side of the wall. The tubercular's bloody rags were already on the street, being sold as clothes.

Chapter Seventy-one

AT TEN IN THE MORNING, the ghetto buzzed with the news of a strike. Parents on the street closely watched their children, who couldn't stand still; the street idlers were on the alert for any sudden movement. At a crossing, a violent shout wrenched everybody around—a storekeeper thought his pocket had been picked when a porter banged against him.

Chatzkel glanced at Clara. "You slept at Shireleh Katz's?"

Clara clapped her hands and laughed. "Listen, when I stay at her house, sleep is impossible. I come in the door, and sleep goes back down the stairs for the night. We three can't stay in the same room—me, Shireleh, and sleep; one of us has to go."

"Yeah, she sounds nice."

"She was in Paris with the street people; it made a *mensh* out of her. The things she told me! We talked for hours, but I smelled she was hiding something. It was a journalist. She wouldn't give me his name, but I'll smell him out. Then I went to another friend of mine, Mindel Garfunk."

"At her place you can sleep?"

"We were too busy going over strategy for today's picketing. The anarchists have sensed the strike coming, especially Zucker. His outfit has been meeting nonstop for two days, figuring how to move in and take over. They think Mindel is one of them, so they tell her everything."

"She's not afraid what can happen when they find out?"

"What can happen? They'll denounce her? She spits at them. They'll beat her up? Then we'll beat them up. Let them start their own strike and not move in on ours, the parasites."

Chatzkel frowned. What was Clara so radiant for? The strike was just getting under way and even he knew much hard work was yet to come. So far, it was just Universal, but the last strike drew a march of fifteen thousand workers to Union Square. This strike was the match that could kindle a hundred other factories and trigger another march. But Clara's happiness was contagious. So she was crazy, but he had just turned sixteen and escorting a *farbrenteh,* hearing her strategy, helping to organize a big strike. His head could be bashed in—but this was America, and he was here. And crazy or not, Clara was a holy woman.

Clara chopped the air with her hand, thinking out loud. "The whole question is, will Zucker's gang come before the police? If they come after, their whole organization is finished; but if they arrive before, then we have to keep them from being arrested. I told Mindel to try and delay them, but if I know Zucker, he'll arrive together with the police and completely tie our hands."

Clara never slowed down, peering from side to side in her indestructible sweater, waving at groups of passing workers, giving a different message with each wave, or just sizing up the street for obstacles. She suddenly stopped. A moment later, a frail fourteen-year-old appeared, springing their way, panting, dodging obstacles. She reached them, and Clara patted her cheek. "What, Mireleh?"

"Misha Feig is on the dock, signing up scabs off the *Neustadt.*"

"How many?"

"He has eight, and looked ready to leave."

"He interviewed close, or took whoever he could get?"

"He took whoever he could get."

"If he took whoever he could get, then they're not solid. Mireleh, I don't want you at the plant today; too much will be happening. But hang around Zucker's headquarters and report back if they start moving."

Mireleh smiled brightly and started in a fresh direction.

Much as Clara made herself a part of the street, she kept a wary distance. People wanted to stop her, to help, to catch an anecdote or a bit of gossip. Clara always shied off, snapping out a bracing word of solidarity. She was the catalyst, the irritant. Nothing happened to her except what she planned out in advance.

The excitement waned for a moment. Restless, Clara gave Chatzkel a long, appraising look, and then started in, not slowing down. "*Bruder,* you're not staying in that café. What's your next move in life? You must have something in mind."

"I want to open an *alles farn shtieb,* everything for the home. The Jews off the boat don't know where anything is, or even what exists in America. I want a store that's an education to the here and now."

Clara grinned broadly. "You know what opening a store makes you."

Chatzkel grinned broadly. "Yeah, a worker."

His naïveté made her delirious with pleasure. "You actually call a storekeeper a worker?"

Chatzkel refused to back down. Talking with her was like riding a wild mare bareback. She kept bucking all the time. The attempt to recruit him was so ridiculous that it made him vehement.

"Look, a swimmer is a man who swims, a walker is a man who walks, and a worker is a man who works. I'll work from morning to night once I open my little store."

"Your little store," Clara repeated, teasing affectionately.

"I'll work a lot harder than anybody at Universal."

Clara had a ready response. "Is a miser who sweats counting money all day a worker, because he counts money? No, he's just a miser. A worker is somebody who makes something; but you won't make anything, just money off somebody else's back that made something."

"I don't know; I'll make a lot of people happy."

"You should be on a Jewish farm, learn what work is."

Chatzkel shrugged. "I've been on a farm."

Clara's face lit up. "Yeah? Where?"

"In Poland my grandfather had a chicken farm. When I was little, I visited a lot. My grandfather, my father, and I all worked together, and walked to the shtetl on Saturday morning for services."

"Your grandfather didn't come over, did he?"

"He was too old; he entered a home in Warsaw."

"My father taught gymnasium in Warsaw, the *Volksverein* behind the train depot."

"Yeah? I passed that school maybe a dozen times."

"But still a storekeeper isn't a worker; he's a distributor, and finally a parasite. He belongs to the parasite middle class, making money out of somebody else's work. Listen, come to one of our meetings at the Yiddish school. You got a lot to learn."

A teacher escorted eight boys to a small square inside an iron fence, with benches all around it against the fence. There fifty ghetto boys were doing calisthenics, in shirt-sleeves and cloth caps or yarmulkes, some with tzitziot bouncing out from under their shirts.

Forgetting everything, Clara and Chatzkel stood side by side, grinning with pleasure, watching, not saying a word.

Then suddenly Clara darted across the street to a burly workman who stood on the pavement with two friends. He shook his head, smiling, his hands on his hips. Chatzkel followed.

Clara embraced him. "Russky!"

"So Clara the Cossack took on Universal."

"The place is shut down."

"Miriam'll use scabs."

"I got word they're on their way. Listen, you're in earshot of Universal. If you hear a scream, will you come running?"

"All eight of us, and before they drag you off."

"And get the scabs off the machines inside. Remember when you were on strike. My head got the first blow when they came at us with clubs."

"You don't have to tell me."

Chatzkel looked at her as they continued. "You'll call him out?"

Clara studied the street. "It depends on Zucker. If he isn't there, we make a *tummel;* but if he shows, I don't want the anarchists in on a general strike. But who gets in Zucker's way? The maniac. Men are such idiots."

Chatzkel grinned. "Yeah."

Clara flashed him a look. "What's funny?"

"I think your mother should have taught you one or two things about how to handle men."

"You're silly."

"I suppose."

They turned the corner onto a sprawling tin hut. Several workers walked with strike placards with four girls Clara's age. She shrieked in glee and ran toward them, talking before she could reach them, as Chatzkel warily followed.

Chapter Seventy-two

BY THE BOWERY, at the western fringes of the garment district, Universal Apparel sat across a square from an Italian district and a police station. The Italian immigrants had planted trees and bushes; a cross over a brick warehouse marked the beginnings of a church. Just below, shipping warehouses with gates wide enough for a wagon faced toward the Hudson River, and winds carried dock noises from the harbor.

At the Universal shed, a sturdy wire fence enclosed fifteen feet of yard, with bales of fabric and a delivery wagon with shipments of finished pants ripped open and sliding out on the rubble. Pigeons flew inside the shed through two broken windows. Several workers had left their machines uncovered; they were now smeared with bird droppings.

258

The square was deserted. The people in the tenements to the north kept their children off the street. Women shopped by the back way. The occasional passerby crossed over with a look of impatience, and the facing shops were locked closed, each with a sign telling customers to return in the evening.

That morning, before picking up Chatzkel, Clara had brought over a heavy ship lock that now sealed the Universal gate. The police would have to cut through the three-foot fence, giving the picketers precious additional time to work on the scabs.

In a morning editorial, the *World* had called the strikers ingrates, allowed into America as guests, who then wasted no time attacking its institutions. Such an editorial would give the police a free hand, and no reporter was around to control the situation. But Mireleh's news that the scabs were hired at random gave their strategy a direction. Clara discussed it at furious speed with her *farbrenteh,* and then with the picketers. They now planned to fix all their attention on the scabs, hanging on to the gate in a tight group and pushing off the police. Otherwise, the police would rush the scabs inside so fast they could claim afterward that what was happening had completely escaped them.

The picketers watched for the strikebreakers from the Italian houses. An approach across the shop district could be cut off, and the police escort could touch off a general strike. The strike committee had tried to negotiate through Tammany Hall, but their messenger had been denied admission. The politicians thought no real votes stood behind the strikers. With the strikebreakers coming from the Italian houses with no reporters around to observe them, the police would have a field day.

Clara kept telling the girls to blame Tammany Hall when attacked, to keep yelling, "Tammany Hall is murdering Jews! Tammany Hall is murdering Jews!" They kept protesting that the bosses were also Jews. This was crazy. Besides, they needed the politicians as friends, and couldn't antagonize them.

Clara clapped her brow. "What do you want, sanity? You're asking sanity from a goy? When you have no power, talk of sanity; here we talk sanity across a negotiating table. Get Poland out of your minds! Here we make the politicians our friends by scaring them! Just label Tammany Hall as anti-Semitic, then the political climate might change. Beg for friendship and you turn into a beggar."

"Yes, but why this shop? It's too isolated, too far out from the Jewish shops."

Clara shook her head. "We didn't pick this place; it picked

259

itself. And we're not that isolated. Russky is within earshot; he'll bring his boys running if there's a real fight. And once they hit the street, every shop in the area will follow."

The girls relaxed and began nodding and smiling in agreement.

The strikers listened without speaking. They were eight, six, chosen by lot, and two volunteers from a work force of sixty-five. They had meetings and discussion groups—six were Socialists—but they couldn't relax into a team of pickets. Ghetto Jews, their heads insisted on working. Every one wore a traditional Jewish hat, but several had thick flaps to shield their ears against a club. Yet they were more uneasy about police authority than about their clubs. They had collective memories of Chmielnicki, the Cossack butcher, to whom entire communities surrendered without a fight, wanting not to provoke him to further slaughter.

As they stood waiting, Shireleh Katz drew Clara aside.

"I just heard."

"What? What?" Clara asked.

"Leah Margolis is back from Vilna and starting a school."

"She brought a principal?"

Shireleh grinned. "Of course, from the Bund; that's her affiliation."

Clara clutched at her heart. "And he'll want teachers."

"They're also a political organization. Still if you get an offer, don't turn it down."

"What do you think I am, crazy?"

"Weren't you and Zucker once a couple?"

"So a little girl once liked his Jewish nose. But this job is interesting. We'll probably get arrested. When we get out on bail, I'm going straight to Leah. I know she'll take me on."

The two girls laughed and continued talking with animation.

The men picketing took short walks, then spun around as if on a leash. They had an exhilarated feeling that America gave them rights, yet not one of them had his final papers. The editorial threw a scare into them, with its hint of deportations. As pickets, they would be thrown in jail. After the strike, the others would be quietly rehired and then blackballed. Walking, they gestured to one another, then sighed and kept quiet. Each picket had a relative in Poland to bring over. Just to strike had a stigma of family betrayal. Their business was to save money.

One picket whittled a stub of wood with a cutter's knife; another had a crowbar handy. They concentrated on the subject in hand, astir like men in synagogue, as the five women stood together, flexing their limbs, giving spasmodic smiles, refusing to be frightened or depressed, though all of them had been clubbed and thrown into jail more than once.

"Hey, what are you?" Clara restlessly asked a picket.

"Right now, I'm a worried Jew."

"Right now, you're a worker on strike, and never forget that! Other workers are with you in . . ."

Clara broke off as a slight, vigorous man started across the street toward them, in a herringbone suit, thick, rimless glasses, and an unruly mustache, bareheaded. Clara saw Shireleh start in surprise and pleasure. Clara grinned from ear to ear; this must be Shireleh's new boyfriend.

"Who are you? Who do you work for?" Clara called out.

He lifted a finger. "Nachum Feld; I write for the *Forward*."

The strikers smiled in relief as he strode to the nearest striker and opened his pad. "Why are you on strike?"

The man spun around. "Think it's money? A dollar more, a dollar less. But a horse in a stable has more respect than we in Universal."

Clara swung up in front. "We want fifteen dollars a week pay for twelve hours a day of work, and equal pay for men and women. We wanted to negotiate, but Tammany Hall returned our message. If you want, I'll get you a copy. We're striking for money to buy our children food . . ."

A bearded Jew pushed her aside. "They doubled the machines in the shed. We sit on each other's heads, and still no lamps. We're going blind."

By now, the reporters were crowding around the reporter:

"Misha Feig, the foreman, won't let me leave from my machine to piss! I'm five minutes late? He docks me a dollar in pay. A dollar for five minutes' late!

"He subcontracts; his wage scale is a lie. To keep my job, I have to take home bundles of work for children to work on at night. And they get paid by the piece at half the day rate."

The bearded Jew grinned. "Even in law, there are side goods, charity for the poor, human dignity, payment on time."

A worker nudged the reporter as he wrote. "When I saw you coming without a head cover, I asked myself, can I trust him? And already you're family."

The reporter gripped his two lapels. "You know what they say; many a yarmulke is to hide a bare head."

"And many a beard is to hide a crooked tongue."

They all laughed. The reporter then turned to a slight man,

261

with hunched shoulders. "And you? You keep yourself a stranger."

The man looked up. "I came so the police can kill me. I won't stop them. My name is Franzel; I'm from the *fusgeyer* from Rumania. We started out fifty strong; ten of us reached Bremen. When we got lost in the Carpathian Mountains, my wife Reizel gave me her last food, to make it out. So she's in the pyramids of Europe, and I'm in New York. I was better off in Rumania. I had a farm; we grew our own food. We were human beings."

"What about the police in Rumania?"

Franzel nodded indifferently. "I'm not sure what's the difference. Only here the police use clubs; in Rumania they use guns and whips."

Clara waved them silent. A group of eight scabs was advancing from behind the Italian houses, escorted by a chain of police, with Miriam at the rear talking very vigorously to the police captain.

As they approached, Mireleh darted alongside the tenements and descended upon them like a swallow. "The anarchists are on their way."

Clara tried to push her away, yelling at her not to stay; but Mireleh pushed among the women.

"Eight scabs?" a striker shrieked. "It's a joke! Eight? What can eight do in that plant?"

"They'll get them started, and find another eight," another answered.

"Believe me, it's us they're after, not the scabs."

The strikers formed a chain around the gate, chanting labor slogans, yelling defiance at the advancing police, calling the scabs traitors, job thieves. Chatzkel linked arms with the others at the gate, pledging allegiance to them in his head over and over. The six girls embraced, shouting together, "If I forget my human dignity, may my right hand be forgotten!"

As the police closed in, brandishing their clubs, the cantor among the strikers began the "If-I-forget-thee-O-Jerusalem" lament for the Fast of Ab, "*Im Eshkacheich Yerushalayim.*" To a man, Chatzkel and the other seven strikers formed a choir. Then the reporter added a tenor accompaniment—he also started out in Hebrew School. The men smiled in solidarity.

An instant later, the police pushed into them, charging to get to the gate. The picketers hung on. The police kept ramming through to get the scabs inside fast, as the picketers grabbed for each other, screaming and pointing at the scabs:

262

"You came to America to join in a pogrom? There you were with Jews, and here you're with the Cossacks?! The Angel of Death should get you! You're stealing my job! Murderers! You came to New York to take away Jewish jobs!"

The scabs shrank back and blinked about as if they heard nothing. Then suddenly a striker recognized one of them. "Yossie Frank! You mamzer! You *treifnyack*! You want to take Nissan Altman's job? I'll tell your mother!"

Dodging a club, the striker broke free and spat in Frank's face. A moment later, he got a club on his head and began to bleed profusely. He fell on his knees, glaring at Frank. Frank silently stepped out and edged away.

"One of them!" Clara sang out, as the strikers let out a cheer.

Mireleh saw a club waving near her. She grabbed for it with a squeal of pleasure. The policeman yanked it free, grabbed her pigtail, and pulled back her head. He then laid her out unconscious and bleeding—keeping it up, blow after blow, tearing hair from her head.

The reporter immediately pushed in, holding up his press card. Chatzkel jumped over and drew Mireleh's head to his breast. He got blows on the head and the shoulder, but the reporter loudly asked the policeman's name and then jumped elsewhere, as Chatzkel guarded Mireleh, making sure that she wasn't tramped on. Chatzkel looked up and saw Miriam pointing to him as one of the strikers.

"Call Russky now!" Shireleh hissed to Clara.

Clara started to scream when she spotted four anarchists scrambling across the street, waving their fists, Zucker half-clowning and yelling, "Strike! Strike! Strike!" Clara closed her mouth. As the police dragged away the last striker, Zucker cried despairingly, "Is there a Socialist among you?! Traitors to Socialism! You came to America to join the capitalist police beating up workers?"

Two scabs stepped out of line without a word.

"Three of them!" Clara shrieked, as the pickets cheered again. But the leading policeman let out a yell. "The lock can't be forced! Get them around the fence!"

Miriam's foreman, hysterical at losing his scabs, let out a scream. "You're the anti-Semites, denying these men jobs!"

"They're our jobs!" And the striker with the crowbar gave a leap and knocked him out with a blow over the head.

The police began swinging their clubs indiscriminately. They knocked down four strikers and left women bleeding and

263

groggy. A fourth scab, trying to step out of line, was clubbed to the ground also. Chatzkel picked up Mireleh as they were herded together to be arrested, when Clara stole over to a still body. She felt him, and let out a low bark: "He's dead!"

A chill stirred through them all. Miriam instantly disapproved. Who had said he was better off in Rumania? It was Franzel, his last wish had been fulfilled. Instantly, the girls began to chant together: "Tammany Hall is murdering Jews! Tammany Hall is murdering Jews!"

Unable to hold back any longer, Clara let out a wail for help that bounced down the street, skidded off the roofs, and sailed in the windows. Workers began swarming from the shops onto the street. The word spread like a whirlwind that a striking worker had been killed. A contingent jumped the fence into the Universal shed and began beating up the scabs and wrecking the insides, as the riot got under way.

Chapter Seventy-three

WITH FRANZEL'S DEATH, Nachum Feld took off at a run, dodging between the workers coming out of the shops. Several asked what was happening. He kept gesturing over his shoulder, throwing his hand to make them hurry, and pushing his glasses back up his nose. Before he arrived at his office, the ghetto streets already knew something tragic had happened at Universal.

Nachum ran down Allen Street to the *Forward* office and pushed inside. He nodded to the secretary and burst into the editor's book-lined office, gasping for breath and waving a full notebook.

Abraham Cahan closed his folder. "It's the strike?"

"It's turning ugly. The police escort clubbed a worker to death. They beat a fourteen-year-old girl unconscious and tore hair out of her head."

"Did you see the policeman who did it?"

"Saw it? I asked his name and he ran off."

Cahan's eyes narrowed. "We won't ignore this."

"They were clubbing and arresting everybody. There was blood all over. All the women were clubbed down. One of the scabs tried to quit; they beat him unconscious."

Cahan tapped his desk top with his glasses. "This was an incident or a pogrom?"

"The women there called it a pogrom; I don't. It got bad when the police saw that their attack wasn't working. The scabs were signed on blind at the dock. Some were Socialists. The pickets kept shouting to them to see what they were doing. Then one of the strikers recognized a scab from Europe; he screamed that he was taking his job away. He spit in his face and got clubbed down, so the scab quit."

Cahan smiled skeptically. "All right, the police don't like being frustrated. But a killing? To tear hair from the head of an unconscious girl?"

Feld shook his head. "What really angered them was when they found a lock on the gate they couldn't open. They felt laughed at; you don't do that to police."

"All right, it's an incident, not a pogrom; but the line isn't always that clear. This strike was organized by the Socialists?"

"The anarchists organized nothing. They did no picketing; they talked to none of the strikers. Then when the police started making arrests, they jumped in to be arrested too."

"I want their names; you can get them off the police blotter, along with the name of the policeman who tore hair off the head of a young girl. Our political activists have to talk to the workers and take them seriously; if they don't, nobody else will. And let the police learn that this isn't Bialystok and Lodz."

"When she saw the dead striker, Clara Lebo let out a call like the shofar up and down the stret. The garment workers started pouring out of the shops, tearing the remaining scabs off the machines in the Universal shed."

"Well, this will start a general strike."

"I think it's started already."

Cahan rose to his feet. "You were the only reporter there, weren't you? And you went out on your own. I won't forget it. Your being there may have saved a few lives and kept it just an incident. Another general strike is on us, and the other papers are all wrapped up in Rabbi Jacob Joseph and his new rabbinic court. We'll see if the Jew on the street knows where his interests are."

"You have an assignment?"

"After this write-up, get down to the jail; I want names, incidents, treatment, attitudes. Then visit union headquarters so it's official that there is a general strike. We'll have an answer waiting for the police statement on Franzel, and coverage for Franzel's funeral. I'm putting the whole paper on this."

"I should worry about incitement in my story?"

"You just tell the truth. The police did the incitement."

An hour later, the *Forward* came out with a full-page spread on the first Jewish worker killed by the New York police, with Franzel's premonition of being killed, and his statement that the police of New York and Rumania were the same, and that New York life was inhuman. The police conduct was described, including the beating of an unconscious girl by a policeman who refused to identify himself. It concluded with the chant of the women dragged off under arrest: "Tammany Hall is murdering Jews!" A separate story described the four anarchists, how they arrived with the police and pushed to be arrested. An editorial denounced exploitation and demanded respect for the worker.

The edition was sold out minutes after it hit the street. Franzel's death sent confusion through the ghetto. The chant about Tammany Hall stirred memories of Old World pogroms, and a fear that their years of work were in vain, years of amassing savings and bringing over others. Amid a memory of old pogroms, older Jews gathered in their synagogues to read Psalms. Several Jewish leaders called the incident exceptional—but to the ghetto, if Tammany Hall admitted no Jews, it was anti-Semitic.

A second edition had a spread on the strike, with a feature on immigrants who returned to the Pale for religious and family reasons, or under the grind of poverty. A fiery editorial demanded more Jews be hired on the police force.

A statement from Police Headquarters insisted the police hired by objective standards; if Jews couldn't pass that test, they couldn't help that. It finished with a statement from Sergeant Cohen that he was proud to serve on the police force. The *Forward* immediately rejected the police statement—its very working showed anti-Semitism—and demanded that notice of police tests be placarded in Jewish neighborhoods. It called Sergeant Cohen the "white jew" of the department, hired to cover prejudice.

At Franzel's funeral, ten thousand workers followed his coffin to the graveyard. His death touched off a general strike that closed the industry for a month. The newspapers were caught by surprise, but they gave the strike full coverage. The Yiddish press generally supported the strikers; the English press denounced radicals and defended the American way of life. But there were too many unions, cutters, cloak makers, pressers; fitters; they took action like pieces glued together to make a ship.

Nachum Feld located a copy of the strike committee letter

asking for arbitration that Tammany Hall refused to read. He translated it into Yiddish and splashed it across the front page. The letter was plastered all over the ghetto. The Socialists then organized a mammoth protest march to Union Square, where Tammany Hall was burned in effigy. The Socialist party signed on a thousand new members. The following day, Tammany Hall invited the entire strike committee for a meeting.

Chapter Seventy-four

THE DISCOVERY OF FRANZEL'S DEATH regularized police procedure for the others who were arrested. The officer in charge supervised the remaining arrests, checking the grounds, allowing nothing out of the ordinary. The reaction would be massive, with an investigation likely. He had to be ready.

Clara had been arrested more than once. Seeing the way they were booked, she murmured to Chatzkel that they would be out soon, and on nominal bail. She kept him close as they waited in the lock-up for their bail bondsman. Seeing the heavy department brass passing their door, she stated she was sure that the post commander was being replaced.

Sitting next to her, Chatzkel felt that Clara was softer somehow. Was it the prospect of a job? Was it the news about Shireleh? He suddenly had an overpowering desire to sleep with her, force her down in her state of confusion. It was wrong; it was very wrong. Yet the opening was there. Her daring had lost its edge. But she probably had some obnoxious boyfriend hidden away already—great women always ended up with obnoxious men.

Chatzkel felt a pang of loneliness. Each person in the lock-up was wrapped in his own world. Not one of them had his hunger for the street. Maybe his role in the strike was just another quirk in the family, part of the Kramer romance.

The four anarchists sat under the barred window, ostracized by the others. Refusing to be ignored, Zucker started speculating in a compulsive Yiddish drone, vaguely aimed at Clara, about whether Irish policemen were circumcised or not. He had it on good authority that they stopped circumcision on coming to America, not wanting to resemble Jews. He called it anti-Semitism. To find out the truth would cost ten dollars; but from the right cop, he could probably get it for nothing, maybe even get paid to have a good look.

Clara touched Shireleh. "It's Nachum Feld, isn't it? His glasses are so dignified; he really has a presence."

"They don't really fit him; I want him to buy another pair."

"But you are seeing him, aren't you?"

"We have met two or three times."

"He came to Universal because of you. And you brought him luck; this story will help him on his job. Oh, he'll end up an editor at least."

There was a stir at the door. Nachum was then admitted with his notebook. Shireleh repressed a squeal of happy surprise. He checked that she was all right, and began collecting information about the arrests, jail treatment, and their thoughts about the coming strike.

Nachum avoided Shireleh, yet every one of the *farbrenteh* caught the exchange. Chatzkel could feel a spasm of jealousy in Clara. She always stayed a step ahead of her group by smelling out what was in the works, and then being the first to make it happen. Now suddenly they were ready to pair off, and Shireleh was the first.

The bail bondsman did his business, and they were released. Chatzkel had stepped toward Clara when Zucker took her arm, talking in his obnoxious Yiddish about the Yiddish schools. Clara walked alongside him like a ghetto wife, listening with patient dignity,

Taking off alone, Chatzkel saw everywhere that the general strike was taking hold. Workers stood in idle clusters on the street; newsboys kept passing, carrying double their usual number of papers, and special editions kept appearing on every fresh wrinkle, and were sold out immediately.

From the talk of storekeepers, the strikers were lucky. It was a boom time. Deadlines hung in the balance on a contract; there were more jobs than available scabs. The bosses would be flexible. The work contract didn't hold that firmly anyway. The workers who signed it would be fired, and nobody could take them to court.

As Chatzkel walked, Shimik materialized alongside him, looking more than ever like a gang member.

"Rabinowitz."

"Where?"

"Twenty-seven Allen Street, third floor, in back. There's no window, only the door. He leaves at ten in the morning."

"I'll carry two dollars; stop me next time."

Shimik's news stirred Shaya to head somewhere. Restless, he

found himself returning to the Pinchas Strauss, looking for Esther. Ellen Binder stood at the door, carrying a box of *teiglach*.

Chatzkel walked up. "Why were you waiting for me?"

"I missed you."

"I thought Sergeant Cohen was your boyfriend."

"I don't understand. How could he be my boyfriend when you're my boyfriend?"

"That's a good question."

Ellen pressed the *teiglach* into his hand. Chatzkel started to laugh, remembering what had happened when Rachel got off the boat. When he laughed, Ellen laughed; when he stopped, she stopped. He suddenly blinked at her, a little frightened. She had staked her soul on him.

"Shall we walk?"

Ellen was relieved as they started walking. She knew he was hers, but he avoided her. Something in him flagellated itself and said happiness wasn't for him. It drew her on.

"Daddy thought you'd come into the store."

"I can't sell clothes."

"You did from the pushcart; you were good at it."

"Those were pushcart clothes."

"So what do you want?"

"I want a store like a great pushcart, an *alles farn shtieb* that will have the whole street inside it."

"You'll get it; I'll talk to daddy."

"Somebody just gave me Rabinowitz' address."

"I know about him. Give it to me. Daddy will get to Immigration. You want to go to Coney Island? Manny Kagan that sells for my father goes every Saturday."

"You're allowed on a Saturday?"

"It's not that big a sin. Manny's engaged to my girlfriend who sells cards at Feuchter's."

"Why are you telling me all this?"

"I don't know; I was just telling you. But I got other news."

"What?"

"Your aunt Esther is expecting a baby."

Chatzkel turned away and viewed the street. The joy was draining out of his life. He was losing his dream, his reliable friend, his real mother. It was all so empty, so utterly pointless.

After a moment, Chatzkel turned back with a look of crazy understanding. "I guess we're getting married."

Ellen took his arm with a quiet joy.

Chapter Seventy-five

CHATZKEL LOOKED AROUND his store, Alles farn Shtieb, its counters stocked with kitchenware, hardware, Primus stoves, wind barriers for walls, knitting equipment, clothing items, serviceable furniture, and endless spools of yarn, with cords of firewood in back. Twenty customers circulated around the counters. He wouldn't have minded another twenty.

A customer held up a cup. "Chatzkel, how much?"

Chatzkel squinted across the store. "Eight cents!"

"If I buy four?"

"Buy a dozen and we talk! Otherwise don't give me a headache!"

Chatzkel believed in quality; his furniture was held together with nails. He scattered his counters with exotic kitchen gadgets that aroused little shrieks of discovery. He hung a message board by the entrance dangling personal messages in eight languages, announcements of vacancy and exchange of rooms. Every day he pinned up the "Bintel Brief" column from the *Forward* so his customers should have something to read.

Stocking one-of-a-kind items and giving credit, he beat out competition at a penny less an article. He knew his customers' temperaments and didn't hesitate to tell them what their homes needed.

Selling on credit involved Chatzkel with his customers in a very personal way. He let the accounts of real charity cases stand, but if one preferred a more expensive version of an item, he started to demand payment. Other people's luxuries didn't come out his pocket.

Chatzkel accepted Ellen as his wife. He even loved her, but he was a man of the street. To keep his marriage from breaking up, he set up living quarters in back of the store, with a bed, and a few dishes with a primus. He made it his escape; his life wasn't really at home. He felt bitter about the estrangement between his mother and Esther, especially after Esther had her first baby and her mother Geula came over to help.

If Chatzkel had cheated on Ellen, he might have been a nicer husband. Being faithful, he made love with all the fury of a cheated man. He kept making her pregnant, refusing to let family pass him by. He did it to keep her out of his hair, to have children to fill the emptiness of his heart, to keep her faithful, even to punish her for being there, in his bed. He had nothing else to do but make her pregnant, to shut up her look of beseeching. Ellen knew the transaction taking place and accepted it, as long as he stayed faithful.

When Ellen was in her period and forbidden to him until she went to the mikvah, he slept over at the store to avoid temptation. His children then stepped in to pay their respect on their way to school. Once he slept with Ellen after her period was over. After they finished, she told him she hadn't gone yet to the mikvah. He said nothing. If she were brighter, he would suspect her of malice, not telling him sooner; but she was just at loose ends without him around. He thought of his father and felt sullied.

Chatzkel was sturdy, vigorous, impatient, with eyes that made special demands, and his voice was edged with biting awareness. He kept a yarmulke on his head and prayed three times a day. He gulped his wine when it was called for, and ate enough at a meal to have something to say grace over. His family in Poland were secret Shabbateans, but New York had its own kind of looseness that tugged at his insides. He clung all the more to his father, yet with an honesty that made him continually defy him. His wife knew not to bother him too much. The store was a scene he could manage. A skeptic about human beings, he made his peace; life offered him nothing better.

Chatzkel spent eighteen hours a day at the store. Summers passed in a steady sift of dust. In the fall, the synagogue competed for attendance at their holiday services. In the winter, animal droppings and ghetto boots chewed up the snow as it fell. Chatzkel managed. This store was where he belonged.

Chatzkel liked having his children with him. They stopped in on their way to school for a kiss; they stayed after school until he shooed them on ahead. In a free moment, he went over their homework, and talked about neighborhoods they could move to to get out of the Lower East Side. He bought special trinkets for his daughters and watched over them; but he was shy with little girls, and perplexed about how to approach them. He set up secret nest eggs for each of them, so they should have something to get started on.

Alles farn Shtieb was a flourishing business, but Chatzkel was too frenzied to keep help. He always demanded too much, leaving his assistants in charge to rush off on some business. But half the items had no price tag—Chatzkel saved time on the floor by barking the prices from memory rather than bothering with cards. So when he returned and found the store berserk, he bawled out his help for not knowing what an item should sell

271

for. They left, calling him crazy. He settled for one or two of his children as help.

He was a businessman with a sense of catastrophe in his soul. Sooner or later, he knew it would come. Unable to prevent it, he reduced his life to his private dirty secret. With a sly sense of humor, he slapped a British cologne under his beard. Having children his way was another of his jokes. The winds of exile kept his family drifters in Galicia; the same winds blew around him on Delancey Street, but he kept the faith.

A part of Chatzkel never left his father's table. Each Friday night he hurried to pay his respect to his father before continuing to make his own kiddush. He accompanied his father to his cantorial engagements and important holiday services. When his father needed ten Jews for a minyan, Chatzkel made sure they were there.

Chatzkel managed the store and remained a Chasid, but now and then an ad for women's clothing caught his attention. He looked at it, singing under his breath, "Rachel's Eyes." An occasional woman customer thought his eyes alive with bewilderment and a deep reserve; they had their own losses and were open to a forceful, emotional man. Some had a shrewd suspicion of the things missing in his life. Women of the ghetto, they spoke their minds. Chatzkel gave no one a flat rejection. His excuse was that it brought customers into the store, but it also maintained his dream that his life had mysteries buried inside it.

Chatzkel's corner of Delancey and Allen streets was something of a local intellectual gathering place. Six Yiddish monthlies had their offices on the block. A Yiddish theater was around the corner; the Socialist *Zukunft* was two doors away. The journalists enjoyed coming in. They ignored him as a storekeeper and spoke freely in his presence, as if he were a piece of furniture. Chatzkel listened with a smile, understanding every word. He didn't think them arrogant; they had an education he lacked. They were lively, always grappling with issues. It was a pleasure having them in his store.

Chatzkel never lost his attachment to his aunt Esther, but he left her alone. She had a husband she loved, and her own children. He refused to give her difficulties. He saw Nathan step into the café once with a strange woman. Esther stopped him at the door and said she didn't have a table for him. Occasionally Chatzkel stepped in with something useful for her home and paid his respects to his grandmother, but he never stayed. He had his own place.

272

Chatzkel's oldest son Saul was his favorite. A decent, agreeable boy, the least aggressive of his children, Saul sensed his father's malaise and was patient with it. Spending a lot of time at the store, he absorbed his father's sense of exile, his alienation from his mother Rachel, his sense of impending catastrophe; but he kept his peace.

Chatzkel picked real estate as a good business for his son and arranged some training in an office. He planned to buy him one or two lots on the West Side, where there were more liberal and Americanized Jews. Saul was a patient, mature boy. He grew up sharing the drama of Chatzkel's life and gave him the scene entirely. He felt very secure; he knew he would be provided for. Meanwhile it was Chatzkel's home, Chatzkel's store. He did what he could to make it work.

Shaya finally died. Chatzkel felt the winds of exile blowing around him as he marched on foot to the cemetery behind the coffin with a thousand Jews marching behind him. For a moment he stopped, shuddering, unable to move, the tears streaming down his face, and then he resumed the march. The ghetto was his life, but his son was moving into real estate. He was the last ghetto Jew his family would have. As they walked he touched his son to comfort him. Saul blinked at him with eyes of adoration.

A long delayed letter came from Warsaw, describing his grandfather's death. The episode wouldn't leave Chatzkel's mind. His grandfather, the founder of the family, died in an old-age home, penniless and abandoned, as he began his life, a foundling in Bessarabia. Our life takes a course; and then we walk it. Does anything ever change? On Ellis Island Chatzkel scarcely remembered Poland, a little boy already looking after his father; and yet Poland would not be escaped. He started awake at night, its shadows folding around him. Was New York another Egypt? He felt himself the last of the patriarchs. Poland had taken the best of them. It had chewed the Kramer family up alive; but they had fought back and gotten out. They had made the odyssey. His children would have a different life.